# THE ANNE BOLEYN CYPHER

### A Timeless Falcon Dual Timeline Series

### Volume One

## PHILLIPA VINCENT-CONNOLLY

Copyright © 2022 Phillipa Vincent-Connolly.
Copyright © 2015 Cover photography Richard Jenkins
Copyright © 2022 Cover design by Megan Sheer: sheerdesignandtypesetting.com

First Edition

The author has asserted their moral right under the Copyright, Designs and Patents Act, 1988, to be identified as the author of this work.

All Rights reserved.

No part of this publication may be reproduced, copied, stored in a retrieval system, or transmitted, in any form or by any means, without the prior written consent of the copyright holder, nor be otherwise circulated in any form of binding or cover other than that in which it is published and without a similar condition being imposed on the subsequent purchaser.

This book is a work of fiction. Names, characters, businesses, organisations, places, and events, other than those clearly in the public domain, are either the product of the author's imagination, or are used fictitiously.

Any resemblances to actual persons, living or dead, events or locales are purely coincidental.

A CIP catalogue record for this title is available from the British Library.

❧   **Gina Clark**   ☙

Thank you for your incredible friendship, warmth, and love.

# One

## Present Day –
## St. Mary's University Twickenham

St. Mary's University isn't a probable venue for misplacing yourself, at least at first glance — unless you're a fresher, lost in the mix of old and modern architecture, from Strawberry Hill House, to sports halls, the Students' Union bar, theatre school, large library, lecture rooms, and chapel.

It's a bright morning in late September, and this year is starting out the same as the last, with all the seminars and tutorials scribbled in my diary. The second year of my BA degree in British Early Modern History has just begun. Later on, I'd like to achieve a PhD. Doctor Elizabeth Wickers — how grand that sounds! Maybe one day.

As I grab my holdall from the passenger seat, I remind myself that I need to focus on the here and now. I secure my iPhone in my pocket and thread the earplug leads up underneath my jacket and over my collar.

A glance towards the building on my left tells me nothing much appears to have changed over the summer, apart from the fact that we are all a little older, and I am no longer one of the newbies, many of whom are now heading towards the reception area, looking discombobulated and nervous, checking maps, their timetables, and room numbers.

The breeze whispers through the nearby trees. I lock my car and turn to join the groups of students heading across the car park. I'm excited. A new year, with so much to look forward to ahead.

Once inside, I pass through the reception, relaxing with the familiar sights that greet me. I make my way towards my tutor room in the history department for my first lecture of the day. Students are massing, with everyone greeting friends they haven't seen since the summer break. I look around, and it's not long before I catch sight of familiar faces. Marc and Sarah are a year ahead of me but we have become quite friendly. As I draw closer, I call out but realise they're engrossed in conversation.

"It's a truth, universally acknowledged, that a historian in possession of authentic primary sources has a yearning to time travel. You know that!" Marc says.

"Yet, you'd agree," Sarah replies, "they should also have the discretion not to meddle with matters out of their control?"

I push in between them. "What on earth are you two talking about?"

"Time travel," Marc answers, smirking. "Well, the film *Back to the Future*, to be precise."

"Michael J. Fox's character messed with his own history," Sarah says, "and look what happened to him — he ended up with several sequels." She laughs.

I roll my eyes. "My parents made me watch that movie as a kid. They assumed because I loved history, I'd love the time-travel aspect."

"Every historian wants to time travel, Beth. Don't you?"

"I suppose so, but I'd only go back in time, not forward, and I'd only travel back to live with a rich family, so they could afford the best clothes, food, and hospital treatment."

"I agree with you." Sarah half smiles. "I wouldn't want to live as a peasant."

Bodies are tight around us as we draw closer to the lecture room.

"Look," Marc continues, "the only way we'd ever truly know about historical events is if we were to witness an event at the time it happened, and even then that's a biased view — from only one point of view. Even contemporary sources of a particular event are never the absolute truth, because history is always written by the victors."

I give him a nervous smile, not knowing the reason for this senseless debate. Sources provide little in the way of known feelings or views of their writers, let alone anyone else. History can be deceptive and complex.

"Did you hear me, Beth?"

"Eh? Oh, sorry, Marc, I was miles away."

He rolls his eyes, then smiles. "I'm going to find Rob. I may catch you later."

They manoeuvre hand in hand through the crowded corridor, and as I watch them walk away, I think of Rob, who I've been friends with since the beginning of my first year here. Recently, I've started to think of him as more than a friend but I would never tell Marc that. Not a chance. All the girls seem to fancy Rob, and I don't think he's interested in me like that. A girl can dream, though, right? Things might be different this year. Who knows?

I push Rob out of my mind and take a seat as Professor Marshall begins to lecture on Tudor history.

"Forget Henry VIII for a moment! Cardinal Wolsey is the man to watch…" He cites examples of sources, declaring what a mastermind Wolsey was, until I raise my hand.

"What about Thomas Cromwell, sir? Is he in the background at this point?"

"Cromwell? Now there's a character! He manoeuvres around the throne and around Wolsey. A clever man, more than a mastermind." He nods. "Later Henry's enforcer, as you will hear in subsequent lectures."

He continues to describe the leading players of the Tudor court. I scribble down copious notes, trying to keep up with his eloquent explanations. The professor reminds me of the historian David Starkey, who is extraordinary when speaking of events and personalities, always able to bring a story to life and put it into context, rather than just spouting dates and facts.

My reasons for studying history are simple I want to teach the subject as a secondary school teacher, but gazing through the window, past the lecture hall and beyond the university grounds, I wish I could experience the events at first hand. Yet I know that if I had lived during the Tudor period, I would most likely have been born into poverty, which constituted a third of the population at that time. Not the best start for anyone in the England of that era.

When the lecture finishes, I pack my books away, bringing my thoughts back into the present, watching the other students bundle out the door, their chatter about their social lives, pub meet-ups, and essay deadlines filling the corridor. Distracted by ideas, criticisms, and evaluations of the topics we've all been discussing, I eventually get to my feet, pulling my holdall onto my shoulder. I could murder a cup of tea right now, but rushing to the canteen to grab a hot drink must wait until after I have shown a group of freshers around the humanities department. My thoughts are broken by the sound of my name being called in an inquiring manner. I glance over, realising the professor is addressing me, as we are the last people left in the hall.

"Miss Wickers, before you go, can I ask a favour?" Professor Marshall smiles, peering over his glasses, as I approach him.

"Yes, sir?"

"I've been having a clear-out and wondered whether you would like to take home a few boxes of books that I don't need anymore. I thought you could put them to good use." He beams at me, knowing my passion for the past. I don't want to sound conceited, but I have a feeling I'm one of his favourite students.

I nod enthusiastically. "Thanks, sir."

"The papers and books are in my study, in a box marked 'TO GO'." He presses his office keyring into my hand. The brass keys are heavy, and the metal is cold to the touch. I didn't realise he'd own so many keys. I hope they are just his office keys, and not his house keys. He must trust me, because he motions me through the hall's open door, into the throng of students and staff passing by in the corridor. He turns to me just before he heads off in the opposite direction. His manner seems strange, excited, and the professor gives me a sort on conspiratorial look as he follows me from the lecture hall.

"Put the keys in the top drawer of my desk. I'm off to a department meeting, so I'll leave you to it. See you tomorrow." As I grin with gratitude, he walks away in the opposite direction, disappearing amongst the groups of students. I watch him disappear through the bustling throng, before I head up the oak stairs. I bury the iPhone earbuds in my ears, then open iTunes just as Bowie's 'Rebel Rebel' blasts through my brain. I find the professor's study, locate a big brass metal key, turn it in the keyhole, and enter.

The room smells of old parchment, solid wood, and red wine, as well as stale tobacco smoke. I tug out both earbuds and leave the dangling lead hanging over the neckline of my jacket. Books are scattered on every available surface, while the computer on the desk hums in idle mode.

Searching for the cardboard box in such disorder is no easy task. As I work my way around the room, I can't help myself, tracing my fingers across the gold-leaf lettering along the leather-boundbooks on the shelves, fascinated by the old artefacts, photocopies of State papers, and marble bust of Henry VIII high on a shelf above my head. Small Tudor portraits cover the walls, among them a copy of the famous 1536 Holbein cartoon of Henry VIII, showing the king with hands on hips, legs apart, his gaze boring into me.

There is also a copy of the National Portrait Gallery painting of Anne Boleyn. The portrait is painfully plain, and she stares wistfully down at me with dark eyes from her vantage point, tight-lipped, keeping her secrets.

I consider the painting for a moment. Her reddish-brown hair is constrained into a tame parting beneath her hood, and that famous 'B' pendant hangs from a string of pearls about her slender neck. I know, of course, that this is not a contemporary likeness — the only surviving one being a medal dating from 1534, commemorating her second pregnancy, and inscribed with her motto "The Moost Happi". It is unfortunate that the medal is severely damaged about the nose and left side of her face.

The professor's love of history permeates the office. If only I could spend all my time in his study, reading his papers, searching for primary sources, and losing myself in academia. I almost trip over a box on the floor, then realise it's the one I've come to find. I lift it onto the desk and remove the lid. Inside, I discover the famous biography, *Anne Boleyn* by Norah Lofts; thumbed-through old copies of the journal, *History Today*; a set of *Letters and Papers, Foreign and Domestic, of the Reign of Henry VIII*, and photocopies of *The Life of Cardinal Wolsey* by George Cavendish.

Why would the professor want me to have these books and papers? Surely, they'd be useful for other students besides me? Unable to believe my luck, I stuff the books and documents into my canvas bag, then dump it back at my feet before continuing to search through the box.

At the bottom, to my surprise, I encounter something harder than a book. I lift the few remaining papers aside and pull out a small wooden casket, my focus sharpening when I raise the embossed lid. Inside, a ring glistens and winks at me as the sunlight from the window illuminates it.

I wet my lips and lift the jewelled ring from its cushion of red velvet, marvelling at the small, individual stones twinkling before me. It is heavy, made in a setting of solid gold. At the centre are the initials "AB", surmounted by a small crown. Looking at the faint engraving on the inside of the ring, I can just make out the date: 1532. I glance at the portrait on the wall.

Of course, Anne's "B" pendant. "AB": Anne Boleyn — that must be the connection.

I can't resist sliding it onto my middle finger to see what it looks like, shuddering as a chill runs through me. It is heavy, bold, and regal. Strangely, within seconds, the metal warms against my skin, and I slide it off to take a closer look. It is hot, but not so warm that it is unbearable to wear, so I push it back on.

Should I find Professor Marshall to return it to him? Maybe he left it in the box in error. But I don't have the time for that, as my afternoon lecture will be starting soon. Remembering the date on the ring, I know some research will be necessary if I'm to get to the bottom of its provenance. If there's one thing I'm good at, it's research.

With my bag in hand, now laden with historical booty, I turn to go and notice, almost in front of me, a copy of Eric Ives' *The Life and Death of Anne Boleyn* jutting out from the middle bookshelf. I have my own much-worn copy, so finding the information I need will take just a second.

I reach for the top of the spine, but the book won't budge. Unusual. I tug at it a little harder, and the exposed end moves, like a pulley. The book continues to be stubborn, and I pull again. Then, suddenly, the whole expanse of the bookcase levers itself into a pitch-black cavity in the wall. The door — it can't be anything else — creaks as it slides into the darkness.

I hold my breath and peer into the gloom, my bag's weight pulling on my shoulder, making me falter. My heart is in my mouth as I blink to adjust to the lack of light. Treading on what feels like flagstone slabs, I take minuscule steps into the murky space beyond, and get the fright of my life when a torch to the right of me flickers into life. I jump again when the bookcase slams shut behind me, the sound resonating in the gloom.

What the hell is going on? I grab the torch from its iron holder and wave it around, feeling a bit of a fool but hopeful that if anything nasty happened to be lying in wait, I might scare it away. Having the light close makes me feel somewhat safer. My heart pounds in my chest as I turn back and press against the wall, trying to find the opening where the bookcase had swung from. It's no use. Even if I could see it, the door would be too heavy to open alone.

The torchlight guides me forward as it cuts through the charcoal darkness. There is a heavy mustiness in the air — remnants of smells I don't recognise.

As I continue down a narrow passageway, the sound of students in the adjoining corridors and communal areas fade and then disappear altogether. When I turn a corner, I discover a large door ahead of me, oak-panelled and ancient-looking. The silence is eerie, and I hesitate, wondering whether to back away from the door. How can I describe the stillness behind me, or beyond the door? All I can say is that it is inconceivable for the university to be so silent.

My heart beats in my ears as I stand before this old oak door, its large handle shaped like a lion's head, its tongue hanging from its mouth, almost smirking at me. I place my free hand on it and, using a little force, pull open the door.

Beyond, a narrow stone staircase spirals upwards. I count the steps, all thirteen of them, and continue my exploration, the excitement biting at my heels, egging me on towards a less-cumbersome door ahead. It is ajar, and the room beyond is partially obscured by heavy tapestry drapes. I see a hint of movement through the gap in the door — a shadow shifting in the room's dim light.

# Two

### STUCK, SOMEWHERE IN TIME

My heart skips when my holdall tangles in the drapes as I lean in to open the door. I release it, and it takes a long moment before I dare to step forward, breath held, ready to apologise for disturbing whoever might be here. What is this place? And how haven't I known about it before?

The movement I thought I saw must have been the light streaming through the lead-paned window to my right. My transition into this oddly familiar place is no abrupt jolt, and I experience no disorientation. However, as I enter deeper, I have an unfathomable feeling of foreboding. I'm not prone to moments of darkness, but something has come over me that hints at things I'm not sure I'm ready for.

I squint, then blink a few times to acclimatise to the change in light, amazed that my torch flickers and stills when I rest it into an empty wrought-iron cradle on the wall. Goodness. What's going on? The hazy light illuminates the few pieces of Renaissance furniture spread about this antechamber. I grip my bag as I risk a look out the window, and my face and neck go cold as I'm met with what I can only refer to as expansive gardens, not the university campus I've just left. Where in God's name am I? I have to still be in part of the university — where else would I be?

I brush the hair from my eyes as I peer through the glass, trying to get a better look. Perhaps it could be a digital, green-screen effect, part of an interactive exhibition facilitated by the university. Whatever it is, it's good — wholly realistic. I circle the room with trepidation, unable to resist running my fingers over the walnut trunks stacked along the walls, and notice, above my head, the half-domed ceiling — which I recognise as a fifteenth-century feature. Everything feels strangely familiar.

The floorboards creak. Rushes, gathered in corners with lavender and herbs, look like they have absorbed a few weeks of dust. Everything — the room, the props — appears like something from a historical film set. So authentic.

When I move forward, beyond this small chamber, I see that oak panelling decorates the walls, much like the linen-fold relief carving of Cardinal Wolsey's lodgings at Hampton Court Palace. So beautiful. Whoever built this set, for that's what it has to be, did their homework.

I breathe in the sensuous, musky atmosphere, with the fresh flowers on the window recess filling the air with their delightful top-notes. I drop my bag and walk through a second door, into what appears to be a bedroom, and over to the large window, to find a similar view to the one that met me in the antechamber. To my left, towards the centre of the wall, stands an impressive four-poster double bed, with a rich red tapestry canopy, and velvet curtain hangings falling around it to the floor.

On the nightstand beside the bed, a burnt-out candle rests next to a cluster of leather-bound books. The inkwell beside it is empty, but not yet dry, giving the impression that its contents were recently used on the nearby blotted parchment, on which lies a beautiful quill. I'm tempted to dip my finger but am wary of tinkering with the sheer quality of this reproduction. I've taken part in a few plays covering this period, but the detail here is remarkable — way beyond our amateur efforts.

To my right, down from the window, is a petite, finely carved fireplace, decorated on the outside with wooden panelling and mounted around a simple stone surround. A small tapestry hangs on the far wall of this modestly adorned bedroom, with its feminine accents.

As quietly as I can, I step over to the four-poster. I'm bound to be missed soon if I don't get back to university, but a folded letter on the bed catches my attention. Beautiful to the touch, I believe it is made of calfskin and, with its large, broken wax seal, it looks significant. The writing proves challenging to decipher, but I manage to make out the first line: *My Dearest Marye*. As I trace each word in the opening sentence with my forefinger, I wish I'd listened more attentively to my first-year lectures on reading Renaissance cursive text. The ink is spider-like as it creeps across the vellum, but I persevere, and my endeavours prove worthwhile.

*It pleaseth me for you to come to court, to serve the queene.*

A trill of laughter from the hallway breaks the stillness, the sound dancing on the air. I have no choice but to move, and quickly. I fling the letter back on the bed. If I'm caught, there may be trouble, but where can I go? My only option is to squeeze into a gap between the bed's headboard and the panelled wall, which I do, hiding behind the excess curtain that hangs from the corner post. Whoever it is, once they go, I promise myself to get back to the professor's study without delay.

Shadows move across the floor, and skirts swish, confirming that a couple of women have entered the room. Who could they be? Will I know them? Maybe they're the curators of this fantastic exhibition? If so, they mightn't be too happy with my tinkering about with their perfectly assembled presentation.

My heart pounds in my chest. As I wait for them to leave, I consider my situation. Nothing has changed, nothing whatever appears to have happened, apart from walking through a variety of doors and passageways to bring me to this rather chilly place. Yet, as I hide in this beautiful bedchamber, I experience an elemental terror so great that I lose all common sense of the situation — not knowing where I am, or what I'm supposed to be doing.

I overhear words spoken by two women. Young women. But though they are evidently speaking English, their dialect is one I've never heard before. I focus on catching the essence of their words.

"Sister, you will return with me to court, will you not?"

"Only if Father wishes it. I do not know the plans he has for me now he has summoned me home. I must wait for news of my betrothal. Perhaps Father will bring word from the cardinal instructing me to go to court with you when he has finally arranged my marriage, and, in any case, I should support you, my beautiful sister. Now that you have finally confided in me of the king's interest in you, we need to keep it that way, in the hope that you might be offered a permanent position in the queen's household, do we not?"

"I suppose so."

"The king cannot possibly be interested in you. Well, not in the way he was with Bessie Blount!"

That last remark is made so decidedly, almost with a sarcastic tone. There is silence. I bite my lip. What kind of production is this? Maybe it's a film, and I've stepped onto the set. Yes, the university must be trying to increase its funding by letting the buildings for filming. But surely we would've been told about it. But I can see no trailing wires, sound or lighting engineers, or hear the noises of film cameras or other equipment essential to such a high-quality production. Apart from the ladies, all I hear are the cries of starlings outside the window.

Hold on, is one of the women speaking with a hint of a French accent? My heart flips as footsteps draw closer. Have I been found out? My lungs burn as I hold my breath. Whoever it is, they stop at the side of the bed, and I can't help risking a careful peek past the velvet hangings. She moves, and I catch sight of the train of a blue silk gown gliding after its owner. A high-quality production, indeed.

"I have read the king's letter summoning you to court. It is Father's influence, I trust?"

"No, Anne, not Father, but our Uncle Norfolk. It is also the king's desire I attend court." There's a smile in those words — I can feel it. "Father has suggested I am summoned because the king desires me."

An audible gasp comes from the other woman — Anne. "What about William?" she asks.

"Is this not an honour, sister?"

"I doubt your husband will see it as such!"

"We have no choice — I mean, I have no choice if this is what the king wants."

"You have every choice — this is not a game!"

"Anne, it is a game I must play if I am to secure my future with William. We need money to remodel our home, to have it ready for the children we might have together."

"Sister, I beg you, not every woman has to sleep with the king to secure wealth and happiness."

More swishing of skirts.

"My happiness is to live in the country with my husband, that is all I want. I shall go down and show Father the king's command directly."

With that, the letter is snatched from the bed, and a scurry of footsteps takes both women from the room. No, wait, one of them has remained. Is she coming over?

I'm afraid I'll draw blood from my lip, but as the footsteps change direction, I take the chance to have another look beyond the velvet drapes. A woman's silhouette is framed in daylight. Beautiful. She steps closer to the window, looking out towards the gardens beyond. Her frame is slender, her reddish, dark-brown hair wound intricately under the coif and French hood perched on her head. I notice her long eyelashes and how they cast shadows on her cheeks as she glances down towards where the voices are coming from outside.

About five-feet, three-inches tall, she stands straight and thin like a mannequin, with no curves, apart from her breasts — like small apples — bobbing over the neckline of her Tudor costume. Her neck is slender and elongated as if she possesses extra vertebrae, and she has olive-coloured skin, which is pale — what some would call sallow. She is unusually lovely, and even the tiny moles on her neck add to her beauty.

She leans forward and peers down at whoever is in the garden below. Conversation rises, but I can't pick out a single word until she opens the casement and makes a reply, nodding with excitement, informing whoever it is that she will be downstairs shortly. She turns and makes her way towards the bedroom door, and I peek out to follow her progress, gasping when she trips over my canvas bag and nearly falls flat on her face. No! I left my holdall on the floor.

I almost choke when she bends and lifts it, and one book after another spills out. Her brows draw together as she picks up *The Real Tudors*, which catalogues the art exhibition previously held at the National Portrait Gallery. I pray she'll drop it and go backstage, or wherever actors go once their scene is finished, but she flicks from a page explaining Holbein's paintings to one showing Katharine of Aragon. Her expression grows darker when she opens a page to the portrait of Anne Boleyn.

No! I squeeze out from my hiding place, race across the room, and lunge at her, pushing the book out of her hands. Then I snatch it off the floor. This woman's resemblance to Anne Boleyn is uncanny.

"I'm sorry, but that is mine," I say, catching my breath as I attempt an apologetic smile. "My personal stuff."

I shove the book back into my bag before she sees another picture. She stands there glaring at me, looking confused and alarmed, scanning me from top to toe. Those eyes, so dark, like jet embedded in the soft cream silk of an evening gown — arresting and alluring. I have never seen eyes that black and beautiful. Silence ensues, for what seems like an eternity.

"What is this? And who are you?" she asks, her chin raised, looking down her nose at me from beneath those long eyelashes, her obvious suspicion conveyed in the twitching of the graceful curvature of her spine.

I don't know what to say. What do I tell her? Who the hell is she? And what's the story with this … place? She watches as I fumble with the zip of my canvas holdall then turn to scarper back to the professor's office.

"Come here!" the woman orders.

Now I've ruined her scene. Obediently, I stand in front of her, waiting for her to have a go at me for being here. Sure of herself, this lady — no, this actress — circles me, her skirts trailing as she flicks the collar of my jacket. I tense when she teases the ends of my sun-bleached, creamy blonde curls, piled up today into a messy topknot that trails loose strands about my neck. She pulls up the cuff of my jacket and stares at my watch.

"What is that?"

The words won't come to form my reply. I'm in shock at being in the presence of a woman who looks so like a historical figure I have so long admired. This must be a re-enactment. It has to be.

We stare at each other, equally nonplussed. I touch the back of my head. No soreness anywhere. I can't be concussed, as I didn't trip or fall over. Or maybe I did and simply don't remember. Perhaps I'm dreaming all this while I lie in the professor's study.

As the woman scrutinises me, my temples throb and I shake my head, then look around to search out the cameras. Damn it, I must be on a film set, there's no other explanation for it. This Anne Boleyn lookalike is an actress. She must be.

I want to escape back to the professor's office before the film crew, and production team come in to berate me, but with the actress glaring, staying in character, it's not going to be easy.

"Well?" she demands. "What is that?"

"It's my watch." My whispery voice is barely audible, and she scowls at me. "It's like a ... sundial." For the life of me, I don't know why I said that because it's not like she doesn't know what a watch is.

"Are you a horse rider?" she asks.

"No." I try not to smirk. Do I look like a horse rider, in my ripped jeans and student-vintage, retro look?

A thought nearly lifts me off my feet. What if she thinks I'm part of the production? Maybe she thinks the director's testing her. That would certainly explain why she's remaining in character.

"Why do you wear such attire? Where is your gown?" She frowns, continuing to circle, before standing face-to-face once more.

"But I don't..." I shake my head and shrug. "I don't have a dress, I'm sorry." My sheepish reply draws her closer as her piercing dark eyes continue to search my face for answers.

"What is your name, and why are you come to Hever?"

As I make no reply, my apparent puzzlement seems to annoy her. "You are a stranger in my family home. I ask you again, what is your name?"

This is beginning to wear thin, but I decide to play along, at least for now. "My name is Elizabeth, but my family call me Beth." I stare back at her, not wanting this 'Tudor' lady to have the upper hand. Hever was Anne Boleyn's home. She's good, being able to stay so deep in character.

"Why are you here?" She begins circling me again, looking me up and down, trying to work me out as much as I'm trying to figure her out.

"I have no idea," I answer. "I'm not from here. I'm not part of this ... production."

She studies me now, her eyes betraying confusion. As good as she is, I realise I don't know this actress, but she certainly plays Anne Boleyn well. I know the Boleyn story — especially how it ends. I wonder if she'll let me watch her next scene. After all, I've read enough books, seen enough films and TV documentaries, and thumbed through enough academic essays to have a fair idea of who Anne was, but staring at this actress now, with her true-to-life portrayal, I realise I may be fooling myself.

"What do you mean by *production*?" Her eyes have become small slits under a furrowed brow.

The best thing to do would be to tell her where I've come from. She'll either laugh at me or think I'm some crazed film fan.

"I am a student at the university. Who are you, *really*?"

"I am Lady Anne Boleyn. What university do you speak of?"

How could she possibly be the *real* Anne Boleyn? "Look, stop messing around. You know you're filming in my university. I came from my professor's office, from behind the tapestry props, along the passageway and up the staircase. All I did was fetch some paperwork and books. Now I've ended up here. For goodness sake, tell me who you really are."

The woman looks at me, blinking, waiting, staring. "I have already told you who I am. I am Anne Boleyn. Now, pray, continue to tell *me* who *you* are, and why you have arrived here, standing in my bedchamber."

"I'm a university student. I study history."

"Whatever do you mean?" Her eyes widen, and a peal of laughter fills the room. But as soon as it starts, it stops. She grabs my hand and guides me to the great bed. "What are these incredible stories?" She looks perplexed, pulling me to sit next to her, patting the furs on the mattress. The reeds inside the mattress move beneath us. "What year were you born, and how did you get here? Are you related to one of the servants?"

She doesn't seem to understand what I've told her. How do I get across to her that I'm nothing to do with her family, her servants, nor the village in which her home sits? I give myself a mental shake. I must still be in the university, I have to be, there is no other explanation for it. However, her manner, the accent, the details on the clothing, the room, it all looks so credible. Production or dream, if she believes she's *the* Anne Boleyn, I need to play along. What harm can it do?

"Mistress, I was born over four hundred years from your time, at the end of the twentieth century. I came through that antechamber door, beyond that tapestry on the wall, just as I told you." I get up and walk into the antechamber, and Anne follows. I point to the door I entered through.

"But that door leads to the servants' quarters and the back stairs." She frowns. "Those stairs are not often in use — hence, the wall hanging." She takes time to study my face again. "Please, you must tell me that you know who I am." She blinks. "I am known well hereabouts. My family are servants to the Crown after all."

"If you are who you … say you are, then I believe you are the second-eldest daughter of Thomas and Elizabeth Boleyn." She doesn't smile back at me, as I'd hoped. So much for my playing along. We return to the bed. As we sit, all I can do is stare at her.

"If you are from the future, Elizabeth," she says, her voice tinged with intelligent guile, "what else do you know of me?"

"Mistress Anne, I know that you can play musical instruments. You can sing. You can dance. You can speak French. You are sophisticated and witty."

Now smiling, she clasps my hand between both of hers, her skin warm. Then she gets up from the bed, releases her grip, and dips into a deep curtsy, a flirtatious look on her face. "Oh, yes, I can indeed be sophisticated." Her gown twirls about her as she performs a galliard she probably learnt in a dance class at her drama school. "Do you think I could catch myself a noble Duke or Lord?" She continues to dance around the room, her head raised and arms gracefully open as she takes each step, showing the toe of her slipper beneath the hem of her skirts.

Admiring her grace, I consider more compliments to please her. "I also know, Mistress Anne, since you have recently been exposed to a world of art and beauty, such as the French court, that it will indeed make you an attractive prospect for a nobleman." I keep my answers positive and light-hearted as if she is who she says she is. I almost chuckle at that, but if it was the case, alerting her to her fate might change the course of history, and I can't afford for that to happen. What am I thinking? Why am I worrying? None of this is *real*!

She dances over to me and leans into my ear. "Is there anything else you could teach me, which the French court has not?"

"I have no idea what you mean, Mistress Anne!" I fail to stifle a laugh, hoping she isn't implying what my twenty-first-century mind is perceiving. I search for something suitable to change the subject. "You speak so beautifully." It's true. Her dialect coach has taught her well.

"Thank you. May I call you Beth?"

"Yes." It's rather sweet of her to be so polite, especially when I'm the one encroaching on her territory.

"How old are you?"

"Nearly twenty-one."

"Then you and I are near the same age!"

That surprises me. "What year is this?"

She frowns at me like I've stepped in something that should've been left outside. "It is the year of Our Lord, 1521, of course."

My breath catches as a cold flush races through my body. I shake it off and focus on our conversation. "The month?"

"December."

Ah, I knew something was different. December is a damn cold month, and as I left the professor's office in September, I'm certainly not dressed for the depths of winter. I wonder why she's jumped three months ahead. It's confusing. I feel embarrassed because when I looked out the window, I should have realised the season from the leaf fall and the lack of life in the hedgerows.

I think of where the *real* Anne Boleyn would have been at around the date of December 1521. "You must be just arrived back from the French court of Queen Claude?"

"How do you know this?"

"Like I said, I study history. I'm from the twenty-first century."

"The twenty-first century," she repeats, looking down, her brows creased as if calculating something beyond her grasp. I unzip my bag, pull out a small notepad and pen and scribble down the year I was born, with this year beneath it.

She stares at me, then points at the top line. "You were born in that year?"

"Yes."

She stares at me like she's seeing me for the first time. "And this year?" She points to the line beneath.

"That's the year I'm living in now."

"Hmm."

She's good. Okay, time to take this up a step or two. "Mistress, were you born at Blickling Hall in Norfolk?" I drop the pen and notepad back in my bag.

"Yes, Norfolk is my birthplace. Why all the questions about me? I thought you knew who I was?"

"Yes, Mistress, but not every detail. In any case, some hist—"

"If you know the year I was born and *are* from the future, you must know the year I die." She wets her lips with the tip of her tongue and leans in. "Do you?"

I'll have to think fast here. Improv was never my strong point, and this actress is keeping me on my toes. "I do know the year you die," I say, "and so should you if you're acting out Anne Boleyn's life." I glance about but catch no sight of her production crew. "You're doing a fantastic job of it, might I say."

She squints and leans away from me as if chewing over my response. "I do not understand you, but no matter! It seems you will not give me a straight answer, but the truth will out." She brings her hands together, pressing her slender fingers into a steeple below her nose. "Have you tried returning from whence you came?"

"Yes, but the doorway I came through is stuck and I can't re-open it."

The actress walks to the window, looks up at the sky, then invites me to join her while she studies me further. As I stand with her, a woman calls up from the other side of the moat.

"Anne! You are requested in the parlour. Your father needs to speak with you."

She kneels up on the window seat and leans over the ledge. "Mother, I will be down presently. Is not the letter from the king exciting?" She casts a huge smile towards whoever is there.

I perch next to 'Anne', leaning behind a drape hanging at the window so I cannot be seen over her shoulder, and watch a woman nod beneath the hood of a heavy cape, who smiles back up at Anne. She's carrying a wicker basket, picking winter roses from a flower border running alongside the moat. My legs turn to jelly at the realisation that the view is anything but a greenscreen special-effect. I can see with my own eyes that everything about this scene is as authentic as the beautiful aroma rising from the fresh, winter blooms.

With Anne beside me, I now scrutinise her up close, and I stare at her right hand, with its long, elegant fingers. I don't expect to see a sixth, as documented by the Catholic propagandist, Nicholas Sander. However, at the side of her little finger is a small extra nail, not fully formed. It's barely noticeable. All these signs point to this woman being the *real* deal.

Goosebumps break out all over my skin, and I need to hold onto the sill to prevent collapse.

This is real. My goodness, this is … 1521!

# Three

### Anne Boleyn's Chambers
### – Hever Castle, 1521

I don't know how I do it, but I pull myself together. The woman outside looks middle-aged and has an air of nobility about her. Anne referred to her as Mother. No, she'd hardly be picking roses, would she? Whoever she is, she's too well-dressed to be a servant.

I let out a quiet sigh and bite my lip at the madness of this new reality. What if the door remains stuck? Does this mean I'm here forever? What about my family? My studies? Rob!

I'm glad the woman hasn't seen me, as I hang back beside Anne.

Despite my concerns, the conversation continues.

"Do not tarry, as your father has much to discuss with you and Mary regarding the king's summons."

I turn and plop onto the window seat. This is *real*. My head is swimming. It's not a film production after all. It's not an exhibition. It's not a dream. It's the *real* thing. I pinch my cheeks to get the blood back into them. What to do? I've got to think of a credible way out of this … dilemma. If I can't go back in the direction I came, and it doesn't seem likely, then I'm going to stick out like a sore thumb.

"Lady Anne." I swallow back a ball of nerves. "If I can't go back to where I came from right this minute, what should I do?"

"Stay here with me, of course." She squeezes my shoulder and smiles as if my enormous life-changing problem doesn't cause her the least bit of worry. "All shall be well, and you will get home, but while you are with us, you cannot stay in those clothes. No, they will never do." She starts pacing up and down the room, her eyes sparkling as she knits her plan together.

She stops and claps. Just the once, but the sound nearly gives me a heart attack. "We will say you are a visitor!"

I force myself not to roll my eyes at her stating the obvious. No point alienating my only hope. "From … the country?"

"Perhaps. Hmm… No, we need to convince my father that you are a distant cousin, related on our mother's side, so he suspects nothing." She cups her mouth with her right hand and taps her cheek as she continues pacing.

"I can't be related to your Uncle Norfolk," I say, sitting back on the bed, my legs still trembling. "It wouldn't work. I'm no Howard, Lady Anne." It seems natural to refer to her this way now that my poor brain has accepted my new reality. Or has it?

She smiles. "No, you are right, you cannot be a Howard. Of course not."

I realise my mouth is hanging open as I watch her. All I can do is shake my head. "You really are Anne Boleyn, aren't you?"

"I told you already, yes." She rubs her hands together. Why isn't she phased by what's happening? If I didn't know better, I'd swear this isn't the first time she's encountered a time-traveller. Perhaps I'm not the first. The professor?

She raises a hand, as if about to make a point at a lecture. "We need to decide who you can be, if not a Howard."

This should be easy for me, what with the million or so hours I've spent studying the people of Tudor England, but not one clear name sticks out from the maelstrom in my head.

"I know!" she says, dancing over to me. "Father is arranging my marriage. Shall we say you are related in some way to my betrothed, James Butler, and that you were sent by his family … to let them know what I am like? You are a spy!"

"That's why you've come back from France … for your marriage?" The details are coming back to me but, again, I can't let her know what I know. "Do you think that would work? What happens when James comes to court, or here to Hever?" I get up and walk around the room, my nerves heightened. "Being related to the Butlers might prove dangerous. I may be found out." My mind is both a jumble and a blank. I shake my head at Anne, willing her to come up with an alternative narrative that will convince her parents we aren't deceiving them.

"Although James is a page in Cardinal Wolsey's household, he is often in Ireland. He is with his family there now. Father does not know everything. We shall say you came back with me from France to be my personal maid. Perhaps suggest you have distant relations here, and in France?" She continues to look me up and down. "It is agreed?"

"Agreed." Although I've no idea what I'm agreeing to, her smile is reassuring, and I'm curious. I want to spend time with her, but I'll have missed my next lecture by now, and what about getting home tonight? What about ever getting home? How in the hell am I going to get back?

Panic grips me, and I run back through the antechamber to the drapes and check behind them, tugging on the door handle, but it's shut fast. My heart is beating so fast as fear for my family wells up. If this is as real as it feels, as it looks, what am I to do? I look around, but there seems to be no other exit back to the professor's office. This is like a bad nightmare I have no idea when I'll wake up from.

My phone! I fumble in my jacket pocket, doubting that I'll get any service on the thing, especially as I have no idea where I am, or whose reality I'm in. Anne watches as I pull it out, yank the earplug lead from its socket, hold it up, poke at the power button, but nothing happens — the phone seems dead.

Anne watches me getting annoyed as I wave it around like a flag. I think her curiosity gets the better of her because she comes closer and snatches it from my hand.

"Hey, that's mine!" I yell.

"What is this strange object?" she asks, turning it over in her hands.

My anger disappears, and I laugh. "Come on, I can't believe you've never seen a mobile ph—"

Then I remember — as if I could forget — she really is the real thing.

"Whatever it does, it looks like a strange contraption." She runs her fingers over the phone's glossy screen. "I have never seen anything as odd as this before. What does it do?"

"It's a mobile phone. You talk to your friends with it. Have conversations. Text people. Send messages, emails, photographs."

The poor woman is baffled. And no wonder, as being from the sixteenth century, she will never have seen any post-industrial technology in her life, let alone a mobile phone. I'm so attached to mine; I could never live without it. I take it back, press the power button again, and the thing springs to life. Whoa! I look at the service bar, but it's non-existent. No matter. I open the camera function, then hold the phone out, facing Anne, and snap a picture of the woman, temporarily blinding her with the flash.

Alarmed, she covers her eyes. "What did you do to me? Am I injured?"

I can't help laughing. "No, I took your photo, silly. Look." I turn the screen to her. She draws closer, peering at the picture of her on the screen.

"This is strange. We do not have such a thing as a *mobile* here. The court painters could not do better than this picture you hold up to me."

"Okay, let's call this my Holbein device. To take the likeness of people quickly and without the use of canvas or brush." I smile at my own joke, but she doesn't get it. I flip the power off and stuff the earplugs, lead, and the phone in my bag, hiding it at the bottom to avoid the temptation of taking it out again, wasting what's left of the battery. For what seems like minutes rather than seconds, I stare at the woman, studying her, stunned that this is Anne. Anne Boleyn.

"You are an unusual girl," she says. "And I wish you would not fix your gaze upon me so." She pulls me to the centre of the room, eyeing me up and down in what can only be described as a conspiratorial manner. "Now, let's get you out of these clothes." She smiles, marches to the open doorway on the other side of the bedchamber and calls out to someone named Agnes.

"My maid will be here directly, and we shall find you a suitable gown. Now, get out of these strange clothes before she sees them."

With that, she pulls my jacket from my shoulders. Everything modern is removed, apart from my bra and knickers, and placed in a pile on her bed. I'm left standing in the middle of the chamber, shivering and almost naked. Anne takes my hands and holds them out from my sides, studying my body. She lets go and scrutinises my lingerie, which doesn't exactly make me comfortable. Then she stares at my vaccination marks on my upper arm, stepping closer to prod at them with her forefinger.

"What are these?"

Fearful she'll think my scars are a mark of Satan, I need to come up with a reason for their presence. "The scars are from a visit to a ... barber-surgeon."

"Like *la saignée*?"

"Bloodletting? Not exactly."

"And this?" She twangs my bra strap, so it snaps back onto my shoulder. "And these?" She stares at my knickers, the cerise lace blaring out like a beacon in a grey world.

"It's my underwear."

My comment amuses her. "We have no such garments like these." She laughs. "You have a pleasing figure, Beth, and we are the same gown size, perhaps."

She's right. We do look a similar size.

"Firstly, you need to take those off." She frowns, transfixed by the shape and design of my knickers. The lace slides to the floor, and I step out of them. Then my bra is discarded, just as fast.

Naked, I stand before her, covering my private parts with my hands.

"Do not be shy. We wear a shift under our gowns. That is our underwear. We are not uncivilised." She retrieves a linen shift from a nearby trunk, then places it over my head, just as her maid appears in the doorway.

"You asked for me, Mistress Anne?" She bobs a curtsy, staring at me, her rosy cheeks glowing, and her short, plump frame conveying an air of healthy vitality.

"Agnes, fetch my gown of frost-upon-green and brown fur. The Mistress Elizabeth will also need matching underskirts and a kirtle."

I find it funny that she calls *me* a mistress. Mistress Elizabeth — how grand that sounds. The maidservant starts to turn away.

"Wait! She will also need fore-sleeves and a hood. Do not tarry too long, for my friend shall catch a cold." Anne beams at me, happy to be transforming me into someone suitably dressed to spend time in her company.

With the shift on, I don't feel so exposed, but the wooden floor is cold, creaking as I shuffle from one foot to the other, impatient to be dressed and warm again. Anne stands close to me once more and hands me red woollen stockings. I pull each one on, up my calves and over my knees, securing them with corded garters.

"Sit. We will need to brush your hair and braid it, for you cannot wear it as it is." She fetches a small silver mirror from the inside of a nearby oak storage chest and passes it to me.

I watch her in the mirror as she starts tugging the tangles from my hair with a wooden comb. Usually, I love having my hair touched, but she isn't exactly gentle. She bends to view my reflection, then stares sideways at me.

"Your eyelashes are strange and long, Mistress Elizabeth." She brushes the tips with her fingernail, examining the coating of mascara I have on them. "And what is that floral scent?"

"My perfume is from a bottle, Lady Anne. Would you like to try some?" I jump up, remembering I have a small sample in the inside pocket of my jacket, but before I can get it, the servant appears in the doorway, almost collapsing under the weight of the kirtle, gown, and fore-sleeves.

Anne beckons to her. "Place the clothes on the bed and help me get the Mistress Elizabeth dressed."

Poor Agnes looks puzzled, staring at my bra and knickers on the floor. I suppose she would because, until now, she's never set eyes on me, or twenty-first-century lingerie. She drops everything onto the bed and picks up my bra from the floor and dangles it in front of herself. She holds its cups against her breasts, her eyes wide in amazement.

"Agnes! Fret not about that. It is a new fashion in France." Well and truly told off, the young woman drops the bra on the bed, before picking up a petticoat.

Anne beckons me to stand closer to her. "This is a petticoat," she says, smiling, as if proud of her ability to teach me about her own fashion items.

I don't let on that I know all about Tudor fashion and dive into the quilted taffeta which, incidentally, is mulberry red to match my stockinged legs. Agnes assists in sorting out the kirtle, and manoeuvres my head and arms through it, helping me slip into the thick fabric, which wafts about me. Then she ladder-laces me in, weaving the cord back and forth until my torso resists the tension, all the while pulling it tighter and tighter. To maintain the sureness of the bodice, the kirtle should be as snug as can be. I stand there, leaning into the walnut bedpost, holding on with trepidation, as if hugging a tree, breathing in as the lacing grows steadfast and secure.

Fascinated, and glad to have paid attention in my Tudor-fashion lectures, I look down at the volume of fabric as Agnes secures the light-green gown over my kirtle, then adds the fore-sleeves with their laces, and rolls back the gown sleeves with their big, turned-back cuffs. These are fur-lined and fastened with individual pins.

The gown's bodice is now tied at my breasts and covered with a placard, which has been hand-sewn on one side, with pins to hold it on the other. The double-pearl habiliment — the beaded trim — glistens against gold braid that is decorated with embroidery on the kirtle's neckline. The layers, when worn on top of one another, are such a weight, I'm going to need to be more graceful when I move. When I extend my arms, looking at the drop of the gown sleeves, Anne smiles, and I realise my face must be a picture.

"You look very fine in this gown, do you not? How do you fare, with your kirtle laced so tight, Mistress Elizabeth?"

"Mistress Anne, I'm not used to it, but it won't take me long to learn to carry myself in it, with your tuition, of course." Not that I'll be here that long. I expect to be out of here and back in university in time for my next lecture.

Pleased with my answer, Agnes tells me to extend each arm in turn, as she pushes on some fore-sleeves, which are covered with pearls. She secures them well, tying them about my upper arms, beneath the gown sleeves. Tudor dressing is complicated stuff.

Before I have a chance to admire my new sleeves, Anne unwraps a pair of beautiful slippers from parchment. "Slide your feet in and see if they fit." Her dark eyes brighten as she guides my stockinged toes into the exquisite shoes. I inspect the soft leather as Agnes fastens the brass buckles. My feet feel so snug.

"Now," Anne says, taking a step back to assess her handiwork, "isn't that better than when you arrived?" She turns to Agnes. "You may go. I will do her hair."

Agnes glances at me, curtsies to Anne, and obediently leaves us alone. I take my seat at her dressing table, and Anne resumes brushing my tangled, product-covered hair.

"Why are you doing this?" I ask.

"Why not?" she says. "For the time being, you cannot get home, and I think you may be able to help me."

"How do you think I could possibly help you?"

"If you are from the future, then you may be able to advise me if I am to catch a rich husband."

I already know that family ambition is paramount with the Boleyns, and Anne is obviously not excluded from feeling the same way.

# Four

### Hever Castle, Kent

Having spent the last few hours here at Hever, I'm learning how to move gracefully in my new garb, even getting used to the weight of the layers, though the pureness of my shift's linen feels itchy and a little rough against my skin.

I'm more settled than when I first arrived, thanks to the warm welcome I've received from Anne. My stomach is churning, not just because I'm hungry, but because she wants to introduce me to her parents and to test her cunning plan. I'm also anxious because I've tried the door back to the professor's office numerous times, but it's still stuck fast.

Anne grins. "I have talked to Father and Mother about you being here."

"And?"

"I explained that because I would soon be a married woman in Ireland, I would need a maid of my own and that you had agreed to come back from France with me."

"But surely they would have noticed had you had company when you returned home?"

"I was clever and told Father you had arrived earlier this morning, while he was in an audience with his tenants and servants, collecting rents and handing out wages."

"He believed you?"

"Yes," she replies, her eyes alive with excitement. "They want to see you."

"Goodness. What, right now?"

"Yes, come on! I think I have done just about all I can with your hair. And my gown definitely becomes you." She takes my hand and leads me along the staircase gallery and downstairs to the parlour.

The woman I'd seen earlier from the window, who I believe to be Anne's mother, Elizabeth Boleyn, greets us at the door, waving us through with a welcoming smile into the parlour, where a man is standing before a roaring fire which snaps and spits in the grate.

"Husband, Anne and her acquaintance are here."

I watch as Lady Boleyn walks up to Thomas Boleyn, who embraces his wife and whispers in her ear before she sits in a cushioned chair next to the fireside.

Anne strides boldly into the parlour and stands before her parents. I loiter at the door, my anxiety getting the better of me. She dips a quick curtsy to her father, who acknowledges her with a smile.

"Daughter, fetch Mistress Wickers. She has no need to be shy."

Anne nods and walks back to me, grabs my wrist, then pulls me in front of her father. I shuffle from one foot to the other, not sure of the correct etiquette for meeting a man like Thomas Boleyn for the first time. Standing near this well-known character of Henry VIII's court allows me to study him up close. He's a middle-aged man by modern standards — mid, or maybe late forties, but closer to old age for this period, who in his youth was probably quite handsome. The elaborate cut of his clothing — soft, dark velvet, modestly embellished — shows him to be a man of culture and well-connected. He brushes his hand through his thick, greying hair and nods at me as I dip a curtsy that is nothing but awkward.

"Mistress Wickers."

"Lord B-Boleyn," I stammer.

He chuckles. "No need for such formality." He takes my hand, then plants an itchy kiss against my skin before turning to Anne, who stands next to me. "Anne has explained your situation and has expressed a desire to have you attend on her as a companion, rather than a servant."

"Yes, sir."

"But we know nothing of your family or your history." He flicks a look towards his wife. "We should like to know what kind of companion you would make to our daughter."

"I am educated," was the first thing I could think of that might please him.

"Good, we consider a girl's education important. And your parents?"

"My dad, erm … I mean, Father works in government, and my mother is a tailor's assistant." Though I lie, it's more like an embellishment of the truth. My dad is a civil servant and my mum works in a clothes shop.

"Your father works for the king?"

Thomas Boleyn is bound to jump to that assumption, so I have to steer him off the scent. "He is a clerk, sir. An assistant to people in government."

He nods. "And his income?"

"My father earns a good wage, as does my mother." I don't provide exact figures, as this would give our game away.

"Where do your family come from?"

"Outside London, sir. South of the river." I glance at Anne, and she nods, smiling with encouragement.

"Father, I told you Mistress Wickers was from a good family."

"It appears so," he says. "Which is a good thing if she is to make a suitable chaperone to you in Ireland, or at court."

"I would love for Mistress Wickers to come with me to court, or to Ireland when my marriage goes ahead. Please say it can be so." She lifts her chin. "But if I am to go to court, can Mother come, too?"

Thomas glances at Anne, then at his wife, who sits up.

"Daughter, we have discussed this matter before," she says. "I would prefer to stay at Hever. The estate needs to be run properly when your father is away on diplomatic business or attending the king. You know this." She frowns, evidently cross at Anne suggesting such a thing.

Most wives of successful courtiers would jump at the opportunity of attending court, but from the sounds of it, Elizabeth doesn't seem to have a regular position there. Maybe this is a personal preference, but I've read reports that at one time she may have been a mistress to the king. If that's true, could it be that she doesn't want to go in the hope of avoiding these rumours resurfacing? She doesn't appear to lack confidence and hasn't hinted that her choice not to return to court in support of her daughters is related to whatever might have given her a poor reputation.

Lady Boleyn waits for her husband to speak. Perhaps they're not the type to use their children as pawns to further their family's plans for power and wealth. Is it possible that history has done them both a disservice? From the corner of my eye, I see Lady Boleyn observing me. She is dressed in a sumptuous velvet gown, the colour of dark cocoa — it's gold trim habiliments twinkling in the firelight. Her red hair, which is greying at the temples, is pulled back under an elaborately decorated gable bonnet, which emphasises her high forehead and prominent cheekbones. You can tell that Lady Elizabeth Boleyn, once a Howard, came from money. Love stole her ambitious nature, and she no longer seems to care for power, only for the well-being of her children. A callous, cold, and calculating parent she is not.

"Dearest Anne, you were returned to England due to worsening relations with France." Thomas gives a knowing look to his wife. "The king has much on his mind, and, because of that, your marriage negotiations have been drawn out, and we feel —" he looks at his wife again, then back to Anne — "that perhaps it may be a good thing for you to experience life at the English court before you go to Ireland."

Anne looks anxious. "I would like that, Father, but why are arrangements for my marriage taking so long?"

"There are financial matters to conclude. Dowries. Property. The king has yet to sign his agreement. Up to now, things have only gone as far as Cardinal Wolsey."

Anne tries to speak, but her father holds his hand up. "Daughter, do not become overwrought. There is much preparation to attend to. In the meantime, you shall attend court."

"And if I go, Mistress Wickers can come with me?"

"Yes, Anne." Thomas smiles. "That is if Mistress Elizabeth wishes it."

Anne grins at her father, her hands fluttering at her sides.

He takes a sip from his goblet, licks his bottom lip with the tip of his tongue, as if to save an errant droplet from slipping away, then captures me with a direct look. "Mistress Wickers, Lady Boleyn and I think it best that you stay with us for some weeks, to get used to the idea and, once arrangements have been made, to see how that would suit you." He places his goblet on the fireplace mantle and turns back to me. "Would you like to attend court with Anne?"

Everything he does is controlled, composed, and considered, but not in a Machiavellian manner. He's quite soft-spoken, with no hint of deviousness about him, as far as I can see. The man is a blank canvass — the consummate diplomat.

"Sir, if that could be arranged, I would be most honoured." What an excellent opportunity. I need to blend in, which will necessitate changing my speech patterns. My twenty-first-century colloquialisms and slang will mark me at every turn. No, I must copy the way this family speaks. I must take on board their mannerisms, dialect, and demeanour to help me assimilate.

"I am sure you have been educated as well as Anne when you were at the French court," Lady Boleyn says. "If you are uncertain of your position or responsibilities at His Majesty's court, Anne will be able to guide you. The court can be a licentious place, and you must guard your honour and reputation at all times."

"Yes, my lady," I reply.

"You will meet my brother there, the Duke of Norfolk. He is an earnest, single-minded, and ambitious man, who seeks power and success at any cost, and will use anyone to aid in his ambitions. I have warned Anne against becoming tangled in his web of intrigues, and caution you, too, in case you fall foul of his scheming."

"I shall take note of your warning, Lady Boleyn."

She nods, looking less perturbed now she has been able to air her grievance over her brother. Elizabeth Boleyn seems a loving mother, who views blind ambition as a sin — anxious that her children will not be used to advance her family, regardless of her brother's personal feelings and desires.

Thomas scoffs under his breath. He seems none too happy with his wife mentioning her brother, but from what I have studied of Thomas Boleyn, he's such a professional that he would never burn bridges. Their opinion of the duke certainly isn't a good one, and I wonder if they'd think so kindly, and be so gracious if they knew who I was, and where I'd come from? How would they react if I was able to take them through the portal and back to the professor's office? I shudder at the thought of the chaos that might cause.

Thomas Boleyn looks at me as he strokes his moustache and beard, then he turns to his daughter. "It is settled then. We shall pay Mistress Wickers and I shall write to the king and await his consent on the matter, then send word to the Comptroller of the queen's household when Mary and I return to London in a day or so."

Anne beams. "Thank you, Father!"

"Thank you, sir," I say. I didn't realise I'd be paid — perhaps it's wrong of me to accept, but before I can speak Anne and I curtsy in unison, then leave their presence.

While I'm relieved that this first meeting is over, my nerves are in tatters. I hope Thomas Boleyn doesn't suspect me of lying to him, and I wonder if the professor knows about his bookcase pivoting to a different place in time. He has to. So much is happening.

For all I know, time may not have even moved forward on the other side of the portal. And if it has, will anyone notice my absence? Mum will worry once she realises I'm not around to give her my dirty laundry. Then there's Rob. What's he going to think if I'm not about to chat to? And I don't want to get behind with my coursework. I've got a deadline looming for an assignment — one that's due in a couple of days. The professor will go nuts if I don't submit it on time. No, I need to get back to my own time.

My heart thumps as I gather up my skirts, rush up the staircase, and back to Anne's room. The urgency is apparent to her as I pull back the tapestry in the antechamber. I clutch the iron handle of the door that leads back to the passageway, the portal, and the professor's office. Flustered, heat surges into my face as I push, tug, and bang on the door. Tears sting my eyes through frustration, self-pity, and the incredulity of my situation.

"What can I do to help you?" Anne asks, no doubt trying to ease my anxiety with her gentle speech. She hands me a small linen handkerchief.

"Nothing." I snatch the handkerchief and dab it against my skin, blubbering as I wipe away my tears. "I'm sorry. The problem is, I don't know if I'll ever be able to return to you if I do get back to the university. I don't want to leave you. I don't want to miss the chance to spend time in your world. What an opportunity it is, but the trouble is, I need to go back to my own time. I have obligations to family, friends, and my studies. I have important assignments to complete!"

"I wondered why you were so insistent on trying the door, especially when you have made promises to my parents. You are obliged to me, too, you know. You can't just arrive, become my companion, and then leave again."

With that, I slide down against the door and draw my knees up against my chest, sinking my face into the frothy green velvet of my skirts. My shoulders shake with long, racking sobs, and I feel Anne's hand on my arm. She doesn't seem to know what to do with me.

I look up. Anne's mood has become as dark as her eyes. She juts her chin out, as is her way when her blood is up. "I feel constrained here, too," she snaps, "if that makes you feel any better?" She turns on the spot and gestures to her room. "Home is not like the French court. This house is too small, cold, and dark."

I'm not the only one who feels stuck. She's right in comparing Hever to Château Royal de Blois. Her mother seems distracted with making Hever Castle as comfortable as she can, and her father, while being a gentle soul, seems stressed and sullen due to diplomatic relations, and details of court and European business which are sent to him every other day.

Anne gazes forlornly at the linen-fold panelled walls and fresh, newly-arranged rushes on the floorboards. "My return to England has been on the summons of either my father or Wolsey." Her chin is still up as a sense of unfairness shadows her features. "England is so dull after my experiences of the French court."

She misses her lifestyle abroad. It's a long time since she has been home. I can tell by the way she looks about the place that she feels stifled, being so fresh from the cultivated hothouse of Renaissance France. She extends her hand to me and pulls me up from the floor.

"Come sit with me. There is nothing we can do, for now. Dry your eyes. All will be well, I promise. I will make it so."

Glancing back at the stubborn door, it dawns on me that my situation may be hopeless. The only thing, for now, is to forget about the damned portal and try again tomorrow. I'll persist every day until the bloody thing opens.

"Take my mind off things, Anne. Tell me why you came back from France."

She pulls me into her room. "I served Mary Tudor, the king's sister, before transferring to the household of Queen Claude, and Father has been arranging my engagement for two years, which is why I am summoned home, in order to marry James Butler, the son of my father's cousin, Piers Butler, who claims to be Earl of Ormond."

From my recollections, I know that the matter of Anne's marriage is far from certain, and Piers Butler, although considerably more distantly related to the previous Earl, is his heir male. I recall that the family had some dispute over the Ormond estate with Thomas Boleyn, and that is the apparent reason why Anne's marriage negotiations are so protracted. She says she has never set eyes on James, yet her father seems content with the match. James Butler is young and rich enough to make a good husband, and while researching this period in the past, I admit I've never read anything bad about him. I think Anne trusts her uncle and father to choose well for her, but, of course, I know the match will never happen and must remind myself never to divulge it.

"I will press my father to write to Wolsey, asking him to push the king to agree to the marriage. Wolsey has a way with the king. I am sure he could settle things. I have grown impatient waiting for a decision on the match. At my age, I should have been married by now."

She is excited to show me the small keepsake, a miniature which she keeps in a little draw in a small bedside table. The portrait is so tiny, it is an exquisite rendition, but she holds it, staring at it as if it will help her discover what her intended is really like.

"What think you of James Butler?" she asks, handing me the little portrait. "Is he not handsome?"

"He's handsome. I think your father has chosen well." I smile as she retrieves the miniature and places it back in the drawer.

"I take the portrait out and stare at it from time to time." Anne sighs. "My only consolation has been to read, sew, or draw, or watch Mother order the servants around, while I wait for my future to unfold." She sighs again, long, and hard, groaning with resentment. "All I do is embroider, practise my riding with one of Father's horses, or kick around the house in my slippers waiting for something to happen, and I loathe it!"

"But it won't be long before your father sends word that we can join Queen Katharine. He said we would be at court in a matter of weeks."

"I know. Although I have my marriage to look forward to, Mother is not great company, for she bustles around the house, never having much time for me. The only thing that alleviates the monotony of the place is knowing that my brother George will soon be here with me."

"When will that be? What's George like?" I try to hide my enthusiasm. "Do you prefer the company of men?"

"Most of the time, although … George can be irritating." She smiles, which is nice to see after her recent griping. "I think I will be glad of your companionship, Beth."

# Five

## Still Stuck in the Sixteenth-Century

I've been here two days now, and while I've tried the door many times, it remains stuck fast. Though I'm still not accustomed to my surroundings, little by little, Anne is helping me adapt to life at Hever. Right now, I'm resigned to remaining here for the foreseeable future. It's not that I've accepted my unforeseen circumstances and taken to Tudor life. Hardly. Sleeping in Anne's four-poster bed with her is weird for me. I'm so used to sleeping like a starfish in my own bed at home, not keeping to one side, or even end. What is weirder is Agnes, the servant, sleeping at the base of our bed, on a pallet pulled out from underneath. I've read about this practice by servants, but the reality isn't so easy to adjust to.

I miss my modern conveniences, like having a shower, or using a toilet instead of a chamber pot, retrieved from under the bed and taken out by poor Agnes. When we aren't caught short in the middle of the night, the family does have a water closet towards the back of the castle, near the moat. I pity the poor sod who has to clean the chamber beneath the seat. The water closet is the strangest thing to get used to, especially with all the layers of petticoats and skirts to tussle and negotiate with. The food is also taking some getting used to. In my twenty-first-century experience, the Kentwell Hall re-enactors are brilliant, and the details and essence of Tudor life superb, but the real thing is truly something to be believed.

With Thomas and Anne's sister Mary now returned to court in London, and brother George arriving from Oxford, I have some time to spend with Anne, who has been helping me work on my new dialect and curtsying.

"Where are we going?" I ask as I follow her through the hallway.

"To find George," she answers. "Mother has just told me he is home!" Her eyes sparkle with excitement as we take the stairs. "George has been considered a man since his fifteenth birthday." Adulthood appears to start early in these Tudor times. "He is well-educated, having attended Oxford, and can speak some Italian as well as Latin and French."

I know from my studies that, as children, the Boleyn siblings spent little time together — usual for the period.

As we walk into the long gallery, I see a man leaning against a windowsill as the sun streams through the panes of coloured glass, causing rainbows of iridescent light to illuminate the copper tones in his dark hair.

"You look beautiful, sister, as ever," he says as we approach.

So, this is George. I must admit to being impressed, at least by his looks and stature. His gaze rests on Anne. Then, as we draw closer, he looks me up and down, admiring my borrowed, French-styled clothes.

"He is a decent, intelligent young man," Anne whispers. "Just be yourself, and he will like you." To the untrained eye, he looks as if his only concern is himself and enjoying life. "Do not be fooled by his appearance," she says as if she has read my mind. "He agrees with me on matters concerning reform and has strong religious convictions, though he leans closer to the teachings of Martin Luther than I do."

George takes his sister's hand, confidently pulling her towards him before placing an affectionate kiss on her cheek.

"Brother." She puts a hand on his shoulder. "It feels like forever since I have seen you."

"Indeed, sister. Not since the king's great celebrations near Calais."

"The Field of the Cloth of Gold?" I say.

"Yes, indeed," he answers, scrutinising me.

"I am sorry, George. Let me introduce you to my friend and companion, Mistress Elizabeth Wickers."

George takes my hand and presses his soft lips to my skin. "I am pleased to meet you." He holds me momentarily under his gaze, his eyes twinkling above a mischievous half-smile. "You have fine, green eyes. Most beautiful."

My cheeks flush with heat. What can I say about George? George Boleyn is a character, and even more flamboyant than Anne. Nearly eighteen, the youngest of the siblings, he is the most charming of them all and seems like a terrible flirt. His personality is much like his clothes: colourful, over-the-top, exuberant, and a little foolish. He stands about five-foot, nine inches, with dark hair like his sister's and incredibly piercing amber eyes.

His demeanour is so mesmerising that I'm finding it difficult to concentrate. It's also challenging, as our meeting progresses, to dodge his questions about my connections to his family. He seems keen to know how I became a companion to his sister. Also, I'm not overly used to admiration from the opposite sex, and blush every time he pays me a compliment, which he finds immensely amusing, teasing me terribly as I try to dismiss his interest.

Anne grows exasperated with him for making me feel uncomfortable. "You know," she whispers, when we are out of earshot, "you need to keep your composure around my brother. It is important to be gracious to him always. And you must never reveal our story."

She takes George's arm as we walk through the long gallery, a room I have fallen in love with during visits to Hever back in the twenty-first century. The pair seem close, and George appears to be his sister's confidant and friend. I watch them, wondering if the accusations made against them in years to come have any truth. At this present moment, it appears not. This seems a healthy, supportive, and loving relationship between a brother and sister. Thank God!

With the sunlight fading outside, I hear his every word as he leads her to the central window seat.

"Has Father told you about the latest rumours at court concerning our sister?" he whispers. I pretend not to listen, gazing into the gardens below from the next window.

"No, brother." Anne grimaces.

"Mary has confided to me that she has been asked to be a lady-in-waiting to the queen."

She nods. "I also read the confirmation of it in the king's letter, commanding Mary return to court."

"I have heard that the king wants her as his mistress!"

"No, George. The letter simply asked Mary to attend court to serve the queen." Anne frowns at her brother. "If Mary is attending court under some other command, she will bring disgrace on the Boleyn name and will be referred to as a prostitute, if she does not take care."

George looks serious. "People will only call Mary such names because of the rumours which circulated a few years ago, about her sharing the bed of the French king."

"No, Mary never did that! I have heard that rumour, too, I grant you, though I never believed it. Besides, Father was with us constantly, on diplomatic duties. I think he would have known if she had slept with François. Father sent her home to protect her reputation."

"I know Father sent Mary home earlier than you, but courtiers think the rumours must be true, sister."

Anne lowers her eyelids, and I discern a hint of a headshake. "George, stop this nonsense! I cannot believe you are discussing our sister in such a way. Courtiers might believe gossip, but I would never believe such a thing of her. Mary never cavorted with François. I heard the French king had tried to kiss her and asked her to his chamber, but she had refused him. Mary was discreet." She looks at her brother. "Even though she is my elder sister, I can assure you, she never said anything to me directly about the French king, apart from the fact he had propositioned her. Besides, I warned her how to deal with men, just as Marguerite of Austria warned me."

"And what did you say?"

"That gentlewomen in our position must, always, remember who we are, or the honour of our family and their hopes for our futures may almost certainly be at stake."

"And?" George urges, leaning in closer.

"I told Mary it is up to us, as ladies of the court, whether it be French or English, to rein in the lusts of men, so they be civilised gentleman, suitably behaved in the presence of royalty. Marguerite advised us about courtly love. We were to flirt, encourage, and even bestow favours — to a point."

George fails to stifle a chuckle. "But the ultimate prize," he says, laughing again, "is a woman's … virginity."

Anne thumps him. "A woman's virtue, as you know, is the greatest gift any woman can give to her husband."

"But the trouble with Mary is that she is too easily led by men."

"How would you know that?"

"I know what most noble ladies are like." I try to stop myself glaring at George as he continues. "And because I know Mary. She loves to please people, but, most of all, she loves to please men." He glances about, and though I'm only a few feet away, I feel almost invisible. I never imagined George would be so rude, unkind, and downright insulting about his own sister. "I too am shocked sister, that such rumours of François still fly about, especially when this 'affair' happened two years ago." Now he's trying to redeem himself!

Anne answers, "But … Mary assured me at the time that nothing happened!"

"Are you sure she did not succumb to his royal charms?" George replies as if he's waiting for Anne to interrupt him. "I know it was Father's reputation and high standing with the king that meant he managed to marry her off respectably to William Carey, without a struggle, but I cannot help but wonder if there was truth in the rumours, especially if it is true that Henry now has his eye on her!"

"George, I heard about the incidents with François from Mary when we were at the French court together, but that does not mean that just because François took a fancy to her, that Henry now sets his sights on her too." She tuts at George. "Father was much relieved that François' pursuit of our sister didn't ruin her marriage prospects, but she was discreet enough to not discuss the French king, except with Father and me." She takes a deep breath and sighs. "You only had to see how François looked at her to know he wanted something to go on between them."

George raises both eyebrows and nods.

"Besides," Anne continues, "Mary was considered sport by François, all the women at the French court were, except his wife, of course! Father did very well in securing her marriage, the negotiations were advantageous, George." The corners of Anne's mouth curl. "Even though William Carey is a man of small fortune, he owns land and is reasonably connected at the English court. Besides, you have seen how happy they are together."

The hint of a smile pulls at George's mouth. "It is true she loves William, but it is rumoured that our king fancies our sister, regardless of her marriage. Would it not be possible that she might fancy the king too?"

"Brother, you presume too much!" Anne grumbles.

"I have told you; Mary has been ordered back to court to serve Queen Katharine."

Anne stiffens. "The king will not look at our sister, not in *that* way. Henry wants her at court to be a servant. A lady of the royal household, nothing more. She is respectable, now that she is a married woman. William will no doubt hope that Mary will start a family with him soon. I should like to become an aunt." She frowns. "It would not do to have these rumours repeating, of her having been a mistress to King François, when she was nothing of the sort, let alone that she might become a mistress to *our king*."

I know Anne is telling half-truths to her brother, and I sigh, thinking of the conversation I heard between the sisters on the day of my arrival. Everyone speaks in whispers here — it takes some getting used to. I edge closer.

George laughs. "It seems Mary Carey enjoys collecting monarchs, as one might collect Aesop's fables."

"Stop it, brother, you are cruel to speak of Mary so. I will not believe she ever slept with King François. I swear, she never accepted his advances, and if she had, I believe she would have told me. No, you add to the gossip, which is all rumour, brother, I assure you. Our sister's reputation will be in ruins if these lies carry on." She sighs and wrings both hands, probably concerned that her sister's reputation might also reflect poorly on her.

I clear my throat. "Maybe Mary feels that if she promises herself to King Henry, she would be doing her courtly duty?"

Anne snaps a look at me. "Now *you* presume too much! Mary has done nothing of the sort, and if she has, she needs to learn her duty by remaining faithful to her husband!"

That shuts me up. I need to learn not to allow my knowledge of their lives to drive my behaviour. Watching these two in conversation, they indeed appear close, and George seems happy to listen to Anne, although at times he loves to make fun of her.

After a light supper of bread and soup, which I must force myself to eat — it is served so differently to modern recipes — Anne and I retire. As I munch on a smuggled piece of gingerbread, I realise that it tastes better than some I've had when re-enacting. They don't quite meet the standard of this Tudor one. I must keep this in mind for my next re-enactment, if I ever get back home.

As we are now accustomed to doing, Anne and I closet ourselves in her bedchamber, away from everyone else in the castle, change into our dressing gowns, in the style of the one Christina of Denmark wears in her full-length portrait by Holbein. They are not just for wearing in the bedchamber and are slightly less formal than the French style.

Anne calls her bedroom her little sanctum, and we sit with the beloved family wolfhound, Griffin, discussing the events of the day — in this case, Mary — but before long, George pops his head in, making his way into the room so he can be the centre of attention. He stands before the hearth, poking and nudging the slumbering coals back to life.

"You do not mind me joining you?"

"No, George," Anne replies, closing her eyes for a moment.

"I thought you would both be getting ready to turn in for the night, but I know you are still discussing Mary. Do not deny it."

"We might have been talking about Mary, what of it?" Anne replies.

"One would think you are jealous, sister."

Anne glares at him. "I am *not* jealous!"

"You are jealous!" George chuckles. "Jealous of Mary already being married. Jealous that she attracts the attention of kings."

"No, brother!" Anne grimaces. "My time will come to marry."

She's not wrong, but she doesn't know it. I try to stifle a laugh, and they both look in my direction.

George persists. "The king fancies himself with all the young, beautiful women of the court," he says, chuckling to himself. "Henry Tudor loves to flirt!" George is certainly cheeky. "And it cannot be denied that dear Mary does attract male attention. The king's attention."

"Brother, you must relent and take up another pursuit."

He smirks at Anne, steps over Griffin, throws himself back into a chair, and stretches his feet towards the flames as the rekindled fire licks the chimney breast. "Mary is beautiful to look at — that you cannot dispute. Her features are pleasing on the eye, unlike the Spanish women at court, who are dull, and never as pretty as our English girls." He laughs. "Besides, Mary isn't cursed with your dark eyes, slender neck, and continental air."

"What is that supposed to mean?" Anne bristles, glaring back at him. "I do *not* look Spanish!" I get the impression she knows very well that he's teasing her. She sits straight, her neck seeming to stretch even more. "Some have said my features are alluring."

"I meant nothing by it," George says, waving her irritation away. "I know my friend Wyatt thinks you are alluring!"

Witnessing these two hurling barbs at one another reminds me of attending Wimbledon with my dad when we watched several fierce rallies. George and Anne make me feel as if I need to referee.

"Brother, do not talk to me of Tom Wyatt!" Anne replies.

"Anne definitely doesn't look Spanish, George. French, perhaps, but never Spanish," I remark, defending my friend, before finishing the last bite of my gingerbread — a useful stalling device to focus on my new Tudor-speak. "You know very well that a certain kind of physical beauty is not always essential — her wit and intellect, as well as her Frenchified manners, so different from the English and Spanish women at court, will stand Anne in good stead, if and when she attends. Besides, I am led to believe Mary is not as well read, nor as accomplished, although she may be able to compete in terms of her beauty, even excel beyond Anne in that regard, concerning the attention of men."

"No, you are right. Beauty is not always essential," he smirks, "but, my goodness, does it not help?" George stares at me, probably wondering why I'm such an authority on his sisters.

"Well, yes," I reply.

"Indeed, Anne is cosmopolitan, I'll grant you. And you are right, Mary may excel with her beauty, but she cannot compete with my younger sister's European education."

Anne shrugs, opening her palms and raising them towards George as if to suggest to her brother, *I am here*.

I glance in her direction. "Mary went to France, but not for as long as you, is that right?"

"That is so," she says, nodding once. "She did not stay, once the Duchess of Suffolk returned home."

I smile to myself over how they often give the full title of everyone, probably because they think I won't understand who they're talking about. How little they know!

"As I said, Mistress Wickers, my sister Mary was never allowed the same opportunities as Anne. Granted, she spent some time in France, but Father knew Mary's looks rather than her intellect would stand her in greater stead in finding a husband." He chuckles. "Besides, Father had heard the rumours about King François and dragged Mary home for the protection of her reputation!"

"No, George, that is not entirely true! We spoke of this earlier. Mary was sent home because she was not asked to stay on in France, as I was." For the time, I imagine that was such an accolade for Anne. Being invited to any court, as a lady-in-waiting, must have been the Tudor equivalent of finding fame. "Do you think I am more of a catch than our sister?" Anne continues.

"Yes, of course, but for your intelligence and wit, rather than your features!" He laughs, but avoids her glare, probably hoping he hasn't overstepped the mark.

George is good at giving back-handed compliments. I'll have to watch out for that. I'm glad he agrees with me, about Anne being the more attractive of the two sisters, and I'm relieved that I haven't revealed too much of what I know of them from my research. I'm fair-haired, but surely George can't suggest that a full-bosomed, blonde-haired beauty is the only ideal woman and option for a man. From the way he describes Mary, you'd think she was the Tudor equivalent of Marilyn Monroe. I reassure Anne that brunettes can also be attractive. This will not be the Tudor version of gentlemen preferring blondes.

"Anne, you have the confidence and abilities to surpass your sister in most things."

"You think so, even though Mary does, from time to time, boast a manner about her that is twice as compassionate, caring, and not as capricious as Anne's?" George asks me.

I force back a twenty-first-century repost and make do with "Yes."

Anne sulks, obviously impacted by her brother's teasing. George, of course, continues smirking at her, delighted at her irritation. He's infuriating me now, and I wish he would be quiet or perhaps change the topic of discussion, but he seems to be enjoying himself too much.

I grab a pomegranate from a nearby plate and throw it at him in the hope it may shut him up! To be honest, I want to knock him clean out with it, but my aim is useless, and he catches the flying fruit with ease, laughing at me. Griffin snaps at his hand but misses. It makes George laugh even more.

"Poor Anne," he continues, slicing open the rich fruit with a sharp knife, then slurping the juices and innards up with a smack of his lips. Considering George is thought of in his time as a man, he appears to be immature to a degree, and I clench my hands in my lap as he continues to goad Anne. "How will you cope with being second-best to Mary?" He smirks in Anne's direction. "Do you think men will flock to you like they do to Mary, if and when you and Mistress Wickers both attend court?"

He chuckles rather unkindly, nearly spewing pomegranate seeds inside the opening of his shirt. "Or do you think James Butler will save you from the attention of other men, sister?" He wipes his chin with his sleeve, staining it in the process. "I am sure he will suffice in time, will he not? Father has made you a good match. I am certain you will get used to the cold in Ireland." He looks at his sister, obviously aware that she wants the matter of her marriage fixed. His dimples dance on his cheeks as he carries on his campaign.

Anne lobs a small cushion at him in retaliation, but it misses, ending up on the floor behind him. Griffin ambles to his feet, thinking it's a game.

"Oh, sister, do not be mad at me!" George laughs. "Although you are not yet at court, you need not worry, dear Anne, nor you, Beth, for soon there will be many of Henry's gentlemen waiting for both of you to just glance their way. You can encourage Henry's courtiers with your fine eyes, Anne, unless, of course, James has married you, and already made you his." George glances at me. "And who could not fancy you, Beth, with your creamy blonde hair, freckles, and deep-green eyes?"

Heat rises in my cheeks as I shift in my seat.

"George, stop teasing Beth so. It's not like you to make our friends feel uncomfortable."

"Anne, I was paying Beth a compliment!"

"Nevertheless, she is our guest, and you *must* be respectful."

"Anne, it's okay," I say, almost apologising for George.

"No, it is not. My brother is younger than you and me, and he needs to learn to be a gentleman."

"So, now you are both ganging up on me!"

"No, let's just stop this petty argument about Mary being better than Anne, or vice versa. Can we?"

"I agree!" Anne smiles. "We two sisters have different attributes but can be equally beguiling!" She chuckles.

I think about a time to come, sometime soon, when it will be the king of England fighting for Anne's attention, but I can't let that gem slip. As much as I try to stop it, my blood burns in my cheeks as George's taunting continues, despite being told off. Goodness knows how this makes Anne feel, because it has me squirming in my seat. Surely this young man can't be such a tormentor.

"Despite my charms, brother, I will never encourage the men of the court, and neither will Mistress Wickers." She lifts her chin in defiance. "I am not like our sister. I do not want a bad reputation."

"I don't think Mary wants a bad reputation." I glance in Anne's direction. "However, you're right about one thing, Anne," I say in support, "I am not looking for a man to ruin my reputation, either. I already have someone interested in me, back home."

George stares at me, his brow raised, and Anne looks surprised, not only as I haven't mentioned a boyfriend before, but probably because I've spoken up for myself.

"I have a pre-contract, but marriage is a long way off," I lie, thinking of Rob, whose face, I must admit, is always etched in my mind. "Anne, your brother must know your father was arranging your match when we were in France?" Hopefully, this will mislead George about my connection to his sister.

"Yes," Anne replies, rather bluntly. She turns to her brother. "James's father and our father spend much time quibbling over details, protracting the arrangement, and leave me waiting. You know this."

"Of course, I do. I apologise for teasing you, Anne, but you must allow me to just a little, as we have not been in each other's company for such a time."

A hint of a smile turns the corner of Anne's mouth — she understands her brother's humour far more than me and, I think, enjoys teasing him a little, too.

Small flames hiss and crackle from the burning wood in the grate and hot tongues spit when George tosses the gutted pomegranate into the hearth. He then leans forward and offers me a plate of sweetmeats, which I refuse, passing them on to Anne, who sits daydreaming beside me. She nibbles at her selection, sliding the morsel into her cheek and chewing it fast, probably hoping she has time to eat it before being called to speak again.

"On a serious point, though, can you imagine our sister in the arms of Henry Tudor?" George asks her. "Because I am not sure I can."

Anne rolls her eyes at me, then shaking her head at George, infuriated by his persistence. "To be honest, I do not want to, brother!"

"Please George, have we not discussed Mary enough?" I plead. He shrugs, and my mind wanders as I consider what the king might look like. Would he be portly, like his Holbein portrait, or athletic, tall, and virtuous, as the historian Suzannah Lipscomb describes him during her talks and television programmes? The thought of meeting Henry VIII in the flesh frightens me, and I wonder how Mary manages to lure a man like him, let alone keep him.

Anne swallows her treat and sniffs. "George, I do not want to imagine Mary even kissing our king."

"I think it is Mary's virtuous and sweet nature that arouses the king's interest," I say, knowing what I know of Mary Carey.

George looks at me beneath his brows. "Unless King François has lied, telling Henry what Mary might be like in bed?" He tries to stifle his laughter.

"George, I cannot believe you would suggest that!" I glare at him.

"I swear it must be that, Beth, for I am surprised she can summon up anything of interest to say. The trouble is, I find Mary far too obliging, fair, and kind. I expect when in royal company, she cannot match the conversation of the king in matters of politics, religion, or music."

"George, please stop it! I am sure she amuses the king in her own way." Anne's dark eyes glint with a mischievous light. "Besides, we do not know that Mary entertains the king in the way you insinuate. She has only received a summons from him, that is all. I have told you repeatedly that I do not believe any of these salacious rumours, which you seem to relish in retelling."

She must know something is going on with King Henry from what Mary said to her when she received the summons, but I'll keep my mouth shut — it's the best way. George, however, insists on continuing the conversation.

He clears his throat and sits back. "Henry will not care what she says or does, so long as she opens her legs and allows him his freedom with her." He laughs, his beautiful amber eyes reflecting the firelight. "The sharpest ambitions are conceived in the softest pouches, or so Uncle Norfolk says." He watches me, aware from precedence that I take offence at his remarks, as does Anne.

I grimace, but it doesn't prevent him from amusing himself at my expense. George Boleyn enjoys winding people up! I need to remember how young he still is. Three years younger than me. Even so, I'd have thought his time at court so far would have made him more mature. Perhaps it's all the excitement of being home, catching Anne up with all the gossip.

With all this banter to the detriment of women, the game of courtly love seems a dangerous one for any courtier to play — I hope not to have to participate in it during my time with the Boleyns, although George insists on practising with me. My attention is still on him, though I try my best not to meet his smug gaze.

Anne sees my discomfort and her chin raises again. "Everyone talks of Mary. Mother, Father, Grandmama. No one talks of me, and I have been away the longest!" She scowls at George. "Mary must be ambitious for this family, and that is why she might accept an invitation to the king's bed. *If* she goes to the king's bed. You are rude, George, insulting our dear sister. There is no reason for you to be so unkind."

George pouts like a child, knowing he's in the wrong. It is a sight I find easy to like.

"Both of you need not concern yourselves with Mary. I have heard that the king's liaisons are soon over," I say. "Is that true?"

"The king has not had many mistresses that we know of, except Bessie Blount."

Anne nods. "Mary will stay in William's bed, you will see. I tell you; I do not believe Mary will succumb to the king!"

Her defiant arguing is a ploy to remove George from the scent. From what I heard of her conversation with her sister when I hid behind the bed, Anne knows full well that Mary would never consider turning down the king if an invitation to share his bed arose. Mary admitted it.

"Ooh, I think I have annoyed my sister, Beth. What say you?"

"You have hacked us off with your unsavoury comments, George. Anne is right about you — you are unkind."

He stares back, understanding my meaning, even if he doesn't recognise the phrase I use. Anne glares at me, and I realise that I should remember to be more sixteenth-century. It's not so easy blending in, but spending time with these siblings is a big help.

I've read that George had a way with women, which I can well believe — Anne has told me he flirts with the female servants, but he isn't at his best here. I've encountered online reports by the American historian Retha Warnicke that he was also attracted to men but observing the way he ogles me, homosexuality seems unlikely. Besides, neither George nor the court musician Mark Smeaton were charged with treason — set out in the Buggery Act of 1533 — when they were arrested in 1536. I shudder at the thought — of the arrest, not the treason.

Sitting with him now, I don't doubt his ability to entice women, as he is good-looking: dark like Anne, but with his mother's gentle features — an irresistible combination. Both Mary and George, it seems, are attractive to the opposite sex, while Anne has confided in me that suitors, despite the licentiousness of François' side of the French court, never lured her. Claude raised Anne in her circle to act virtuously and chaste. I wonder if she's still a virgin. I almost roll my eyes at that — I must remember not to judge Anne or her sister by twenty-first-century standards.

"As I said," George says to me, obviously deciding to continue, "you cannot blame a man for taking a fancy to any young and beautiful woman. Not when the prize could be so delightful."

I wish George would just shut up! He's difficult to ignore with his crude remarks, and I force my thoughts towards Mary's husband. "My sympathies are with William Carey, not his wife. I'm sure he hates the rumours that are circulating and must find it difficult hearing that Mary might have been with the French king, before him. What must he be feeling? They've not been married a long time, have they?"

"William and Mary married last year, in the Chapel Royal at Greenwich Palace," Anne says, unaware that I would know the exact date.

"Carey is an Esquire of the Body," George states. "A relative and close friend of the king, which made it a pre-requisite that Henry attend the wedding."

"The king made an offering at the ceremony," Anne says. "Even though I did not return home for her nuptials, Mary wrote to me, telling me all about it."

"What kind of offering?" I ask.

"A financial one, and very generous, too," Anne replies.

I remember having read that Henry was known to make financial offerings to family who wed, but have no idea of the amount given to William and Mary.

George pokes at the fire. "William Carey shares the king's appreciation of art, is assembling his own collection, and has introduced the Dutch artist, Lucas van Horenbolte to the court."

Anne stares at her brother for a moment, then turns to me. "I must assure you, Beth, that the marriage of Mary to William has been no hasty affair, and never designed to cover up any interest the king might have in her."

"I believe you, Anne," I say.

George throws another shovel of coal on the fire, then prods the embers back to life. He sits back and takes us in. "Indeed, William Carey is a great match for Mary, he always was. As well as holding one of the most coveted positions in the royal household, he is a major figure at court, and is in high favour with the king." George speaks ten to the dozen, rambling on, before stuffing another portion of sweetmeats into his mouth.

"We know William is not the first husband to be so used by the king, if indeed Mary may go to Henry's bed." Anne glares once again at her brother. "And if Henry were to use his wife, and make a cuckold of him, he will probably not be the last."

George rubs Griffin's head. "To be cuckolded by a king is no insult, Anne. William should be grateful. If the king wants to honour such a man by using his wife, regardless of her marriage, he will have her, and besides, we do not even know if the king has so honoured our sister by taking her to his bed, do we?"

"So far, brother, as I have repeated before, Mary has decided to accept an invitation to court, nothing more."

"Would Mary hold the king at arm's length to save her marriage?" I ask, approaching the situation from my modern standpoint.

George smiles. "Only if she wishes to cling to what remains of her chaste reputation."

"So, you think the king will just talk with Mary in his privy chambers?" My tone reveals my exasperation.

"Probably not," he says, his eyes glinting once more. "Not going by the king's reputation with women, anyway."

Anne gasps. "George, are you suggesting the king is not honourable when it comes to women?"

"The king makes demands of women, like any man," George replies, his manner matter of fact.

"Do you think Mary would refuse the king if he asks? Surely Father would disown her if she did not have the strength of character to refuse him, would he not?"

"My dear sister, please." George shakes his head and looks to the ceiling. "You think Father would never speak to Mary again if she became the king's mistress? Admittedly, Father is not as ambitious as our Uncle Norfolk, and he would certainly never deliberately push Mary in the king's way." He leans towards his sister. "Look, Carey has a good position, but his family is not very rich. Mary's dowry has been spent and, as a family, we must use this situation to our benefit. Father is realistic enough to know that even if Mary refuses the king, as one of Henry's most trusted ambassadors, the family would never lose its royal connection, but to save face, he will need to make sure Mary does not refuse Henry, even if he hates the idea of her being in the king's bed. He must make sure the king is pleased with our sister. The king usually looks after his whores and pays well for a virgin's sweet cherry."

I roll my eyes, fully aware that as a married woman, Mary could no longer be a virgin.

Yawning, I watch as Anne flings another cushion, this time hitting her target. She is furious with her brother, as she knows, as does he, that the family has been on the rise for years.

"I do not like the fact that you underestimate Father's standing at court, and as a diplomat in France. Do you not remember how Father was rushed in, led by the hand of Louise of Savoy, to greet Queen Claude when she was in confinement?"

"Yes, how could I forget?" George strokes Griffin, who rests his head against his leg. "I know Father is a man of influence and wields enormous respect." His grin lights up his face, knowing well of his father's diplomatic efforts. Neither George nor Anne underestimate Boleyn's standing at court, in England and abroad. George knows that the elevation of the family has nothing to do with the king's interest in his eldest sister. Thomas Boleyn is Treasurer of Henry's household — he doesn't need his daughters in any royal bed.

Anne sighs, pulling at her dressing-gown sleeves. "George, Father would never allow Mary to be so used and would certainly never encourage it. Now, can we stop all this talk of our sister?"

"I agree, Anne," I say. "Let us change the subject." I'm shocked by George's manner. How can he speak of his own sister in such a way? I wonder if it's perfectly normal for the men of this period to talk of their women in such a manner. If it is, this is something of a behavioural revelation to me, but how could I take it back to my time and prove it? If I included it in an assignment, how could I back it up?

Mary's virginity must have been lost to her husband, and will her honour eventually be lost to the king? My mind drifts back to what I've read of Henry. Does he really have the overwhelming presence so many of his contemporaries described? Maybe I can ask George to shed some light on life at the English court. I catch his eye.

"I have heard it said that being in the king's presence is like being reflected in the constant rays of the sun and that when he speaks to you, you alone feel like you are the only one who has his attention. Is this true, George?"

"Being in the company of the king is like no other experience on earth," he replies, leaning back against a cushion. "He has an opinion on many subjects, and is interested in all his courtiers, knowing them all by name."

"He knows everyone?" I ask, surprised.

"Of course he does — his favour is granted to many, and with exuberance. He embraces his courtiers without ceremony, and converses for a long while, very familiarly, on various subjects, in good Latin, and in fluent French." He smiles, his teeth gleaming. "I swear to you, His Majesty is the handsomest man at court and above the usual height, with an extremely fine calf to his leg. His complexion is very fair and bright, and his auburn hair is usually combed straight and short, in the French fashion."

"He sounds wonderful."

"And he plays well on the lute and harpsichord, sings from a music book at sight, draws the bow with greater strength than any man in England, and jousts marvellously. Believe me, he is in every respect a most accomplished prince, if not the greatest sovereign in Christendom." George's smile conveys his confidence that he has answered my question.

I stifle a laugh — he talks about King Henry as if he's writing some kind of dating ad — George will never discover how I already know his king!

"I know I have bored you both with conversations about Mary," he says, "and I know neither of you wishes to discuss the matter any further, but you will be better able to assess the king and his countenance, as well as Mary's situation, in a month or so when I accompany you both to court. You will find it very different from life at Hever. The king is clever, sometimes impetuous, and has a habit of dancing with his courtiers' ideas, but never in a straight line to reach his target. However, once achieved, his claws can take a callous grip. Also, His Majesty desires to be liked — he is as vulnerable as he is hard-nosed."

He seems to know what he's talking about and, for so young a person, comes across as on-the-ball, which is both charming and disconcerting. My thoughts wander to Anne. I can't imagine how she will have the power to resist Henry for the seven years of their fateful courtship. The king doesn't sound like a man who can ever be denied anything. It makes me consider my companion in a different light — to hold the king's interest and prolong it for so long, seems unbelievable.

George gains my attention when he cracks a walnut in his palms and begins to separate the innards from the outer shell. For a man with such an athletic figure, he has no trouble putting away quantities of food. My thoughts are interrupted by a knock at the door.

"Ladies, are you decent?"

"Yes, Father," Anne answers, as Thomas steps into the room. He looks at us in our damask dressing gowns, surprised by our informal attire. He then sees George with his lap full of walnut shell and eyes him suspiciously.

"No wonder my purse feels light!" he exclaims, frowning. "Perhaps you should just eat my money instead?" he growls. "Stop smuggling food up here!"

George looks rather sheepishly at his father, then brushes some of the walnut shell off his lap, mixing them with the herbs and rushes that cover the floorboards, probably in the hope his misdemeanour will be forgotten.

"Do not be long to bed, George," Thomas says. "Anne and Elizabeth need their rest." Thomas plants a kiss on Anne's forehead, and smiles gently in my direction. He seems like a gentle soul, so different from how history has painted him.

"I will not, Father, I promise." George grins, knowing he has avoided a good telling off.

"Goodnight, Papa." Anne replies to his affectionate kiss.

"Goodnight," Thomas says.

"Goodnight, sir!" I call out to Thomas, who closes the bedroom door behind him as he leaves. I smirk at George. His face is flushed, no doubt because he's embarrassed his father rebuked him in front of me. I hold back a smile and carry on our conversation before we were interrupted.

"So, George, you compare your king to a crab — hard-shelled, yet inwardly soft and pliable?" I nervously nudge a stray piece of walnut shell across the floor with my toes. Panic bubbles in my tummy as I realise the enormity of visiting the Tudor version of Camelot. George looks at me, probably concerned he may have overstepped the mark again, as he so often seems to do.

He finally nods. "The king can be changeable."

"At least Father is not," Anne coughs into her hand. "Father told me yesterday that I am to be part of the queen's household as a maid-of-honour."

"You never told me," I say, a little put out at not being included in her confidence.

George flings the remaining nutshells into the fire. "Now that King Henry has negotiated a rapprochement with the Emperor, Anne is no longer required at the French court."

"Will there be a war between England and France?" I ask, striving to keep any hint of foreknowledge out of my eyes.

"Almost certainly," George replies. "It is imperative that Father continues to make a way for our family in England, now that diplomatic relations with France have broken down."

As he talks, I almost have to pinch myself, still finding it hard to believe that I'm here, witnessing the very history I'm so in love with. "As I will be accompanying Anne, what about my position at court?" I ask, fearful of being excluded further.

"Father will negotiate a place for you, and I suspect you will also be a maid-of-honour to the queen."

"Really? I thought I would only assist Anne."

George smiles. "Yes, you might do both. Besides, the queen prefers her ladies to be beautiful."

"You are certainly that, Mistress Wickers," Anne says.

The room shifts and my head feels light, as if I'm about to faint.

"Are you unwell, Beth?" George asks, reaching over and rubbing my hand.

"George, ask Agnes to bring some ale, and some bread and cheese. Elizabeth looks pale. She has not eaten much today and perhaps sits too close to the fire."

With that, George almost runs from the room, calling for a snack of bread, cheese, and a jug of ale for me. Anne leads me to the bed, where I'm encouraged to make myself comfortable.

Minutes later, Agnes enters and places the food and drink on the bedside table, as George bows and scrapes to me, looking like an unwanted lapdog. He pulls a chair up beside the bed, and Anne waves Agnes out of the room. It seems the servant has taken to me — the poor girl has been fussing around me for the last couple of minutes and reluctantly takes herself away.

"Mistress Elizabeth, I am so sorry for causing you any distress. I am not rude, just honest. I apologise if you felt I was lewd. I am not normally that way. Would you forgive me?" He takes my hand, which is a surprise to both Anne and me.

"Yes, of course. Do not worry, I did not take too much offence. I'm just hungry and tired." I bite back the urge to say '*hangry*'. "I'll feel better once I've had some sleep."

I get off the bed and stand. For all George's annoying little habits, I can't help but like him.

"Please leave us be now, brother. Beth needs rest, and your conversation has vexed us. She will be well on the morrow. Until then, we both bid you goodnight." Anne bends to kiss his forehead. He gets up from the chair and says goodnight, looking appropriately apologetic.

As he leaves, Anne's mother enters. She stares at George, glancing at the pomegranate stains on the neckline of his shirt.

"George, you were told not to bring food up here!" She starts fiddling with his shirt. "Look at that linen! I will never get that stain out!" She smirks at him. "Be off to bed with you!" Lady Boleyn inclines her face towards George so he can kiss her goodnight.

"Sleep well."

"Goodnight, Mother."

Her entrance and George's departure awakens Griffin from his slumber, he lifts his head and thumps his tail on the floor as Lady Boleyn sits.

I dip a curtsy before sitting back on the bed, where I pick at the cheese from the pewter plate on the nightstand.

"Girls, are you going to bed?"

"Soon," Anne replies.

"Have you everything you both need?"

"Yes, Lady Boleyn." I smile.

"Mother, will Father join us at court? I am worried because George says he is taking us."

"Your father shall be waiting in Richmond for you, then he will take you to York Place," Lady Boleyn replies. "Everything has been planned. You will be safe with George on your journey."

"What am I to wear to London, Lady Boleyn?" I ask, daunted by the enormity of attending the English court. I'm worried I'll stick out like a sore thumb and draw attention to myself.

"I am certain Anne will have something you can borrow."

"Mother, would Father allow Beth and me to speak to the court tailor, Skutt, and ask for new gowns and shifts? Beth has nothing. Her trunks were lost in France." She lies well.

"Girls, my husband told me a few weeks ago that his money will not stretch to new silks, velvets, and the use of an embroiderer, and if you both go together, he has suggested you should share, and make do with what you already have."

"Mother, please talk to Father again. Beth certainly needs new gowns."

"Anne! For the time being, you must share. You have such wonderful gowns. What is wrong with sharing? You must not be so ungrateful."

Anne sniffs, and I frown back at her.

"Lady Boleyn, I am really grateful for everything that you and Sir Thomas are doing for me, you are both very kind."

"Elizabeth, we are glad to be of assistance in this matter, as you will be chaperoning our daughter."

"Lady Elizabeth, please call me Beth." I smile. "It will lead to less confusion, with both of us having the same name!"

Lady Boleyn smiles. "Of course, if you are happy with us being so informal, dear?"

"Yes, Mistress." I really hope I'm addressing Lady Elizabeth as I should be. No one has explained the etiquette expected within the Tudor home, and I hope I'm not making any mistakes. "You have taken me in and have treated me like family, which I do not deserve."

"Beth, it is our pleasure." Lady Boleyn returns to the matter of clothing. "As you know, Anne has trunks full of clothes, and more fore-sleeves, French hoods, and slippers than the Great Royal Wardrobe. Believe me, neither of you will look ill-turned out. It is a good job you and Anne are of similar stature."

She's right, as I have enjoyed my time spent in Anne's dressing room, which is full of divine silks and satins, lined with pelts of miniver and encrusted with jewels. Anne's real creations bear little comparison to the costumes I've used in my re-enactments. Maybe, after seeing and wearing the real thing, I can make some improvements to my own, if and when I'm able to return home.

"We will find something for you to wear, Beth." Lady Boleyn turns to Anne. "Besides, Anne, you have many gowns. You can't wear each one at the same time!"

Anne grimaces at her mother again, yet I find myself cheered. I sit back against the walnut headboard, smooth out my dressing gown, and wipe the crumbs from my lap. My energy has increased, but I'll not risk my light-headedness returning so stretch my legs out on the bed furs and kick off my kid-leather and satin-slashed slippers.

"And there will be no other ladies with gowns cut in the French mode," Lady Elizabeth continues. "The queen of France would never have allowed her ladies to be dressed in anything but the latest fashions. We sent you to the Netherlands and then France so you would have the best education, language tutors, access to the best tailors, artists, and music teachers. Everything I did not have as a girl."

I'm surprised Lady Boleyn had little agency in her youth. After all, her family had money when she was young. Perhaps it was her marriage to Thomas that meant she had to do with less. I wonder if she ever regrets the choices she made? Maybe, like most Tudor women, even though she married for love, she has had little control over how her life has turned out. Griffin wanders over to Lady Boleyn's feet and slumps on the floor.

"I am grateful, Mother. I learnt so much whilst with Marguerite, and with Claude, who is pious and knows how to behave, despite the behaviour of her husband's side of the court, and how her court mocks the French queen's physical deformities." In a tender moment, Anne presses her hand into her mother's. "Do you remember The Château de Chambord? It has a spectacular spiral staircase, ornamented with classical statues and filigree. The French court is at the heart of all culture — François even invited the artist Leonardo da Vinci to visit — and in spending time there, I had the chance of watching him draw and paint."

I realise my mouth is hanging open as I listen to this conversation. I never knew Anne had met da Vinci!

"You have been fortunate to meet such important people, but you must know I missed you growing up." Lady Boleyn looks like she's about to tear up. "Yet, for the time lost between us, you have been fortunate to have opportunities I never experienced, and it has been money well spent. Your Father is proud of you, too."

Lady Boleyn sighs. "Anne, you may not be the prettiest girl at court, but you and Beth will certainly both be the most stylish of the queen's ladies, with Beth's beauty, and, in your case, Anne, your particular wit, you will amuse everyone."

Anne beams at her mother, then at me, reassured by the praise we are receiving. Lady Boleyn seems to enjoy giving backhanded compliments, like George.

"We were so proud, too, when Marguerite of Austria wrote from her summer palace at La Vure to your father. She found you so bright and pleasant for your young age that she felt more beholden to your father and me for sending you to her, than we should have been to her. She trained you exceedingly well. The letter you wrote to your father at such a young age was well composed." Pride radiates from her smiling face.

It is fascinating listening to Lady Boleyn talk to her daughter and gives me a great insight into their relationship. I need to savour such moments, because they are the ones the history books will never record.

"You will impress the ambassadors if no one else. You excel at speaking French."

Anne grimaces, folding her arms across her chest. "My French vocabulary was terrible! How could you say it was good?"

"For your age, when you were younger, you were accomplished." Lady Boleyn pats Anne's arm. "Now, you excel. But it will not impress the queen if you speak French in front of her. You must work on your Spanish."

Anne usually is the graceful epitome of courtly life. But she's complaining, obviously wanting to escape her rural life at Hever. I know from the records she is only at Hever in short intervals. I wonder how she'd have coped if she'd ended up in Ireland? I'm the only one who knows that will never happen. She still has an opportunity to shine at the English court, to show off her ability to dance, play the lute, converse in French, and read some Latin and Greek. All these graces, I know, will entrance the English king.

"I want to be accepted with Queen Katharine in the same way, Mother, and I hope I will be of all virtuous repute when I arrive at court. I am looking forward to conversing with the queen — someone so wise and good, from whom I can learn so much."

"Lady Boleyn, what is Queen Katharine like?" I ask.

"As the daughter of two reigning monarchs, she is highly educated, as is to be expected. The queen is cunning, with an unflinching fighting spirit, no doubt gained from her mother, Isabella of Castile. She does not understand failure and reigns alongside the king in most matters."

"A formidable woman, then," Anne says, nodding to herself. "Much like Marguerite of Navarre."

"What of her religion?" I ask, curious to have some aspects of Katharine's stoic character revealed.

"Katharine is of the faith," Lady Boleyn replies, continuing to pat her daughter's hand. "She follows doctrine unswervingly."

"What of her relationship with the king?" Anne asks, somewhat unexpectedly.

Elizabeth Boleyn looks at her daughter, her shock at the question evident in her widened eyes. "The queen believes, like all good women, that after God, we must obey our husbands."

Anne nods.

Contemplating the conversation tonight, I find it easy to see why Katharine's desire to rule alongside Henry, whilst obeying her husband, is a source of conflict that runs like a silken thread throughout her life.

"Now girls, do not think on all these things." Lady Boleyn smiles. "It will make it difficult for you to sleep!"

Griffin follows Elizabeth Boleyn around the bedroom as she kisses her daughter and me goodnight before Agnes helps us undress down to our shifts, ready for bed. I share the four-poster with Anne, while Agnes eventually slumbers on a pallet at the foot of our bed.

Today has revealed that Anne has many different sides to her character. She is innocent, yet sophisticated, with polished manners, as well as being pious and at the same time worldly. I'm hoping she will astonish both English king and court with her cosmopolitan style and wit, just as the history books recorded — then perhaps the gossips will leave Mary — and her reputation — alone for a while.

I snuff the candle out with one blow. Once I'm certain both Anne and Agnes are asleep, I slip out from under the coverlets, onto the moonlit floorboards, and tiptoe out into the cold antechamber, taking the opportunity to check the portal. Tonight, again, my efforts are to no avail — the door is still jammed shut.

# Six

## Stuck, Forever it seems, at Hever Castle

I've tried the door to the portal on several occasions. The strange thing is that whenever I approach it, the ring on my finger heats up, but not enough to become unbearably uncomfortable. It makes me wonder whether it has something to do with the portal opening? It's a serious piece of jewellery, and I'm beginning to think that it must, in some way, be connected, yet while it remains on my middle finger, the blasted door has *still* failed to open, even with me twisting it round and round each time. Nothing happens.

I've been in the sixteenth century for over seven weeks. Seven weeks! What must my family and friends think of my disappearance? For all I know, there's a colossal search across the nation. Or has time there stopped since I slipped through the portal? Have I taken a quantum leap into a parallel world where time moves at a different rate? The only way I'll know the answer is to return to my twenty-first-century life, but that won't happen for the foreseeable future now that my path in Tudor England has taken something of a radical turn.

With mixed feelings, I have accepted Thomas Boleyn's invitation to attend court. While I'm buzzing with excitement, I'm also anxious at the thought of leaving the portal, my only connection to the twenty-first century, behind. As I help Agnes and the other servants load the trunks, Anne and George are still inside, saying goodbye to their mother. The servants assist us into the litter. Agnes steps up first and sits at the curtained window on the far side. Then I nudge up next to her. She squeezes my hand, obviously aware of my anxiety.

"Mistress Wickers, I am as nervous as you about attending court. I will always be there to look after you and the Lady Anne, and I promise that I will behave in a way that will make you both proud of me."

I watch the corner of her mouth turn up in a reassuring smile and consider how different Agnes's country accent is to Anne's French one. This sweet-natured, comforting creature has such a sensitive character and seems the most caring young woman I have ever come across. As I embrace her, she stiffens. I don't think she knows how to take my show of affection.

"You are lucky, Agnes," I say, breaking my embrace.

"Why might that be, Mistress?"

"Because servants such as you can stay back in the shadows, undetected and unnoticed by important men and women. Out of any danger, so long as you do not get embroiled in the intrigues of court."

"Lady Boleyn, Anne's mother, instructed me in matters about serving at court. I have been warned that if I do anything to distress Mistress Anne, then I will be sent home, to be a burden to my parents."

"Agnes, that will never happen. You have no need to fear."

My own fear stems from the fact that I am leaving Hever and the portal behind. It is my only way back. The prospect of being separated from my only means of returning home — of being miles away in London — has my stomach fluttering.

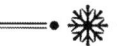

---

The bright spring sunshine warms the air as George and Anne appear, walking arm in arm under the portcullis and over the drawbridge. Anne enters the litter, with George's assistance. She straightens out the knotted silks of her gown and sits on the seat opposite, while George proudly squeezes in next to me.

Our journey, first to Richmond Palace, then York Place — Cardinal Wolsey's London house — starts off somewhat arduous. The litter, like a primitive carriage, burdened with our baggage, constantly lurches from side to side. Agnes slumbers next to me, her head on my shoulder. I'm surprised she can doze with the jolting. Though bumpy, the journey hasn't been too bad since leaving Hever, which embodies for me all that is typically English.

The village of Edenbridge, which dominates the area, as it will do for centuries, creates a timeless contrast of church, inn, and castle, with a few typically medieval cottages dotted about, all surrounded by the lush green Kent countryside.

Anne sits upright, opposite me, with a whole seat to herself. George rests against me — I can feel his body heat — and as we pass Penshurst Place on the way to Tonbridge, which is just a couple of miles from Hever, he leans across me and Agnes, reaching to pull back the curtain to stick his head out the window. His action reveals the elegant exterior of Penshurst — well, the entrance gate, at least.

He is so close that his thigh is pressing into mine. I can't move, trapped between Agnes and this young, virile man. He probably means nothing by such a move, and it's possibly all in my twenty-first-century mind. I could push him away but, secretly, I'm enjoying this unintended intimacy. I know I shouldn't, but there is something that attracts me to him. George's over-familiarity mustn't surprise me, because he's so confident by nature. Perhaps that's why I like him. I press my spine against the seat while he points out the view.

"Penshurst Place has recently been returned to the king," he says, gesturing to the entrance gate. "As the estate belonged to the traitor, Buckingham, Penshurst has now become the property of the Crown."

Agnes shifts in her seat without opening her eyes and rests against the side of the litter.

"What will Henry use the house for?" I lean across Agnes to poke my head out, craning my neck for a better look, aware of the lack of space between Agnes, George, and me.

"I'm sure the king will use it as a hunting lodge. I know his friend, the Duke of Suffolk, stays here regularly."

We move on from the castle's mellow stone walls, which drowse in the leafy valley of lush vegetation; a paradise of orchards and hidden gardens, its vine-shaded walks and rose gardens echoing the fragrances of a familiar England. I listen in wondrous excitement as George relays his stories of Tudor life, people, and places.

Having explored Hever with Anne, I had been loathed to leave its rooms, but George assures me that I will find court far more fascinating. Of course, Hever Castle is entirely different from its existence in modern times. There is no visitors' centre, no shop, no Astor Wing, and none of the Tudor portraits that will be collected and displayed centuries later, hang upon the walls. Some of the original furniture that Anne and her family use daily is still in the castle in modern England, but because of the coachloads of tourists, visitors are forbidden to touch anything. For an historian-in-training like me, it is the most magical experience to see and use such artefacts in context, when they are in their prime condition.

George witters on about the people we are likely to meet. He explains that he must pick up his own valet to take with him to London. Anne listens politely until she can get a word in edgeways, and Agnes starts snoring as her head rattles against the side of the litter. We all chuckle at the noises she's making.

"I hope you are happy, dear Beth, with the gowns and shifts I have given you," Anne says, her words gushing with excitement. "It is only right that you have your own wardrobe at court."

I almost have to pinch myself at the reality that I am living part of this history that enthrals so many of us in the twenty-first century. I keep trying to make a mental note, take pictures in my mind of every detail, of the smells, of the textures of Tudor life and wish my mobile phone, which I've left back at Hever tucked away with my modern clothes, would work. But there is no signal, of course, and I don't want to waste what is left of the battery's life.

I have taken many photographs when alone, and sneakily when Anne wasn't watching me. Imagine the stir it would cause at university if the students knew I have actual pictures of Anne Boleyn. Trouble is, if my secret becomes common knowledge, details of the portal, and so many other things, will come to light. There would likely be an investigation, and I would have no evidence other than the photographs, which I'd never be able to prove were the real thing.

"I am so very grateful." I smile back at her, turning the ring on my index finger. I've been clever at hiding the cypher while in company, twisting the band, keeping the initials tucked beneath my finger.

"Do not mind my sister — Anne will want you looking a poor reflection against her, as she will not want you to outshine her!"

"George!" I glare at him.

"It is a good job I am leaving you both to travel from Tonbridge alone, otherwise by the time we reach London, I would be covered in bruises!" He laughs, eyeing me with relief.

Anne scowls. "Father was under the impression you would escort us the whole way to Richmond, and then on to York Place."

"No, sister, I have business to attend to." He traces his forefinger across his upper lip. "Besides, the driver will keep you all from harm. The country roads are peaceful in comparison to the city."

Anne, obviously put out, frowns at her brother all the way to Tonbridge. When we arrive at the inn, a young man steps to the door.

"George Boleyn?" he asks as we step down from the litter.

"Yes. You are John?"

"Yes, sir." John bows.

"No need for formalities, boy. At least not until we arrive in London." George smiles, probably tickled that he is not much older than this poor servant standing before him. He indicates which trunks are his and orders John to reload them onto another litter. "Sister, I will stop at the inn for an hour, share a jug of ale, then follow on with my servant. I need to acquaint him with the ways of court, sort out his attire, and wait for horses to be prepared."

Anne's mood brightens, probably because she knows George will not be far behind us. "Very well, brother, but do not tarry. Beth and I do not want to be lone travellers on the road."

"Do not worry, Anne, all is arranged." He nods to the driver before embracing his sister, then kisses my hand. He laughs as colour rises in my cheeks; even with my schooling from Anne and George, I'm still not used to the ways of courtly etiquette.

Agnes is now wide awake, having stepped out into the crisp air. "Mistress Anne, may I ride upfront, alongside the driver? It will give you and Mistress Wickers the chance to sleep if you both need to."

"I do not see why you cannot," Anne replies as we step back into the litter.

We set off again, without George, which is probably a good thing, as after an hour or so, the horses tire, so we must take a break at the side of the road, giving us time to stretch our legs, relieve ourselves behind a tree, and drink a little wine we have been saving in a leather bombard. I wonder what Rob would think if he could see me grappling with my petticoats and skirts, trying to negotiate long grass and mud underfoot!

As we journey on, Anne and I discuss many topics, but most of all, she wants to know why historians are so interested in her.

"Is it because I am to be a lady-in-waiting to Queen Katharine that learned men in your time discuss me?"

I wince inwardly, wondering how I can answer her questions without revealing too much. "Mistress Anne, the Tudor court and the reign of King Henry VIII and his heirs have a massive impact on England and its history." I pause for a second, trying to think of what else I can say. "Anyone so connected with the court is read, written, and debated about, even five hundred years since."

"So, I am studied by scholars and students? Women go to university where you come from?"

"Yes, they do, and you are studied, Mistress Anne. Female historians, in particular, are fascinated with you."

She looks at me, puzzled by my comments. Reading her expression, I really feel as if I should explain.

"Women have the same rights as men, Anne. They can make decisions, they can earn money, buy their own homes, marry whomever they choose, and even have children without marrying, should they so decide."

Her eyes widen at my revelations. "When in France," she says, "I read the work of Christine de Pisan. She was a fourteenth-century Italian writer who became a speaker for the rights of women during her lifetime."

The fact that Anne has read some of her work sheds light on why she will become so forthright in her views, and be a mistress who will go on to say 'no' to a king.

"All rights of inheritance go to men, don't they?" I ask. "When a woman marries, all her property becomes her husband's?"

"Indeed, it does. Women have always been restricted where inheritance of land is concerned, and they are restricted from membership of guilds. And what of God, of faith, in your time?"

"Well, we still have some factions within our religious beliefs in my time, as you do between Catholics and Reformers, but faith is not seen as important as it is now. We also have other religions."

Anne raises an eyebrow and looks dismayed at my answer.

"We are a multicultural society, Mistress, made up of different faiths and races."

"You mean you live alongside Saracens, such as the English fought against in the Holy Wars?"

"Yes, Mistress."

She stares at me in astonishment. "At present, we struggle against ancient thinking as we try to reform the Catholic faith. Father has told me that not a few days ago, Bishop Warham wrote to Wolsey, who has received letters from Oxford, and in them, Warham has written that the university is infected with Lutheranism, and many books forbidden by Wolsey are obtained and have circulation there."

She glances about and urges me closer, obviously worried she might be overheard by Agnes, upfront with the driver, but the clatter of livery means no one can hear our conversation.

"Is this where George learnt about Luther?" I ask.

"Yes, and in France. Tracts are circulating in places such as Oxford, which are things pleasant to the Lutherans beyond the sea, and a great encouragement if the two universities — Oxford, which has been void of all heresies, and the other, Cambridge, which boasts it has never been defiled — should embrace these tenets."

"So, literature is circulating against Catholicism?" I ask as if I didn't know.

"The university has requested the bishops of Rochester or London to draw up a table of Lutheran writers who are to be avoided. It seems that this new religion is beset with setbacks at this time, and I am sure any pamphlets or books smuggled in by Lutherans will be burned."

I concentrate on what she says, knowing how ardently she will support reform. I know George will come quite near to becoming a Lutheran, but that Anne and her father will die as orthodox Catholics — the Boleyns will become zealous for the cause of reform within the Church and, eventually, evangelical rather than Lutheran.

Luther launched an attack on the Pope in 1517 by translating the Bible into German. His radical ideas spread across Germany and Europe as his 'doctrine of grace' struck at the heart of the Catholic Church. Luther believed that people obtained eternal life, not by the Church holding the keys to the gates of heaven, but through justification by faith. What is happening now is not just a war of words and manuscripts back and forth between clerics, but a battle for souls. Henry has become 'Defender of the Faith' through arguing in written doctrines against Luther's subversive beliefs. But the new ideas suggest that the only way to save a person's soul is to read the word of God and to understand it in their own language.

"Luther will make it his life's work to ensure the Bible is available to all," I continue, and wish I could reassure her with all that I know, but I should remain discreet and silent on matters so as not to attract attention once I'm at court.

"Our old faith twists everything, Beth. Christ crucified does not transfigure into bread. Did Jesus suggest he was a door or a vine?"

"No, Mistress Anne, Jesus never meant that he was literally a door or a vine, or even that his body was bread or his blood wine. The Catholics have translated the word of God and changed its meaning, but everything will turn out well. Soon there will be an English bible in black and white." It's not that I'm an agnostic or an atheist — I'm glad my own beliefs mean that I don't have to keep up any pretences, having to assuage Anne that everything will be okay when the likes of Galileo and all that entails is just around the corner. For fear of alarming her, I mustn't let her know that a sizable chunk of the modern world doesn't believe in the 'God' of her world, and that science will go on to reveal the wonders of the universe.

"Beth, sympathisers of an English bible being printed will face severe punishment."

"You wait, Anne. Things will change. Give God time. Tyndale will introduce a New Testament from Cologne three years from now, for anyone who can read the truth, so that scriptures will be plainly placed before the eyes of lay people in their mother tongue. Despite the dangers and expense of the endeavour and the quashing of the printer's workshop, three thousand copies of the pernicious merchandise will eventually be smuggled on to our shores."

"Be careful, Beth, that is heresy!" she exclaims as the litter lurches. She wrings her hands and looks to the window. "Who will be so Bedlam mad to keep people in dark ignorance when they can have access to true light by reading the word of God?"

"Mistress, it is the truth. In a few years, Tyndale will smuggle in copies of his translation of the New Testament in barrels from the ports. The book will be small enough to be hidden away in clothes, carried around surreptitiously to protect its readers because they could be tortured and sometimes executed for even possessing it."

Her eyes widen as she moves across the litter to sit beside me, leaning in close to ensure our conversation is exclusive. She looks at me excitedly as I carry on.

"Tyndale's Bible will be a translation that will have a powerful effect on your friends and relatives. The word of God is destined to be read by all, as Tyndale's simple language is resonant, and he keeps sentences short and simple, translated from the Greek. For the ordinary people of our country, it will be an education and a revelation. My Lady, I know it is hard now for you to imagine the effect the English translation will have on the minds of the people who read it. They will understand the stories, the conflicts, the nuances, the arguments, the characters — the difficulties in the New Testament, which will be all theirs to debate and discuss amongst themselves — even the potboy will have an opinion." Have I said too much already? I must think of something to say to reassure her. "I sympathise with you," I continue, "as I believe in a personal faith with God and that we are saved by grace alone. I also believe that it is acceptable before God when two or three evangelicals gather in his name, He hears their prayers."

Anne's composure grows calmer as she rests against me, shoulder to shoulder. "Then we are of the same mind, Mistress Elizabeth, are we not?"

"You need not fear, Anne, I am your faithful servant."

She smiles, showing her understanding as she hands me her personal copy of a Book of Hours, the calfskin pages of which, to my astonishment, look fresh and feel crisp, the illuminations so vibrant. It takes my breath away as I turn each page, trying to read the devotions and examine the illustrations, which are perfect with the gold leaf and inks so intertwined.

"This Book of Hours," she explains, "was made in Bruges in around 1450, and was a present from my father. He handed it down to me from his family."

I turn to the page that bears the inscription *Le Temps Viendra — the time will come —* and Anne's signature, *Je Anne Boleyn*, which is written beneath a miniature of the Last Judgement. There is also a drawing of an astrolabe in dark ink.

"This," she says, pointing, "symbolises time."

I trace my finger over the black ink, which is as pitch as night. My hands tremble as I realise that this priceless object is in my possession — book historians would go crazy over. I hand it back, not wanting to damage it.

"Please read it anytime you should wish, and take great nourishment from it, as I do."

"Thank you. Can you please explain to me why you have written *Le Temps Viendra* in your prayer book?"

She smiles, and replies almost prophetically, "I know that one day, God has something special in mind for me. I have always believed it so, which is why I have such faith. God will not fail me, and I will not falter. My time will come, and God will grant me His grace to do His bidding."

"You impress me, Mistress, and I will pray daily that God grants you your heart's desires, as you are faithful to Him."

She places the book beside her on the seat, leans into me, grasping my hands in hers. "Oh, dearest Beth, I know you understand me! We are kindred spirits, you and me. We shall be friends forever."

During these hours of travelling by litter, we discuss many topics. We talk of the poet Thomas Wyatt, with whom Anne spends a lot of time, and

George, who she insists is infatuated with me. Our conversation turns to etiquette at court and what is expected of us when we are in the company of the king or queen.

After some time, we leave the countryside behind and approach the streets of London. I'm excited but also shocked. The streets are crowded and stink of stale food and human waste. The noise outside the litter is an intrusive cacophony as we drown in a babble of voices, with traders packing up their wares and rowdy drunkards spilling from tightly packed alehouses, hanging around in the doorways, trying to pick up whores ready for the approaching dusk.

Looking up, I notice something rather odd. A clear sky. Yes, there are clouds, but no contrails. London's sky is usually full of them, not to mention the planes attached. I must remind myself that we are not in modern-day England, but a Renaissance, Tudor land, where everything is so beautiful, yet alien, like the blue, London sky.

Candles flicker in the cloudy windows of merchants and tailors, who sit cross-legged in their establishments as they work under the strain of bad light, showing their talent and wares.

The cobbled and muddy lanes are filled with a different kind of pollution. Not car fumes, but the stench of excrement and urine thrown from upstairs windows. There is also the unmistakable pong of perspiring bodies crushing around the last of the market stalls, looking for a bargain.

I chuckle to myself, thinking of the hustle and bustle of modern Oxford Street and the throngs of people there on a Saturday afternoon, which is not so different, apart from the veil of time that separates the fashions, stock on sale, and the politics of capitalism. Oxford Street, during this time, is called Oxford Road, and it leads to Tyburn, where most traitors die a public death, either by burning or hanging. I'm hoping and praying that our litter won't make its way past such a notorious site, where bodies are left hanging and in cages until they rot.

For the first few days, Anne tells me, we are to stay at the Palace of Richmond. She has been assigned a tailor from the Wardrobe of Robes, a Master John Skutt and his apprentice, Paul Cotton, to prepare gowns at twenty-eight pounds each, ready for our debut. Contrary to popular belief, the people of the sixteenth century are more civilised than I'd been led to believe. Anne says she will teach me how to mix rosewater for bathing, and she tells me her mother has packed and prepared potions for our use. So, these noblewomen behave like any modern woman would do — why am I so surprised?

Luckily, I had my make-up bag in my holdall when I passed through the portal, and I've brought it with me so we can stay as fresh as possible with some modern toiletries. As we near the end of our journey, I spray myself with my floral-scented perfume.

Anne scrutinises everything I do, fascinated as I explain how she can use my moisturiser on her skin, a touch of mascara on her eyelashes, and a dusting of blusher to her cheeks to enhance her olive-toned complexion — not such an easy task with the litter rocking as it does. She seems most impressed by my bottle of perfume, snatching it from me and spraying it on her décolleté.

Then she rubs a dab of toothpaste onto her front teeth, and I smile, watching her enjoy the tingle of the paste on the tip of her tongue. She tells me that she usually uses soot, which she rubs on her teeth with a small linen cloth. But from the delight on her face, I can tell that she thinks the toothpaste is much more effective. I couldn't bear to use soot and, it appears, neither can Anne now that she has experienced the sensation of a smidgen of borrowed toothpaste.

I have decided there's no harm in encouraging her to enhance her beauty with modern toiletries. I am merely aiding her cause to become the most celebrated woman at Henry's court. I pack everything away as the litter comes to a halt on the gravel, and my heart flutters as we sit in the shadow of such a prestigious palace.

I'm excited about meeting the king. I look about for anyone important, but the page who greets us informs us that the king and his courtiers are due to arrive at Richmond in the next day or two, so my efforts to catch sight of him about the place are in vain. Anne and I have been thrown into the stillness before the mayhem, which, thankfully, gives us time to prepare ourselves.

I am delighted at having the opportunity to visit the old palace of Richmond, of which there are few records. To see it in its prime is an honour. It's an architectural wonder — a vast collection of passageways, gardens, closets, and private chambers, which Anne and I are bound to get lost in. I hope some kind gentlewoman of the queen's household will be gracious enough to eventually show us where we need to be.

As our belongings are unloaded, and Agnes follows Anne and me to our apartment, my mind drifts back to Hever, university, and home. Now I'm here, just outside central London, there's absolutely no chance of getting back to see my family or friends, or to complete my studies. I haven't forgotten my acquaintances and loved ones, but it's hard to stay focused on my dilemma when faced with this alternate reality — this supreme wonder of Tudor England.

# Seven

### Early Spring, 1522

Anne and Agnes have very kindly filled me in on how things run here. To say it is a complex society would be an understatement. Henry's court is something of a nomadic one, always on the move, travelling from one palace to another every three months or so.

The royal couple's entourage consists of many courtiers, who are companions to them, playing cards, hawking, jousting, wrestling, fencing, and playing tennis with the king, just as the women sew with the queen, or read to her, maybe learn music or dance, and continuously serve her needs. I'm shocked to learn this can mean up to two hundred women, and even more men, joining Their Majesties at court at any one time.

Anne's first post at the English court will be with the Royal Wardrobe. Thanks to her father's position, and his closeness to Henry VIII, she is to become one of Katharine of Aragon's ladies-in-waiting. We will be joining the court as companions to the queen, thrown into a mix of one thousand noblemen who serve Henry in the broader court.

Anne has warned me that we will belong to a heady melting pot of politics, intrigue, and theatre — a formal, serious, religious, and dangerous institution, enhanced by parties and enjoyment, involving throngs of courtiers, mostly young people of a similar age to Anne and me, who have too much time on their hands, which, she says, has the court awash with sexual tension and wanton desire.

She has explained that, as a form of entertainment and promotion, entanglements are the way to be elevated at court and in politics. Some see courtly love as a safety device, preventing this critical mass from exploding. The fictions of courtly love are based on the same ideal which disposes men to attend the king: service.

The courtier is supposed to sublimate his relations with the women of the court by choosing a mistress and serving her faithfully and exclusively. He forms part of her circle, wooing her with poems, songs, and gifts, and if she is gracious enough to recognise the link, he might wear her favour and joust in her honour. Though he might have a wife at home, that is a separate life. In return, the suitor must look for one thing only — a platonic friendship.

A woman might, in fact, be older than her lover, and she would then act as his patron and launch him into court society. Courtly love is essential psychologically, meeting the need for emotional ties. I'm not sure I fully understand — maybe it's my twenty-first-century outlook — but Anne assures me that it works well enough to regulate gender relations at an acceptable level, especially in this hotbed of potential promiscuity.

Courtly love is a game where Henry plays the leading courtly lover and, at present, Anne's sister is his object of desire. Competition for this role is intense, and Bessie Blount, although considered a great beauty, has now been replaced, having recently given the king an illegitimate son, named Henry Fitzroy. For Henry VIII, having mistresses is expected, but not an everyday event within his court, as it is with the French one — so if Mary is in such a position, it is something of a surprise. Queen Katharine, I am told, gracefully turns a blind eye, pretending that the king only has eyes for her.

---

My first taste of the Tudor court is to assist Anne as she, amongst other women, will entertain Spanish ambassadors at the cardinal's house of York Place.

When we arrive, the residence is crowded — faces aglow with a thousand burning candles, their smoky fumes making my throat tight and dry. As we are shown to a curtained area, the intoxicating smell, the heat, and the flickering light entrances me, transporting me back to a childhood memory, back in the twentieth century, of my grandmother snuffing out flames in her dinner-table candelabra, and of me following behind and dipping my fingertips into the warm candle wax, annoying my poor grandmother as I'd squish it between my fingers and accidentally let the remnants drip onto her carpet. Luckily, she knew how to remove the evidence with brown paper and a hot iron. Since then, I've never touched a candle, but I'm always mesmerised by the intensity of their warm glow.

My mind snaps back to the present. I laugh with Anne at the confused conversations of the players around us, which amuse us as we join them. We are squashed in the middle of a bustling crush of bodies as they prepare for their parts in the masque. The leaping shadows of wall torches become our audience, and the corridors and rooms ooze fevered excitement.

Anne dresses in the curtained side-chamber with some of the other women, stepping into her satin and damask gown of white cloth with Milan-point lace and gold thread. Even after several weeks in Tudor England, I am still easily astounded and astonished by the beauty and extravagance of the clothing and style around me. The name of Anne's character is embroidered on a silk caul of Venetian gold, and on a Milanese bonnet, encrusted with jewels, which will adorn her head.

"Mistress Anne, are these masque characters related to the *commedia dell'arte* characters?" I ask, securing this magnificent cap onto her plaited, dark-chestnut hair.

"No, Beth, I do not think so." She shakes her head lightly, turning to face me, her hands pressing against the edges of the bonnet. "The cap feels secure." She smiles, straightening the silk caul across her torso, looking delighted with herself. "You take advice easily." She smooths down the caul, then looks around at the other players, as if comparing her appearance to theirs. "It will not take you long to feel part of life here at Court. I know I have more experience than you, but we can learn together."

This pleases me. Being a fast learner allows me to excel at taking on the etiquette of dressing as a Tudor woman and the behaviour expected by this society.

Mary is at the other side of the chamber, being fussed over by a young, brown-haired woman, who seems eager to please. Anne notices me watching them and, as if she has read my mind, leans closer.

"Mary is the same as she ever was. If she is in a liaison with the king, it will not change her."

Her voice is so low, I have to strain to catch each word. "Is that a good thing?" I ask. From what I can see, she puts on no airs or graces and, if you didn't know, you wouldn't think Henry had his eye on her to be his new mistress.

Apart from the Boleyn family slowly being raised to noble ranks — which will be an expected consequence of such a relationship — Mary asks the king for nothing. Moreover, Thomas Boleyn knows his accomplishments as a diplomat aid the Boleyn family's rise at court. Mary is still Anne's gentle sister and supports us, overseeing our arrival at court, ensuring we are happily settled and have everything we need.

"She believed your story, did she not? My sister will always be sweet-natured to all. You, nor my family, have nothing to worry about where Mary and the king are concerned."

"You seem very sure of that." Admittedly, like the rest of her family in the last few weeks, Mary has welcomed me into her confidence. I have seen for myself just how beautiful she is, inside and out. I realise why the king has his heart set on her, hoping she will be his next mistress — Mary's star is ascending, and fast.

## 4TH MARCH 1522 – YORK PLACE

I see Cardinal Archbishop Thomas Wolsey looking on as the preparations continue. It is going to be an extravaganza, as is the case with much of what happens here.

A couple of days earlier, Anne and I sat alongside the queen in the royal stand above the tiltyard, with the colours and ribbons of combatants and spectators waving as we avidly watched Henry Tudor ride into the lists, bowing in his saddle to Her Majesty Queen Katharine, and acknowledging and admiring the applause of the assembled crowd. Anne watched open mouthed as he reined his mount, a beautiful stallion, and turned to enter the joust. We all saw the motto — *Elle mon Coeur a Navera* — *She has Wounded my Heart* — on a cloth-of-silver caparison, which included a picture of a wounded heart embroidered on the trappings of his horse. No one spoke aloud, instead, the people watching whispered behind their hands. The spectators seemed surprised. Many audibly gasped. I was not sure how I should react.

Of all the crowd gathered, it was Queen Katharine who looked the more surprised, shocked even, probably wondering what on earth she had done to upset her husband. I watched uncomfortably as she tried to regain her composure, wiping her brow with a linen kerchief, trying to focus on the contest. I was sat close enough to discern she was watching through what appeared to be tear-filled eyes.

To me, she seemed proud, not the kind of woman who would show her emotions in public. It was in this moment that I realised that all these people I had read so much about were real human beings, with the ability to feel, and be touched by genuine emotions, such emotions that can never really be evoked from any document in any historical archive. Perhaps she realised that Henry's display must have been meant for someone else, possibly Mary Carey, Anne's sister, who hadn't confided with either of us exactly what had happened between her and the king.

As we looked about the crowd, Anne and I were in an excellent position to notice the reactions of others. However, even Anne was uncertain of the meaning of the silver caparison. The queen looked visibly shaken, and Maria de Salinas, her maid-of-honour and friend, discreetly leaned in to ask if she felt unwell.

Anne whispered to me that, according to other ladies-in-waiting, Katharine was not used to Henry being indiscreet. We had no confirmation from Mary that the regalia was directed at her. However, as soon as we noticed Mary, who was sat further down the stands from us, beside her husband, we could see she was flustered. Her face was flushed, and her gaze fixed on the banner flapping in the breeze in front of her. We realised then that the motto was aimed at her.

As King Henry trotted passed, he stared directly at her, and tried to meet her gaze. William leaned in close to his wife, as Mary sat motionless in her seat. I noticed that William must have growled something in her ear, because Mary visibly squirmed. How she managed not to snap back at him, and stayed so composed, I have no idea. For the rest of the tournament, she had sat biting her lip.

Anne whispered to me that the king, though known for his ways, had never openly practised the art of courtly love, and Anne assured me he had never so blatantly flaunted any mistress at court before now. Apparently, it was so out of character for him to proclaim to the world in such an unconventional manner that he was pursuing a lady of the court, that many of his courtiers whispered behind their hands throughout the afternoon's proceedings. Anne found the situation fascinating, especially as she already had an idea that her sister Mary was the object of such attentions.

Regardless, the queen, ever the professional, ignored the salacious murmurings around her, and cheered when the crowd did, as we all did. Then, afterwards, she presented gifts graciously when the winners came up to claim what was due to them.

How she managed to lovingly smile at the king is beyond me. Katharine masked her disappointment with smiles, and applauded the loudest when her husband had unseated most of his opponents. They had to let him win, it was their duty.

Anne and I watched the queen closely because we both realised that she was probably mortified with the way in which Henry was behaving. Anne had already told me that the court considers the game of courtly love as nothing but harmless fun, but such games are often a cover for something more dangerous. We also know, as must the queen, that there are numerous women within her household who would be only too willing to give themselves without hesitation to such a charismatic, handsome, irresistible, athletic, and powerful monarch as Henry.

Besides the joust, there have been feasts, dances and festivities. Today is Shrove Tuesday — to mark the beginning of Lent. Sadly, there is not a plate filled with any pancakes in sight, that tradition is yet to come.

However, the Great Hall has now been cleared in readiness for Cardinal Wolsey to honour the Spanish Ambassador, Mendoza, who, on behalf of the Emperor, is visiting court to discuss his suit for the future marriage to Princess Mary, who is still a young child.

Master Cornish and his group of actors and choristers are putting on a production of a play called *Château Vert*. I have read accounts of this event many times, but to be here, witnessing it in person, is unbelievable. I watch Mary and Anne, as they stand together with the other female courtiers, and follow them to where other players are now preparing their outfits, behind a heavy curtain. These players must be dressing themselves, ready to play the eight female Virtues. I thought it wise not to participate, to give Anne and Mary all the limelight.

As the evening masque begins, I observe, keeping to the shadows to avoid eye contact with anyone, especially Wolsey. He intrigues me. He does not simply walk into the hall but, instead, creates a spectacle by his procession, full of pomp and finery, with dignitaries and courtiers swarming around him — a massive performance for the benefit of the onlookers. Men bow and doff their caps as fanfares announce his presence, and women curtsy, lowering their eyes as he passes.

Anne points out the writer George Cavendish, as I squint through the gap in the curtain. Cavendish bows and scrapes to Wolsey with gusto, which, with all the added ceremony, makes the cardinal look like Europe's greatest statesman. His face is kind, and he stands straight and splendid rather than stout and portly. He is a renowned man of culture, as grand as any of his counterparts in Rome. His household has pulled out all the stops today to create an exquisite display, fit for any noble prince.

In this setting, the cardinal appears like an alternative king — influential, suave, authoritative, worldly-wise, ostentatious, and affluent. The hall at York Place is packed to overflow, and I wish the palace had air conditioning as I stand here, stifled in my velvet gown and voluminous skirts. Standing with the rest of the female players, Anne and I hide behind the curtain, glancing around, reading the names embroidered in gold on the sashes of some of the women taking part in the great masque: there is the king's sister, Mary, the Dowager Queen of France, who represents Beauty; Gertrude Blount is Honour, while Mary is Kindness, and Jane Parker, the young woman I'd seen fussing over Mary earlier, is Constancy.

"Jane Parker is infatuated with George," Anne says, cutting her eyes towards her.

I know Jane will later become George's wife, and as I watch her adjust the caul attached to her costume, a surprising spark of jealousy flashes across my heart. I focus on the names to ensure this unexpected flutter doesn't make it to my eyes. All the names surreptitiously match the wearer, and Anne is to play Perseverance, which, in the future, will sum up who she is.

I feel safe from prying male eyes, standing inside this inner sanctum, and I see Mary finishing her preparations, as are the other women of the masque. They are all dressed identically and are as excited as I am as they push past me to peek behind the heavy fall of brocade that screens us from the assembly.

"I wonder if anyone will invite me to dance with them once the masque is performed," Jane Parker shrieks from over my shoulder. "This evening is going to be incredibly splendid!" She's bursting with nervous delight, as are all the female players, thrilled with the excitement of taking part. They have never seen stage props like it. The atmosphere is electric, full of expectation, enhanced by the sound of the musicians warming their instruments up.

The makeshift fortification has been wheeled in and takes up most of the hall. It stands proud, like a small medieval playground consisting of three towers, from which hang three banners. One has three broken hearts, with the second displaying a lady's hand holding a man's heart, and the third portraying a lady's hand turning a man's heart.

The wooden and plaster life-size model of the castle is how I imagine the fortification at the Field of the Cloth of Gold to have looked, but obviously on a much grander scale. The magnificent structure of the little château is painted red, yellow, green, and gold, and is adorned and decorated with leaves, flowers, hearts, and motifs, with its battlements shining as the whole set becomes brightly lit by flaming torches on branches. The natural light from the flames is so much softer than the theatrical lighting used in twenty-first-century re-enactments, and Tudor plays. The atmosphere of this authentic experience is nothing less than remarkable.

"Jane, all the ladies, once unmasked, will not be without a dance partner," Gertrude Blount declares, hardly containing her excitement as she shuffles next to Jane Parker. "I hope George Boleyn will ask me!"

"No," Jane says. "He will ask me first!" She glares at Gertrude. "Do you not think Château Vert looks like a smaller, pretend version of Windsor Castle?"

Gertrude nods. Everyone is on tenterhooks as the players wait in anticipation for the event to unfold.

The fluttering in my stomach heightens as I help draw back the draped curtain so the Dowager Queen, Mary Tudor, the king's sister, can lead out the Captive Virtues. My mouth is dry as I watch them walk to their allotted positions, where they'll wait to be rescued by the king and his retinue.

The task of guarding the female Virtues — stopping them from being recovered — is awarded to the contrary feminine Vices, but really, they are young chorister boys, dressed all in black.

The rest of the participants in the hall, and those not taking part in the masque, jostle each other from the sidelines to get a closer look at the spectacle. I join them, elbowing past several in the excitement of observing the celebrations.

The masked Vices wait for the music to stop so that Master Cornish can introduce the pageant to the ambassadors. The group bow to the ambassadors, then turn to pose in the silence, looking directly at the Captive Virtues, of whom Anne, Mary Carey, Mary, Duchess of Suffolk, and Jane Parker are a part of, waiting to win them from their captors.

The male Virtues represent Amorousness, Nobleness, Youth, Attendance, Loyalty, Pleasure, Love, Gentleness, and Liberty. The trumpets sound as Anne and the other ladies adjust masks and gather their skirts, with the Duchess of Suffolk standing in front, ready to lead the dancers. I'm a tad lightheaded at the prospect of witnessing at first-hand such a prestigious event. What a profound privilege it is to be standing where I am.

At this end of the hall stands the vast canopy of estate, and the musicians conceal themselves in the minstrels' gallery above our heads as they finish playing *Saltarello*, followed by *Branle des la Guerre*, bringing the drama to its formal introduction. What I find fascinating is that amongst the musicians stands a trumpeter, but this trumpeter is Black. He stands proudly, in full court livery, looking down on all who are gathered.

"Who is he?" I ask the woman standing next to me.

Her eyes follow my upwards gaze. "The trumpeter is John Blanke. Have you not seen a man of colour before?"

"Many a time," I reply as I look out into the crowd, who are beginning to take their places in the masque. "Who is the king portraying?" I ask, pretending I don't know, as I watch Anne take her place in the battlements of Château Vert.

The female courtier beside me places her mouth close to my ear. "You cannot miss the king. Look, see him over there?" She points to the tallest man in the room, even though he is in disguise.

I am speechless, seeing straight away who Henry is, as he waits to enter the fray.

The king is more than six-feet two-inches in height and towers over all his court, able to command attention without effort. He's a virtuous-looking prince, better than he's shown to be in his portraits — he is a beautiful figure of a man, with a round, gentle face — good-looking, with bright blue eyes.

I can now see why the Venetian Ambassador praises him so highly, saying his face is like that of a pretty woman, though his fiery red hair and broad chest show him to be a fierce specimen of a man, and his well-turned leg is not easily disguised, with his silk tights clinging to the definite curve of his calf; nothing dissuades him from enjoying imitation games.

The women about me, knowing I am new to the court, instruct me on how I must act when the king finally reveals his identity. One of the women nudges closer to me as she stands in the crowd, and whispers, "Mistress Wickers, you must act surprised when the king shows himself to the crowd during the unmasking, it is a requirement."

"Very well. I understand." I reply, as silence falls within the Great Hall of York Place as the Master of Choristers of the Chapel Royal, now as Ardent

Desire, the genius who has devised the court revel, steps forward to address the gathered crowd.

"It gives me great pleasure to introduce to the Spanish Ambassadors, Her Majesty, Queen Katharine, and His Grace, Cardinal Wolsey, our pageant, *Château Vert!*"

Dressed in dark crimson satin, embroidered with burning flames of gold, on which his name is emblazoned, Master Cornish steps closer to the wooden castle, opens his arms, and looks towards the battlements, where Anne, Mary, and the women are waiting, poised for the masque to begin.

"Lady Scorn and Lady Disdain," he cries, "I beg you to surrender your prisoners and come down to me — otherwise we will breach your defences."

We all laugh, as 'ladies' Scorn and Distain, who are actually two of the young, male choristers, sneer at the gathered onlookers.

"No knight will ever breach our defences!" they cry.

Everyone breaks into raucous laughter at this double entendre.

"Then, *ladies*," Master Cornish snarls, "you give us no choice."

Ardent Desire's voice rattles the rafters, "We must make siege of your beautiful castle, forcing it down around your ears. You will be at our mercy!"

As the lords charge forward from the far end of the hall, the Virtues try to retreat, but pandemonium ensues as the lords rush the walls to cries of invented alarm, while great explosions of gunfire resonate. The Virtues jump into the revels of discord, defending the castle with passion and energy, laughing, and shaking with excitement, their heads thrown back in hysteria at the drama.

But Mary Carey looks distraught in the mayhem, standing solitary and silent. Perhaps she is hoping Henry will come for her before anyone else. She likes to be dramatic, it's her way of gaining attention.

Meanwhile, the court is in an uproar, and Cardinal Wolsey's rotund face screws up with laughter as Mendoza, the Spanish Ambassador, looks on. Even the queen enjoys the masque, laughing and clapping while she sits on her throne under the Canopy of Estate, surrounded by the rest of her ladies-in-waiting. She looks to be in better spirits than when she observed the joust. Perhaps her mood has improved because of the proposed Spanish marriage of her daughter, Mary, which will reinforce and further the alliance with her family.

The actors charge around the hall as the king's men, splendid in caps of gold cloth and capes of blue satin, hurl dates, rotten apples, and other fruits at the castle's defences. The chorister boys, Jealousy, Distain and Scorn, who are holding Mary, Duchess of Sussex, Mary Carey, Jane Parker, Anne, and others captive, return a hail of fruits, sweetmeats, and comfits with rosewater, at the besiegers, filling the hall with a great flourish of projectiles.

I've read of this night so many times in the historical records, but to see this in real-time, as it happens, astonishes me. Butterflies erupt in my stomach, filling me with a nervous excitement I haven't experienced before.

The scene is like one of comedy and torture; some just stand and laugh, like me, while many of the women scream at the top of their lungs, running in different directions. Some of the young choristers, with their costumes all dishevelled, slip and slide, almost falling on their backsides because of the rosewater covering the floor.

Mr Cornish is red-faced, exasperated, and visibly sweating. His reputation is at stake as the crowd becomes uncontrollable, the masque now in ruins. His face is flushed with anger, yet there is nothing he can do but surrender to a hail of missiles. He waves his arms and shouts towards Anne as she leans over the battlements, screaming encouragement at the men coming to her rescue.

Then, a monster of a man, who cannot be mistaken for anyone but the king, chases Disdain, Scorn and Jealousy out of his way, scaring them half to death, stopping them from continuing their brutal attack against George Boleyn and Sir Antony Denny. The Duke of Suffolk pulls both George and Sir Antony from the battlements, who fall to the floor in a heap of laughter, after which, Brandon, Duke of Suffolk, and His Majesty breach the inner wall.

A triumphant cheer erupts from the crowd about me, and the spectators see Brandon making off with one of the Virtues by the arm. I can't work out who the lucky woman is but she is not his wife.

By tradition, because of rank, Sir Loyal Heart, or Love, played by the king, should rescue Mary, his sister, first, but no, William Compton liberates her before him, and the Duke of Suffolk looks shocked that someone else has managed to liberate his wife.

The king then races for Mary Boleyn. I watch open-mouthed as the king scrambles up the wooden facade, dagger in hand, the ouches from his doublet scraping the paint on the decorated castle wall, and roars like a lion after his kill.

It is a job well done. Henry is still athletic; otherwise, his weight might have brought the walls toppling around him. He lunges for who he thinks is Mary, but Mary is stood looking confused as she watches him grab Anne's hand, pulling her to him, grunting with satisfaction. Anne tries to draw back, but he is too strong for her. Henry Tudor seems determined not to be ignored, despite his disguise.

Mary looks as if she will burst into tears as she watches the king fling her younger sister about his shoulder, the satin of her gown tangling as he dashes with his cargo away from the inner battlements.

I wince as Anne bounces hard in the king's vice-like hold. Her Milanese bonnet falls, and I lift my skirts, running to make a grab for it, hoping not to collide with the king, whose great hand is now gripping Anne's buttocks to stop her slipping from his grasp. He drags her, now dishevelled, from his shoulder, but fails to hold her, and she slides down his body to the floor, inadvertently pulling him down with her. Probably not what he'd intended at all.

He's now kneeling with her, his face flushed as he catches his breath, their brows almost touching. They both look flustered. He bows his head, then looks up as Anne gets to her feet and defiantly removes her mask. His eyes widen, his gaze transfixed.

"I am sorry. I … think I have made a mistake." He grunts, shifts back, and gets to his feet. "You are not who I thought you were."

"Perhaps you mistook me for Mary Carey, Your Grace. As you can see, Your Majesty, I am not her, I am her younger sister. My name is Anne. Anne Boleyn."

Henry looks ruffled. Anne, however, doesn't. The king turns his head, probably glancing around to see where Mary might be. He'd obviously grabbed the nearest woman to him in the confusion, not considering Anne's dark, European looks and continental manners, which are in great contrast to her sister. With not a little embarrassment, he realises his hand is still held fast around her waist. He removes it quickly, hesitates, then bows, before scrutinising her in a way a man should not look at a woman.

I watch as Anne sinks in a curtsy before him. After a long pause, he raises her to her feet.

"I am pleased to meet you again, Mistress Boleyn." He smiles. "I think it is some time since I saw you last, in France."

"Yes, Your Grace."

Mesmerised, it is some moments before she can tear her eyes from him and turn them to where she thinks she last saw her sister. But Mary is gone. I turn and look back towards the far end of the hall, where I spot her. She has removed her mask, her forlorn look of hurt and disappointment at being sidelined plain for all to see.

The drama has diminished around her. She doesn't appear to like not being the centre of attention, now that all focus is on Anne, and the king. She looks as if she is about to burst into floods of tears.

In a corner of the opposite end of the hall, I catch a glimpse of Thomas Boleyn on the fringes of the crowd, in conversation with a tall, thin, important-looking man with dark hair and piercing eyes. Thomas looks apprehensive, he nods in my direction, and his shoulders curl forward as he fiddles with the collar of his shirt. Anne glances over at her father, but she is still in the snare of Henry's gaze; gracefully and defiantly standing before him, she now looks directly at him, her chin high. She inclines her head, a boldness in her eyes.

"You must return to the little château, and the battle, as it is not yet over. You need to save Mary, Your Majesty. The honour of your beautiful mistress is still at stake. You have left her all alone." Her voice is strong yet alluring.

"Ah, yes. But first, Mistress Anne, please accept this small gift." He smiles. "As an appreciation of your beauty." Henry's gaze lingers as he pulls a token from his doublet and thrusts it into her hand. He suddenly turns, retreating from her and, with a loud cry, turns once more into the melee of the evening, where, eventually, he finds Mary waiting for him.

The *king's Pavan* rings out its melody from the minstrels' gallery as the drama continues. I watch as the king bows to Mary, and she returns his salute with a timid curtsy. To my surprise, he strokes her cheek, and she smiles. I continue to scrutinise them as he whispers something in her ear, which makes her blush. Henry then takes her hand, leading her towards the dance. Anne is standing, rooted to the spot, unable to move.

Giving myself a mental shake, realising I have just witnessed Henry's first proper encounter with Anne, and his pursuit of Mary as an invitation as mistress. I watch spellbound as Anne turns the etui in her fingers, before she pins the small whistle, with its decorative case used for needles, toilet articles, and the like, to her gown. The little jewel is exquisite.

I stand next to her, where the spectators are gathered. In the fracas, I hope the queen hasn't observed the exchange between her husband and my friend. When Anne and the other ladies are led by the hand onto the dancefloor, I notice Katharine watching intently.

As the dancers take up positions, all curtsy to their partners and move to the music, I hang back, as if glued to the edge of the dancefloor, and cast a sideways glance at George, his face chiselled in the candlelight. He's standing with two other men. They are all laughing at some joke, their faces flushed with wine. One of the men, I don't know who he is, spies me looking at them from the corner of his eye, nods in acknowledgement, then nudges George, who returns my smile, teasing me as his gaze takes in my breasts, raised high beneath my bodice, and makes a leg as he bows in my direction, then walks towards me.

"Mistress Elizabeth, may I have this dance?"

I swallow and nod, then spy Anne being guided in and out on the periphery of the dance, and as she passes me, she smiles and nods, showing her approval to my dance partner.

I curtsy and take George's hand, my fingers balanced on his palm. The minstrels strike up their rendition of Joan Ambrosio Dalza's *Pavana Alla Venetiana*, and the king, partnered now by a much-brighter looking Mary Carey, joins the dance. I focus on the couple, fascinated by the spectacle they create. The costumes, coiffured ladies, and the music all jab at my doubts and my ability to blend in. I hope my re-enacting skills will hold up to the real thing. Anne has schooled me as best she can, but now that I'm amongst this crowd, I'm scared my inexperience will betray me.

There are so many unfamiliar faces and, as we pass them in the dance, George explains who many of these strangers are. The king and Mary weave their way in and out of the other dancers, bowing, turning, leaping, and the happiness is restored to her face as she glides around the hall with Henry. The king is the centre of attention, as he is easily the tallest among all the dancers, and the most recognisable.

George leads me out onto the floor, and I rest my palm over his warm knuckles as he guides my steps. It's clear that he's enjoying this, and he pushes himself close whenever he gets the opportunity. I continue smiling, blushing every time our eyes meet, as they often do. It must have taken him no courage at all to ask me to dance with him, as he reinforces my view that he is capable of being a terrible flirt. From the corner of my eye, I spy Jane Parker glaring daggers at me, as if I've stolen her man. He laughs when he sees her watching us.

"You should ask Jane Parker to dance with you — she seems to like you."

"Does she? I had not noticed." He smiles, ignoring his obsessed spectator as we glide passed her.

"Do you not like her?"

"She is fair enough, but not as beautiful as you."

My heart races at this remark and my face feels hot, I'm sure everyone in the hall will notice. "So, how did you enjoy the pageant?" I ask, shifting the subject in a safer direction.

"I liked it very well." He beams, aware of my embarrassment as we promenade before the dance forces us apart.

Now and then, the serpentine steps lead us towards other partners, allowing me to touch other hands and exchange pleasantries with other men. I feel self-conscious when some look at me as if they are trying to imagine me naked — I certainly didn't expect the English court to be so licentious! Anne seems the most confident of all the women present and she smiles graciously as she dances with a nobleman of high rank. Her gaze meets mine when we cross the dancefloor.

"You are a credit to me," she says, laughing as we almost rub shoulders. The dark-haired man she dances with gives me a sideways glance and a nod, to acknowledge me, but his gaze is fixed on Anne — she has more grace than me and is more experienced at the steps, but all the while I am aware of George watching me, leading me through the dance.

Anne glides back and forth across the room, her head high, her feet light as air as her partner, with a galliard, gathers her into the entertainment.

I toss my head with more spirit as George lifts me with ease into the air during the dance. I doubt my ability to carry this off. Perhaps I'm trying too hard to match Anne's moves. Her presence fills the room with admiration at her acquired French ways. I hear people commenting from the periphery of the dance on her graceful ability. A few courtiers debate on whether she is indeed English, as women comment on her gown and manners. They must know she is one of the Boleyn girls. From the centre of the dance, I sense the king watching her. I'm not sure if she notices, but if she does, it doesn't show.

When the music ends, George makes a bow. My stomach gives a leap when he rises and fixes me with a predatory look. Tiny beads of perspiration glimmer on his brow, probably from lifting me during the dance.

"For a novice, Mistress Wickers, you dance very well."

"I think it is more a case of having an experienced partner." I smile, though I'm sure it's more of a smirk. "George, please call me Beth. I think you know me better than to be so formal?"

"Indeed, Beth." His gaze remains direct. "You know how to flatter a man. Has Anne also trained you in the ways of courtly love?"

"No, most definitely not." I try to think of something else to say. "I am on my best behaviour." My face flushes with the weight of his attentions. "I forgot to ask if you retrieved your cap." I laugh, wondering why all the other men's caps were on their heads, yet George's has been misplaced.

"No, I am afraid it was lost in the confusion." He chuckles. "Did you not see me trying to rescue Sir Anthony Denny while all those missiles were exchanged?"

I nod. "I did see some confusion."

He grins. "I'll wager you were laughing."

"I couldn't help it — everyone was laughing. You were deep in the action, trying to rescue a gentleman who had half of his body hooked over the castle wall!"

"I was determined to save Denny, but had to give up because I was being pulled into the fray — that's when I lost my cap."

"I wanted to help, but was frozen to the spot."

"That is an excuse. You watched me being hit! You allowed Ladies Scorn and Disdain to steal my cap."

"I was some distance away. What could I do?" I smile. "Did you suffer any bruising at their hands?"

"I have not checked." He sighs. "You allowed those young boys dressed as women to mock me. What an indignity. Some friend you are!"

"I'm sorry."

"You must have seen that choirboy bash me over my head." He looks somewhat despondent.

"Yes, I did notice him waving your cap violently above his head." George's doublet is stained with the juice of missiles. I pull a handkerchief from my silk purse and try to wipe some of it away. He stares at what I'm doing.

"Since when did you care what I look like?"

"Since you are covered in the stains of assault weapons used against you!"

"I did not think you would notice, Beth!" His eyes lock with mine for what seems like forever, and I have to look away in case my feelings might betray me. I push the dirty handkerchief back into the small purse attached to the sash of my gown. "I think Master Cornish owes me a new cap!" George pats my shoulder. "Can I get you a cup of wine, Mistress?" He wipes sweat from his forehead with his sleeve.

I hope my answering smile is almost as beguiling as Anne's as he leads me to the refreshments and hands me a Venetian glass goblet full of red wine. He chuckles as he watches me take slow sips.

"Are you not wanting it to go to your head?" His eyebrows wiggle. Every time he insinuates something about me, it infuriates and thrills me in equal measure.

I need to remind myself who I am. I need to calm down. "I can control myself." I snort with a burst of short, dismissive laughter.

He smiles at me. His eyes are bright and glossy as he applauds the dancers, now the masque and dancing have finished. I put my glass down on the table behind me and follow his example.

We clap as Henry leads Queen Katharine to a chamber appointed for her by Wolsey, where she will host a lavish feast for the visiting Spanish ambassadors. If she is suspicious that her husband might have a new mistress, it doesn't show, and Henry hasn't betrayed himself, even though he has danced with most of the ladies of the court.

There are only two ladies who have not taken his hand this evening — Mistress Anne Boleyn and me.

# Eight

### Late Evening, Richmond Palace – 4th March 1522

The small fire in the grate provides welcome heat and light as I sit with Anne at Richmond Palace. Everyone who has returned from York Place is settling to sleep after the busy evening. The other maids-of-honour have already retired to the dormitory, and it's nice to have some quiet time on our own.

I want to go home, but I can't lose sight of how things are developing for Anne. She's my reason for being here — I'm convinced of it. But there's nothing I can do to help her without changing history, and I certainly don't want to do that. Do I?

Something about the ill-lit chamber urges me to wrap my dressing gown tighter. It's not just the cold. Tucking my feet up beneath me brings a bit of needed comfort. Mum always does it. Mum. God, I can't believe it's been so long since I've seen her. She must be in a terrible state, not knowing what's become of me.

The twenty-first century tugs at my heart, creating a dull ache in the pit of my stomach. I need to return, even though I'm enjoying my experience in this Tudor world. Tonight's entertainment was majestic, but I can't possibly stay for much longer.

I stretch my arms out towards the fire, which crackles and spits, hoping to catch the warmth from the flickering flames. The rubies on my cypher ring twinkle, reflecting those same flames. I sigh and tuck a cushion into the small of my back as I relax into the settle.

All I can think about is how I must get back to my own life soon. How can continuing with this situation lead to a positive outcome? On the one hand, the predictable claw of history is reaching across time to Anne. I feel it, like a black shadow creeping around our ankles. She deserves a happy ending, rather than the established one history will hand her, but I can do nothing against what is an inevitable conclusion.

I'm trapped between the indeterminate reality that I can't change her fate, though I dearly want to, and putting my poor family through so much confusion, worry, and anguish. Yet what can I do if I can't get the bloody portal to open, or even get to it?

My hands tremble as I imagine the possibility of being able to manifest a future more magnificent than could be conceived for my dear friend Anne.

Thing is, I can't risk sharing my thoughts and fears with her for obvious reasons.

The prospect of never being able to return to my normal life and family evokes frustration and anxiety. Are they devastated at my unexplained absence? How are my poor parents coping? Is Rob directing a nationwide campaign to find me? What about Professor Marshall? Does he know what's happened? Might he be able to open the portal the way I did?

Movement next to me brings a halt to my thoughts. Anne looks relaxed, snuggled into the settle, lounging here next to me with a bit of a mysterious look in her eyes.

"You look pleased with yourself, Mistress Anne. Anything you'd like to share?"

She leans closer, brushing her hair from her eyes, then glances about, as if she's got a secret to divulge. "I hope Mary does not think I outshined her tonight." Our heads are close as she speaks in whispers before the dwindling hearth fire. She smiles, looking me directly in the eye. "Well?"

"Why would she think that? She was the centre of attention and danced with the king, not you. Are you worried you have offended her somehow?"

"Yes. I know how sensitive my sister is. I did not look for the king's attentions when he singled me out, rescuing me during the pageant." She rests her hands in her lap and stares into the fire. "I may not have been a partner to the king, but all eyes were on me. Did you not see?"

"Of course — everyone noticed. The crowd were watching the king's reaction to you." I hope she will divulge how his attention made her feel. She glances at me, and the corners of her mouth turn up into a little smile.

"I did enjoy being under his gaze, if only for a moment. It was a pleasure to be the focus of the king's admiration. But —" her smile broadens — "I felt almost as favoured when I yielded my hand in the dance, with one who will bear the title of Earl."

I stifle a yawn as I remember the events of the evening. "Yes, I think I recall that. An earl, no less, but what will he expect for such attentions?"

"As a woman, I am not expected to give sexual favours, just the impression, a hint of possibility, and the lover who offers service to me is then allowed to threaten to possess me."

"Aren't you afraid the impression might be taken literally?"

"It depends on how you manage such attention. Marguerite of Austria advised us to keep men at a distance, to treat their advances with a light touch."

However dismissive her remarks, I realise that after tonight, Henry Percy may be in her sights. This wasn't what she had initially intended. What about James Butler? Has she forgotten him already?

"Henry Percy, the heir to the earldom of Northumberland, is a similar age to us," she declares.

I already know Percy is connected to Wolsey. George had pointed him out to me, explaining who he was. He also told me Wolsey thinks little of Percy's abilities as a nobleman and is waiting to be disappointed by him. From what George has observed, Henry Percy is a muddle-headed lightweight, full of emotion, unreliable, and not of sound judgement. In some circles at court, he's called an unthrift waster. I need to put Anne off him so she has no need to bear a grudge in the future — that kind of feeling will only lead to trouble.

On the other hand, perhaps it's best if I just keep my mouth shut and let fate take its course. This is the *big* question I'm always wrestling with — what to do?

Anne lifts her chin. "Henry Percy may be the match for me."

"You would do well, Mistress Anne, to remember that your hand is pledged elsewhere." My words might force her to consider my warning. Our eyes lock while I decide whether to be frank, or to feign innocence. The direct approach is probably better, as I know she appreciates the characteristic, similar as it is to hers. "Percy is just a young man playing the game of love … as our betters do." I take a quick look around to ensure we're alone. "The game is dangerous, Anne. You do not want your name thrown about … like Mary's. It will not do to have you both linked to easy virtue. Think what your father will say if you jeopardise the match with Ormond."

"I am certain the match with James Butler will fall through." She frowns. "Father has not said a word about the betrothal in weeks. Besides, I believe Henry Percy is a man of his word — an honest man — his adoration is so fervent that I feel I cannot escape it." She smiles broadly, clasping her hands against her chest. "I could fall in love with such a man."

"Anne, how can you tell that after one evening of dancing?" She glares at me, her disapproval evident, but I carry on regardless. "Saying you could love Henry Percy, when you are promised to another, is dangerous!" I keep my voice low, trying to show my concern without chiding her. "In any case, it is rumoured that Percy has mountains of debt, even for a nobleman." She needs to understand what she may be getting into. "Understand, in the wilds of Northumberland, you will not be able to wear fine silks. Instead, you will be lumbered with home-spun gowns, sewn by your own hand. All your accomplishments will be wasted, for you will have no one to entertain. If you elope with Henry Percy, you will spend your time skinning rabbits for the pot, stewing in juices of your own making."

"Who said anything about eloping?" She laughs, clutching her side. "Oh, Beth, you fret too much. What of you, dancing with my brother?" She smirks, takes a sip of wine, and tucks her feet beneath the hem of her shift.

"I only danced with him and shared a cup of wine." The longer I am here, the easier it is to lie, and blatantly. I concentrate on the way the firelight plays upon her face and try not to think of George.

"You like him, I can tell. Never have I seen your cheeks blush beneath a fellow's gaze. He will be betrothed soon, I am certain. Father will see that he makes a good match, especially now Mary is married. Hmm, perhaps I could suggest to Father that George marries you."

"What?" I look at her in disbelief. "You know marriage in your time would be impossible, Anne. I do not know why you are making such a fuss about George, anyway — it was only a dance." I pick up my glass of wine from a nearby table and raise it to my lips, take a sip, then close my eyes to remember again the softness of George's hand brushing mine, the excellent cut of his leg, the way his Adam's apple bobs when he laughs, and the infuriating way he stares at my breasts. I have no idea why I'm deceiving Anne, who is party to some, though not all, my secrets.

Anne is aware of the effect she has on men since we've arrived at court. She seems pensive tonight as we sit discussing her life.

"Beth, I find myself with more suitors than I expected. Men did not leave me alone tonight."

"My Lady, surely it is nothing you cannot handle?"

She looks up and flutters her eyelashes. "Tom Wyatt lusts after me. I have known him for years — since childhood. He and I are neighbours in Kent."

"Do you like him?" I ask innocently, as if I know nothing about him.

"He has a desperately handsome face." She giggles, her hand covering her mouth. "And he writes beautiful poetry. But I am not attracted to him — not in the same way that I am drawn to Henry Percy."

I rest my hands in my lap. "Isn't Thomas Wyatt a married man?"

"Yes, he is," she answers.

"How is Henry Percy different?"

"When I am with him, he makes me feel alive. When I am close to him, it is as if my blood runs faster in my veins."

"I wish you didn't feel that way, Mistress."

"Why ever not?" she asks, her voice almost inaudible. "Am I in love?"

"Only you know whether you are in love, Anne." I smile and pat the back of her hand, trying to think of something that might take her mind off Henry Percy. From what she's shared over the previous weeks, I know love isn't something she's felt before.

She questions me, wondering what it feels to be in love. I share with her how I've fancied my best friend Rob for ages, but friendship is all he seems to want. I can't say I love him — I'd not go that far, but…

Anne chatters into the night about Percy, yet I haven't the heart to tell her it will all be to no avail. I daren't mention the king, as she will read far too much into my comments, and her future will be out.

As much as I'm tempted, I can't put thoughts into her mind that could potentially change her life path. To mess with history could be disastrous, and I shudder to think of what might happen. I don't want to think about it, the same way I don't want to think about May 1536, and her appearance on the scaffold. The thought horrifies me. Could I prevent her death? What would happen if I did? What will happen if I stay here? My head hurts as these questions whirl around my brain. Maybe I should blame the wine. It's doing more than making me feel dizzy.

"Of course," Anne continues, "should his betrothal with Mary Talbot be broken, he would be as fine a match as I could ask for or my father could arrange. But I fear such an arrangement will never be revoked."

Henry Percy will one day come into a vast inheritance, despite his debts. A prize indeed if he were to ask for Anne's hand, but I know — we both know — that such a thing is impossible, for such bonds cannot be broken. Besides, her cause is doubly hopeless since they are both promised elsewhere.

I place my glass on the table, gather myself, and turn to Anne. "You know it has been months since I arrived at Hever."

"Indeed," she says, "I remember it well."

"As do I. And it has been an amazing experience. But … it has been so long now. What if I cannot get home?"

"You mean, to your time?"

"Yes." I turn the cypher ring. "I … think this ring has something to do with it."

"Really?" She leans closer and studies it. "I have seen you fiddling with it. Where did it come from?"

I explain how I came to have it, and how once the ring was on my finger, the metal heated up, as it did again each time I tried the door back to the passage. I've concealed the nature of it from her since I arrived, purely because I didn't want to broadcast too much about myself in case my mouth ran away with me. But it seems apt to show the ring to her now because she may be able to shed some light on its origin. This must be the only ring of its kind, as it's so unique — dated 1532 — and she couldn't possibly have the original in her jewellery box. Maybe it will be a gift from the king — but in this future, that might mean two rings existing at the same time. How could that be possible? I rub my forehead, feeling the blood pumping hard — the wine and the stress are bringing a migraine on.

"I know this ring has something to do with you, Anne, because of the initials." I continue turning it.

She stretches out her hand. "Let me see it." Something inside warns me against showing her, but I push it to the back of my mind and slip the ring off. She takes it and gives it close scrutiny. The jewels twinkle in the low firelight as she places it on her finger, opening her hand out and admiring it.

I stare at the small extra nail on the side of the little finger of her right hand. She catches me looking and tries to hide it in the cuff of her shift. "It is a fine ring, Beth. Father has not given me a present of a ring such as this. Do you think this is meant to belong to me in the future, seeing as it has my initials on it?"

"Maybe," is all I can think to reply.

She takes it off and studies the engraving inside. "1532." She looks into the shadows as if trying to catch a glimpse of her future. "I wonder what that signifies." Her brow creases and her mouth purses as the cogs of her mind whir.

Of course, I have some idea what the date means, but it's not my place to suggest or meddle.

"I have no clue," I lie. "The ring will come into your possession at some point, but who gives it to you, I do not know. All I know is that I have been away from my family for a long time and they must think I am dead."

"Dead?" she says, her hand at her mouth. "We cannot have your family suffering so." She touches my hand, a welcome gesture of support. "You must endeavour to return to your time. I will be fine — George will look after me. I will tell him you have been summoned home."

"But what if I cannot open the portal. I have tried so many times, always without success."

"Well, Beth, we shall keep trying until we achieve the result you are searching for."

Anxious questions tumble through my mind. What if I can't get back? What if I can? How will I explain my absence? My head throbs with the migraine. "I am going to bed, Mistress Anne. I will think about the best way forward. We need sleep, it is very late. Where is Mary? Have you seen her?"

"She entertains the king, no doubt." She gets up, placing the ring back in my hand.

"Perhaps the king has gone to the queen," I say, "out of duty, rather than be with Mary?"

"The Boleyns tread carefully at Court, Beth. We will fare well whatever the king does, but if you go, I will miss you. George will miss you."

"Shush now. Do not concern yourself. Let's get some sleep."

We enter the dormitory, trying not to disturb the other women. Agnes is snoring on a pallet bed, and Anne doesn't want to wake her as she dumps her dressing gown at the end of our bed. I remove my own dressing gown and drape it over the back of a chair, after snuffing out any remaining candles. The sheets are cold, and my linen smock gives me no warmth as I clamber into bed. Once Anne and I are settled, we wish each other sweet dreams.

The trouble is, I can't sleep. My mind is racing ten to the dozen, fretting about how I need to get home. I twist and press the cypher ring as it sits on my middle finger, and as I do so, the metal begins to warm up. I keep my eyes closed, visualizing Professor Marshall's study and wish for all I'm worth that I could be back there.

# Nine

## Professor Marshall's Office – Present Day

I can't believe it as I stare down at my bare feet. Shivering, I realise I've somehow managed to transport myself back to the professor's study, with the use of the ring. I blink at the fluorescent lights, unaccustomed to their brightness. I'm feeling giddy, the whole experience shocking and disorientating.

Professor Marshall is sitting at his desk, scribbling red pen across a thesis. He turns to me nonchalantly, as if my appearance is nothing out of the ordinary.

"So, you found the ring then?"

"Erm, yes," I reply coyly, my shoulders shuddering with the cold. I look down at myself and realise the reason I'm shivering is that I'm standing in his office with my body covered in only a linen shift, and a very thin one at that. I hope he can't see through it — that would be embarrassing.

I can't believe I've discovered the secret of the ring. All I had to do was rub on the cypher, wishing myself in a specific place, at a particular time. It is the key to creating the time slips and my way to transport myself between centuries and locations. I stand here now, back in the professor's study, somewhat bemused at the modern surroundings, as it seems a lifetime ago since I was in the twenty-first century.

Realising that I've left my holdall at Richmond, and all the rest of my belongings, including my mobile phone, at Hever, back in the sixteenth century, my heart pounds at the thought of who might find the books and papers, as well as all my modern stuff. I can only hope that Anne has the good sense to keep it all hidden and not look through any of it. What a problem that would cause if she did!

I stare at the professor as I turn the ring, worried that I have done something terribly wrong.

"I guessed as much when you missed your second lecture this morning. Professor Hughes was visiting today."

For a moment, I wonder if I might have misheard him. "I'm sorry, Professor, but how long have I been away?"

He looks over to the bookcase — the entrance to the portal. "Oh, a few hours."

I have to lean against his desk, not sure my trembling legs will hold me upright. How can this be? "Are you sure, Professor?"

"Positive," he says, his brows knitted as he studies my attire.

I self-consciously cross my arms over myself. "Am I … in a lot of trouble?"

"What? No, no, not at all. I deliberately allowed you to find the ring and use it to travel back in time, as I knew you would learn so much from the experience."

"You're not kidding," I say, knowing it to be the understatement of the century, though I'm not too sure which. I stare at him and wonder why he chose me. I'm hardly his best student. Or am I?

"You can't travel into the future, though." His tone is cautionary.

I spot a bunch of keys on the desk, and I realise they're mine. I grab them up, knowing they are a physical link to home. "My interest lies only in the past, Professor." A thought occurs to me. "Have you also travelled back in time?"

He watches me turning the bunch of keys, his focus sharp, waiting, probably pondering whether he should answer my question or not. "Absolutely," he says, after what feels like ages, "but I can only travel between the period Elizabeth the First was born and died. I can't shag Lady Godiva or Marie Antoinette!" He chuckles at his own joke.

I don't. My mind spins, struggling to grasp the disturbing reality that I haven't been missing for months, or that my family and friends haven't been driven to despair over my unexplained absence. "How is it possible that I've only been gone a few hours, when I've spent the last few months living with Mistress Anne Boleyn?"

"All I can say is that the bearer of the ring's relationship with time works differently. I cannot fully explain it. Also, the ring chooses where to send the wearer."

I twist the ring and pull it off my finger. Its rubies sparkle in the overhead light. "I have no control over it?"

"Yes, you do. Well, to an extent, but the ring does most of the work."

"I … I kept pressing on the cypher, and rubbing the stones, wishing I could be standing here. So how does the ring make it happen?"

"*How* is the easy bit. You go into a dark space, like a wardrobe, or an alcove, then twist the ring and think about a specific time in Anne Boleyn's lifetime you'd like to return to." He smiles, then shrugs. "That's it. Well, there's a bit of a rumble and a tumble with this method of travel if you don't come directly through the portal, but trust me, it works."

"That's what happened, just now." I sigh, my shoulders dropping. "But how did my love of history send me to Anne at Hever after her return from France?"

He nods. "Ah, so that's how far back you went. Good. To answer your question, your desire to seek the truth of history, and of Anne Boleyn, drew the ring to you."

I realise my mouth is open. "My…?"

"Your desire to learn," he continues, "to understand. The power within the ring picked up on your admiration of and passion for Anne's life. When I wore it, it took me to Elizabeth, Anne's daughter."

To my disappointment, he doesn't seem to want to divulge any further information on it. He leans forward in his chair, his fingers steepled beneath his chin as he looks at me intently for a long moment, until my face flushes under the heat of his scrutiny. "I hope you have not divulged anything of Anne's future to her?"

"Oh, my goodness, I struggled so much to ensure that didn't happen. To be responsible for a change in her life and future — for changing history — I must tell you, it wasn't easy. The more I learnt of her and got to know her, the more difficult I found it to allow her destiny to play out." I collapse into a chair opposite the professor, a jumble of questions tumbling through my mind. "I wasn't sure how it worked. What about the butterfly effect?"

He opens his hands, their heels together, framing his face. "I don't seem to have messed up civilisation yet."

"It's scary. I'm finding it a tad difficult believing that up to a few minutes ago, I had lived almost six months of my life in sixteenth-century Tudor England, yet now I'm here, with you, and only a few hours have actually passed."

He takes a deep breath and nods again. "Yes, my dear, I understand how … troublesome that might be. And if you decide to continue this path of discovery, it's going to be something of a complicated time for you."

I lean towards him, eager to understand. "How have you coped with it?"

"I've soaked up every experience of Elizabeth's reign that I can. Listened to every conversation. Learnt things about her that no one knows."

"So … what should I do?"

"You must observe, Beth. Use the experience to help you understand history as it happens. You cannot save Anne from her fate — you mustn't even try. You have the Tudor dynasty to consider in Edward, Mary, and Elizabeth. Don't let Anne stray from her path or you may interfere or change things so much that you could completely transform our reality."

My mind races through a flurry of memories, trying to pinpoint any time I may have contravened this regulation. "Though the temptation and opportunity were there, I told Anne nothing of her fate. She was gracious at giving me the liberty to speak boldly with her, and I advised her to the best of my ability, allowing her to make her own choices."

"Hmm, she is a stubborn woman," Professor Marshall says, crossing his legs at the ankles. "Intelligent for sure, but her only saviour is the love the king has for her. Once that is gone, I'm afraid there will be nothing left for poor Anne, nor anything you or her faction can do."

My stomach lurches at the truth of his words. "Professor, I have grown to love her, for all her stubbornness and strong will — her ideas on religion inspire me. Her love of life compels me to wish she will be around to see her daughter crowned."

"You know that won't happen, Beth. All you can do is support her and advise her to curb her sharp tongue, especially once she is queen, because she will find it difficult to make the transition from mistress to monarch. Guide her as best you can and no more. Above all, conceal your real identity from all, especially from the king and from Cromwell." He stares directly at me. "I do not want to have to come and save you from the Tower, or from the Swordsman of Calais!"

I wince, tugging at the cuff of my shift. "Surely it wouldn't come to that?"

He wiggles his eyebrows.

"Oh, Professor, I can't believe I will soon be able to recount and witness one of the most sensational episodes in English history. Anne seems such a courageous, determined woman, it's such a disaster that she will run headlong into tragedy. I so want to help change the outcome."

"I suggest you go home for a while. Rest, have a bath, then spend some time with your family. Give yourself space to decide what you'd like to do." He stands and hands me his trench coat. "Here, you can borrow my coat. If you should decide to return to Anne, you will need to devise something else to wear, unless you go back again in modern clothes." With that, he bids me goodbye and shuts the door behind him.

With the professor's departure, I cover my linen shift with his long coat. It swamps me right down to my ankles, making me look a little strange, with my bare feet popping out from below the hem.

I find it a unique experience walking to the student car park, jabbing my toes over the bare tarmac. It's surreal that my little Figaro car is exactly where I left it months ago, or at least what I thought was months ago. Thankfully, the battery won't be dead. The seat is comfortable and familiar, yet turning the key in the ignition and hearing the engine jump to life feels so weird having come from a world where no such things exist.

Driving home to Carshalton, the rain comes down in sheets. I switch on the demister and sigh as the realisation hits me that I may never be able to help Anne, to change her fate, or save her from the path set out for her. Accepting it is the hard part, and I guess that whilst I can continue to return to Tudor England, I will always have to take things as they are.

I need to learn from the experience, as Professor Marshall said, and help and advise Anne where I can. I hope I can stay within those parameters.

I feel refreshed after a warm shower, washing my hair, and having the chance to do all those twenty-first-century things people do: tweezing eyebrows, waxing legs, using deodorant, drinking copious cups of hot tea, and eating toast with Marmite. Having realised I'd left my holdall back in the sixteenth century, packing a new bag to aid me against the perils of Renaissance life is essential — I need to be ready for when I get the opportunity to go back, and I must go back, even if it's just to retrieve my mobile phone.

I can't just wear my shift if I go back through the portal — that would attract too much attention. I pull open my wardrobe doors and grapple around with a few large, zipped storage bags at the bottom. I grab one and pull it out onto the middle of my bedroom floor. It's got my re-enactors Tudor gown inside that I bought from Gina Clark, the Tudor Dreams Historical Costumier, who advertises on social media. I've watched her Facebook Live videos many times — her dresses are as historically accurate as you'll get, and my best choice if I'm going to return to Anne.

I grab a big holdall, folding the dress and its underpinnings inside, along with the matching hood and velvet cloak. I've also got some cow-mouth shoes, which will be ideal to finish off the outfit. It's not as beautiful as one of Anne's actual dresses, but it's close to it, and will do the job, which is a big relief. I stuff aspirins and other necessities into a plain linen bag, as well as make-up, more toothpaste, a decent hairbrush, and a transparent lip-gloss.

I wish I hadn't left my iPhone at Hever; otherwise, I'd have plugged it into my laptop and downloaded the photographs of Anne. Sitting at my desk, I open my laptop, log into social media, and check what I've missed. Nothing much. Just the same stuff I'd viewed before my time-travelling escapade. I decide to do some research to aid me on my return and check something about George, giggling to myself when I see portraits thought to be him, knowing none of them are a good likeness.

Mum pops her head around the door, and I slam the laptop lid shut.

My mum is lovely, quirky, and intelligent. To me she's perfect. A lecturer at the London College of Fashion, she is svelte and typically English, always dressing head-to-toe in navy or black. Her fashion hero is Christian Dior. She is the mother of style, and is always busy, tending to delegate to save time, and is unsentimental with colleagues and students. The only time she shows any affection is when she's around her family.

"Do you have to sneak up on me like that?" I'm hoping my sarcastic tone hides the fact that I've missed her — she has no idea how long I've been gone.

"Sorry, did I startle you?" she asks, coming over to my bed and picking up some dirty clothes.

"Yes, you did!" I grin.

"Is this for the wash?" She picks up my Tudor shift from the bed, eyeing it curiously. "Gosh, this looks really authentic! Where did you get it from — Ninya, at The Tudor Tailor? It looks absolutely accurate, and perfect."

I hope her seeing that undergarment doesn't give the game away. My mum, the fashion historian, is looking at an artefact that's technically over four hundred years old, and in perfect condition!

She examines the stitching of the seams. "All hand-done, too. I will wash it by hand, to be on the safe side. Is that okay?" She looks at me with a hint of curiosity.

"Yes, if you wouldn't mind?"

"Have you eaten?"

"Yes."

She looks at me, lifting my chin with her free hand. "You look pale. Are you sure you aren't working too hard?"

"I'm fine, Mum. Honestly." I shrug her off as she questions my comings and goings, and I brush off her curiosity by making excuses about spending time in the university library reading copious journals and papers, researching for my next assignment. In any case, she can't grumble, as I'm a studious student, intent on achieving the best I can with my dissertations. "Shouldn't you be teaching?" I ask. "Why are you home?"

"I have time owed for all the overtime I've done lately," she says, releasing a long sigh, "but when I come home, all I seem to do is housework!" She slumps on the edge of my bed, still clutching the dirty washing.

"*You* work way too hard." She looks tired, and dark circles have started to form under her eyes. Why haven't I noticed them before? "Perhaps you should think about getting a cleaner?" I lean towards her. "I would help you, but I just don't have the time."

"I know, sweetheart. Your father and I want you to do well, so I don't want to put any other pressures on you." She retrieves a sock she's just dropped on the floor. "But you should take a break from the study sometimes and have some fun. Go out with your friends. Haven't you met any nice boys yet? You haven't brought a boyfriend home in such a long time," she teases, obviously hoping I'll take the bait. George's face wafts into my brain, as does Rob's, but its best to keep my thoughts to myself.

"Seriously, Mum, how old do you think I am? Just because I live at home, you still think I'm your little girl!" I laugh, wishing she'd be more grateful that I care about my degree and doing well for myself.

"Trust me, there's plenty of time for men. I've got some fantastic friends from school and uni. Just because I don't tell you where I am every second of every day, doesn't mean I'm not having fun or even a few drinks in the pub with friends after lectures."

"Okay, okay," she says, her arms full of clothes. "I was just checking, as your dad and I haven't seen you that much of late. I was beginning to think you consider this house more of a hotel than your home."

I am slightly surprised. Dad says little — his schedule doesn't allow him to notice much at home, with his work keeping him occupied. He treats me more like an adult, because he chooses to, which makes my life easier. "Oi, I'm not that disrespectful," I say, grinning and brushing my hand down her forearm.

Apart from university, I have a few hobbies, like joining my re-enactor friends when they're up for visiting Sudeley Castle or Penshurst Place, usually in my costume. Apart from that, I'm a normal young woman who likes watching stuff on iPlayer or streaming something from the TV, as well as going to the gym and doing dance and fitness.

And then, of course, there's Rob. We met in the Students' Union during my first year of university and bonded over our mutual love of music (especially Bowie) and history, and socials, which are a big part of our lives, whether it's a night out, a quiet drink, or a day trip, or even just hanging out somewhere green and peaceful, like The Grove — the park opposite my house.

# Ten

The following morning, I head back to the university for an exciting lecture, which I must not miss. We have an exceptional guest tutor, the historian Suzannah Lipscomb, who I've met before and who has taught me so much.

The refreshments' area adjacent to the lecture hall is awash with humanities' students, hanging around with blank notepads at the ready, chomping at the bit to be allowed access to the university's premier arts' lecture theatre.

I stand shoulder to shoulder with familiar faces as we filter through the doors to the large, well-lit hall, with its excellent audio-visual facilities. It is typically used for prestigious events and visiting speakers during term time and is much sought after for conferences the rest of the year. I secure a central spot a few steps up the tiered seating system, placing myself amid the action. After fifteen minutes of activity, everything finally stills, and the room is filled with a buzzing anticipation.

Professor Marshall enters, as does the head of the faculty, to introduce our guest speaker for the afternoon.

"Welcome to you all. Please seat yourselves quickly and quietly." Both staff look around the room, observing the throng, waiting for respectful silence.

Professor Marshall steps onto the podium, looking smart, his glasses wiped clean of smears and fingerprints. He seems excited and somewhat animated as he introduces our lecturer. "Students and guests, along with the humanities' faculty, it gives me the very great privilege to introduce to you the historian, author, broadcaster, and award-winning academic, based at the University of Roehampton, Professor Suzannah Lipscomb."

We break into an enthusiastic round of applause as Professor Lipscomb wafts into the lecture hall, her floral perfume announcing her entrance. She takes the stage, the epitome of an intelligent, witty, and beautiful scholar, with such an enquiring mind.

Professor Lipscomb introduces herself. Her blonde, Pre-Raphaelite curls cascade around her face and shoulders and her piercing blue eyes engage with every student as she removes her fuchsia coat and places it over the back of her chair, then unwraps her thick wool scarf from about her neck. Next, she secures her laptop on the table, and begins her lecture on '1536: The Year that Changed Henry VIII'.

"Good afternoon. I'd like to thank Professor Marshall for inviting me to come and speak with you lovely lot." She smiles graciously to the gathering, and another short but loud round of applause fills the room as she opens her PowerPoint presentation. "Today we are going to discuss the big man himself, Henry VIII. There is something about Henry that makes us feel that we know him, although Hollywood does have a habit of reintroducing us."

The screen fills with pictures of Richard Burton, Keith Michell, Eric Bana and, of course, Jonathan Rhys Meyers. Chuckles fill the room, the noise diminishing as she clicks forward to show another image. We look at a portrait of Henry VIII, *c.*1536, by Hans Holbein the Younger. It's the quintessential painting of the infamous Tudor monarch.

Professor Lipscomb points to the portrait: "I'd like to suggest that when you think of Henry VIII, this is what you actually visualise, and you attach to it all sorts of values, none of them particularly positive."

I pull out a large notebook from my bag and begin jotting down details of the last decade of Henry's life, while Professor Lipscomb elaborates on the stereotypes surrounding him during that time. She smiles, almost knowingly, but not as knowingly as I smile back at her. If only she knew.

My thoughts drift, but I pull myself together and continue scribbling notes on how, when Henry came to the throne, he was known for being good-looking, accomplished, and kind. Professor Lipscomb clicks on several other portraits by unknown artists.

"Perhaps we have to rely slightly more on the documentary evidence than the pictures!"

This makes us all laugh. I know the chronicler Edward Hall said that he had a 'goodly personage, an amiable façade, a princely countenance', and the Venetian ambassador Sebastian Giustinian said the king had 'a round face so very beautiful that it would become a pretty woman'.

According to Professor Lipscomb, the king wasn't just good-looking, he was also very accomplished. Therefore, he could surpass all the archers of his guard. He was said to be a fine jouster and a capital equestrian, and could play musical instruments — in fact, he could play every single instrument in the room when entertaining visiting French ambassadors.

"Henry was also gentle in debate," she says. "He acts more like a companion than a king. Apparently, the Venetian ambassador once said that he was 'affable and gracious — a man that harmed no one'. In fact, it seems as if Henry, in the first twenty or so years of his reign, was the perfect golden-Renaissance prince."

It's funny, because the way she describes Henry is precisely how he appeared at the *Château Vert* masque, and I'm anxious that if I go back through the portal, I won't like the later prince — the king we know of as being savage, obese, cruel, and ruthless. I can't imagine him being irascible, irritated, or capricious.

The lecture is enlightening and engages all the students, who write down questions they want to ask Professor Lipscomb at the end of her talk. I want to know why she thinks 1536 was a pivotal year in the king's life. My pages are full of spider-diagrams, crossings out, dates, and context.

The ensuing question-and-answer session goes on for over an hour, which is excellent, and Professor Marshall looks pleased that Professor Lipscomb has given up so much of her time to be with us.

As students begin to filter from the hall, Rob is standing in the doorway waiting for me. He's not what you'd think of as obviously good-looking; however, he is tall and dark, with a charisma that could charm the birds out of the trees. One thing I adore about him is his dress sense: those crisp, pastel linen shirts, and the tight jeans that sculpt his bum — and yes, I've looked!

But what has attracted me to him the most is our mutual passion for history and his profound intelligence on all matters concerning it.

We met in my first year at university. He is in the year above me studying History and Classics but some of our modules overlap and we share an equal enthusiasm for the Tudor period.

We often debate topics at the pub for hours on end, he nursing his pint and me with my usual alcopop — the blue variety. Everyone says Rob and I are an obvious match, and I agreed … before I ended up in Tudor England, spending so much time around George Boleyn.

"What happened to you yesterday?" he asks. "Are you all right?" He stares at me.

"It's nothing." I can't look him in the face. I can't tell him I was with Anne Boleyn or he'll think I've lost it. Not only am I finding it difficult to adjust to the time-slipping, but it's also difficult to reconcile the length of time I've been gone with the reality that I seem to have lost only a few hours in my modern life. "I've been in the library. I had some work to catch up on." I pinch my nostrils, trying to hide my dishonesty.

"Ah, okay. So how was the lecture?" He looks back towards the hall.

"Good, thanks. A great scoop for Professor Marshall to get Professor Lipscomb here." I smile. Now I pluck up the courage to look at him, and I feel my cheeks flush.

"I'm sorry I couldn't go, but it clashed with a Classics' lecture."

"I thought as much. What are you up to now?"

"I was going to make a start on the three-thousand-word intro I have to write for my next module. I'm going to the library. What about you?"

"I'm not sure." I'm finding it difficult to settle back into life with my friends and family, back into my *real* life. I worry whether the time-slip will work in reverse. If I spend too much time in the present, will I lose a year or more with Anne? I pull the strap of my bag higher onto my shoulder. People nudge past us as they filter from the lecture hall.

"Rob, are you coming into town with us tonight?" Marc asks as he passes in the doorway. "You can join us, Beth, if you fancy it?"

We both shake our heads.

"Not tonight," Rob says. "I have other plans."

"No worries," Marc calls out to him as he joins his friends and heads down the corridor.

Rob turns back to me, guiding me out of the doorway by my elbow. "How about coming for a meal with me at The Greyhound?" His eyes twinkle under the fluorescent lights.

"Why not?" Another evening here won't make much difference to the portal. It never seems to open when I want it to, at least that's how things were back in Tudor England, and I can't be thinking about my studies all the time. Besides, who's to say the portal will work in the same way again?

"That's settled then, I'll pick you up at eight." He smiles and walks away.

Hearing Rob's car pull up outside my house, I grab my wool coat and scarf and rush down the stairs to open the front door before Mum gets there.

"Hey, where are you off to? Aren't you having dinner with your dad and me?" She stands in the kitchen doorway, apron on, a half-peeled potato in one hand and the metal peeler in the other.

Mum never cooks tea — she's never usually home early enough — which means Dad and I often fend for ourselves. Again, tonight, she's home late, which explains her preparing food at an odd hour. It doesn't bother me, but she detests it. Mum eats like a sparrow, anyway.

"Sorry, I've planned to go to the pub with friends. Is that okay?" I kiss her on the cheek, hoping she'll be appeased.

"You best say goodnight to your dad." She nods at the lounge door.

I look in and find Dad engrossed in today's copy of *The Times*. When I enter, he looks up at me. "Are you off out?" he asks, disappointment obvious in his tone.

"Yes, Dad. I'll see you later." I bend to give him a peck on the forehead, then rush out to the front door. On opening it, I see Rob already halfway up the path, and I'm glad I've caught him before he rings the bell.

"You ready?" he asks.

"Yes, ready as I'll ever be." I button my coat up and secure my scarf in a knot around my neck.

The sky is dazzling tonight, with starry constellations filling the cloudless heavens. Rob stands with hands deep in his pockets, waiting to escort me out through the garden gate. He seems in a jovial mood, and we meander between the bollards at the end of the road and cross over to the other side of the street, walking in relative silence, our path illuminated by the streetlights. The pavement is covered in crisp dead leaves, which crunch underfoot as we make our way towards the pub in The Greyhound Hotel, opposite The Ponds in Carshalton, a stone's throw from my house here in Westcroft Road.

"You seem quiet tonight. Is everything okay?"

"Yes, I'm fine," I say, not meeting his eyes. Everything, of course, is not okay. All I can think about is how soon I can reasonably return to Anne? I need to get back to my *other* life. I can't share anything about my Tudor adventure with Rob, as he'd never believe me, and if he did, he'd only want to come with me, and that could ruin everything. That's a chance I cannot take.

"You didn't seem so earlier." He glances at me, patiently awaiting my response.

All I can do is shrug. "I've been all over the place — busy with research, assignments."

"I guess you haven't got much time for anything else." He strides along beside me. "Or boyfriends?"

"What?" I stare at him, glad of the lamp above us not working because I feel heat spreading through my cheeks.

"I just wondered," he says, "if a lovely girl like you had time for dating?" He looks away for a moment, then back at me. "But maybe not, if you are so … busy?"

I laugh. It's either that or choke. "Well, you know what university life is like?"

He sniffs. "It depends if you are interested in having a social life, or are happy always studying."

"I suppose so." I don't know what else to say. I knew Rob liked me, but I didn't expect such an approach. Or did I? How often have I wished for it? But that was before the portal.

We continue strolling, and it isn't long before we're met by the sound of music pumping through the pub's open windows.

The place is heaving, and I'm so glad Rob booked a table; otherwise, we would have been disappointed. Ever the gentleman, he escorts me through the doors, and we order our drinks at the bar before being taken to a niche in the far corner of the restaurant. I pull my coat and scarf off, fold them neatly, and leave them on the bench beside Rob. He takes two menus from the holder and passes me one.

"What do you fancy?"

I love his smile. "The steak looks good." I wish I had the guts to say that I fancied him, as some kind of truthful joke, but things are different now, and my mouth salivates as I realise this will be the first proper meal I've eaten since arriving back from Tudor England.

He beckons the waitress over.

"What would you like to order?" she asks, taking out her little notepad and pen.

"Ladies first." Rob motions to me with his hand.

"I'll have the steak with chips, please."

"How do you like your steak?"

"Medium to well done, please."

She turns to Rob. "And for you, sir?"

"Steak and kidney pie with mash."

She takes the menus from us and saunters off towards the kitchens through the packed restaurant.

Rob takes a gulp of his lager, nursing the glass in both hands. He smiles. "Did you enjoy the lecture this afternoon?"

"Yeah, I did, thanks." I look around the bar, hoping to see some familiar faces from university, but no one but us seems to be here yet. Music blasts from the speakers overhead and, in the far corner of the bar, football supporters raise their beer bottles and shout at the match on the big screen in the hope it will encourage their side to do better.

"What was Professor Lipscomb speaking on?" Rob raises his voice, so I'll hear him over the din.

"She was explaining how and why things went so terribly wrong for Henry at the beginning of 1536."

"Did she discuss the wives, or was it a talk on the politics of the time?" He brushes his hand through his dark hair, then folds his arms as he leans back against the bench.

"She talked about her favourite subject." I smile. "You know? The king, about how the events of that year changed him, turning him from being affable and gracious to becoming a tyrant and a despot." I'm aware that Rob is studying me, and I tuck a long strand of hair behind my ear, looking anywhere but at his eyes. His half-smile is delightful. He must sense my awkwardness. To my relief, he keeps the discussion on things he knows I'm confident debating.

"Ah, so the theory of the jousting accident causing him brain damage and a permanent change to his character?" He leans forward, shifting the table candle between us, watching its small flame flicker. The soft glow makes me think back to evenings spent with George Boleyn, discussing the latest political issues and religious matters at court. I miss him. I look at Rob, who is scrutinising me, and I realise he's waiting for my answer.

"Erm, yes." I fiddle with the strap on my watch, and I wonder where the waitress has got to with our order. "Although I don't agree with all her theories, I do wish one were true, that Henry didn't want to get rid of Anne at all, and that he still loved her."

"Aha! A romantic at heart." Rob laughs, leans back, and scratches his side through his T-shirt. He looks more casual than usual tonight. The plain, natural fabrics suit him. He could wear a bin liner and still look good. T-shirts, teamed with jeans, and an old tweed jacket can never be a fashion faux pas for men, nor for women — well, that's what Mum has always taught me.

"What's wrong with being romantic?" I ask, unable to hide my grin.

"Nothing." His cheeks flush scarlet. It makes me laugh that he gets embarrassed so quickly.

"Anyway, I always hope that Henry's dalliance with Jane Seymour would be just that, a game of courtly love and that he was never responsible for Anne's execution." I stifle a yawn and look around the room, hoping our food order will be here soon. I'm tired and starving.

"Sorry, am I boring you?" He laughs, though his eyes tell a different story.

"No, Rob, I'm just exhausted and hungry." I lean back against my seat, unfolding the serviette in anticipation of our meal.

"Hungry, eh? Hopefully our food will be here soon. Take your mind off your stomach for a minute and return to the evidence."

"Um, okay. Question is, have you read the new evidence, recently discovered by the author Sandra Vasoli?" I continue playing with the serviette, trying to create some kind of swan design, but Rob snatches it and proceeds to create a fantail ... just like that.

"There you go!" He laughs, placing the serviette back on the table. "You were saying something about an author? What's her new evidence?"

"Vasoli suggests that Henry, on his deathbed, acknowledged Anne's innocence, regretting the punishment he'd invoked." I straighten my back, feeling confident discussing this.

He looks intrigued. "Where did she find the evidence?"

"In the British Library. Henry had apparently confessed to Brother André Thévet, saying he hoped he would be pardoned for his *great sin*."

"Sin against who? Anne?" I notice a man at the next table, who is eating a steak with his hands. It reminds me of meals back at Hever and at court. I long to be back there, but I'm looking forward to some modern cuisine, which is all too obvious as my stomach continues to rumble.

"Yes," I reply, clutching my stomach, "and Vasoli goes on to suggest that Bishop White Kennett then recorded the truth of Thévet's knowledge."

Rob is wide-eyed. He leans in closer. "So, you're telling me that all we know of Henry and Anne is wrong? That we can now regard Henry's last hours with a sense of compassion?" He locks his fingers together in front of him and rests them on the table. "Interesting."

"It's crazy, isn't it? But it certainly sounds compelling, and may also confirm Anne's innocence, so she would forever be known and remembered in that light." I brush my hand through my hair. It feels strange having it loose. In Anne's world, my hair is mostly braided and rarely left hanging free around my shoulders. "What do you think of that?"

"It certainly sheds new light on his relationship with Anne. Yet it's so unlike Henry to show any remorse, don't you think?"

"I know, but wouldn't it be thrilling for this evidence to be true?" From what I've seen of the king, he is a romantic and attentive man when it comes to women, so the new evidence does seem plausible.

I lean towards Rob. I should be pleased. I'm here with him. Alone. Being spoilt. Having dinner. It's what I've waited for, for so long — for him to take notice of me and be interested. And here I am ruining the evening with my indifference.

He takes his phone from his inside jacket pocket. "It would be interesting to see the sources for ourselves. Do you fancy taking a trip to the British Library or the Archives at Kew one day and we can see if the evidence adds up?" He seems genuinely enthusiastic, which is excellent. "It would work around uni commitments. The opening times are here on their website." He turns his phone to me.

"Okay, yeah, I'd love to go. We could also look for evidence about Cromwell, as I'm still of a mind that he was the minister behind Anne's downfall." I smile. If I get the chance to return to Anne, I'll be keeping a close eye on him, with his rolled-up parchments, conspiracies, and scheming. I'm sure once we meet, I won't like him, but we'll see.

Rob looks up, his beautiful eyes flickering as if he's viewing something in the air above him. "I know that later, after Anne's execution, Chapuys will write in his dispatches, which are included in *Letters and Papers* about Cromwell, saying: 'He said it was he who had discovered and followed up the affair of the Concubine, in which he had taken a great deal of trouble, and that, owing to the displeasure and anger he had incurred upon the reply given to me by the king on the third day of Easter, he had set himself to arrange the plot.'"

I love how he does that. An encyclopaedic knowledge that I envy. He stuffs his phone back in his jacket pocket and leans on the table.

"Stop showing off, Rob. That's the evidence historians have often cited in their work. As far as I'm concerned, there was nothing in this plot to suggest the king had a hand in the matter." I'm confident the evidence shows Henry's innocence in the matter, and as I lean towards Rob, I'm determined to prove myself correct.

"You know there are several translations of this particular dispatch?" he says, flicking a fly into the proverbial ointment. "The source, *Letters and Papers*, differs slightly in translation to the one from *Calendar of State Papers*."

"I know. Professor Lipscomb suggested this source —" I dig the notes I took during her lecture out of the bottom of my bag — "which says: 'He, himself, meaning Cromwell, had been authorised and commissioned by the king to prosecute and bring to an end the mistress's trial, to do which he had taken considerable trouble. It was he who, in consequence of the disappointment and anger he had felt on hearing the king's answer to me on the third day of Easter, had planned and brought about the whole affair.'"

"It's interesting how two similar sources could mean the exact opposite if particular wording and lines are omitted." Rob grins as if he's in the know. "I understand that the king might have suggested that Cromwell would be up for the chop if the allegations against Anne proved to be false."

I lean forward. "But Henry was still championing Anne as late as April 19th. I believe her to have been innocent. These were trumped-up charges, orchestrated by Cromwell to get her out of the way. The evidence clearly supports it. I don't believe the king was behind it." I feel my face flush as my passion rises. "And I don't believe the king wanted to be rid of Anne. In fact, I'd go as far as to say that he still loved her, right up until the end!"

Rob frowns. "You really think that?" He looks me directly in the eye.

"Yes, he never wanted to marry Jane Seymour — she was a courtly love interest — he just wanted her in his bed, nothing more." I take a breath and drink some of my alcopop. "It's not until that musician Smeaton confesses to sleeping with Anne three times that the king changes his mind and everything snowballs."

Rob waves to someone over the other side of the bar, and whoever it is, they come over to say hello.

The guy smiles, pulling up a stool beside our table. I've never seen him before. He isn't from university and talks with a thick South London accent.

"What's up, cuz?" he says.

"Hey, mate! I'm good. Just here for dinner." Rob turns to me. "This is Beth, a friend of mine from my history course."

"Nice to meet you, Beth." He grins, his teeth gleaming. "I'm Josh." He offers me his hand to shake. I tentatively return his greeting. The calluses on his hand scrape my palm. He's obviously a builder, evidenced by his crisp tan. I like his twinkling eyes. He's a bit older than us — I'd say early-thirties.

"Look, I hope I'm not disturbing you two? I couldn't ignore you and not say hello."

"It's okay," I say, feeling a tad awkward being in the company of Rob's family when we're meant to be out for a meal for two. But it's not a date, is it?

"Anyway, you guys, I'd better go — my other half and our friends are waiting at the bar. We're heading up west later."

"Have a great time. I'll give you a call soon." Rob nods and smiles, getting up from his seat.

Josh slaps him on the shoulder. "Cheers, mate." He turns to me and grins. "Nice to meet you, Beth. Great to see Rob with a decent girl." He chuckles and wanders off back to his friends. The music continues to thump out, and the football crowd's fervour rises with their match on TV.

"Sorry about that," Rob says, fiddling with the lapel of his jacket, "Where were we?"

"Talking about the lecture."

"Yes, that's right!" He smiles and leans back against the bench again.

I shift in my seat, staring at the candle between us, and take another sip of my drink. I really don't want this to be awkward. "I've come across no evidence that Henry put pressure on Cromwell to frame Anne, and the letter to Charles V from Chapuys has always indicated the opposite."

"You have such strong opinions on this." Rob touches my hand, a brief contact, and I like it. "But you're omitting a line, written in that letter to Chapuys."

"And that is?" I feel my brows crease as I await his reply. I twist the ends of a strand of hair around my finger — a bad habit, that makes me look childish, but I can't help it as I wait for Rob to argue his case. He gulps back some more lager and licks his lips. It makes me think of Thomas Boleyn and how he enjoys his goblet of wine while sitting by the fire in the parlour. My mind wanders at the thought of when I will be able to see them all again.

"Hey, Beth, did you hear what I said?"

"Erm, sorry, I was miles away."

He shakes his head. "Anyone would think you didn't like the company."

"Oh, Rob, of course I do. I wouldn't be here otherwise, would I?"

He shrugs. "I suppose not."

The waitress finally turns up, placing our meals under our noses. The steam rising from our dishes brings with it a beautiful bouquet of flavours, and my stomach rumbles again as I cut the steak to take my first bite. Not a word is heard from either of us as we tuck into our food, until Rob starts to talk.

"I've just got to say, this is delicious." He swallows his food before forking up another mouthful.

I laugh at his terrible table manners. When we finish, I push my cutlery to the centre of my plate and relax against the high-backed bench.

Rob fidgets with his napkin. "Beth, I, um … brought you here for more than just the food. I want to ask you something." He looks so nervous, which is strange because he's usually a confident person.

"What is it?" I ask, not sure if I want to hear what he has to say.

"We get on well, don't we?"

"Silly. Of course, we do. Why do you ask?"

He bites his bottom lip. "You know I really like you?"

"Yes." Heat rushes to my face, and I know I've gone a deep red.

"Well, how would you feel if I was to ask you if we could date each other regularly?"

I wasn't expecting this. He wants to date me. Me? So many of the girls on our course have been trying to date him for a year or more, yet he wants me?

"I'm flattered, but I'm not really sure I have time for a relationship, what with our workload." It's not that I want to say no, it's just that it seems selfish of me to say yes to a relationship, to then realise I don't have the time for one. Maybe I'm unsure because of George. What a mess. Although I could keep my options open, couldn't I? After all, I'm a modern girl. Well, most of the time.

"Maybe you're right," he says, shrugging. "Could we take it more casually then? See how that goes." He motions to the waitress for the bill.

"I don't see why not." I smile. "I wouldn't want you getting jealous of the time I spend studying. It's not fair on anyone."

"You're right, as usual, and I do have to study, too." He nods — I think more to himself than me. He takes the last gulp of his lager and places the empty glass on the table. "Shall I walk you home?"

"Yes, come on then." I grab my coat and scarf, putting them on as we head out into the cold evening air.

The sky is filled with a thousand stars and the moonlight dances on the surface of the ponds opposite the pub, the water reflecting the nightscape's speckled brilliance. Rob puts his jacket on as he strides along beside me. This time, however, his hands are not stuffed in his pockets. He offers me one to hold, his touch warm and secure — his romantic gesture flushing heat through my cheeks. We keep up a brisk pace, the streetlights illuminating our way.

When we arrive outside my garden gate, Rob is still holding my hand, but now faces me. "Shall I see you tomorrow? What's your timetable like?"

"I think I have a mentor meeting with Professor Marshall about my last few assignments." I know this is the only way I'll be able to have access to the portal to see if it will work its magic again.

"Can I catch you later on, then?" he asks, looking down at me.

"Yep, no problem." I smile. "But don't text me, I've mislaid my phone."

"I'll find you," he says, leaning in for a kiss, which I wasn't expecting. His soft lips brush against mine and from the corner of my eye, I see the silhouette of my mother as she peers through the net curtains of the living-room window. With that, I pull away and the metal grates as I lift the latch on the gate.

"Don't look to your right, but we have my mother watching our every move."

"Oh, God. Sorry." He turns bright scarlet, not knowing quite what to do.

"I'd best go in. I shall see you tomorrow." I swing the gate open and make a dash for the front door.

Mum and Dad greet me in the hallway before I have a chance to make a run for my bedroom. Mum is full of smiles, pressing for information, while Dad stands beside her, looking apologetic, as if not wanting to embarrass me.

Dad, well, he is the most conventional of my parents. A socialist civil servant, who works in the office of the Leader of the Opposition. Contrary to his affiliations, he dresses impeccably and, if not working, always has his nose deep in *The Times*. He is politically astute and, when not in the city, spends his days just being … *Dad* — a most charming, clever man, and my hero. His mind is forever on other things, although I've never discovered what.

"Your sister has just left," he says. Joanna, or Jo-Jo as she likes to be called, is the opposite of me: a single mum, with elfin eyes, pink T-shirts, and eternally bare feet — she tends to be even more eccentric than the rest of my peculiar family.

"I'm sorry I've missed her. I didn't know she was coming round. Is she okay?"

"Yes, darling, she's fine," Dad replies. He wanders into the kitchen, grabs a bar of chocolate from the cupboard, breaks off a couple of squares, and bites into it as Mum continues to stand in the hallway, beginning her tirade of questions.

"So, you do have a boyfriend!" She smirks, locking the front door behind me.

"Mum, he's just a mate."

Dad has wandered back into the lounge to find his newspaper. From his demeanour, I can tell he isn't impressed with Mum's interrogation of me.

"You looked more than mates from where I was standing."

"Well, you shouldn't have been spying." I enjoy telling her off. I don't get to do it too often.

"Will you stay up for a nightcap with us?"

"No, I'm off to bed. I'm shattered. Will you say goodnight to Dad for me?"

"Yes, of course." She smiles. "Night, darling." She kisses my cheek and, as I make my way up the stairs, calls out after me. "Love you!"

Finally, in the quiet of my room, I collapse on the bed, only to be meowed at by Rutterkin, who reprimands me for spoiling his sleep. He has been comatose in my duvet where I left him earlier this evening. My bag of stuff sits at the foot of my bed, full with provisions for my next adventure.

I'm ready to face Tudor England once more. Will it be ready for me?

# Eleven

## Richmond Palace, London – September 1522

I resolve wholeheartedly to return to Henry VIII's court at Richmond Palace. Once back in Professor Marshall's office, dressed in my Tudor re-enactors' costume, I twist and press the ring, thinking of Anne and where she might be in 1522. I last saw her at Richmond Palace. I'll think of that and hope to return to the same point in time, but the process seems to be more random than I wish.

With one twist of the ring, it's as if I take off in my head, with everything around me swirling and tumbling, until I am here, out of breath, still clutching my bag to my breast.

To regain my equilibrium, I sit on the grass beneath the golden foliage of a large oak tree and marvel at the sight of the Royal residence that dominates the lush landscape between what must be Richmond Green and the River Thames — its white stone beckoning me in the bright sunlight. The octagonal towers, capped with pepper-pot domes, are magnificent with their delicate strapwork and brass weathervanes.

I'm dying to get to the palace, and hope the ring has done its work and I'll be reunited with my mistress. But I am glad to catch my breath for just a minute under the dappled shade, as the branches rustle and whisper in the light breeze.

My chest is tight, my side sore. Did I lace my kirtle too tight? The rough bark scratches me as I arch and stretch my back against the tree trunk, somewhat alleviating the tension between my shoulder blades. My lungs fill with the most pristine fresh air, so alien to the London I come from.

Time to get moving. Amber leaves crunch beneath my soles as I cross the grass, which splays out like a green blanket before me. I straighten my hood and adjust my cloak, then lift the hem of my skirts so they don't trail in the mud. If Gina could see me now, in her creation, in Tudor England, she really wouldn't believe it! When I reach the stony track that leads towards the palace entrance, the sun hides behind a cloud, stealing the cheering warmth from my cheeks.

The redbrick walls rise towards me as I approach the palace gates. All this Tudor architecture excites me, and I'm reminded of reading at the archives at Kew, in the 'Great Chronicle', that in 1506 a fire broke out in King

Henry VII's chamber, destroying the room but luckily not damaging the structure of the building itself.

On the opposing side of the castle entrance, there are a few small, round tents erected, with people sitting outside peddling their wares. Beggars approach the main gates but are unceremoniously chided and given their marching orders.

A range of double-storey, brick-built apartments — with half-turrets at intervals along the outer wall — extend for almost the full length of the frontage facing me. Once I'm within touching distance, I brush my hand along the bricks, stare at their beauty, and think of how Henry VIII, then a prince, had also escaped death by fire within these same walls. I'd read an account from 1507, that the teenage Prince Henry had just finished walking through the galleries when, for no reason, they collapsed, almost killing the would-be king. Furious, he had the builders imprisoned and the whole palace renovated.

I'm jolted from my thoughts when I'm prodded by a man I assume to be the gatekeeper. His clothes are dull, dark wool, and the only signs of his hierarchy is the Tudor rose embroidered on his chest, and his crisp, white linen collar poking up from his doublet. He rubs his chin and hacks up a wad of phlegm, which he proceeds to spit into the nearby grass. Gross. The last thing I want is to become ill here, so I try not to get too close in case he has a cold.

"My Lady." He looks me up and down, staring at my gown. "Who might your business be with, here at Richmond?" He pulls me closer to him, to allow for a group of courtiers leading horses on reins to be ushered through. One or two of the visitors doff their caps, but their faces aren't familiar. I nod in acknowledgement. The gatekeeper, his hand now resting on the hilt of his smallsword, pulls his cheeks in, waiting for me to reply. "Well?"

"I am come to see Mistress Anne Boleyn." I give him my best smile in the hope that he'll wave me through the gate. Swords rattle as they clip brickwork, and livery colours and luxurious damasks flash against the redness of the walls as visitors hurry past me and are questioned by servants, who direct them on.

"Is Mistress Boleyn expecting you?" He threads his thumbs beneath the leatherwork of his belt and stares at me. He's obviously a busy man, and suspicious of anyone he doesn't know.

"Yes," I lie.

"Well then, go and find Sir Henry Guildford, and he will take you to the privy lodgings and to your mistress."

"Thank you, sir."

With that, he hurries past me, barking orders at servants and interrogating those who should not be so close to the palace. My heart pounds as I walk beneath the gatehouse, and I'm surprised to find myself in an expansive cobbled courtyard called the 'Great Court', which is not dissimilar to 'Base

Court' at Hampton Court Palace, as it is in my time. The Great Court has redbrick buildings on the east, west, and north sides. On the east side is the palace wardrobe, where the soft furnishings are stored, while on the west are rooms for officials and courtiers.

I follow the flagstone path. Courtiers to the left of me tether their horses against the lodgings, giving orders to the stable hands. Hoofs clip the cobbles and tails flap, swiping flies as the animals wait to be fed and watered.

As I head towards the middle gate, which is turreted and adorned with the stone figures of two trumpeters, I see familiar faces and hope one of the Boleyns might be amongst them. However, it's not to be. Courtiers and servants hurry everywhere.

I pass through the gate and into Fountain Court, pulling my bag closer as I go. In this bustle, I must look lost, because as I enter another central courtyard, Sir Henry Guildford, flanked by other court officials, notices me. I recognise him because of his portly stature, so expertly captured in Holbein's painting. He strides towards me, passing the Great Hall.

Sir Henry Guildford, Comptroller of the Household and Master of the Horse, makes a short bow and politely smiles, oozing confidence. He is a well-dressed gentleman in sumptuous velvets of gold and green, his chain of office dazzling in the intermittent sunlight. I guess he is in his early thirties — middle-aged for the time. His cheeks are ruddy, his eyes dark brown, and he has a cleft in his chin. He wears his hair in the straight fashion, long enough to help disguise his undefined jowls. On the other side of the courtyard, the chapel's bells peal out a charming sound every so often, calling those who wish to observe daily Mass.

"Mistress, can I help you?" he asks. "My name is Henry Guildford. I usually reside at Leeds Castle as Comptroller of His Majesty's Household." He is animated and appears to enjoy letting me know exactly who he is.

I dip a small curtsy in deference, which he seems to appreciate. "Sir Henry, I am Mistress Beth Wickers, I am a lady-in-waiting, and I have come to stay with Mistress Anne Boleyn."

He frowns, and the cleft in his chin deepens as he purses his lips. "We were not expecting you."

I nod. "I apologise, sir. I had no time to write to Mistress Boleyn to let her know she was to expect me."

"Ah, well, you are here now." He clutches the hilt of his dagger, eyeing me up and down, squinting at my gown. "John will carry your belongings." He gestures to an usher, but I clutch my linen bag as tightly as I can to my chest.

"Sir, I am quite capable of carrying my own bag!"

Henry Guildford frowns again and shakes his head. "If you are sure?"

"Yes, I am."

He stares at me, then at his servant, who looks somewhat bemused, not knowing whether he should have grabbed my bag before I had a chance to decline. I breathe a sigh of relief that I had the hindsight to swop my personal belongings into a handmade linen bag, which looks more historically accurate than the holdall I'd had with me back when I entered the portal in the professor's study. With all my twenty-first-century goodies inside it, I couldn't possibly risk anyone else seeing them — there's too much to lose — I might be burned at the stake as a witch if they catch me with such modern conveniences. How could I possibly explain them? Heat rushes into my cheeks and for the second time today, I must lie.

"Mistress, are you well?" Guildford asks, rubbing his forehead.

"Perfectly fine, thank you. I have a gift for Mistress Anne, that is all."

It isn't that bad a lie, and if it means me keeping my true identity safe, then I don't feel so bad.

"You look in need of some refreshment. John will take you to Mistress Anne." He smiles, and I'm confident he's bought it. What a good job he doesn't think I'm smuggling Lutheran tracts or other religious propaganda.

"Mistress Anne will be delighted to see you." He bows again, then turns and walks away into a crowd of waiting ambassadors and their respective entourages, who, no doubt, are requiring food and lodgings.

I follow John, the usher, who proceeds to lead me past the chapel and the Great Hall, then over a bridge which crosses the moat. I'm out of breath as I try to keep up with this equally flustered man, while he talks ten to the dozen. The bridge seems sturdy enough, which is good because it survives from Edward III's time, linking the Privy Lodgings to the central courtyard.

John explains where the public and private kitchens are and informs me that there is a library should I wish to collect any books my royal mistress — he means Queen Katharine — may be interested in reading.

The palace gardens are extensive, and as we enter the Privy Lodgings, it smells musky and damp. Through the windows, I see courtiers walking, playing games, and admiring the late-blooming roses. John hurries me to the rooms being used by the queen's ladies-in-waiting — up three storeys, which are set in a rectangular block with twelve rooms on each floor, and set around an internal court. This part of the palace contains staterooms and private apartments, while the ground floor is entirely given over to accommodation for palace officials. Servants and ushers bark orders at each other behind us as they carry caskets and trunks to the upper lodgings.

The rooms are bustling with servants, and I need a moment to gather my thoughts and pull myself together, still a tad disoriented after my tumbling, time-travelling experience. Will I ever get used to it? Now that I'm here, I realise that I must look a terrible sight.

John opens the door to a series of small dormitories and introduces me to one of Katharine's mistresses of her household. It isn't Maria de Salinas — I would have recognised her. This woman, in black velvet and silver damask, looks down her nose at me, her dark eyes assessing my obvious disarray. My face flushes and I tug at my cloak, pulling it tidier around my shoulders. How would this Spanish lady feel if she'd been flung head over heels through time? I want to return the sneer but hold myself back, knowing she'd be unable to grasp anything I've been through. It would be so much better if time-travelling entailed a quick 'Hey presto!' from there to here but, unfortunately, that isn't the case. Maybe walking through that hidden door is a better way to proceed. I'll have to keep it in mind for when I see Professor Marshall again.

"This is where you shall sleep." The woman indicates with a wave of her hand. "Mistress Boleyn shall make you aware of your duties."

I nod. "Thank you, Madam." My mind is a jumble as I remind myself how to sound like a sixteenth-century noblewoman. She sniffs, looking dismissively at me in my French apparel, then leaves the room, closing the door behind her.

I hope Anne had the foresight to pack some of my gowns; otherwise, it will be an expensive journey, having to re-order clothing out of her father's purse.

The chamber is cosy and inviting, with an established fire crackling and hissing in the grate. Anne's belongings, now familiar to me, are scattered about the room: books in various places, small, half-empty vials of rosewater on a dresser, and a couple of velvet and damask gowns laid upon the four-poster bed. Floorboards creak underfoot as I go to the window facing out over the gardens and down towards the bank of the Thames. The river is busy with boats heading towards the city. Several look like they belong to merchants, filled with all kinds of cargo, with some stopped at the bank edge, making deliveries to the palace. Servants unload goods into carts, while others push them back towards the bridge and courtyard.

A delightfully familiar voice in the outer corridor catches my attention, and the latch on the doors lift and Anne enters the room. Her face lights up, and she runs to embrace me.

"Beth, you are back!" She grins, her eyes sparkling. "I am glad of you being here. Welcome home. I am so pleased to see you." She hugs me so tight it feels like she might not let me go. I grin at her mention of this being my home, and, yes, I suppose being with her, I am home. She looks me up and down, frowning. "What are you wearing?"

"Erm, well, when I returned to my time, all I was wearing was my shift. Remember? We went to bed after the *Château Vert* celebrations, so I was in my night things." I wave a hand across my face, trying to hide my embarrassment.

"I see." She smiles. "I did wonder what had happened to you." She frowns. "You left me no message, and you were gone."

"I'm sorry."

"So, what is this you are wearing?" She tugs at my cloak, and glances at my gown beneath it.

"It's my costume I use when I re-enact."

Her brows knit together. "What do you mean, re-enact?"

"Well, in my time, people who love history dress up as people from history, and walk around palaces and castles, teaching children and their families about those times. It's for tourists mostly, from Amer… I mean, the New World, sometimes France, Spain."

"Really?" She looks puzzled. "You do *that*?" She laughs.

I grimace. "Yes, why not?"

"If I was a re-enactor, I might be a queen, like Philippa of Hainault or Catherine of Valois."

I'm not sure if that was a question or a statement, and I begin to laugh.

Much time seems to have passed here, even though I've been away in my time for two nights only — there's probably no point trying to explain this concept to Anne, as I think it might be too complicated for her to grasp.

"You will need to change out of that *costume*," she says. "You must be hungry and need refreshment." She offers me a goblet of wine, and a seat padded with luxurious cushions.

I pull at the ribbon tying my cloak and shrug the thick velvet off my shoulders so I can relax, letting it fall over the back of my chair.

"Pass me your cloak." She takes it from beneath me as I half stand, then lays it across a trunk at the side of the room.

How much time has passed? She looks like she's lost a little weight. Her waist seems smaller, and she's casually dressed in an ivory silk kirtle and watchet-blue velvet gown, which looks like some kind of dressing gown with a squirrel-fur trim.

I take my first sip of the wine and shiver as my palate adjusts to its heady bouquet. I'm so used to alcopops and other modern drinks; I'd forgotten how strong the wine at court is. But this is all there is on offer, so I take small sips, almost having to force myself to drink it.

Anne leans towards me and grasps my hand. "I must tell you all my news."

I sink back into my seat, thankful for comfortable cushions and the chance to settle myself. She stands before me, resplendent in her silks and velvet. Her smile is radiant, and she relays her stories with enthusiasm, her arms animated.

"You must know that I am admired by all for my excellent gestures and behaviour. The court adores me."

I'm sure courtiers are jealous of her, too, but she doesn't mention it. The sunlight through the window accentuates the chestnut highlights in her dark hair, which today she wears loose, down to her waist. "Didn't your mother imply that is how it might be?"

"She did, indeed." She walks to the door, leans out, then turns back to me. "Where did all the servants go?" She steps out into the corridor, looks around, then stops a passing page and asks for some cheeses and bread, before returning and warming herself in front of the crackling fire. From the décor of her rooms and her proximity to the royal apartments, it seems she has officially become one of the queen's women and is doing better than all the others. What else has changed?

"What month is it?"

"September."

"1522?"

"Of course, dear Beth." She chuckles behind her hand. "You are so funny."

I make a mental note about the timings. Nearly seven months, or thereabouts. I wonder how this time-travel thing decides how the months shift in comparison to my twenty-first-century timeline. The whole experience is confusing, not helped by Professor Marshall never making it clear how the actual timing works. Perhaps he doesn't know? Maybe I'm not meant to know?

I lift the goblet from the small table beside me. "What have I missed?"

"Well, only months ago, Father was appointed Treasurer of the Household, and in April he was granted the Manor of Fobbing in Essex, as well as becoming the Steward of Tunbridge, the Receiver of Bransted, and Keeper of the Manor of Penshurst." She rubs her hands with excitement.

"Ah, I remember George mentioning something about Penshurst. Something to do with the appointment being awarded due to the fall of the Duke of Buckingham."

"Yes." She nods and sits back in the settle opposite me. "The king has trusted Father more and more with his affairs over the past few months."

The wine refreshes my dry throat. "He will be pleased to have been so well rewarded."

"It is no more than Father deserves. He is a skilled diplomat. His appointments are for his long service to the king and his assistance in indicting the Duke of Buckingham last year."

"So, these titles and favours have nothing at all to do with Mary?"

She glances towards the door, probably checking that we will not be overheard. "It would appear not. But that may change if Mary finds herself with child. The king takes her to his bed most nights. Of course, the courtiers gossip that Father is being rewarded for her services to the king, and Father is furious that the affair gives the impression that there may be truth in it."

"Is he not suffocated with pride?"

"No, Father believes he deserves such elevation because of his due diligence."

I take another sip of wine. Hmm, it all seems so coincidental that her father's accolades have come at the same time that Mary is in the king's favour. "Is he here?"

"No, he is away on diplomatic missions with Spain." She sighs, looking into the bottom of her empty goblet.

"Spain?" I always thought Thomas Boleyn's diplomatic duties favoured France.

"You missed the visit of Emperor Charles, travelling from the Low Countries on his way to Spain."

"Charles V? Why was he here? What was he like?"

"Charles?" She giggles, and I wonder has she been sipping too much wine. "He is tall, with that famous Hapsburg chin that you cannot miss!"

I smile. "Not very attractive, then?"

"Ha, no. You know how I detest the Spanish."

"And your father, what are his thoughts on a Spanish alliance?"

"He prefers the French, as I do." She gets up, refills her goblet, and stands by the window, peering out at the courtyard below. "I had to attend the queen when His Majesty met with Charles at Dover, to inspect the new flagship, *Henry Grace à Dieu*."

"How did that go?" I ask, forgetting to speak like a native Tudor. My stomach grumbles as I grab my belly. Where's the damned page with that cheese?

"I was part of Katharine's retinue, and we accompanied Their Majesties to London. We had such a gay time, being entertained along the way by banquets, pageants, jousts, and attending church services."

"What was the reason for the emperor's visit?"

"I think it was to discuss their mutual campaign for the French war." She stands in profile and raises her brows, probably thinking how her mistress, the queen, would revel in a war against the French.

Ah, I should have remembered. "What was the outcome of their discussions?"

"In May, the king declared war on the French."

"So, your father was right to bring you back to England when he did." I take another sip of my wine, which I'm quickly becoming accustomed to.

"I told you, Beth, Father is ever the diplomat. I trusted his judgement, and he has proved himself." She places her goblet on the sill and closes the casement window, then turns to me and beams with pride. "Father is presently away on diplomatic matters with a Doctor Sampson, to visit the Spanish Emperor to promote joint action in the war against France. I have been bored here at court without you or him."

"Bored? Why?"

She picks up her goblet and takes another sip. "Because I am spending most of my time in the company of the queen. I know that is what I was to expect when I came here, but she is so pious, all the ladies have so little fun."

"It can't be that bad, surely?" I sink back into my seat, getting used to the feeling of my heavy clothes again.

"No, it is not bad all the time, especially not when the gentlemen of the court join us." She walks over and sits facing me. "What of you? What of your home?"

"Life carries on as normal. My father is working. Mum, too. My sister and my niece, I rarely see. Rob took me out to dinner."

Anne sees me smile to myself. "Who is Rob?" She leans forward, evidently intrigued.

"Just a friend."

"Your gentleman friend you mentioned before?"

I shrug in what I hope is a noncommittal manner. Our relationship isn't something I want to dwell on at this moment. I'm where I want to be, and I need to focus on everything that surrounds me.

Anne gets up and walks to the door, opens it, and peers out, presumably looking for the page she sent for our cheese. She closes it and turns to me. "Why did you not tell me much of this man before? Is he like the men of the court?"

"No. He's a student like me. Life is … different. Men and women are much more equal in my time."

"Equal, you say. How intriguing." She half-smiles. "I cannot imagine how different your life must be when you are home, instead of the stuffiness of this court." She looks around at the walnut-panelled walls. "If only Queen Katharine could be like the French." I stifle a laugh. "If only she enjoyed dancing or riding." She raises her goblet and takes another sip. "Instead, all she does is pray or read her bible, and argue that the Catholic faith is the one true faith."

"I heard it said that the queen was once very beautiful and even wore her red hair, as you do, down to her waist for all to see. She was as admired as you are. But you cannot blame Katharine for being pious." I shrug. "That is the way she has been brought up."

"I do have sympathy for her, but her piousness does make her dull."

"You follow religious doctrine — perhaps not the same as the queen, but in a manner where your prayer book dictates your waking hours — it's all part of the routine of daily court life, is it not?"

"Yes, but…"

There is a knock at the door, and a serving boy is there when Anne opens it.

"Mistress Boleyn," he says, looking rather sheepish. "I am sorry I have taken so long, but I was serving Her Majesty upstairs." He half smiles. "I have brought some cheeses and fresh bread for you."

She opens the door fully and he walks in, patently nervous. He must be all of twelve years of age but looks quite handsome in his embellished white and green liveries.

"Thank you, Stephen."

He places the platter on the table in the centre of the room, and Anne presses a penny into his small, waiting hand. As he slips it into his side pouch, he looks at me from the corner of his eye and smiles, then disappears back out into the hubbub of the passageway.

"Do not be so hard on Katharine, Anne. The queen only understands her religious rituals in terms of her place in court and her duty. It is expected of her to be pious and to set a precedent for how her household runs. You know this from your time at the court of Marguerite of Austria." She looks annoyed. "Mistress Anne, did Queen Claude teach you nothing in France? To them, routine and piety is everything."

Perhaps I'm too hard on her. Maybe I'm teaching her things she already knows, but all the same, I wish she would be more charitable to Katharine and show some tolerance about why the queen behaves as she does.

"I am sorry — I do not mean to be disrespectful to our queen. I just wish there was more gaiety here." She sighs. "Besides, court life does not dazzle me, nor does it intimidate me. I would prefer that things were more spontaneous, is all."

"You mean you'd rather have a room full of gallants pining for you."

"No! Courtly love is the routine."

"Routine or not, how could there not be fun around here with you?"

We both laugh, realising how serious our conversation has become. Anne puts her goblet down on the table and offers me the platter of bread and cheese. I pull a piece of crusty bread from the end of the loaf and begin to chew it.

"We shall have fun!" she says. "We shall dance, play music, write poetry and plays — pluck the queen's apartments out of their gloom, just by bringing ourselves into their midst." She gets to her feet and twirls around the room like a dervish, with a cushion in her arms as the latest gallant to set his heart on her. The sunlight catches the metallics of the embroidery in her gown, and her radiant smile fills the room with joyous happiness. She is mesmerising.

"I didn't plan on being away for so long, but I'm looking forward to settling into the routine again."

She throws the cushion back on the settle, then grabs my hand and pulls me to my feet. "You are a confident woman."

"You are more confident than me."

Her eyes are bright, and she looks more beautiful than ever.

"Only in so much that I keep my indifference to the king to myself. I do not like how he uses my sister." A shadow falls across her eyes. "In the months since his seduction of Mary, I have barely been able to bring myself to glance at him. Even though he is our king, I … think badly of him for what he has done to her. He is a lustful and overpowering man, who does not care whose feelings he hurts to get his own way."

"Surely that isn't true?"

She sits back in the settle and clasps her hands in her lap. "He is loathsome. I hate him for how he uses my sister. He even had the cheek to single me out when I was serving the queen in her apartments recently, and asked me how I was finding life at court."

I sit next to her, intrigued. "Is that such a bad thing? What was your reply?"

"I passed pleasantries with him, nothing more." She glances at the door as voices trail off down the passageway, then wets her lower lip with her tongue. "I kept my lashes lowered so he could not see how much contempt I feel for him."

"Probably the best way to play things, under the circumstances."

"I notice how he keeps looking at me when I am in his presence. It irritates me so."

"Perhaps he is trying to assess your feelings towards his relationship with your sister?"

"Relationship?" She laughs. "He is using her."

"Okay." I grab a piece of cheese from the platter, hoping it will satisfy my pangs of hunger. Delicious, and nothing like any modern creations I've experienced. I follow this with a swig of wine. "Now, what of your betrothal to James Butler? How are things progressing?" I ask this, of course, as if I don't have a clue what her answer might be.

"That!" She jerks her head back with disdain. "The cardinal has dragged out the negotiations so much I believe it might never happen."

Do I sense a hint of hope in that statement? "I don't suppose your father is pleased."

"He is furious. So much so, he says if the cardinal fails to reach an agreement by the end of this year, then he is going to pull out of the arrangement." She looks delighted at that and glances up at the door again, obviously concerned she might be overheard. "I told Father I have not yet decided on the man I should like to marry."

"Anne, you are so defiant."

"How so? I told Father he is clever enough to demand the Earldom of Ormond for himself. His mood was somewhat soothed when I buttered up his pride." The chimes of the courtyard clock ring out and she jumps to her feet and rushes over to the door. "I did not realise the time!" She looks down at herself, realising she cannot go out in such a state of undress. "Beth, quick, help me into a gown."

She rushes over to the far side of the chamber, throws my cloak onto her bed, opens the trunk, and hands me a green velvet gown and matching damask sleeves from the pile of clothes inside. With all haste, her dressing gown is off, then I pull the overgown about her shoulders, pinning them to her kirtle as she ladder-laces the bodice. Anglets tucked away, I begin pinning the placard, digging my fingers in between the velvet of her gown and the silk of her kirtle.

"Damn! My finger." I suck the pinprick of blood from my forefinger and continue dressing her. "Why are we in such a hurry? What's the rush?"

"Mass," she replies. "The queen hates it if we are late." She's finally ready and now looks more respectable. "I am sorry to be so rude, dear Beth. I will relate more news to you another time." She lifts her Book of Hours from the table, then goes to the door and peeks out. "I know you probably need to rest after your journey, and I have so much to discuss with you, but we must join the queen." She adjusts my hood and thrusts a prayer book from the shelf into my hands.

I follow her to the Chapel Royal, feeling a tad awkward with my heavy skirts trailing behind me as we rush to the back pews. We swish and slide into our seats, settle ourselves, then observe the queen kneeling on the altar steps, twisting at her paternoster and tugging on each bead as she whispers the creed, pleading with the saints to her Catholic god, who seems to be ignoring her. I listen to the Latin wording, something that is rarely heard in my time:

"*Áve María, grátia pléna, Dóminus técum.
Benedícta tu in muliéribus,
et benedíctus frúctus véntris túi, Iésus.
Sáncta María, Máter Déi,
óra pro nóbis peccatóribus,
nunc et in hóra mórtis nóstrae.
Ámen.*"

There is an eerie feel to the scene as we ladies-in-waiting watch Katharine from our huddle. Her gable hood wavers as she pleads with St Mary and God to bless her barren womb — a womb that no longer bleeds and will bear no more fruit.

"The queen has known her destiny since she was a small child," Anne whispers as the choristers sing out their perfect-pitched harmonies and melodies. "She knows her duty and what is expected of her."

"Didn't she come to England as a teenager, to marry King Henry's older brother?"

Of course, once again, I'm pretending to not already know. Tilting my head heavenwards, I stare at the chequered timber ceiling and plaster, decorated with roses and portcullis badges. Such craftwork. I hope they don't all assume I'm bored. I'm not. How could I be, when admiring architecture which, in my time, has long since disappeared? Anne looks at me, her eyes full of curiosity.

"Beth, you must know Katharine was an object of prestige for Henry VII and his alliance with Spain." She nudges my side. "Queen Katherine's presence was meant to cement the new and struggling dynasty because of its weak claim to the throne."

"It's a shame she hasn't had any sons," I say, feeling quite sorry for the woman.

Anne covers her mouth with her hand and leans closer. "Heirs were expected, but her ladies-in-waiting say they were never certain whether the queen consummated her marriage to Arthur." She glances at me. I'm fascinated at having a history lesson from her point of view. Despite being in the presence of the queen and God, she carries on chatting: "Henry, as the younger prince, never knew what to do with Katharine, and his father certainly never wanted to lose her dowry."

"Henry VII was a penny-pincher," I say. "It was Henry VIII's choice to rescue Katharine when he became King."

Anne nods. "His Majesty and Katharine were very much in love, apparently. Mother told me that Katharine went to the marital bed a virgin, but I am not so sure. Sexual relations between the king and queen were more than acceptable. In fact, Katharine clearly adored her new husband."

I tilt my face towards her. "Isn't it a shame the relationship has soured between them?"

"At the root of it all is the fact that some of her babies died, and Katharine's constant petitions for a son have so far only brought her the Duke of Cornwall, who lasted but fifty-two days. She has suffered a string of stillbirths, and the Princess Mary is a useless, young, and spikey-faced girl who is prickly and pious, instead of the strong, virile son the king craves." She clenches her hands in her lap.

I stare at her, a tad shocked. "Anne, isn't that a bit hurtful?"

"It is the truth. Katharine's only duty is to produce an heir to the throne. Her parents would have raised her to know this. Queen Claude was a cripple, yet she produced sons for the king of France. She knew her duty."

This is the first time I have heard her speak in a derogatory way about Katharine. It's shocking, but she does have a point. Queen Claude was a good role model for Anne, showing her what was to be expected if married to a monarch. It is a role that Katharine has not been able to carve out for herself, at least not successfully.

When the ornamental ritual and choral music finishes, the queen is helped from her knees, and I stare at the floor as I follow everyone to her private apartments.

"Elizabeth, what is the matter?" Anne whispers.

I wince as she rubs the top of my arm — bruising from my time-flip. I glance in the queen's direction. "I feel sorry for her, that's all."

Anne leans closer. "There is nothing any of us can do for her."

The queen stares at us as she passes. Her apartments are large and airy. Even with the brilliantly coloured tapestries, the walnut linenfold walls make the chambers dark, but the fires create a hearty-enough welcome. There is a small oratory, with an altar, a brass crucifix, and lots of candlesticks. Queen Katharine sits beside the low-burning fire as everyone else spreads out on cushions around her.

"Lady Anne, Mistress Wickers, please come and sit with us. Please share your earlier conversation with us."

I can't help myself and feel the colour rising in my cheeks as we nervously sit with the rest of the queen's ladies-in-waiting. "We were just saying that, with your faithfulness, Your Majesty, there is no reason why God would not answer your prayers." She could have been praying for anything, not just for the Holy Spirit to fill her empty womb, so I am truthful.

The queen smiles graciously, and I'm glad I was quick-witted enough to twist my response into a compliment. Anne stares at me, probably in disbelief that I've managed to be as outspoken as her.

Anne and I, with everyone else, sit and sew, making garments for the poor while the queen works on a collar of blackwork embroidery.

I lean closer to Anne. "I can't do this kind of sewing. I have never been taught it."

"Follow what I do," she says, poking her needle in and out of the linen, showing me in slow motion exactly how to count the stitches.

I try to copy, then pass it to her for inspection. "Who is the woman sat to the queen's right?"

"Margery Horsman."

I watch her, knowing I will have to keep a close eye on her, on everyone, having read in Eric Ives' book about an anonymous person, listed with Anne Cobham and Lady Worcester, as being sources of information against Anne in 1536.

"Who is that woman in the berry-colour dress?"

Anne smirks. "You mean the Mulberry gown?"

I nod. I need to remember to speak 'Tudor'. I seem to have forgotten their vocabulary.

"That would be Jane Seymour."

The young woman sits demurely on the queen's left. I stare at her, now I know who she is, and am shocked that this mousy girl will one day be Queen of England. She is not a beautiful woman. Far from it. Her face is plain, her skin whitish — she has a long, big nose and a receding, yet slightly pointed chin. Her cheeks are rounded, and her mouth is small.

Jane keeps her lips pursed as she sews, and favours the conservative gable-style bonnet. I've read somewhere that Chapuys, the Spanish ambassador, will later describe her as "proud and haughty" in her demeanour, which doesn't quite mesh with the tranquil picture history has passed down.

As I study her, thoughts of changing history flit across my mind. Maybe I could encourage Jane to fall in love with someone way before Henry sets his sights on her. If I could somehow persuade her to marry a rich man who is too stupid to interfere in politics or live at court, then perhaps she might be happy and not lose her life in childbirth. Without Jane to distract the king, maybe Henry might give Anne a second chance, instead of throwing her in the Tower.

My heart skips at the implications of Jane not blessing Henry with little Prince Edward, and Anne bearing a healthy son, and I daydream about how my actions could prevent the succession being awarded to Lady Jane Grey, which would mean she'd never be executed!

Goodness, I really need to control my intervention fantasies and heed the professor's warnings about interfering, as I could seriously disrupt the course of history. Anne nudges me, and I banish a visual of a furious Professor Marshall from my mind.

"You seem deep in thought. What is it?"

"Nothing," I lie, but I'm not sure she buys it.

"Have you met Mistress Seymour before?" she asks. Her brows knit together as she leans closer to hear my whispered response.

"No, never," I answer, shaking my head, "but … I have heard of her."

She stares at me. "Oh, do you mean in future terms?"

I nod. "You could say that."

Her lips spread into a thin smile. "Tell me more."

"All I shall say is … she will be connected with you."

"Really?" Her eyes widen. "In what way?"

"You will serve Queen Katharine together, as ladies-in-waiting." At least I've kept to the truth.

"But Mistress Seymour has not yet officially joined us as one of the queen's attendants." She frowns. "I believe she is here while her father, Sir John Seymour, has an audience with the king."

Anne seems to be well clued in with everything that's been going on at court during my absence. Being so quiet spoken, no one really notices Jane — I haven't heard her laugh, nor seen her smile. She seems self-effacing, even humble, and looks desperately unattractive.

"Jane can ride and hunt well but has few other accomplishments to recommend her," Anne says, keeping her voice low.

Both she and Jane are direct opposites, and, in later years, Henry will swing like a pendulum from one to the other. I cringe at the thought, observing the circle of women: one queen, and two others who will later assume that role, providing I don't meddle.

My eyes sting through concentrating on the close needlework. I would generally listen to music on my iPhone when studying, and being able to do so now would be fantastic as my brain screams with boredom.

It seems I'm not the only one who is bored. Anne moans about it being as dull as ditchwater, and while I agree, I shouldn't take for granted the company I'm in, even if I can't expect lively court entertainment. However, I take every opportunity to observe behaviour, speech patterns, décor, even the tedious stitchwork. I'm fascinated with every second, despite Anne's complaints.

My enthusiasm is dulled by our little group's stifling piety and pity for a woman who is adored by her subjects. Katharine looks worn out and almost old for her age. Her gable hood and Spanish attire don't help with her beautification, and she sits stiff and statuesque in comparison to the sophisticated, witty Anne in her French silks, resting beside me on a velvet cushion.

Katharine ignores us when she's in a contemplative mood, and her muted mutterings of prayer continue on and off. I've heard that she shuts herself away in the oratory, praying late into the night.

Anne nudges my ribs again, drawing me to her. "Katharine would do better to get up off her knees, stand straight, lighten her mood and expression, and even attempt to lure the king to visit her bed at night."

"Does he not accept her invitations?"

"Not as often as he used to. He has my sister now to keep him busy."

As I observe the queen, I suspect that she might be menopausal. For the life of me, I can't remember the exact reference to it from my studies. At this stage, it must be evident to Henry that she will not bring him an heir. She behaves more like his mother than his wife, and he must blame her for not providing him with a living son and successor.

"If I were Queen, I would try and fight for him," Anne whispers. "But I am not Queen, and Katharine's piety, prayers and silence will get her nowhere." She flicks a look at the group to make sure we're not being observed. "I have seen the queen casting an envious eye on Mary when she is around."

"Really?"

"Yes, she knows something is going on, but says nothing."

The queen grimaces at us for our whispering. We are obviously grating on her mood, which is made worse by the stifling air in her apartments.

My throat is dry for breathing in the fumes from the burning logs on the fire, and I try to stifle a cough. Anne and I bow our heads over our sewing.

Katharine sighs continually until, finally, she drops the embroidered collar she's working on into her lap and closes her eyes. Above her nose, crevice lines deepen, and her jawline droops.

"The queen was beautiful once," Anne whispers. "As a young woman, she was a golden-haired beauty. Apparently, everyone at court admired her. Now she is faded, like a worn-out husk, unable to give the king what he most desires."

"Anne, shush, she will hear you." I nudge her, and she scowls back at me, but there is a hint of a smile in her eyes.

"I only speak the truth."

# Twelve

### RICHMOND PALACE, LONDON 1522
### – ANNE'S CHAMBERS

My bones ache. I've not slept well because Anne has been tossing and turning next to me all night. Although I've only been back a week, I need to adjust to my Tudor life, and fast.

As the sun breaks through the boarded window, Anne stretches out under the linen sheets, sits up, then pounds the pillow with her fist and thumps her head back into the crevice she has made. She groans, staring at the whitewashed ceiling. "I cannot sleep. I have barely slept all night."

"Why, what's bothering you?" I ask, propping myself up on my elbow.

"Mary. I wonder how William Carey is coping with the situation, and I worry if Mary is happy with the king."

"You care for your sister, don't you?"

"Of course I do, but I also worry about what problems her liaison might create for me."

"Nothing will touch you, Anne," I assure her, hoping my tone doesn't reflect the fact that every day I hide the truth of her fate from her.

"I bumped into William only yesterday when he was leaving the king's apartments. He seemed in a hurry, probably on His Majesty's business." She sighs. "He has no choice in the matter, but I can't help but be concerned about Mary's marriage. I hope my Uncle Norfolk did not scheme to get her into the king's bed."

"Perhaps Norfolk persuaded your father that the opportunity would be a good one for Mary?"

"No. Father is not my uncle's puppet, and neither is Mary." She swings her legs out from under the bedcovers, sits on the edge of the bed, and rubs her brow. "I have a terrible headache."

"Perhaps you shouldn't attend Mass this morning?"

"I should go. *We* should go."

I fumble through my bag, grab my make-up pouch, and take out a strip of paracetamol from their box, releasing two pills into my palm. "Here, swallow these with a little wine."

She takes them and turns the white tablets between her fingers. "What are they?"

"They will get rid of your headache."

She does as I tell her and, too late, I wonder what effect paracetamol would have on someone who has never had a drug in her life. She watches me fuss around my belongings while I find my brush from the bottom of my bag.

"Even if this gets rid of the pain, I still do not want to go to Mass. I would rather stay here and talk to you." She tugs her shift off over her head and stands before me naked, goosebumps rising with the cold. These people are more robust than me or my contemporaries. She pulls a clean shift from her trunk and slides is over her head, shoving her arms through both sleeves simultaneously, then adjusts the neckline.

As she dresses, I continue searching through my belongings, until my nails jab against metal. I look in and smile to myself at the sight of the two power banks I brought for my iPhone.

"What is that?" Anne asks, lacing up the anglets on the side of her kirtle.

"To be honest, Mistress Anne, it's pointless explaining."

"Why?" She plucks the bank from my grip, turning it in her hand and running her fingers over its smooth surface.

"You remember the device I had when we first met, where I was able to take your portrait instantly? My phone?"

"Yes, I remember." She passes me back the power bank.

I wave it in the air. "These are used to charge and provide power to the phone, so it can be used." Her face contorts. I knew I shouldn't have tried to explain. How would she understand the concept of electricity and battery packs? "For me, it means that if and when I get back to Hever and find my phone, I can take a few sly 'portraits' to help me document my experience of living with you."

The odd photo along the way wouldn't hurt, so long as I keep them to myself. I could take a few, at least until the power runs out. I've accumulated too much twenty-first-century stuff in my time-travelling escapades: my holdall back at Hever, with all the papers from Professor Marshall's office, along with my books and iPhone. The only items I brought on my first visit to Tudor London were the few bits of make-up, toothpaste, and toiletries Anne tested during our carriage journey, and which she has all but used up in my absence. It's a good job I've brought more this time.

I stash the paracetamol and power bank back in the bag. Anne stares at the plastic make-up bag, then squeals.

"You brought more things to make me beautiful!" She reaches for the bag, but I snatch it off the bed.

"Yes, but you must make them last. After all, I don't know how long I'm to be here." I open the bag and her eyes light up, like a child at Christmas wanting to open her presents early. "Let me apply some to you to remind you how to use it, because you must not look like a painted doll."

She nods and sits on a stool facing the window, the sunlight streaming in as she holds a small mirror up to her face, remaining still until I've worked my magic. I'm satisfied, and it doesn't look too much.

"Where can we hide all my belongings so no one will find them?" I ask as I stuff everything back into the linen bag.

After admiring herself in the mirror one final time, she gets up and tiptoes to a corner of the room, where she presses a couple of floorboards with the ball of her foot. "There is a loose floorboard here — we can lift it and put your things in."

I follow her over. "What a great idea! No one will think of that."

She lifts the edge of the floorboard with a small dagger. "See. But it is our little secret."

I tuck the bag beneath, and we seal the floorboard back in place, covering the spot with a small Turkish rug.

Once we have helped each other to dress and be presentable, we go to the queen's privy chambers and sit in front of the cold cuts, bread, and ale that have been laid out in the dining room for breakfast. The queen is already in the chapel saying her prayers.

"Will Mary be joining us?"

"Shortly, I expect," Anne says, nibbling on a corner of bread. "You worry, as I do, but I am sure my sister can look after herself."

"Like you, I want her to be happy."

She closes her eyes for a moment, then swallows back a mouthful of ale. "I am sure she is."

I tear at a slice of bread and nibble on the crust. "Come, Mistress Anne, William is a good man and will be there for her when it all falls apart with the king. It will not be the last affair for Henry Tudor."

"You know that for certain?"

"I am from the future, after all."

She glances behind. "Be careful what you say, Beth, someone will hear you."

The door opens and a few servants scurry about, bringing in fresh linens, replacing wilted flowers, or tidying away dirty gold plates and Viennese goblets. All is silent again until Mary enters.

"Where have you been?" Anne asks.

"With His Majesty." She looks about the room, cautious. "Where is the queen?"

"At her prayers," I answer, beckoning her to come and sit with us.

"And Maria de Salinas and the other ladies?"

"In the chapel hearing Mass. They will be an hour or so."

"Why are you both not there?"

"I had a headache," Anne says, hiding a smirk behind her hand. "I could not bear to watch the queen on her knees yet again."

I hold my tongue as two servants clear the table of leftovers. When they leave, I look at Mary. "And I got out of accompanying them by saying I felt weak and needed to eat."

"You should both be ashamed of yourselves, not doing your duty."

"What?" Anne frowns. "Oh, I forgot, you are such an obedient lady-in-waiting, defying the queen when you are in the king's bed and doing his bidding!"

I nudge her arm. "Anne, don't be so harsh."

"Anne is just jealous!" Mary declares.

Anne glares at her but says nothing. If only Mary knew how much Anne detests the king.

Mary looks around in a panic and leans closer. "Please, you must understand, my lover may be the king, but I do not like betraying my husband. I did not want to. But how could I refuse Henry?"

"Did he force himself on you?" Anne asks. "We have never really spoken about it."

"At first, I felt unsure of him, but Henry, I mean the king, is not like François. He is gentle and attentive."

"And how does your husband feel about that?"

"William could not look me in the face, at first, but Uncle Norfolk talked him around, explaining that it is an honour for his wife to be chosen by the king."

"Does your husband not mind sharing you in such a way?" I ask.

"William often wants his pleasure with me, but it makes me feel unclean, being with two men concurrently, so I feign a headache when I have been with Henry. However, I do admit that sometimes I am terrified Will might succumb to his temper and lose patience with me."

"You can refuse to go," Anne says, fire in her words.

"Refuse the king?" Mary coughs into her hand and glances around. "Are you mad, sister?" She stares at her in disbelief. "I dare not refuse Henry, and besides, he is so good to our family."

"Father has achieved much without you having to resort to sharing a bed with the king."

"That may be the case, but the king might withdraw any future favour from us, or worse. Where would we Boleyns be then?"

Anne snaps her napkin out, the noise filling the sparsely populated dining room. "If you are unhappy with your lot, why do you not go home to Hever?"

"Have you lost your mind? Leave the king? Never." Mary fluffs out her dress and squares her shoulders. "I love Henry. There, I said it — I love the king."

Anne's mouth falls open, just as the double doors swing open and we jump to our feet and dip into curtsies as the queen enters.

"Ah, the Boleyn girls," she says. Anne and Mary nod and smile. "And how are you this morning, Mistress Wickers? I heard you were unwell."

"I am feeling much better now, Your Majesty."

The queen extends her hand for me to kiss her ring. Her skin smells of sweet roses. She is dressed ornately in luxurious damask, and her velvet hood — in the style of a traditional gable bonnet, with long lappets —frames her face, which is pale and lined with care, but her expression is sweetness itself.

Katharine's chief lady-in-waiting, the Countess of Salisbury, looks gaunt and just as aristocratic — she is of the Plantagenet line, after all. They are great friends. I am quickly reacquainting myself with how things operate in royal society, and which relationships are the most important in the queen's chambers, filled with prayers and supplications.

Anne finds Katharine's ladies dour and avoids conversing with the most conservative of them. She has said as much over the last few days and prefers the company of her books. According to her, the English court's routine is much like that of the pious Queen Claude than that of Marguerite of Austria's, and I have been warned to be punctual, devoted, and, above all, charitable.

Most of the time, we spend our days sewing altar frontals, garments for the poor, or embroidering shifts for ourselves. Sometimes the queen enjoys dancing if the mood takes her. At other times, she becomes deeply embroiled in intellectual discussions with her ladies, much to Anne's delight, even though Katharine's views are strictly orthodox. I know Anne will never be able to discuss controversial subjects, and she is wise enough to never mention religious reform or the march of women.

What surprises me, though, is how Katharine allows her ladies to have much more freedom where men are concerned, as the younger gentlemen of Henry's household are often invited into her chambers to enjoy the entertainments.

The cardinal makes visits at times, even though they are short, and he seems to get along well with the queen. Everything happens under her benevolent eye in a controlled and honourable way. Anne is always busy, but she makes time to teach me how to help her look after the queen's wardrobe and personal effects. The queen returns our obedience with praise, appreciation, and a warm smile. She is not difficult to admire, and I find myself warming to her.

The Princess Mary is a delightful child and is often with her mother when she is not at her studies. She is well-spoken, graceful, and entrancing — a slip of a girl, with a pale face and red hair, like her father's.

Anne seems to be enjoying her time here. She relishes the company of men but knows discretion is the watchword because promiscuity is frowned upon and we are to follow the example of the queen; the court can be sober, and decorum is often strictly observed.

Both of us have become the centre of attention in the court at large, mostly because of Anne's Frenchified ways — her mode of dress, manners, speech, and grace. She teaches me all she knows, and we stand head and shoulders above the other ladies because of the way we carry ourselves. It's not long before the men come circling, like moths attracted to flickering flames. These courtiers try it on, but my head won't be turned, unless, of course, George is at court. Anne won't look at anyone unless it is Henry Percy, the heir to the Earldom of Northumberland. We are paradigms of virtue against other men's attentions.

In our free time, we sometimes resort to sitting with Anne's sister, Mary, in the lodging in the palace's outer court, which has been assigned to her and her husband. We mostly compare notes on the latest court gossip, sip wine, and eat the favourite Tudor sweet delicacy of marchpane — what I know as marzipan. It tastes sharper than the modern version I'm used to, and I actually like it.

Mary giggles. "Anne, the men call you a saint, after Saint Agnes, because of your constant virginity!"

Anne snorts. "Just because I will not share myself with the likes of them?"

"Well, we all know Anne is like a Frenchwoman born," I say.

"Not too French!" Anne remarks. "I do not sleep around like the French do."

"I've noticed that some ladies have copied your dress sense."

Anne's cheeks flush. "I am flattered, but I do have good taste."

I bow my head in acknowledgement.

"You must recall, Beth, how Father would not stretch to buying me a wardrobe of English-style clothes, so I adapted the gowns I have before we left Hever. Don't you remember?"

"I do, Mistress. Now, I think we must get sewing. I cannot keep borrowing your gowns." I'm hoping my suggestion may mean a visit to the apprentice tailor. I have bought some old gold jewellery from home that could be melted down to be resold to pay my way in society, and Anne has kept a chest of money which Sir Thomas has been giving Anne to pay me. I feel guilty about it.

"Indeed," Anne says, "Master John Skutt is an excellent craftsman. He is an apprentice within the Wardrobe of Robes. Have you seen some of the designs he has brought to life? And his clerk, Master Paul Cotton, is very talented, too."

"I could ask Henry for some new bolts of fabric. What say you?"

"That is an excellent idea, sister!" Anne smiles. "It's about time you got something out of your liaison with the king." She chuckles, nudging Mary.

"Mary, what is it like to be the king's mistress?" I ask.

"It is thrilling," she answers, almost dreamily, smiling as she turns an opal ring on her finger. "The way he speaks to me in public, with people watching, knowing how some of the women must envy me! Beth, it is that covert glance, the excitement of a fleeting touch, and everyone really knowing what is going on."

Anne stares at Mary's hands. "Sister, where did you get that ring?"

"It belongs to the king; he gave it to me."

Anne pulls at Mary's hand for a closer look.

Our chatter is broken when someone wraps on the door. William's manservant, who always keeps a discreet distance, goes to answer. He comes through to announce George, and Mary asks that he be welcomed in.

"Afternoon, ladies," George says as he stands before us. He looks delighted to see me, and I admire his amber eyes when his gaze meets mine after resting on my décolleté. "And how are you all? Mary?"

Mary stands and gives him a hug. "I am well, George."

"Anne." He kisses her on the cheek. "You look charming as ever." Anne beams at him. "And here is Mistress Wickers." He stands tall, his chin up. "It looks like court suits you. You look even more beautiful than last I saw you." He stoops to kiss my offered hand. "The king is in the queen's chambers, entertaining everyone. I have come to fetch you all."

"Have we been summoned?" Anne asks.

"Yes, you are all missed." With that, he leads me by the elbow, and we hustle along the passageways to the queen's apartments, where we find the king in a relaxed mood.

He looks broader and taller than ever, his majestic presence filling the room as the ladies of the court laugh and blush around him. Strumming a lute, he recites a poem he has recently written, captivating all with his rendition. His red hair burns bright in the sunlight which streams through the windows, and I catch Mary's grimace when he bends to lovingly kiss the queen, speaking to her in fluent Spanish, for all to hear.

To my surprise, the queen calls me over to present me. As Henry fixes me with his piercing blue gaze, I must acknowledge that despite his reputation as a dangerous despot, from a twenty-first-century perspective, I find myself attracted to his palpable magnetism. The man is accomplished and witty, and it is easy to see why Mary cares for him so, what with his considerable political acumen, artistic talents, and his powerful sense of authority. No doubt there have been other women, like Bessie Blount, and there will be others, but he is not as promiscuous as the king of France. The Spanish marriage still seems a good one and has been for a long time.

Mary cannot take her eyes off him, and she barely blinks as he addresses me.

"So, you are Elizabeth Wickers, the lady-in-waiting I have heard so much about." He flicks a glance at Mary. "You are an accomplished young woman, I think."

"Your Grace, you pay me much honour by giving me such a compliment."

"The queen tells me you are educated and well-read."

"I am not as well-educated as Her Grace, or indeed, many of her ladies."

He chuckles and nods. "I will be the judge of that." He seems to have bought it, enjoying my bashfulness. "I am sure we will see more of you." Then he offers me his ring, and I oblige by kissing it.

His skin smells of musk, and as he smiles and turns away, he moves with a quick, light tread, surprising in one so powerfully built. His hugely puffed sleeve brushes my arm as he passes, and the scent follows him as he walks into the attentions of the other ladies, chatting with them momentarily before being called away by Wolsey, who now holds the king's full attention, leading him out of the room towards the council chambers. There are always meetings to attend, and it seems the king spends little time with his wife, busying himself instead with state affairs, especially when the Star Chamber is in session. But when he is amongst his courtiers, he has only to raise a beckoning finger, and any one of them will come running. Henry has a way, with his red hair, vivid clothing, and glistening jewels, of making other people appear drab, and colourless.

With the king gone, I notice some of the men dawdling within the queen's apartments, one of whom is the young man Anne danced with at *Château Vert* — Henry Percy. Katharine makes the gallants feel welcome, and I watch as Percy makes a beeline for Anne, who is standing near the window seat, waiting for permission from the queen to converse with him. Katharine nods and looks on indulgently as Percy's face flushes when he takes Anne's offered hand and kisses it.

"Mistress Boleyn, may I sit with you?"

"You may," she says, returning to her seat, making room for Percy.

"Ladies, you may entertain our visitors," Katharine commands. "Pour ale and wine for anyone who desires it." She looks towards her minstrels. "Play the lute for my ladies so they might try a new dance."

The musicians take up their instruments and fill the room with their delicate melodies, at which point couples join hands for the dance.

I fidget, like a spare part, then notice Mary sneaking out of the chamber, probably to attend the king, unless he's gone with Wolsey to deal with his political business. Standing at the edge of the entertainments, I overhear several ladies in conversation with Katharine as they sit sewing — Margaret Plantagenet, the Countess of Salisbury, with Maud Green, Lady Parr, mother of Catherine Parr.

The queen picks up her embroidery and speaks loud enough for most in the room to hear. "I do not mind when the king's household comes to make entertainment with my ladies. Indeed, I encourage it. If the men behave with propriety, there can be no harm in it."

Lady Maud clears her throat. "The parents of your ladies-in-waiting are hoping that by being in your service, their daughters will secure good marriages."

The queen nods. "Is that not the way of things, Lady Parr?" She looks about her chambers. "I hope all my ladies shall make happy marriages, just as I have."

"You are a champion of true love, Your Majesty," chirps the Countess of Salisbury. "I remember how hard won the king's heart was, in the face of his father's stubbornness."

Katharine squeezes Lady Salisbury's hand. "Henry's heart was always mine — it was his father who needed to be convinced of me." She smiles, looking about the chamber.

"I think Henry's father would have married you given half of a chance!"

"No," Katharine answers, "he was only ever concerned with my dowry. It was my husband who was in love." The queen basks in her influence, though it is not as strong as during her halcyon days when she first married Henry.

"As always, Your Grace, you are right."

With my attention on the queen's conversation, I have been separated from George in the throng of gallants. Melodies fill the chamber, while new partners join hands, and Anne is now on her feet with Henry Percy, which makes many stop to watch her elegant steps while Percy holds her tiny waist.

As I wander around the room, I spot George in the doorway of the outer chamber. He sees me and approaches through the small crowd. George has been part of court life since he was eleven years old and is comfortable in the company of courtiers. He took part with his father in the revels during the Christmas season of 1514–15, so he is an old hand at it. Having been a page in the king's household for some time, he is the best person to keep company with, proving this as he steers me away from the wolves at court.

"Mistress Wickers, I do not like to see you alone," he says as he guides me around the chamber, sipping from his glass of wine as we promenade.

"I'm not alone, now you are here," I whisper.

"I feel as if I have neglected you of late." He frowns. "And because you have been away, I have not been able to spend any time with you. Where have you been?"

"Visiting family." It's the only reply I can make, but at least it's not a lie.

"Your family is in good health?"

I smile. "Yes, George, very well. And your mother and father?"

"Father has me running errands for him and helping him attend to his business. Mother attends to business at Hever."

"That is to be expected," I reply. He seems relaxed and in a conspiratorial mood, though he keeps glancing at Anne and Henry Percy. "I understand you need to learn the ways of court, for how will you ever succeed if you do not learn from someone as experienced in the ways of a diplomat as your father is?"

"You are very wise, Mistress."

"Call me Beth, please."

He leans in so close his warm breath brushes my cheek. "Beth, what think you of my sister's attachment with Henry Percy?" He stares over his glass at them.

"She seems to like him."

"No doubt helped by the fact he will inherit the Earldom of Northumberland once his father dies."

"Perhaps Anne just likes his face," I say, giving George a reproving look.

"And will you marry for love?" he presses, searching my face for a truthful reply.

"I hope so." Heat flushes my cheeks as I return his gaze. "Although I'm not sure I want to marry, at least not yet." His interest in me needs to be discouraged. It's not fair to tease him with my attentions, though I did put Rob off for his sake, even as I know there is no future for any intimate relationship.

---

Every day is more or less the same: breakfast, prayers, Mass, sewing in the queen's company, walking in the gardens, trying my hand at archery, hawking or horse riding, and meeting the men of the court — so much it all begins to blend into one.

Anne seems to live in a dream-like state in-between clandestine meetings with Henry Percy. I warn her to keep her distance from him, but she takes no notice. On another visit to the queen's chambers, Percy comes again to Anne and pays her special attention. It hasn't gone unnoticed by other ladies of the chamber.

As one of the queen's ladies strikes up a tune on the lute, Percy is soon standing before Anne, asking her to dance. This is becoming a habit. Should

I warn her off? Even though Anne considers me a friend, maybe it's not my place. Perhaps the reprimand is better coming from her older sister. I've said my piece before, and it has obviously made no difference. Harry, as Anne likes to call him, is a lanky young man, with dark, curly hair and bright, hazel eyes. His features are strong, with a long, admirable nose, and his manner is charming — his face honest.

"Mistress Anne, would you partner me in this dance?" he asks.

She looks up at him, accepting his hand. "I would be happy to."

The queen watches closely as Percy leads Anne in the new steps her ladies are learning. Some whisper behind their hands at the intimacy of the Basse dance, likely wondering what the couple must be discussing as they go through their paces.

Percy takes the opportunity to ask Anne for another dance, then another. They seem close, as if they have known each other for years. Does anyone suspect how deep their attachment is? As I sit on a cushioned seat in one of the tall windows, all are watching them — even the queen, who smiles, clearly approving of such a match. When the dance finishes, Anne leads Percy to me, to introduce us.

"Mistress Wickers, forgive me for never introducing you before, properly. This is my friend, Harry Percy, son and heir to the Earl of Northumberland."

"Harry, I am pleased to meet you." I extend my hand. "I am sorry we have not spoken much before."

"I have seen you dancing with Mistress Anne's brother, George, during the *Château Vert* pageant."

I smile. "That's right."

"I am currently serving the cardinal as a gentleman of his household. I sometimes have the honour of serving the king."

"You have done well, sir," I say.

"I hope to do even better —" he looks to Anne — "just as Master Carey has done well with Mary. William is my cousin. It would seem the right thing to do, to marry into the same family." He smirks and lowers his gaze, no doubt in the hope of gaining preferment from Anne. Her cheeks flush a rosy hue.

"Did William encourage you to pursue me?" Anne asks.

"He might have done," Percy replies.

"He is right to encourage you, as I am unattached. My father's agreement with James Butler, the heir to the Ormond estate, looks to have fallen through."

"Hmm." Percy fiddles with an anglet on his doublet.

"Mistress Anne's father has recently been honoured with more titles," I say, "which he richly deserves."

"He must be very proud," Percy replies.

Anne nods. "Father is a modest man. We are proud of him."

"I would feel the same of myself if I were him." He grins. "I, too, shall make my family proud of me."

Anne seems to really like Henry Percy, and he is plainly smitten with her. Perhaps I should encourage the match — he seems genuine, sincere, and would never let her down, like, eventually, the king will do.

# Thirteen

### DECEMBER 1522

Although months have passed, the routine of the court is very much the same as usual. I left to go home for an overnight stay — a fleeting visit — but again, when I returned to Tudor England, time had galloped by.

I'm concerned by the absurd way the ring interprets the passing of time, but I'm glad I've had the chance to return to my modern life. I was homesick, missing my family, especially Mum. The strange thing was, when I went home, no one had missed me. I was still in the same day as when I'd left. The whole time-shift thing confuses the hell out of me, but the way it works means that no one in my twenty-first-century life seems to be aware that I'm missing for long periods, which is just as well. Thank goodness the ring always seems to work, and I reach home safely. Each time I think of it, I give its band a gentle rub.

Within weeks, the Royal Court is on the move again, away from Richmond and back into the centre of London. The allure and pull of being with Anne, and forever in her company, is far stronger than I ever anticipated. I'm often riddled with guilt for feeling like this — I should be missing my family, being with Rob, my lectures, but I can't help myself. I'm like a sponge, absorbing all the experiences just as Professor Marshall advised.

We arrive in London, and John Parker, who is, among other things, Yeoman of the Wardrobe and Keeper of the Palace, has honoured me by giving me my own private rooms adjoining Anne's so we may stay together. Sometimes I sleep alone in my rooms, while other times I sleep on a pallet-bed beside Anne in case she requires me. We have become inseparable.

I'm surprised at how far she has risen in society in the few months since my last visit. As a young socialite, she has already developed a reputation within the narrow world of the English upper classes for the excellent food and wines she serves during her dinner parties, as well as the dances, gambling parties, and hunting afternoons she organises.

Thanks to her childhood in France, she has acquired a gourmet's palette. Concerned to remain thin, she does not eat very much, but what she does eat seems to be of an exceptionally high standard. Above all else, of course, she is famous for her sense of fashion, both as a debutante and, now, as a lady-in-waiting to Katharine of Aragon. She is the most observed of all observers.

When she becomes queen, I know she will strike such a glamorous figure that even one of her bitterest enemies will call her 'The Rose of State.'

"I have been gone but two days and your life has moved forward a few months."

"This time-travelling adventure of yours is extraordinary, Mistress Elizabeth. I would one day like to experience it." She raises a brow at me, as if tempting me to say yes to her request.

"That is not possible, Anne. I would hate to jeopardise any card that fate will deal." I can't even imagine what would happen if she were to come to twenty-first-century London. Professor Marshall warned me not to mess with the time-slip.

"You think fate has something great in store for me, do you? What are you not telling me, pray?" She fixes her gaze on me, no doubt hoping it may break my resolve and I might share more than I ought with her.

"Lady Anne, I have nothing further to share with you. I am here to support you and no more. Would you rather I go back to my time?"

"No, of course not. I do not trust many women — I prefer the company of men — but I very much appreciate your friendship."

"I thank you for that," I reply, relieved she doesn't push me.

"I must tell you the latest gossip," she says, thankfully changing the subject.

"Please do." I start unpacking the trunks of gowns that have been placed at the side of the bed. At least she had the foresight to keep the dresses she'd had altered for me.

"The palace," she claims, "is awash with rumour since I promised myself to Henry Percy, caused, I imagine, by the fact that he is never out of my company. We are always together, whenever possible."

"Really?" I can't hide my amusement, though I succeed in holding back a full smile. "If you are together often, then no wonder you provide gossip." The cat is out of the bag. I pass her a pile of her undergarments and a couple of silk girdle belts to place into a chest of drawers.

"What was that?" she asks, her tone unexpectedly sharp.

"What I mean to say is that it's a shame you couldn't keep your friendship secret, as when I left, it was not known that you had made any promises."

She looks intently at me — not happy. "I know I can trust you, Beth." She grimaces, placing her toiletries on her dressing table. "But how can anyone keep secrets at court? It is impossible. We are always surrounded by others." She turns to me and grips my elbows. "You must know I trust you?"

"I do, otherwise I am positive I wouldn't still be here in your service." I half-smile at her.

She grabs both of my hands in hers. "I have so much to tell you, my sides are fit to burst."

I go back to sorting through the chest of clothing. "Mistress Anne, I cannot wait to hear every morsel."

She arranges her hair accessories in another drawer. In between unpacking, she relays the details, her energy lighting the room as she shares her hopes and dreams. "You should be aware that Harry Percy and I plan to marry."

"I gathered that, Mistress Anne, but you cannot do it, can you?" I follow her every step across the creaking oak floorboards as she potters about the room.

"I am sure that when the news has broken of my impending marriage to a duke, Father will be well pleased with me." She half-smiles, almost as if reassuring herself that she has done the right thing.

Silence surrounds us as I consider the fact that the king has not shown or declared his interest in their potential match. "You cannot marry Henry Percy, at least not without your father's consent, or indeed, the king's. It would be unthinkable for you to proceed."

"Maybe, but we are in love," she insists, "and love overcomes all. And besides, he has a title." I get the impression she's trying too hard to convince me that her intentions are good and right. She stands in front of the small casement window, looking out into the cobbled yard below. "Before anything else, I am a woman — a woman capable of passion, who has a need to be loved and a desire to love."

"Don't all women want to be loved?" I smile. "I suspect that he is infatuated, Anne, and nothing more." I sink back into the chair, knowing it is best I concede defeat, as, no doubt, she will try her best to get what she wants — to become the Duchess of Northumberland.

"You have seen the way he looks at me, Beth. He woos me at every opportunity and comes to find me when I walk in the gardens with the ladies of the court and the queen." Sighing, she plops into the cushioned seat opposite me, her skirts billowing out around her.

"Anne, you must be careful that others don't see how intimate you are together." I know it won't make any difference. She is headstrong, and once she sets her mind to something, everything else fades into insignificance.

She glances at me a few times as she fiddles with the fragrance-filled pomander on her girdle, then leans back and closes her eyes. Is she reminiscing? Are her heart and mind full of memories of stolen moments with Percy?

"What goes on at court and in parliament?"

She opens her eyes. "Politics. Always politics."

I smile. "The politics of snakes is what we have to watch."

"Vipers, indeed." Her familiar and unique laughter fills the room. "Talking of vipers, I have heard the king is angry with some of his ministers."

"What have they done to offend him?"

"A newcomer, from Wolsey's household — a lawyer, I think — has openly conveyed his doubts on the value of war, and others have raised their fears that the country would be denuded of coin if a tax to fund it was to go ahead."

"Which lawyer?" I ask, as if I didn't know.

She picks up her wine-filled glass and takes a sip. "A man named Cromwell, I think."

Cromwell. So, he is now in Wolsey's household. That's the first time she has mentioned him. I stare into space, thinking about all these famous people, and that sooner or later I will be crossing paths with them. My thoughts turn back to the most famous Tudor of all. "And what news of the king and your sister?"

Her mouth drops open for a moment. "Of course, you have not heard. She is pregnant."

I feign shock, covering my mouth with my hand.

"Unfortunately, the king is fickle and seems to have lost interest now she is with child. He has sent her several gifts as tokens, but his passion for her is waning."

"I don't mean to be impertinent, but does your sister know who the father is?"

She shrugs. "I have not asked her. If the baby is the king's, surely he will claim the child as his own?"

"Perhaps," I lie, knowing full well that history will never get to the truth of the child's paternity.

# Fourteen

### November 1523

As I look out of the casement windows of Anne's lodgings, the trees are bare, and frost bites at the glass. The weather has turned wintry, and I think about those soldiers who have been fighting the French with the Duke of Suffolk, knowing from my studies that many of them will have died of the cold or frostbite.

Anne has heard that things are not going as well as expected, and the English army has been depleted through deaths from the plague. There is talk of Suffolk returning home, which will no doubt please the king, who is said to be planning a new expedition to France in the spring.

My focus is drawn down to the courtyard, to a young man wearing Wolsey's household livery. He walks up from the direction of the river, across the cobbles, and towards the entrance to the queen's apartments. I'm intrigued by the stern and determined look on his face.

It is a beautiful crisp morning, and I consider taking a walk. The air is so clean in Tudor England, no doubt doing my health the world of good after living in polluted London. The pre-Industrial Revolution cleanliness and the quietness — due to the lower population number in Tudor England — remind me of the lockdown during the coronavirus pandemic. However, it's difficult to say whether the Sweating Sickness which will fall on the Tudor population a few years from now will mean as many will die or fall ill as have done from COVID-19 in my time.

I will need to guard Anne and myself from the 'Sweat' in the coming years and make sure if I do go back home again, to bring as many medicines back through the portal to help get us through the outbreak. I wonder if knowing what I know about the 'Sweat', I could save William Carey from dying from the illness? What would the implications of that be for Mary, and for the Boleyn family? Perhaps it's too dangerous to even consider meddling in stopping Anne or her loved ones contracting the Sweat.

I think of home often, of my family and my friends, back in the twenty-first century, but I am so engulfed in my experience here that I don't long to return home as much as I did in the beginning. Perhaps this is because when I went back for the first time, I realised I'd only been gone a few hours, when I'd been living in Tudor England for months. Maybe the time-travelling process will carry on in the same way? I hope so. I'm hoping no one will miss me.

I turn to Anne, who sits at the fire, being nourished by the flames as they swirl and swish through the logs. She is wrapped in furs, flicking through her prayer book. A loud knock on the door distracts her. When I open it, I face the same man I'd just seen below our window.

"Mistress Anne Boleyn?"

I shake my head, and Anne jumps up and comes over.

"I am Mistress Anne Boleyn." She pulls the door open wider. "What can I do for you?"

"Madam, my name is James Melton. I am a friend of Henry Percy."

"Yes, I know who you are." Her brows knit together. "Why are you here?" She covers her mouth with her hand. "Is Harry unwell?"

"Henry Percy is in good health." Melton's manner is awkward. "It is not he I have come about, but rather his Eminence, Cardinal Wolsey. He has asked me to fetch you on a matter of urgency."

"What would the cardinal want with me?"

"I do not know, Madam." He lowers his gaze, revealing his lie. "Henry Percy is with the cardinal now, and I need you to come with me."

She blinks several times, her face pale, then turns to me. "Beth, I need you to accompany me."

I step back around the door and beckon her to me, out of sight of young Melton. "Are you sure, Mistress?" I tilt my head, guessing this must have something to do with her and Percy's arrangement.

Melton steps into view. "Madam, Henry Percy is at York Place. There is a barge waiting to take you to Wolsey. I need you to come with me now."

Anne fixes me with a pleading look. I have a fair idea of what this is about, but I'm not sure I can do anything to help. Whatever happens, though, I need to support her.

"I will come," I say, grabbing my cloak and wrapping it around my shoulders.

Anne smooths her gown and checks her appearance in a small hand-mirror, then takes my hand, and we follow James Melton down the labyrinth of corridors and out through the gardens, past the gatehouse and up to an awaiting barge. Melton offers me his arm as I step onto the vessel bearing Wolsey's colours.

The cardinal's men are ready with their oars. These six burly lads begin rowing in unison, propelling us down the Thames. Anne laughs at my reaction, my mouth agog at the activity on the water — small and large vessels weaving and bobbing, the bigger ones carrying goods, possibly to the likes of Deptford and Woolwich. So many people travel in the smaller boats — with no trains or buses, this is obviously a primary mode of transport for them.

On arrival at York Place, after a couple of hours on board the barge, we are greeted at the steps and assisted off the vessel.

"I have orders to bring these ladies to the cardinal," James Melton states to the guard at the entrance to the gardens. He waits, hands on hips, and bids us follow him. "Come, ladies, do not tarry. The cardinal is waiting."

We are waved through.

I scurry obediently behind Anne as she strides ahead. York House is a maze of passageways and corridors, lit sparsely with beeswax candles, our shadows looming and ebbing as we pass them.

When we arrive, religious men in dark clothing and black coifs huddle in groups in the corridor and stare at us as we wait outside Wolsey's audience chamber. Wolsey's voice carries through the open doorway, past his servants and nobles. He is chastising someone unseen, and I know I wouldn't want to be on the receiving end of his ire.

I inch forward and, in the moving shadows through the open door, I spy first a cat curled up on a cushioned chair in the corner of the room. I never knew Wolsey was a cat lover — that was a surprise I wasn't expecting. Then I can't help but notice Wolsey nose to nose with Percy, the poor lad withering under a spray of spittle. Wolsey is tall by Tudor standards; maybe five-foot-nine, but he is rotund, too. He seems exactly as I imagined him to be — effective in his demeanour, as, through Henry VIII, the cardinal has become the most ambitious and dedicated right-hand man. And like Cromwell, who will come after him, Wolsey is omnipotent in knowing everything, confirmed by the reams of parchments strewn across his desk. The only problem for Wolsey is that he serves two masters — the Pope in Rome, and the king.

"I marvel not a little," he says, "of your peevish folly, that you would tangle and involve yourself with a foolish girl in the court like Anne Boleyn."

"My Lord —"

"No! Do you not consider the estate that God has called you into in this world? For after the death of your noble father, you are most likely the one to inherit and possess one of the worthiest earldoms of this realm."

"That is true, my Lord," Percy answers, his voice barely audible.

Anne shifts by me, trying to move closer to the gap in the doorway without being detected.

"How could you think that your intentions towards the Lady Anne would not come to the king's knowledge? Have I not told you that he is much offended?"

"What did Wolsey just say?" Anne whispers, tugging on my arm.

"Apparently, the king is offended by Percy's interest in you."

"Offended? Why?"

"Shush, I can't hear Percy's reply!"

"You have, my Lord. I am sorry if I have offended the king," Percy answers.

"I cannot believe that you did not think to seek the consent of your father in relation to this match. If that is not bad enough, you then failed to make His Highness privy to these matters, which require his agreement."

Anne glances at me, the worry lines on her forehead clearly marked. We hear pacing in the chamber and presume it is Wolsey as he continues his lecture.

"How could you be so foolish? His Majesty would have listened to your submission, I assure you, and would have provided a resolution on the matter."

The gallery falls silent and Anne grabs my hand. Then the pacing continues.

"The king would have agreed to the match if you had found someone of the same nobility as you, according to your estate and honour. This way, you might have grown in the king's high estimation, had you consulted him in the first place."

"Yes, my Lord."

"Now see what you have done through your wilfulness! How many times do I have to repeat that you have offended not only your father, but also your most gracious sovereign lord, and matched yourself with someone who neither the king nor your father will be agreeable to? I put you in no doubt that I will send for your father, and at his coming, he shall either break this unadvised contract or disinherit you forever."

"Please, my Lord, no!"

Anne's grip on my hand tightens as Percy's heart-breaking sobs fill our ears. The cardinal continues his dressing down of this lovesick puppy.

"You must know that the king has a secret affection for the Lady Anne, and he intends that you marry Mary Talbot."

I fear for my bones as Anne's grip turns vice-like. "What was that?"

"Apparently, Wolsey says the king has an affectionate interest in you."

"No, never! It cannot be!"

"Shush, they will hear you."

"Sir," Percy says between sniffles, "I knew nothing of the king's pleasure towards Anne. If I have offended His Majesty, I am very sorry. I considered that I was of mature years, and thought myself sufficient to acquire a convenient wife, whereas my fancy served me best, not doubting that my father would have been well persuaded for me to be married to Mistress Anne. Though she be a simple maid and having but a knight to her father, Anne is of good parentage on her mother's side — she is of the Norfolk blood — and of her father's side, lineally descended of the Earl of Ormond. Why should it be a problem then, sir, if her descent is equivalent with mine?"

A short silence ensues as we stand in a huddle outside the door. I suspect our presence has been forgotten by Wolsey's servants in their own desire to hear what is going on.

"Therefore," Percy continues, "I most humbly require Your Grace of your special favour, and also to persuade the king's most Royal Majesty most lowly on my behalf, for his benevolence in this matter."

"Sirs," the cardinal says, obviously speaking to his counsellors inside his chambers, "this boy is very wilful and foolish. He has no wisdom in his head. I thought that when he heard me declare the king's intended pleasure, he would have given up his pursuit of the Lady Anne and wholly submitted himself to His Majesty's will."

"Sir, so I would," Percy says, "but in this matter, I have gone so far, before many so worthy witnesses, that I know not how to discharge my conscience."

"Why, do you think that the king does not know what we have to do in a matter as important as this?"

"No," Percy answers. "If it pleases you, I will submit myself wholly to the king's Majesty and Your Grace in this matter."

"Well then," Wolsey says, "I will send for your father out of the north parts, and he and we shall sort out this foolish mess. And in the meantime, I urge you, and in the king's name command you, that you will never see Anne Boleyn again if you intend not to stir the king to anger."

This said, Wolsey asks Henry Percy to leave but before he can, Anne releases my hand and bursts into the chamber, past Wolsey's guards, with me following behind.

The cardinal glares at her. He is a stout man, proud-looking — not the humble, pious man, with gracious nature, as would be supposed. His scarlet robes swish around him as he stands before Percy, his eyes piercing, scanning those who keep his company in his magnificent chamber. If it were not for his robes, you would take his manner for a king, with all his giving of orders and diligent tongue. His desk is lit by candles, the surface covered with piles of large parchment scrolls and leather-bound books. There is not a matter concerning the king that does not pass over his desk. From what I've read of him, he has a finger in every pie, ready to manipulate, to grant the king's commands.

Anne curtsies, as do I. "We had hoped you would speak for us, My Lord Cardinal. My father has much love and respect for you as, I am sure, does the Earl —"

"If your father weren't in Europe," he snaps, "he would have spotted this ill-matched attachment and stopped it the moment it began. Percy here would be safely married, and you'd be at Hever nursing yourself from a hard whipping!" He turns back to Percy. "I will summon your father to court. He will put you straight. Meanwhile, you are not to look upon this … girl again."

Anne turns to Percy, who reaches for her outstretched hands.

Wolsey steps between them. "You are never to touch her again!" He looks to Anne, his eyes full of venom. "Get you to the queen, Mistress." He nods to me. "Go with Mistress Wickers and don't let me see or hear of you in this boy's company again."

"Harry!" Anne wails, as Wolsey edges her towards the door.

Percy will not look at her as he is edged away by Melton. His head is lowered, his focus on the floor.

The cardinal stands his ground, his girth blocking a distraught Anne's view. Her eyes fill with tears as Lord Percy is guided through a door at the far end of the chamber, leaving her cheeks sodden and, as I look at her, I realise that she is just a young woman in the pains of first love.

She storms through those gathered in the doorway and strides down the corridor, with me chasing after her. I catch up and am not surprised to see that her face is scarlet with rage. Tears stream down her face when she stops and turns to me, snarling and cursing, threatening such venomous hurts that I haven't heard in the darkest and toughest places of my hometown. Anne is indignant knowing Wolsey will tell all and sundry that she is not worthy of marrying into the Percy clan or becoming the next duchess.

However angry she is with that insult, though, I get the impression that the loss of Percy as a marriage prospect doesn't leave her completely broken. I think it's more a case of her not being keen on the prospect of banishment to the freezing, windswept wilds of Northumberland, nor of being affiliated in any way with a man as mean and uncaring as Percy's father. Moreover, I'm not sure she is actually in love with Percy — I suspect she just enjoyed being worshipped by him and the fact he has a title. Yes, she is attracted to him, with his expressive boyish face and his dark hazel eyes, and while it is undeniable that he has the lovely, lithe physique of youth, her hurt is more about the loss of reputation and standing at court.

---

"If it ever lays in my power," Anne spits, "I swear I will work the cardinal into disgrace to show him my utter displeasure."

She is now lying on her bed, weeping inconsolably, and I don't know how to comfort her.

"What can I do?" I ask.

"Leave me be!" she sobs through her tears.

Anne won't listen to me. I have no choice but to run to the queen, and my heart pounds in my chest as I dash from privy chamber to privy chamber, disturbing servants inside Katharine's most private rooms, but I can't find her. I've been informed that she is at her prayers. Who else can I find who will deal with Anne in a kind way? Suddenly, out of the corner of my eye, I spot the Countess of Salisbury. Margaret Pole will have to do.

"Countess —" I bob a curtsy — "would you mind coming with me?" Margaret seems like a kind woman, I'm sure she could come up with a plan to help Anne.

"Now, Mistress Wickers?" She looks at me curiously. "Why, pray tell?"

"It's Mistress Anne Boleyn, she will not let me comfort her, she is heartbroken. I don't know what to do."

"What upsets her so?" the countess asks.

I lean closer. "She has been ordered home to Hever, My Lady."

"But why?" Her eyes are wide, probably fearing the worst. "By whom?"

"His Eminence, Cardinal Wolsey. Anne entered into a pre-contract with Henry Percy. They have fallen in love, but Cardinal Wolsey will not allow the match. He is banishing her from court."

"Hmm, I have seen how Henry Percy has turned his attentions on Anne these last months. Her Majesty has noticed too. Take me to Mistress Anne."

"Yes, Madam."

She walks beside me, down the passageway, towards Anne's bedchamber, where we find Anne still lying on her bed, her face stained with fresh tears. When the countess enters, Anne pulls herself up, getting to her feet to curtsy.

"Countess."

"Tell me why you have been crying." She takes Anne's hand in hers.

"I am to leave the queen and go home to Hever," Anne whispers.

"Mistress Wickers has told me," the countess says, her voice low. "I will tell the queen. She will not be angry with you. Her Majesty is responsible for you. Your welfare is her concern, being that you are a maid in her household."

"I have been foolish. Well, Wolsey says I am foolish having entered into a pre-contract with Henry Percy, heir to the Earldom of Northumberland."

"Who else knows of this?"

"No one, Madam, not even my parents. Only Wolsey, Mistress Wickers, and now you."

"Erm… Anne," I say, "you forgot to tell the countess that the king knows, too." And everyone within earshot of Wolsey's chambers. I would roll my eyes only I don't know how it might be taken.

The countess tuts. "You did not think, did you, Mistress Anne?"

"No. *We* did not." She bows her head. "Percy and I are in love."

"Wolsey is right. You and Henry Percy have been most misguided in this matter. His father will not be pleased. To enter into such a pre-contract without both your parents' permission is unthinkable. You must know that a pre-contract is just as binding as a marriage, do you not?" the countess replies.

Anne sobs. "Yes. I know, I know."

"Henry Percy did his best to plead with the cardinal, Countess, but Wolsey commanded them both not to see one another again. Anne has been told to leave the court," I add.

Anne is beside herself. "Countess, I swear, I love Henry Percy, truly I do. I cannot lose him. I have loved him for a long time, more than anything in the world." Her shoulders heave, and she buries her face in her hands.

"Anne does not know what to do. She does not want to leave the royal household. Can you help her?" I place my arm about Anne's shoulders, knowing that anything the countess does in this matter will probably come to no avail.

"I will speak with Her Majesty," the countess says, "but I doubt that it will do Anne or Henry Percy any good."

Anne looks up, wiping away the tears from her cheeks. "Thank you, Madam, thank you."

What can I do? Professor Marshall told me not to interfere. Anyway, I don't know whether I have the strategic ability to alter events without affecting history.

I give Anne's shoulder a squeeze, glad the countess, Queen Katharine and her ladies don't know who I really am, or what century I was born in, or the effect I could have on the queen's fate or that of her lady-in-waiting.

# Fifteen

### December 1523 -
### Travelling Back to Hever Castle

I pull back the drape as we pass St Peter's Church and peer through the wooden coach's window opening, straining my neck to see Hever come into view through the foliage of the trees ahead.

Anne stretches and pulls her cloak about herself, looking through the window from the opposite seat, pinching her cheeks to take away the pallor of sleep. My back aches, but the air is fresh and crisp and, as I shift under my furs, I'm relieved and surprisingly excited after a long, tedious trip. Perhaps it's because I can try the portal once more, and this time I might have better luck. I must admit, I prefer being able to just walk back into the future, rather than being catapulted into the mind-bending, tumbling experience the ring offers me.

"What a long and tiresome journey, Beth." Anne steps down from the coach. "I feel bruised to my very bones!" She groans, straightening her skirts.

The coachman offers me his hand, and my shoes compact the snow underfoot as I alight upon more familiar territory. "Me too, Anne." I give her a sympathetic smile. "Are you not glad to be home, now that we're here?"

She smiles. "Of course!"

I long to see my family, yet here I am, smiling as I watch Anne pick up her skirts and race like a child under the portcullis, down the stone stairs, and through the ice-covered courtyard.

I follow, surprised she doesn't slip as she tears off her heavy cloak, running into the front hallway, then up the narrow staircase. As usual, I'm on her heels like a loyal lapdog, chasing her trailing velvet skirts. I thought she'd be somewhat subdued, coming home in disgrace, but she probably feels relieved to be back, away from gossip, accusation, and her uncle's anger.

The lady of the house is in her chamber, which is sombrely lit with two flickering candles on sconces either side of the Boleyn four-poster bed. Hardly any light comes through the draped casement windows from the oppressive gloom outside as Anne rushes over and hugs her mother in a tight embrace.

I peer through the window and see George in the courtyard below. He's talking with a tall, thin young man. Maybe it's William Carey, Mary's husband. I strain to watch them in conversation, but my focus is broken by Anne's exuberance.

"Mother, I am so delighted to see you. I have missed you!"

Lady Boleyn smiles and smooths the skirts of her gown.

"Beth and I are excited for Christmastide — I cannot wait for her to experience the season as we do." Anne releases her mother and turns, sharing a conspiratorial smile with me while I hang back from the family familiarity.

"Yes, indeed." Lady Boleyn smiles at me, beckoning me over. Her warm embrace and her soft kiss on my cheek helps me to relax. "I am happy to see you, happy to see the both of you." She gets up and walks over to the door to call Mrs Orchard, then turns back to face Anne. Her smile fades. "I received your letters. However, I am unhappy that you are returning to us under a cloud of such controversy." She wrings her hands.

Anne lowers her eyes beneath her mother's critical gaze. Lady Boleyn looks concerned, but all I see in Anne's expression is frustration and anger. She must know her mother wouldn't be pleased about her being scolded by Wolsey.

"Controversy, Mother? What controversy? I fell in love." Anne looks as if she is about to burst into tears. "I had an arrangement with Henry Percy, and Cardinal Wolsey blocked it!" She shrugs, her hands outstretched, emphasising her disquiet.

"Your father has written. He is concerned about your situation. Mary and George have told me everything. We shall discuss it later." Lady Boleyn gives her daughter's shoulder a reassuring tap, no doubt knowing that Anne's temper will cool in time.

Anne exhales, clearly exasperated by her mother's brush-off. She sees me shake my head, and I mouth, "Change the subject." A familiar friend brushes up against her skirts, and she ruffles Griffin's ears as the wolfhound stares adoringly up at us.

"Is George here? And Mary, is she here with her husband?" Anne is decidedly excited about spending time with her family, as am I with George.

"Your brother arrived this morning, along with Mary and William." Lady Boleyn looks at me, and her lovely face brightens with an amused smile, making me feel most welcome. "So, Beth, how are you?"

"I'm very well, Madam, and very happy to be here again."

"I have heard you behaved beautifully at court, unlike my younger daughter!"

Anne bristles, but says nothing. Her expression is easy to read, and she doesn't look happy, but her mother continues. "Dear Beth, despite Anne's behaviour, we will all be sure to have a lively time together, as a family."

Later, in the afternoon, while sitting reading with Anne, our peacefulness is broken by the sound of footsteps pounding up the stairs, and the door at the end of the long gallery is flung open, though the force of the gesture is contrary to the young man who makes it.

George strides over to us, bows in salutation, then bends to kiss his sister on her cheek. A slow smile crosses his lips as he makes a beeline for me in the hope he can share the same deference with me, but Anne blocks him with her arm.

"No, brother. Show some restraint."

He groans under his breath and straightens his back. "Ladies, William and I have put your trunks in your bedchamber."

I close my book. "Thank you, George."

"That is most kind of you," Anne says. "Are Mrs Orchard and Agnes unpacking for us?"

"I believe so. What are you reading?" He reaches for Anne's copy of *Treatise of Love*, then snuggles in between us on the window seat and thumbs through its pages until he arrives at a section in Part One. He begins reading it out loud: "And see the inclination of his head to kiss you; see the spreading of his arms to embrace you; behold the opening of his fair side and the crucifying of his fair body, and with great affection of your holy love, turn it and turn it again from side to side, from the head to the feet, and you shall find that there never was sorrow or pain like that to that pain our Lord Jesus Christ endured for your love."

Almost all he does is measured, considered, and perfect. Everything seems to have changed about him over the last couple of years — he's matured and is now accomplished and articulate. He's twenty-one now, but looks older.

"Sister, this is not very light-hearted reading! Can you not find something a little more entertaining to occupy your time?"

Anne smiles. "'Tis poetry, George."

"Anne has been reading this book to me. She is teaching me the ways of a noblewoman," I say.

He chuckles. "Is she now?" He smiles at me. "I think you are becoming very accomplished, Beth Wickers." He grins even more. "But I have yet to see you ride a horse, handle a hawk, or play the lute!"

"Brother, do not pester Beth so."

I smile. "Well, from this book, I have learnt that the text contains three main parts that deal with divine love, which are largely based on the early thirteenth-century *Ancrene Wisse*, and seven brief sections dealing with other aspects of 'religious' love. This book is meant to be used as religious advice, written for aristocratic women, but then you probably already know that, George."

"Indeed, I do."

There's not much he doesn't appear to know for his age. He's well-educated, which doesn't surprise me in the least. Considering I'm living life in sixteenth-century England, I feel fantastic. My knowledge is challenged at every turn, without people knowing they are doing it. I'm absorbing all I can at an indeterminant rate, and while I have so many questions, I often have to curb my enthusiasm in case I should come across as a little weird.

The only headaches I have are ones brought about by the fact that I feel as if my brain might explode from the information overload. Other than that, I feel quite healthy — radiant even. Perhaps this is because of the absence of pollution, and the lack of processed food and so much sugar in my diet. Another noticeable difference is that I'm not actually ageing, or at least not beyond the one or two days I've been away in the twenty-first century.

George runs his hand through his hair and notices me watching. He smirks, but his eyes are serious. "What is it, Beth? Why do you watch me so?"

"No reason. You seem different than when I last saw you."

"In a good way?" He eases the book closed, then nurses it in his lap.

I know he's teasing me.

"Master Boleyn, you seem to have matured." My stomach ties itself in knots when he even glances at me. I fancy Rob, too, but he doesn't make me feel the way George does. No one makes me feel like George does. Anne stares at me, rolling her eyes before shaking her head, then smiling. I must be so easy to read — like an open book.

"Oh, so I am not George anymore?" He grunts. "You prefer to call me, Master Boleyn?"

"Sorry for being so formal. I have grown used to the ways of court."

"First you praise me, then you wound me by being so unfamiliar." His eyes narrow, as if he's trying to work out what I'm really thinking. "My sister has taught you the ways of women well." He chuckles and nudges Anne's elbow.

I hope my expression doesn't betray my feelings for him as I consider his amber eyes, their golden flecks almost sparkling, and I lower my gaze for fear of getting lost in them. When I look back, he flicks his hair from his face, his stare now intense. Something touches my side, then his arm is about my waist.

"George, stop it!" I whisper, shrugging him off, hoping Anne hasn't noticed. His mouth lifts into a slow smile, and his seductive eyes view me with amusement.

I squirm inwardly as Anne turns to me and raises an eyebrow. A fleeting look of concern passes over her features.

"Hever is going to seem so inestimably dull," she says, groaning as she brushes the open page in her book, changing the course of the conversation, much to my relief. "I love being home to see Mother, but it has been far more entertaining to be at court."

"I'm sure there are many advantages to be gained from living so far distant from the prying eyes of court, eh, Anne?"

"Brother, I am certain you could not name one!"

"Why, that is easy!" He laughs. "'Tis being here … with you two." He's trying to brighten the afternoon, but with Anne, at this moment in time, it's not working. Her mood is so changeable that I don't think it matters where she is now that Wolsey and the king have quashed the debacle of her engagement with Henry Percy.

The day is grey, a mirror of her melancholy. It doesn't help that her father is embarrassed by the whole sorry business.

"Wolsey has robbed me of my future," she complains. "How dare that insufferable man do such a thing to me." She throws down the book and gets up to gaze out the window at the white blanket of snow gripping the countryside; spring is far off, and the snowdrops have yet to arrive.

I walk over to her and pat the middle of her back — a comfort I know she likes. She looks out through the glass as she traces the intricate leadwork of the casement with her fingertip. The pane mists as I speak, momentarily obscuring the view of the trees, and St Peter's Church in the distance.

"I know you think things are bleak," I say, hoping to reassure her, "but be encouraged, things never stay the same for very long."

She releases a long sigh, and I despair that she is ever going to pull herself out of this depressed state. "The trouble is, Beth," she whispers, "I know you must know about my life, but you do not tell me!"

"I don't know everything," I lie, trying to keep my voice low so George doesn't hear me.

"You will tell me, eventually. You must!" A sharpness has crept into her voice, and it cracks as if she is about to cry.

"Listen," I whisper, rubbing her arm, "you may not have Henry Percy, but God may grant you a better husband than you thought possible, trust me." I try to smile, hoping I haven't said too much.

"Better than a duke?" She screws her nose up at me. It looks like she doesn't believe me — thank goodness!

"Just trust in your education and your abilities, and the right person will present themselves to you."

"You believe that?"

"I know it!" She looks like she wants to press me for more answers, but I turn to look out of the window again, to distract her. "Look, it's snowing again!" I sound like an over-excited child. Great flakes flutter down, adding to the accumulation below, making the manor look beautifully romantic. However, I long to see the golden hue of daffodils poking their heads through the lush green foliage, and bluebells springing up in woodland and the surrounding parks, carpeting the grass in a mass of purple.

George joins us, staring out at the big silver sky. I don't think he overheard our whispers. "Ladies, you seem melancholy. It cannot be all bad — we have festive views. It will soon be Christmastide, and we have so many amusements to look forward to, and I am here with you for a while, unless, of course, Father calls me back to court. I will cheer you both." His beams a dazzling smile at us.

---

Christmas Eve and Christmas Day are the happiest of times in the house, and, indeed, they are filled with the festive warmth Lady Boleyn has promised. It is a joy to celebrate the season as it is meant, surrounded by the people you love — by family. But, at times, my heart is heavy at the thought of my own dear family back in twenty-first-century South London.

I miss my sister and my little niece. But, of course, it isn't Christmas there — the time lapse means I've been gone for probably two days at most, if that's how this time-travelling stuff works. Mum and Dad will think I'm studying and won't even notice I'm gone.

Occasionally, without telling Anne, I try the door back to the passageway and the professor's study, but my efforts come to nothing, with the door always sticking fast every time. Even when I stand before it, gripping the cyphered ring upon my finger, nothing happens. Why isn't the ring working? Perhaps the bloody thing only works of its own volition? Maybe it chooses what I should and shouldn't experience of these time-bending adventures? Mind you, I remember Professor Marshall warning me to use the portal rather than the ring when trying to return home.

My finger is red and swollen as I tug and twist, and swearing under my breath doesn't help matters, either. As my frustration builds, my palms become clammy, and I double my efforts. Then, without warning, the ring releases and flies off my finger.

As I squeal, it rolls across the floorboards and falls through a gap under the curtain. My stomach flips. *No!* I scramble around on my hands and knees in the rush matting, hoping it might have got caught between the skirting and a floorboard, but there's no sign of it. My heart thunders as I realise it has disappeared.

"What on earth are you doing?" a familiar voice asks.

"Anne, you nearly gave me a heart… You made me jump!" I look up at her, still on my hands and knees. "I've lost the ring."

"What ring?"

"*The* ring."

"Oh, that ring!"

Before I know it, she's joined me on her hands and knees, searching around the floor. Her tiny hands thrash at the dry lavender as I explain what's happened.

She laughs.

"What's so funny?"

"It would not be so bad if you were permanently stuck here with me, would it?"

"Erm, no." I keep telling myself it's not so bad, as I am excited to be witnessing a Tudor Christmas and need to remember what a privileged position Professor Marshall has put me in.

"George would not mind — do you not think?"

"What?" I grin. "Me being permanently stuck here?" She laughs at me, and I look away. "I wouldn't know!"

"Oh, I think you know exactly!" She sits back on her haunches, her skirts crumpled about her. A short silence ensues before she glances up at the door. "Would you be willing to take me through there?"

"Definitely not!" My grimace is too apparent.

She frowns. "Why ever not?" Then leans forward, a twinkle in her eye. "What could possibly go wrong?"

"Everything!" I answer, getting to my feet, still scanning the floor for the missing ring. I need to put her off thinking she could time-travel with me. Nothing good would ever come of it. Besides, I need to think of the future — the history of the House of Tudor. If there was no 'Gloriana', what would that mean? I shudder at the thought.

"Whenever I try the door, the stairs and the parlour below are the same as they ever were." She sighs.

"Look," I say, "if you were meant to accompany me to my time, I'm sure it would have happened by now." I close my arms across my chest. "But you have so much to sort out here."

"I want to see what you experience, in your life and at your home. I want to meet your family. To meet your friend. Rob, is it not?" She is almost begging. "Please, let me come with you."

"I wasn't planning on going back to my time, at least not at this moment. I'd tell you if I was." I avert my eyes for a moment. Maybe she realises I'm lying, which I'm useless at. If I had confided in Professor Marshall that I'm not so good at hiding a truth, he might never have allowed me to find the ring in the first place. Mind you if I can't find this bloody ring…

"But Beth…"

"Stop pestering me! If I don't find the ring, then I'm never going to get back home. Ever!"

"You cannot go back to your own time. Not now. Not yet. I need you. And what about George?"

She's clever. *You're no fool, Anne. Use your brother to pull me back to the Boleyns — to keep me here at your beck and call. You know what buttons to press.* "What about George?"

"Come on, Beth, you know he likes you."

"He has never said as much," I splutter.

"Believe me," she says, "I have stopped him declaring himself to you on numerous occasions. It has not been easy keeping him quiet." She stares at me, and I wonder if she's playing me. "When you disappear, I have terrible trouble explaining to him where you have gone."

"What do you tell him?"

"I make something up — usually that one of your parents is unwell, or your niece needs you to go home and care for her." She winces. "I say anything that will stop his infatuation for you from growing."

"You hope that me being absent from you, and him, will take his mind off me?"

"Exactly!" She nods. "But George still insists he loves you, no matter what I say."

"Why don't you want him to share with me how he feels?" My voice quivers. News of George's feelings is a revelation, even though he always flirts with me.

"I do not want either of you to get hurt."

Her answer surprises me. That is the first time she has shown genuine, heartfelt affection for George in front of me. Perhaps their bond is as strong as the historical texts suggest? I shake my head, hoping it's not in the way they might be accused of committing treason with each other. I shiver at the thought.

"What is wrong?" She's now on her feet — her arm around my shoulder. "What vexes you?"

"George vexes me." What else can I say? Not what I'm thinking, that's for sure.

George, however, is not my only problem. I'm now trapped in Tudor England, in all probability never to see my family, or Rob, again. I need to find that ring.

# Sixteen

## Hever Castle

More months pass and George has been summoned back to court by his father, who has stayed with the king. They will arrive home for the New Year season.

The week rolls by, and to make myself useful, I help Agnes and the other servants prepare the house, throwing open the casements, changing the beds with clean, fresh linen, sweeping the floors, as well as refreshing the rushes, while Mary huddles before a slow-burning fire. Sometimes I massage her feet with some essential oil to alleviate the swelling in her ankles. At other times, I busy myself turning down the covers of her and William's bed so she might enjoy an afternoon nap, as she tires quickly — her belly now well-rounded; she must be due soon.

Mary is indeed a beauty — far prettier than Anne — and we often talk as she shares her experiences of France, attending the Field of the Cloth of Gold, and, of course, her stolen and secret arrangements when she has been with Henry Tudor. One afternoon, I press her on the subject of kings as I tuck her toes under her coverlets and plump up her pillows.

"Mary, what was François like?"

"What do you mean?" She sinks back into her pillows.

"Is he affable and gracious, like King Henry?"

"No one is like Harry," she purrs as she rubs her belly through her dressing gown.

"Did you love him, as you do Henry?"

She stares at me for asking such an impertinent question. "Shh, William might hear you!"

"Do not worry, I think he is out."

"Are you certain?" she asks, whispering again. "I do not want to hurt my husband any more than is necessary."

"I promise I will not say a word." I lean forward and squeeze her delicate fingers. To my surprise, she carries on talking. Perhaps she is relieved she has someone to share her secrets with. I feel privileged that she can unburden herself.

"François flirts," she confesses. "He is attentive when he wants to steal a kiss, but he does not make you believe you are his only love."

"And Henry does?" I whisper, leaning closer.

"Henry is wonderful!" she says, beaming. "When I have spent time with His Majesty, he makes me feel special, wanted. Do you understand?"

I watch her stroking her bump and wonder if the baby might be Henry's. "Yes, I think I might do," I answer, thinking of George, but then Rob's face flits across my mind. I mustn't think about either of them in that way — not anymore. I want to ask her so many questions, but if I press her for the answers, she might become suspicious.

Anne enters the chamber carrying fresh linens, which she places in a large wooden coffer at the foot of the bed. "What are you both whispering about?"

Mary sighs. "Nothing."

"Sister, have you had anything to eat or drink?"

"I think I need some water, mixed with a little wine." Mary heaves herself up against her pillows.

Anne walks to the door and calls for Agnes, who sounds as if she is at the end of the passageway. "Fetch Madam Carey a flagon of water, with a little wine."

"Yes, Mistress Anne."

"And, Agnes, do not forget a clean goblet."

"No, Mistress. I mean, I will not forget it!" The poor woman is flustered, her footsteps resounding as she scurries off down the stairs. The door swings open as Anne returns, followed by Griffin, who plonks himself at the side of the bed.

"Now, you be a good boy." Anne waggles her finger at him, and he stares up at her with his big brown eyes.

"Oh, Anne, leave him be. I think he is protective of me."

"You don't need that dog bothering you, sister."

"Anne, he isn't doing anyone any harm."

"Very well." Anne nods. "I think I shall go and help Mother with preparing dinner." Her eyes light up, and before Mary has a chance to reply, she's gone.

"I think Anne is jealous of my condition," Mary states, fiddling with the dainty flower design embroidered on her bedclothes.

"No, Mary, she is just frustrated at being shut here at Hever."

"Me, too, Elizabeth. Me, too."

———— ❄ ————

At every available opportunity, without others seeing me, I endeavour to locate the ring, but I still can't find the bloody thing. I've been filled with terror ever since I lost it and my nerves are in tatters thinking about the consequences of not being able to return home. It has got to the stage where I'm finding it difficult to eat or sleep. Anne, of course, has noticed how drained and ill I'm looking. Every chance she gets, she thrusts food under my nose, but I have little appetite for it.

Another day has rolled past and it's mid-morning, and I'm walking around like a zombie as I help Anne and Lady Boleyn with menial tasks in the kitchen. The faggots in the fire heat the stone in the smaller of the kitchen ovens, ready to bake pies. Lady Boleyn beckons me over and shows me how to grind down the sugar mountain and prepare the ingredient for cooking; it's not like they have a bag of Tate and Lyle in the cupboard. Sugar is an expensive commodity, and I put the pestle and mortar to work under the watchful eye of my mistress.

Anne organises herself, covering coins made from sugar with silver leaf, delicately coating their surfaces using a short, squirrel-haired brush, before placing them in a decorative group on a pewter plate. The kitchens are bustling with servants as preparations are made for the family feast, with all kinds of fragrances filling the small larder.

A servant hurries in with a folded parchment, its wax seal embossed with Thomas Boleyn's cypher. She dips a curtsy to Lady Boleyn, and the steam dissipates as she closes the door behind her. Lady Boleyn opens and reads the letter, then folds it and tucks it away in her apron pocket. I'm naturally curious but keep it to myself.

There's another interruption as the cook and a servant carry in a swan, which has been taxidermized, to present to Lady Boleyn for her inspection.

"I must say this is a magnificent display." She strokes the swan's plumes. "Take it to the Hall."

I'm shocked at the sight of this now-protected bird, stuffed and stiff, laid out on a large silver platter, and I feel a little faint. Lady Boleyn stares at me, and I feel Anne's arm about my shoulders.

"Are you unwell?" she asks.

"I feel a little sick," I reply. A wave of nausea sweeps over me, not only because of the swan but at the stench of gutted fish wafting through from the kitchen. I daren't tell Lady Boleyn how tired I am. The stress of losing the cypher ring is having such a detrimental effect on my sleeping patterns.

"Take her outside," Lady Boleyn insists.

I watch the cook carry the swan away, and Anne and I follow them as they walk through the kitchen towards the Hall. The spit boy smiles at me while he checks a pigeon as it roasts on the large kitchen fire, which sits in the wall alongside a small bread oven.

Lady Boleyn has locked the larder room and now follows us. Anne grumbles to me about having to do the chores. She's more interested in her books or debating a topic with George. But with him gone, we have no such opportunity.

"Anne, do not think for one moment you are being let off helping with the plucking of our chickens," her mother says. "You will be punished for your wilfulness at court."

She feels that by keeping Anne close, and busy, she will not cause any further embarrassment to her, especially if she helps prepare the family meals and assists the servants with household chores.

Lady Boleyn checks the presentation of the swan on the table. "She just needs a freshly baked pie to sit inside her wings and she will be ready." She walks back through to the kitchens, with us following. "Anne, when your father arrives home, you must behave compliantly. He must see you are sorry for your disobedience." Lady Boleyn looks back at us. "You would still be at court if it was not for your wilfulness."

Anne scowls, but her mother is unmoved.

"I have one child who has been whoring in public with an adulterer, and the other banished from court!" Lady Boleyn's nostrils flare. "My only consolation is that George is maturing well and learning from his father." She now has her hands on her hips and rolls her eyes. "My brother, however, uses Mary for his own ends. It vexes me so."

Anne nods and sighs.

So, Lady Boleyn thinks her brother, Thomas, Duke of Norfolk, is behind prostituting Mary to the king? This is an exciting development. I smile to myself. So, all those historians are wrong about Thomas Boleyn. He is ever the diplomat, and the brother-in-law is the pimp!

Anne stares at me, her brows furrowed. "What is it? Why are you smiling so?"

"It is nothing," I reply. I want to laugh but hold it in. Anne sulks, probably annoyed I've not let her in on my little joke.

Lady Boleyn ignores Anne's petulant mood and goes to talk to the cook to make sure the other preparations are progressing well.

The serving hatch is laid out with sweet foods, which they call sweetmeats — the fact they can afford such delights shows their standing in society. It is a magnificent presentation, set with preserved fruit, gingerbread, sugared almonds, and jelly, while marzipan paste made of almonds and sugar is used to make edible sculptures of animals, castles, trees, and people, referred to as 'subtleties'. The Boleyns must have spent a large sum of money for the New Year Celebrations, and it's a good job Sir Thomas has deep pockets.

As I listen to Lady Boleyn complaining about her children, I want to laugh aloud. I wish I could tell her all I know. It's all very well observing history as it happens, but sometimes my frustration at not being able to say a word to anyone threatens to bubble over and I must stifle any urge to comment. One day, I will let rip, and everyone will know my secrets, and then where will I be? At this moment, I can't hold my tongue.

"Why, My Lady, do you want Anne to be like her sister? Mary's adultery has never given your family any advancement at court. In fact, it is your husband's loyalty and hard work that has brought you the benefits of being close to the king."

Lady Boleyn stares at me, probably unsure what to say in return.

"It is true, Mother," Anne says. "For all the king's generosity this family has been awarded, it's certainly not Mary's attention-seeking behaviour we have to thank for it. Father is the closest to the king in this family. He is the diplomat. Mary will not use her relationship with the king to better herself or involve herself in political discourse. If the truth be known, she does not know how to do that."

"Do not be disrespectful of your sister!"

"I am not. You should not be complaining about Mary — she chooses her own path."

"Anne, I think you need some fresh air, the warmth of the fire seems to be boiling your blood! Take Beth, you both need to clear your heads. Go into the garden and gather a few sprigs of holly."

Lady Boleyn is right, the atmosphere in the manor's kitchen is draining, hot, and confining. We tie our cloaks about our shoulders and cover our heads with our hoods, then slip out the kitchen door and hasten through the hallway, before ducking out the inner door to the timber-framed and brick courtyard. The layer of ice that caps the cobblestones takes us unawares and we both slip, gripping each other's arm to stop ourselves from falling. The wall of frosty air that slaps my face is a merciful relief.

"Father and Mother expect so much of me," Anne says, shaking her head. "It is not my fault that the marriage to James Butler fell through. Father gives me no explanation for it. I am wasting so much time here at home. How will Father ever find a match for me when I am not at court?"

She swings the empty wicker basket from side to side. We take our time, carefully making our way up the stairs and under the portcullis, over the drawbridge, and across the outer entrance to the castle, walking in the direction of the church.

Eventually, I spot the red berries of a holly bush poking through the dusting of snow on the foliage. Anne hands me the basket, then huffs and puffs, snapping each fragment into a growing pile. The silence is deafening. I hope she isn't going to sulk for long — I hadn't expected her to be quite so moody when faced with adversity, thinking she would be somewhat more determined, forthright, and straightforward. Maybe she is. Perhaps I will see a different side to her when her father gets home.

"I think it would be better if you accept the way things are. It won't do you much good being in such a temper."

She flashes me a look that silences me and we return to the steam and heat of the kitchen, where she places the basket on the oak table. We waste no time in leaving, as we don't want Lady Boleyn to find us other chores to be continuing with.

When we step out into the fresh air again, the courtyard is bustling with servants — some who have come to see if Sir Thomas has returned home, and some who are helping to prepare for his arrival. Beyond the portcullis, a young woman is helping an older woman unload a cart filled with produce from the village market. We watch as they struggle to carry the bundles back and forth, across the courtyard and towards the kitchens.

They pause to let us pass. The young woman is red in the face from the exertions of carrying heavy produce, and she barely looks up at us as Anne addresses her.

"How are you today, Jayne?"

"Well, thank you, Mistress Anne," she replies in a gruff manner. She is heavy-set, with short hair, which has been shaven under her coif and woollen bonnet. Shy and unsure of herself, she obviously has learning disabilities and has the features associated with Down Syndrome. Her ruddy cheeks betray her station in life, and she shivers as she waits for the old woman, who approaches.

"Good morrow, ladies." She heaves more produce down the stone steps towards the open doorway.

"Good morning," I reply. "Should one of the men-servants carry those for you?"

"No, Mistress, I be well used to heavy loads such as this."

"Good morrow, Joan," Anne says, beckoning me on. "I hope you are well."

"Yes, Mistress." Joan smiles at us both. "Fresh today, isn't it, ladies?" she nods. "I would be careful not to slip on the ice!" The woman is like an old mother hen, clucking around a brood of chicks.

"It is cold, I agree," I reply.

"We will take care, Joan. Thank you." Anne smiles.

With some trepidation, we negotiate a thick blanket of snow which still covers the garden, and Joan is right, the paths are slippery and dangerous underfoot. Shrubs have grown unkempt, with small red berries the only nourishment for the birds to feast on. The gardener is trying to prune the rose bushes and moves aside as we pass him. He holds his bonnet to his ears and pulls his doublet around him to keep warm.

We avoid exchanging long pleasantries with him, and don't stop as we continue towards the orchard, ducking beneath the outstretched skeletal branches of trees, and take the path through the gate and into the meadow. Here, the grass is covered in deep snow, compacting under our feet, and my toes turn cold inside the kid leather of my shoes. Now we are free from the stuffiness and control of the house and can breathe again; the warm breath of our chatter swirls between us when it meets the chill of the wind.

"Who was that young woman with Joan?"

"Jayne," Anne answers. "She lives in the village. She is what we call a 'natural fool', or innocent, because she has problems with her memory and her mind."

"In my time, her condition is called Down Syndrome, after the doctor who identified the disorder." I pull my cloak about me to fend off the chill.

"And is there a cure during your time? Would bloodletting help?"

"I'm afraid not — the condition is caused as the child is formed in the womb." I could explain in more detail, but I'm sure chromosomes would be beyond her understanding.

"That is a pity. Jayne has lived near the Hever estate all her life."

"Is her mother alive?"

"Sadly not," she says, walking with care beside me, waddling like a penguin across the white carpet. "Her mother had her when she was much older. Our servant, John, is her father. Jayne lives in one of the estate cottages with him. I worry for her if anything should happen to John and wonder if I should take her to court with me when I return."

"That would be generous of you."

"I think Jayne deserves kindness." She pulls the edge of her hood around her face. "In any case, Mary, George, and I have grown up with her. We have all played games together, crawling through the long grass as children, here in the meadow."

"Not in this cold weather, I hope?"

"No! George and I would play hide and seek with Jayne and Mary, and we would all hide from Father in and around the woods. I'd be bold and stand out in the open just as Father appeared, then dart behind the nearest tree, even though George would warn me Father was coming."

"It sounds like you had so much fun as children."

"We did have fun." Anne smiles.

Despite the chill, Anne is in better spirits. The warmth of the sun is a welcome contrast to the cold breath filling me and, as I look around, I realise the conditions create a serenity that can't be ignored. There is no hint of dark deeds to come, no breath of treason or bloody retribution, and no whisper of a kingly wraith. We are far from the gaudy Tudor court and all its tainted splendour, and a long way from the Tower and its ravens.

We stop in a meadow at the edge of the estate, beneath a stand of trees, and I hold my ribcage as I scan the horizon, trying to spot St. Peter's Church through the gap in the trees, while the pain caused by a stitch grips me. The fabric of my dress is straining as I struggle for breath — my muscles aching through exhaustion. I'm fit enough, but not used to walking outdoors for long periods, in heavy fabrics that suck up the moisture from the snow — the hems of my skirts are soaked.

Sitting for long periods reading or sewing with Anne has robbed me of my natural vitality, debilitating my fitness levels, as has my current lack of sleep and appetite. The wind is blowing my cape about, and I must look like a sight as Anne delicately tucks loose strands of my hair back under my hood. My feet are beneath the fresh snow, and I feel rooted to the spot.

"I knew I should have braided your hair for you this morning!" she says, tutting and smiling at me. She looks out across the meadow and back towards the castle. We can just about make out the gardener as he tends the rose bushes, pruning to make way for their spring and summer growth. The sight of the castle in its period perfection pulls at my heartstrings, knowing how it will be ground down into almost ruins before Lord Astor saves it. It all looks so postcard-perfect now: no commercialism, no cars, no tarmac, and no tourists!

"I wonder when Father will be home?" Her comment snaps me back to the moment.

"Soon, your mother said. I know you are worried about how he will be with you." Anne hasn't seen him since her return to Hever.

At the bottom of the meadow, a chestnut courser canters in our direction, but I can't make out who its rider is. The man is almost upon us when his horse grinds to a sharp halt, whipping clouds of snow around us, making us squeal in fear. To my surprise, it's George, who we weren't expecting home so soon.

Anne gasps, holding her hand to her décolleté. "What are you doing here? You scared us half to death!"

"I thought you were at court," I say, delighted to see him.

"I was. I asked Father if I could take my leave of him — I have some news to relay to Mother."

"What news?" Anne asks. "Is there news of Henry Percy?"

"No, Anne." He dismounts and leads his horse back down the meadow towards the stables. Anne clambers through the snow after him. "Go inside," he says, waving towards the castle. "I will be with you both presently." He doesn't look happy. In fact, he seems decidedly miserable.

"What could be wrong with him?"

"I do not know," Anne says. "But whatever it is, it cannot be good news." She tucks long wisps of hair back under the hood of her cape.

We make it back inside and run up to her bedroom, leaving wet drag marks on the stairs from our sodden hems. Agnes helps us change out of our damp gowns and wet stockings, and it feels so good to don fresh, dry clothes.

While Anne is changing, I sit before the fire, my eyes closed, stretching my toes out towards the flames flickering in the grate. By the time we enter the parlour, George is stood in front of the hearth, and Lady Boleyn is sat in a chair, leaning against a cushion. Her stern expression tells me this is a serious conversation we are barging in on.

"Sit," she says, motioning to us as we curtsy. I rest back on the cushioned settle, with Anne next to me.

"Firstly," George says, looking at Anne, "Father has told me to tell you that you must not be so ashamed of your disgrace. He is not unsympathetic, and I am to tell you that time will heal the wounds you have suffered of late. He understands you trying to make the match, but because you'd not taken your petition of marriage to Wolsey first, the pre-contract between Percy and you could never be allowed."

Anne rises to her feet. "But, George, you don't know how devious Wolsey can be!" She sighs. "He made up the pre-existing contract between Mary Talbot and Henry Percy to dissuade me from pursuing the matter. I am certain of it. I have heard of no ceremony taking place."

"Anne, you knew about the pre-existing contract with Mary Talbot long before your audience with Wolsey! There is nothing Father can do to stop that marriage, if and when it happens. In any case, he will find you a man to make a good match yet, so forget about Harry Percy. That is all I can say on the matter."

"Anne, sit down," Lady Boleyn urges, a hint of frustration in her voice. "What other news do you have, George?"

Now George looks uncomfortable. I notice a muscle in his jaw twitch.

"You will never believe it." He swings around to look at the door, probably to check he is not overheard, then apprehensively turns back to us. "It must be a secret for now, between us four." A grim expression wafts over his face, and he glances at me as if waiting to see my reaction to what he is about to say.

"Well, what is it?" Lady Boleyn asks. "What could be so bad? Spit it out!"

George coughs into his hand, then takes a deep breath, his hand on his heart. "Father told me a few days ago that I am to be married. It has just been finalised, and he is going to tell you, Mother, when he returns home."

My heart plummets like a stone in deep water, and I grab Anne's hand at my side. She squeezes it back, probably realising the devastation this news will cause me. Heat surges to my face, and beads of perspiration form on my forehead and the back of my neck. My mouth is dry as I wait for him to say her name.

"Who is the young lady?" Lady Boleyn asks, unaware of how cutting his answer will be to me.

"Mistress Jane Parker. Lord Morley's daughter."

"She is a pretty young woman," his mother says, "and her father is educated."

George's obvious discomfort lifts some of the darkness from my heart.

"Surely Father is not serious about this match, Mother?" Anne looks from her mother to her brother, then back again. "When we were at court, Jane could not stop looking at him. It was embarrassing." She brushes her skirts, her anger evident. "Father could choose someone far more suitable, surely?"

Lady Boleyn frowns. "He has settled matters with Lord Morley, and he informed me by letter how the negotiations into the arrangement were going. Your Father is delighted by the match. After all, Lord Morley is cousin to the king." She folds her hands in her lap and gives Anne that look we're all familiar with. Then she stiffens in her seat. "Now, George, what could possibly be wrong with you marrying Jane Parker?"

George groans. "Father has told you already?"

"Of course. I received the letter this very morning."

I knew something was up with that letter.

"Mother, you said nothing to me!" Anne says.

Her mother sniffs. "Jane Parker will be a fine match."

"She is passable, but I don't fancy the girl." George tugs at his cuff, shifting his weight from one foot to the other, accidentally nudging Griffin, who yelps at being disturbed. "Sorry, boy." He bends and ruffles the dog's ears. Then he straightens, his eyes wide. "I will speak with Father about this matter when he gets home. I cannot marry Jane Parker!"

"Why ever not?" Lady Boleyn asks. She doesn't look happy. "It is your father's greatest wish — we want grandchildren by you — a Boleyn heir for this estate."

"That may not happen with Jane, Mother. I am in love with someone else!" He bites his bottom lip, and it's the first time I've seen him so anxious.

Hearing him declare himself out loud makes my heart skip, and my face flushes so hot it burns the back of my eyes. Could he mean me? The way he glances at me gives the game away, and I hope his mother hasn't noticed. I have no choice but to break from Anne's tight grasp. My heart thuds, like my feet on the floorboards, as I race up the stairs, lifting my skirts so I can get back to Anne's bedchamber as fast as possible.

Raised voices filter up from the parlour, and Mrs Orchard scurries to the landing.

"What is all the commotion about, child?"

"It's George, Mrs Orchard, he's betrothed to be married!"

Seeing the state of my tear-streaked face, she must realise my feelings for him as she puts a reassuring arm about my shoulder. "Mistress, you must dry your tears. Do not let Sir Thomas come home and see you in such a state — he's already told George he cannot have you."

I look back at her in disbelief. Thomas Boleyn knows George loves me? George has told his father he wants me. If Thomas knew that my income from my student loans, savings, and inheritance left by my nan was over twenty thousand pounds a year, he might change his mind! But he can't know, ever.

This is a disaster. I've entirely ruined history now. I have got to get back home to my family. At least I know who I am there. "I'm sorry," I blurt out through my tears. I break free of her embrace and rush into Anne's rooms, through to the antechamber and the tapestry.

As I try to pull the thick drapes back to get to the door, someone reaches to stop me.

George. I know his touch so well.

"Forgive me," he says, holding my shoulders and turning me to face him. "I did not want you to find out like this." He can see the silvery traces of my tears.

Ashamed, I bury my face in the warmth of his doublet. Trembling as fear grips me, I realise that I have nearly revealed who I am to him. One more second and I might have been back through the portal. What if he had followed me? I can't believe I've nearly given myself away through my childish emotions. I know this isn't going to end well. My heart thumps as I try to backtrack.

"I'm sorry, George. I can't stay here anymore, not now. The news of your betrothal was such a surprise." I say this knowing full well his announcement was inevitable. How could I have forgotten? I pretend shock to him, but my emotions are real. I knew the news of his engagement would break eventually — I've just been living in my own dreamworld, hoping history might run differently, maybe to suit my hopes and needs. How stupid I am.

As he lifts my chin and looks down at me with those dark amber eyes, I am rooted to the spot. To my surprise, he moves in closer and brushes my cheek with his lips.

"I'm sorry, my love." His heart thuds through his doublet as he presses me against the tapestry hangings, and I'm helpless as his lips linger over mine, his eyes full of desire.

"Let me kiss you, just this once," he whispers, tucking a stray blonde curl behind my ear, "before I become a married man." He doesn't wait for an answer.

Before I know it, the air is being forced from my lungs as he presses against me and kisses me fully on the mouth. There's no point resisting. His attentions stir such feelings for him that when he breaks his kiss from mine, I gasp for breath and equilibrium.

From the crooked smile on his face, he seems to have enjoyed the chaste sensation as he attempts a more persistent and lingering kiss this time, pulling me to him, his hand brushing up my neck, holding my head to gain leverage, making it easier for him to part my lips with his tongue, kissing me harder, deeper, with growing passion.

I wrap my arm around his neck and run my free hand through his hair, allowing myself to become immersed in the moment. He presses against me, pinning me to the drapes, his free hand in the small of my back, pulling me up against him. Our embrace is so intense, I don't notice anyone enter the room until we both hear a loud cough.

To our mutual embarrassment, Anne stands before us looking somewhat stunned. George breaks our embrace, his face flushed, his eyes fluttering.

"What is this?" she asks, her hands now on her hips.

"Sister, you know how I feel about Beth."

"Yes, I do. Is that not even more reason now to stay away from her?" She looks angry. I thought she didn't mind that George had taken a fancy to me. I shrink back behind him to hide my embarrassment.

"Anne, I just wanted this one moment, nothing more."

"I know how you care for one another — it's been obvious since the first day you met — but if Father hears of this incident, he will banish Beth from Hever and from court, and that cannot be allowed to happen." She hands me her linen handkerchief. "You had best wipe your eyes. Better yet, clean your face."

I nod and walk through to her bedroom, where I splash my face with water from her nightstand. She comes and stares out the window, with George beside her. They look out into the gardens, the silence lingering.

"Forgive my behaviour, sister, but I cannot say it was nothing."

"Brother, you should know better." She squeezes his shoulder. "You are betrothed now. It may end up being a year before your wedding is set, but you are a grown man and should behave as such. You have responsibilities." She softens, her compassion shining through her eyes. "I only repeat to you what Father would say."

"I know." With that, he bows and walks away, yet lingers in the doorway. He watches me press the dry linen cloth against my face as I try to pull myself together.

"I'm sorry," I whisper. "I've never encouraged you."

A half-smile of regret forms across his lips before he turns and leaves.

Anne shuts the bedchamber door, and I turn to grab her hand.

"What am I to do, Anne?" In response, she huffs under her breath. The problem is, my feelings are written all over my face. "I can't help myself where George is concerned."

She lifts her chin. Her blood is up. "Well, Beth, you are going to have to curb your lusts for my brother and he for you, for Father expects the marriage to the Parker girl to go ahead, and he will not be best pleased if you scupper it." She pulls herself from my grasp.

This is the first time she has chastised me. Shame, guilt, and not a little remorse combines to wrench my heart. I push back the urge to cry so she won't see how utterly distraught I am. When she opens the door, I see George is still in the passageway. Has he been listening to our conversation? I hope not.

As I stroke the crumpled handkerchief across my cheeks, I wish I'd had the ring instead of running for the portal. I would have been out of this situation sooner, and not had the bittersweet joy of George's passionate attempt at seducing me. I must get home. Where is that bloody ring?

Anne is out of sight, talking to George in the hallway, probably persuading him to go back down to the parlour. As she does so, I realise this is my opportunity to escape this mess, so my existence here won't cause any more problems.

I make another attempt at searching for the ring, to no avail. Blasted thing! I run over and pull back the drapes that hide the door in the antechamber. I'm amazed that it opens, and my skin tingles all over.

As I walk through, I wonder whether it would be wise for me to return to Hever again.

# Seventeen

### Professor Marshall's Office

The fact that the ring is lost yet the door to the portal has worked, confuses me. Maybe the door reacts to my emotional state, but in a different way to the ring? Or perhaps it's my overwhelming need to return to my own time? Whatever the reason, as the bookcase bangs closed behind me, I'm glad, for once, of familiar office smells, the smooth feel of plastic and metal, and crisp white paper, as well as the chatter beyond the office door.

This time, I have nothing to change into, because my bag of modern clothes has disappeared. I stand amongst the books, the whirring computer, and piles of unmarked student dissertations, not knowing what to do.

I grab my car keys from Professor Marshall's desk drawer and stare at the portrait of Anne Boleyn on the wall. Tears threaten again, and I blink them away, swallowing down the surge of disappointment at how things have turned out. Should I ever go back to her? Maybe I should just leave her and George to their fates.

My heart aches as I step out into the throng of students. I keep my head down, their collective glare boring into my back. Some whisper between themselves, commenting on me being dressed in my Tudor finery. A few laugh. My cheeks burn at the indignation of it all, and I up my pace to get away.

As I pass the monitor, which acts as a noticeboard, I glance up at the screen and see the date. It's two days after my date with Rob. I'm shocked that hardly any time has passed. It really is difficult to grasp. I rush towards the exit doors, my focus on the car park and my escape, but I step on the hem of my dress and almost topple over. *Damn!*

"Beth, is that you?" I look back, mortified to see Rob staring at me, his face a picture of confusion. He looks me up and down. "Why are you wearing *that*?"

Tears prick the back of my eyes, and I swallow hard to hold them back. I can't reveal where I've been, so I'm going to have to lie, fast. There has to be a credible reason for being dressed this way. "I … I've joined the local re-enactment society."

He stares at me, and I can see he doesn't believe me.

"What are you talking about?" he says, frowning. "There is no re-enactment society attached to the university."

"There is," I shoot back. "I needed a … costume-student friend of mine to check the fit of my dress."

He shakes his head, obviously puzzled. Now I'm looking like a fool. "Beth, there is no way the university has a re-enactment group." He tilts his head to one side. "Besides, if there had been, don't you think we would have both joined it during Freshers' Week for a laugh?"

Great! Now he's making fun of me. I scowl back at him, furious that he's choosing to mock me.

He grabs my hand and leads me towards the car park. "Where's your car?"

I point to where I last parked the Figaro and he takes the keys from my other hand.

"I don't know what's going on —" he runs his hand through his hair — "but I'm driving you home." He unlocks the passenger door and, as I struggle in, pushes the excess train and hem of my skirts into the footwell.

The door slams as a tear escapes and runs down my cheek. I wipe it away, so he doesn't see.

He gets in, starts the engine, and snaps the gearstick into first, setting off at quite a pace with the engine revving. Within half an hour, we stop outside my front door. In that time, I haven't said a word.

I somehow manage to extricate myself from the car without falling over. The elderly neighbour's net curtain twitches as I walk up the garden path. I feel their eyes bore into me when I reach the front door.

Rob takes control of the situation by glaring at them before he unlocks my door and steps inside, the junk mail and letters on the mat crunching beneath his feet. My parents are at work. Thank God for that! I couldn't imagine my mother's reaction to me dressed like this. I pick up the post and shut the front door behind me. As I place the mail on the hall table, Rob reaches for my hand.

"Are you going to talk to me?" He pulls me closer and looks me straight in the eye. My face is hot, and my eyes sting. "Beth, what's going on?"

I stare at the carpet, cornered. The best thing to do is say nothing, then I won't feel forced to reveal the truth. Instead, I reiterate what I've already said.

"I told you, I'm part of the university re-enactment group. It's new."

He stares at me. "I know you sometimes go out with your re-enactor friends to Hatfield, Berkeley, or Sudeley Castle in the summer holidays, but there's no way you'd do an event on a weekday, let alone a study day."

I don't answer. Instead, I walk through to the kitchen to find Rutterkin on the worktop meowing his head off. I stroke him between his ears, and he bobs up at my face in an attempt to persuade me to feed him. His bowl is empty. Rob follows me and leans against the doorframe. He watches me grab the cat treats from the cupboard and tip a good handful into the bowl.

"Come on, Rutterkin, here's some dinner." He jumps off the worktop, purring around my feet as I place his filled bowl on the mat next to his water.

"Why on earth have you called your cat Rutterkin?" Rob asks, his frown showing his state of confusion.

"You mean to say, as a history undergraduate, you don't know?" I smile to myself. "He's named after the cat who was said to have helped the Belvoir witches. You know, Joan Flower and her daughters, who carried out their spells in James I's reign?"

"Yes, I remember now." He smiles, but I'm not sure whether he really does remember or is just humouring me.

"The cat was called Rutterkin. As my study partner, I thought you would have remembered me talking about him?"

"Your cat, or the witches' cat?"

"Both!" I reply, as flippantly as I can.

"Anyway, who said I was your study partner? I thought we were friends?"

"We are!" I shove the cat biscuits back in the cupboard, turn around, and clench the worktop to control my frustration.

"What's going on?" He stands in front of me. "What the hell has happened to you that you are dressed like that?"

"Nothing."

"Nothing?" His voice cracks in annoyance. God, I've pissed him off. "This," he says, pointing at my outfit, "doesn't look like nothing!"

"Why are you so cross with me?" How in the hell am I going to get out of this?

"I haven't seen you for two days. You don't call or text me, and you haven't been in our lectures."

"Is that any of your business?"

"Well, I'd like to think so, considering we went out together!"

"What? Rob, we went for dinner."

"Yes, but…"

"And you agreed we'd be better as casual friends."

His shoulders slump. "Yes, I know, but…"

"But what?" I'm growing in confidence now.

He takes a deep breath, his shoulders rising. "Well, we did kiss."

"Yes, we did, didn't we? So, you like me? Like … that?"

"I might." He smirks. "But I'm finding you very frustrating at the moment."

"Why?"

"You don't answer me, and you won't explain yourself."

"I don't have to."

"Are you kidding me?"

"No."

"So, you are going to force me to confess to something that I don't want to?"

"Can you blame me?" His voice reaches a pitch I haven't heard from him before. "I don't hear from you, then you turn up at university in this get-up!" He moves closer, looking me up and down. "I was worried about you!"

"So?" I say.

He moves away and walks towards the kitchen door, stops, then turns to me. "If you don't tell me what's going on, I swear to God, I will walk out that door and never see or speak to you again!"

I stare at him for what seems like ages. "You mean that?"

"If you can't confide in me when I am worried about you, what kind of relationship would we have?" He looks up at the ceiling and sighs. "It would be one without trust."

"I'm such an idiot. I'm sorry."

"Don't be, this obviously isn't going to work, especially if you can't be honest with me — even as a friend." He walks towards the front door and reaches for the latch.

"Don't go!"

He turns to face me. "So, are you going to tell me what's going on?"

I take a deep breath and release it in one gush. "You wouldn't believe me."

"Try me."

"It's the Boleyns."

He stares at me. "The Boleyns? What do you mean?"

"The Boleyn family," I say, then I hear myself utter the words, "George Boleyn."

Rob walks towards me until he is so close I can smell the mint flavour of his chewing gum on his breath. He cups my chin with his hand. "What did you say?"

"I had to get away from Anne. I had to —"

"Anne who?" He's now holding my shoulders. "You had to what?"

"Leave Hever and George. I had to get away from George Boleyn."

He steps back and stares at my dress again. "What are you on about?" He shakes his head. "You aren't a drama student. I know that lot are rehearsing Hilary Mantel's *Wolf Hall*, but you aren't involved with them. Besides, the theatre is on another campus."

"I'm not talking about the drama production!"

"Then why are you dressed like that?"

"Like I said, if I told you, you would never believe me."

"Just be honest, Beth." He stares at me. "Try me."

I shrug free and walk into the front room, where I plop myself down in the armchair. I feel so out of place, still in my gown, surrounded by my parents' modern furniture. Rob sits opposite me, on the edge of the sofa, leaning forward with his hands clenched in his lap.

There's only one way to go about this. I take a deep breath and relay the whole story to him. He shakes his head in disbelief many times, especially when I mention how Professor Marshall is involved, and he has me repeat many details over and over.

"Beth, you can't tell me all this and not show me. Do you know how important a find this portal is?"

"Professor Marshall swore me to secrecy. No one else must know about it." I tug on the neckline of my gown, wishing to be out of it and in something comfortable. Normal. I want to feel ordinary without the weight of history upon me.

"Let me come back through the portal with you. If what you are saying is true, show me. Let me see it for myself."

"You believe me?"

"Well, look at you!" he says, both hands out. "I've never seen such an authentic costume before."

"Why do you believe me so readily?"

"I know you aren't mad, and I wouldn't have thought you a natural-born liar." He half-smiles. "And if what you are telling me is true, you can take me to the portal so I can see for myself."

"No, Rob, it's not possible." There is no way in the world he can go through the portal with me. I must put him off it.

"You can't tell me such a fantasy and not show me the truth behind it."

"After how George has behaved towards me, there is no way I am going back to the Boleyns." I'm telling the truth now — he must see that in my eyes. I have to put him off in whatever way I can.

"Look, the only way you're going to convince me you're telling the truth is if you show me the portal, *and* we go through it together."

"I can't!"

"Think about it, Beth — would you believe someone if they told you such a story?"

"Probably not."

"Well, then, you have no choice but to prove yourself right. Otherwise, I will think you've gone stark raving mad."

"I said, no!" I can be just as stubborn as him, but then, if I don't agree, what do I lose? My chance with him. I've lost my chance with George, and if I say no to Rob, too, over this, then I risk the possibility of losing any opportunity I might have with him. I cover my face with my hands and groan, then drop them in my lap and look at him, letting out a long sigh. "I can't anyway. The other thing is, I've … I've lost the cypher ring. Professor Marshall is going to kill me."

"Well, in that case, you really do need to go back to Hever to find it!" He looks delighted with my plight. Oh, why couldn't I keep my mouth shut? I don't want to give him an excuse to go to Hever with me.

"What if I just show you the portal?" Maybe that won't be so bad. Oh, this is terrible. I feel as if I'm betraying the professor, Anne, and everyone else.

He claps, his eyes wide with excitement. "We can tell Professor Marshall we've gone. We can leave him a note."

"No, we can't!" I shout. "Didn't you hear me?" The enormity of it hits me. I could never betray Professor Marshall like that. It would be so wrong, and besides, I couldn't possibly go back, not now.

"We won't be missed for a day. I bet the professor would cover for us."

"It's absolutely out of the question!" I stammer, refusing to consider the matter, even for a moment. "I can't even manoeuvre my way through their world without causing chaos, let alone introduce a total stranger to it."

"No, no, Beth, you said you'd show me the portal. You can't go back on your word now."

"But…" I lean back and sigh. Would it really hurt, just for a day in their time? Anne knows about Rob so it wouldn't surprise her if I brought him through with me, would it? It may deter George from pursuing anything further with me. And it might work to leave a note with the professor, so he knows what's happening.

"I'm no stranger to history," Rob says.

"You don't understand, Rob. Living it is so completely different to studying it."

He gets to his feet and looks down at me. "Don't you trust me?"

"It's not that I don't trust you. It's if you mess up the history — cause it to go in a different direction."

"I swear, I won't interfere. Hey, what do you take me for?"

I study him as he stands over me, his eyes pleading. "Okay, but only if you promise that it won't be for long, and you won't breathe a word of it to anyone. It can only be for a couple of hours, and just the once." His eyes widen even more, and he jumps about with excitement.

"Really?"

"On one condition."

He grows still. "What might that be?"

"That you promise not to punch George Boleyn."

Realisation dawns, and the silence is deafening as he stares at me. "I … I'm not sure I can promise that."

"Then you can't come."

"Okay, Okay!" He sniffs and blinks several times. "I promise, I won't lay a hand on him."

I'm exhausted from arguing. While he makes something to eat for us both, I go upstairs and take a quick shower to refresh myself. I've only been away for one day, but in my reality, I haven't had a real shower in months. By the time I'm ready, back in modern clothes, with Anne's dress packed in a large bag, Rob has made soup, a sandwich, and cut up the cake Mum had hidden in a tin in the cupboard.

"You certainly know your way around a kitchen."

He laughs. "The benefits of having a brother as a qualified chef."

I run my fingers through my freshly washed hair, which cascades down my back. It feels so good, and the smell of conditioner fills the room. We sit at the dining table and nourish ourselves with the steaming broth.

"What shall I do about clothes?" he asks, wiping his mouth with a napkin. "I can hardly go undetected in jeans, can I?"

I laugh at him. "No. Perhaps I can ask Anne to pinch some of George's clothes from his travelling trunks. You're about the same size."

"Are we?" He chuckles. "I guess you would know!"

I glare at him, the way I usually do to George when he makes a rude remark.

"I must say, you did look the part, with the dress and your hair. So authentic. And attractive."

Warmth flushes my cheeks. I should be used to the compliments of men, after George, but coming from Rob, it feels a bit strange. Will I be able to cope having the two of them in the same room? In the same time?

When I finish eating, I clear the table and take our empty bowls and plates to the kitchen. Rutterkin darts back through the cat flap and rubs up against my leg. He meows, his actions becoming more insistent. When I bend to stroke him, I notice his drinking bowl is empty, so I fill it to the brim with fresh water. Rob stands in the doorway and laughs while I load the dishwasher.

"What's so funny?"

"You looked like the funniest anachronism I've seen all year, standing in here earlier with that dress on."

"Oh, shut up!" As he passes me the last of the knives and forks, I flick a tea towel at him.

"I was paying you a compliment." He grins. "You looked so 'proper' in that get-up — made you look out of place in your own home."

I laugh. "The dress does belong to Anne Boleyn, so what do you expect?"

"Should you leave a note for your parents, before we go?" He raises a brow.

"I suppose I could. I still don't know how this time-travel stuff works. The timelines never run parallel — years pass by in the Tudor slip, while little changes here. I still don't get it." I scribble a note on a piece of paper and leave it on the worktop, where I know Mum will see it.

*Mum, Gone out with Rob — not sure when I will be back. Love, Beth. PS. Don't worry about dinner.*

As Rob drives us back to the university, twilight falls and I try to convince myself that everything will be all right.

"Why didn't you tell me about your time-travelling adventures when they first happened?" he asks, trying to manage the gear stick, which sticks whenever you decide to change it. My gown is packed in its bag, along with more toiletries, and stored on the back seat.

"Why do you think?" I stare at him. He glances at me, then fixes his gaze back on the road, turning on the windscreen wipers as the rain starts to spit.

In some ways, I'm glad I've shared my experiences with him — it's like a weight has been lifted off my shoulders — but in another way, the situation makes me feel as if I'm drowning in a deep pool of my own making. I could completely ruin history — if I haven't already. Oh my God, what am I doing?

"Turn around, Rob!" My voice betrays my fear. He's never seen me in such a state as he has today. What must he think of me? He's probably going to forget about asking me out again after all this. Surely all he wants is a way into the portal, then, after that, he'll forget I ever existed.

"Why do you want me to turn around?"

"Just … just stop the bloody car!"

He pulls into the side of the road and parks, leaving the engine ticking over.

"We shouldn't be doing this — it's against the professor's rules."

"If we risk nothing, we gain nothing."

I don't know what to say to that, because I know he's right. If I hadn't taken the initial step, I would never have met Anne and experienced her world. He looks cross. "What?" I say. "Why are you looking at me like that?"

"Come on, Beth, you can't blame me for wanting to experience where you've been and what you've seen."

The guilt is burning into the back of my eyes. Why should I deny him the right to do precisely as I've done? If we stick to the rules, what harm can it do? However, now that I no longer have the ring, I hope the portal will get us both back if an extra-quick exit is called for.

# Eighteen

### Professor Marshall's Office

We stand side by side in the professor's office. My finger feels naked without the cypher ring. Rob snatches a sheet of paper from the professor's printer and a biro from the desk. I put the big bag on the floor and scribble out a note.

*Sir,*
*Please don't be angry with me, but I have taken Robert Dryden through the portal. I PROMISE we won't compromise ANYTHING!*
*Beth Wickers*

I put the letter on the professor's desk, where I know he will find it, then reach for the copy of Eric Ives' Anne Boleyn book and tip the top of its spine towards me. Thank God that mechanism works, as I was worried the entrance to the portal would remain closed without the ring. Just as before, the bookcase swings open, allowing me to grab the flaming torch and lead Rob down the passageway, up the stone stairs, and towards the antechamber at Hever.

My heart pounds, not only because Rob's hold on my hand is tight, but because something back in the darkness piques my attention — a noise from the office. Whatever it was, it dissipates, and we continue forward through the dimly lit passageway and up the thirteen steps that have become so familiar to me. I hope Anne is still here, and that time will not have leapt too far forward. My hand shakes as I push the door to the antechamber open.

"Who is there?" Anne cries out as she walks from her bedroom into the antechamber. "Is that you, Beth?"

"Yes, Mistress Anne."

"Beth! I am so glad you are back. When you disappear, I have such a task explaining to my parents where you have gone."

"I'm sorry," I whisper. Her cheeks are rosy, and her eyes are red. She looks upset, and I wonder if am I to blame, or was she like this before my arrival.

"Whenever I try that door, it is stuck fast! Beth, you left without a word — how could you?" She's mad with me, and who could blame her?

"Erm, I've brought a friend with me."

She stops in her tracks when Rob steps out of the shadows.

"Hello, good sir. Beth, I ... I thought you were gone for good! How could you do this to me, when I need you?" She doesn't shout, but her words are tinged with anger and hurt. "I thought you had abandoned me, just when I need you to help me negotiate with Father, to get back to court."

"I know, Anne. I'm sorry." I feel bad, but glad that time doesn't seem to have moved on too much since I left. I stuff my hands into my jeans' pockets as she stares at me, then at Rob. He is so obviously shocked, his jaw flapping as he glances around the small room, at Anne, then back to me.

Anne wipes her eyes and laughs. "I am glad you are back, Mistress Wickers, but did not think you would bring company."

She stares at Rob, and for a moment he looks trapped, like a rabbit in the headlights, transfixed by her gaze. It is true what the ambassadors reported about her, that she knows how to entrap a man with the use of her fine, dark eyes.

"Robert, I presume?" She holds out her hand that he might kiss it. He steps forward, lays my bag on top of a trunk, and brushes his lips across the back of her knuckles, still speechless.

"Is he shy?" she asks, laughing again.

"Not normally." I prod him in the back. "Say something."

"It's ... nice to meet you." He grins like a Cheshire cat.

"Robert, it is a pleasure to meet you." He just gawks, and I can see that he's utterly hooked. She turns to me and laughs, her expression as bright as I have ever seen it. "I see he is wearing his horse-riding clothes, the same as you did ... and now are." She studies us, in our fashionably ripped jeans, and covers her mouth as she laughs.

"About that," I say, "he can't stay in those clothes. It will make him too conspicuous."

"Who said anything about him staying?" Her gaze hardens on me. She waves her hands in the air. "And you, Beth, you need to change." She nods to the bag filled with necessities I've brought from home. "And how do I explain his presence?"

That's the second time she has reprimanded me in as many days. "While he's here, can he borrow some of George's clothes?"

"Lady Anne, if it's going to be a problem, I will go." Rob looks at me, then back to Anne. "I just wanted to see if what Beth had told me was true."

Anne circles him, the same way she did with me when I first arrived.

Rob looks unnerved by it and folds his arms across his chest.

"Father and George will not like it, you bringing a man to Hever."

The passageway door shoots open, and the tapestry is pulled aside as Professor Marshall strides in. Like Rob and me, he looks out of place in twenty-first-century clothes but nevertheless is reverent to Anne, taking a deep bow and addressing her in front of us.

"Madam, please forgive my intrusion. I am Mister Marshall, a friend of Beth Wickers and Robert Dryden. I have come to take them both home."

"Sir, I have heard of you." She approaches him. "You are Beth's university professor, are you not?"

"Yes, Mistress Anne."

"You are welcome to take Robert back from whence you came, but I will not allow you to take Beth from me." She seems resolute.

I need to tell Professor Marshall I've lost the ring. He's going to kill me, but he needs to know. Whatever troubles Anne is going through now are irrelevant — it's my future I need to be concerned with, not hers.

"But, My Lady, it is not possible for Mistress Wickers to remain here. In doing so, she is damaging your future happiness." With that comment, he glares at me and I know I've messed up big time.

"Mister Marshall," I start, "I nee—"

"No, Beth. I think you have done enough."

"Sir, it's my fault," Rob says. "I persuaded Beth to bring me through the portal." He straightens and trails his fingers through his hair. "I didn't mean for anyone to get into any sort of trouble."

"I will talk with you later, Mr Dryden." His anger burns into me as he grabs my wrist. "You are coming!"

"Let me go! Sir, I've los—"

"Be quiet! Can't you see what you've done? You have put everyone involved in danger. I asked you to keep things between us, to support the Lady Anne and nothing more. You are meddling, and I warned you not to." His grip on my wrist tightens and I grimace.

"Stop it!" Anne snaps. "Let Beth go now!"

Professor Marshall stares at her, and his grip weakens. I'm just glad he can't see my other hand, missing the lost ring.

"Sir, she has been a great help to me, and we are firm friends." Anne steps closer to me. "You cannot expect me to give her up now, just when I need her."

Rob loiters in the background, blatantly unsure of what to make of the scene unfolding before his eyes.

"Very well, Mistress, as you wish, but I will only leave Miss Wickers with you if she makes a solemn promise to never interfere or to meddle, just as I told her the first afternoon she came here to you."

Anne scurries into her bedroom.

"What are you doing?" I call to her.

"Looking for my prayer book so you can swear on it."

Seconds later, she comes back into the antechamber carrying her precious Book of Hours and passes it to me. Professor Marshall releases my wrist, which is reddened and burning. The sight of it sends a shock of realisation through me. What have I done? If we're all found, the potential for disaster is enormous. But what am I to do? Stay or go? I certainly don't want to put Anne at risk.

Right now, I wish the ground would swallow me up. I'm torn between my loyalty to Professor Marshall and to Anne, but I need to find the ring. I can't go back with Professor Marshall without it — he'd kill me! The reality hits me: I need to stay — I need to find that bloody ring — I need to save my own neck now, not just Anne's. The professor can't know I've lost his precious jewel. I must protect myself and Anne, and guard both our futures.

the book in my left hand, I keep my ring finger beneath and place my right upon the embossed leather cover. "I swear upon this Holy book that I will do as Professor Marshall has asked and not mess with history's plan for Anne Boleyn, her family, nor their futures, so help me God."

The grim look of retribution fades from the professor's brow, and the relief that tensions have eased almost topples me. I find it fascinating that even now, after nearly five hundred years of time passing, that swearing on the word of God is as profound to onlookers as it was then. It reminds me of Anne swearing her innocence on the sacrament, and I vow to myself that I will prevent her from ever having to do that. But then, haven't I sworn that I won't meddle with her future? God help me, how did I get myself into this mess?

I snap back to the moment to see Rob retreat towards the passageway door. He catches my eye and mouths "I'm sorry." Then he stops, a pained look in his eyes. "Forgive me?"

"Be quiet!" Professor Marshall snaps. "You have done enough damage."

The ensuing silence is broken by a knock on the bedchamber door.

"I will answer it," Anne says. "You can't go dressed like that, Beth. You had all best be quiet." She scans the three of us before leaving to answer the door. A long-held breath later, I hear mumbling apologies to her.

"Mrs Orchard, what is it?"

"Supper will be ready shortly, Mistress Anne."

"Very well, I shall be down presently."

"Mistress, do you need me to help you change for dinner?"

I hold my breath again as the door creaks. Mrs Orchard can't see me in modern clothes — that would take too much explaining. And how on earth would we explain the presence of two men in the antechamber?

"A rider sent a dispatch earlier. Sir Thomas and your brother are expected back tonight."

"Thank you," Anne says. "And … Mrs Orchard, tell Mother to set another place for Beth."

"Very well. Are you sure you wouldn't like some help changing your gown?"

"No, Mrs Orchard. That will be all, thank you. Tell Mother Beth and I will be down presently."

I wonder if Mrs Orchard is aware that I have been absent from Hever? How has Anne explained that? It must have been plausible, as Mrs Orchard's tone remains as it always is.

"Very well, Mistress Anne." With that, her apron flaps as she scurries off down the passageway.

I'm lucky George hasn't turned up. It wouldn't be right if he just barged into Anne's rooms in his usual style. That would not go down well with Rob, not to mention the repercussions of George seeing two male strangers in his sister's rooms.

Anne returns to the antechamber. "It was only Mrs Orchard. Father will be home soon, so I best get you changed into something more suitable." Her brows raise as she stares at me, then at Professor Marshall and Rob. "Mother is expecting us for supper."

"Well, gentlemen," I say, "you heard the lady. I suggest you both make your way home."

Professor Marshall frowns. "I'm not happy about this, but if you want to stay…?" He bows to Anne again, then Rob tries to make an effort at Tudor etiquette by kissing her hand.

"My Lady, we are so sorry to have disturbed you," Professor Marshall says. He smiles at her, then looks to me. "You know where I am if you need me, right?"

"Yes, sir."

"Remember what I've said — don't meddle."

I nod. With that, he ushers Rob through the passageway.

As they disappear into the darkness, Rob glances over his shoulder, looking somewhat lost and perturbed at being sent off. I can't look him in the eye — I'm still angry that he persuaded me to defy the professor, and I'm gutted that I've broken a trust. But I need to forget about it, and the only way to do that is to shut the door on the portal. I pull the tapestry over, relieved that the whole episode is over, at least for now.

I grab the bag and pull the gown out onto Anne's bed. Then I undress and fling my clothes into the bag, also removing any modern-day jewellery, while Anne finds a shift for me and throws it over my head.

"Thanks!" I sigh, feeling better now that I'm not so obtrusive. I stuff the bag right in under the bed. It still contains many modern conveniences: toothpaste, aspirin, mascara, and some leftover antibiotics and heavy-duty painkillers. I never know what I might need, so I thought it best to pack everything but the kitchen sink.

As Anne helps lace my kirtle, she sounds pensive. "You would not have left me again, would you?" She ties the lacing tight as I pull my stomach in.

"I didn't want to, but I thought I had to go back with them. I thought the professor wouldn't allow me to stay with you again because I brought Rob through the portal."

"Mister Marshall seemed placated." She smiles. "I have a way with men!"

"Yes, so I noticed. It is those eyes of yours."

"And what of you with Robert? He is very handsome, is he not?"

"Yes," I reply, "and very intelligent."

"But…?"

"I'm afraid that after today, I have messed all that up." I push my arms through the sleeves of my overgown as Anne lifts its weight onto my shoulders. It feels good to be back in these clothes — back at Hever. When I turn around, she tugs on the lacing of my bodice.

"You could not have had a passion for two men. That would not be fair."

"Can a woman not love two men at the same time?" I meet her gaze. "Didn't you love two men simultaneously? Or have you forgotten Harry Percy and Thomas Wyatt already?"

"Now you are rude!" she says with indignation.

"No, I'm just honest," I reply, unable to prevent a smirk. She knots the bodice laces hard and hides them under the placard of my overgown. With my hair having been recently washed, she helps me 'restyle' it, so it matches my clothes. I finish making myself presentable, tucking my toes into my soft leather slippers and securing my silk girdle belt about the waist of my gown.

Anne leads the way down to supper and, as we reach the dining room, it's hard not to hear Sir Thomas and George arguing in the library. We hover outside, peering through the small gap in the panelled door. George is standing in the candlelight, chewing on a toothpick, which seems to have become a regular habit. He looks confident as he stands before his father, who is sat at his worktable, now covered in fresh paperwork from court.

"When we spoke of marriage before, just as Anne returned from France, you were happy for me to decide for you. What has changed?" Thomas leans back in his chair, stroking his beard. The man sounds exhausted.

"Everything has changed, Father."

"In what way?" He picks up a Venetian wine glass and takes a gulp of its ruby contents, then wipes his mouth with the back of his hand. "Well, boy?"

"I do not love Jane Parker." George paces the room, the toothpick still between his lips.

"I know not all marriages are as blessed as mine was with your mother. She married me for love and was happy to give up her ambitions to have your brothers and sisters."

"You married Mother to fulfil your ambitions first and foremost, Father."

"The marriage may have been to my advantage, George, but it was a love match — with that there is no doubt." He gets to his feet, his cheeks flushed. "You will marry Jane Parker, and you will beget a child once the girl has become a Boleyn." He tugs on his wedding ring and twists it about his finger, no doubt to prevent himself from completely losing his temper.

George does not shrink back from his father's insistence. "She likes to gossip!"

Thomas chuckles. "And you and Anne do not?"

"But, Father, when I am at court, she stares at me. She does not let me out of her sight." He tugs at the cuff of his shirt. I notice he always does that when he's angry or anxious. "She asks my friends about me. Tom, Francis Bryan, and others."

"Jane likes you, George." Thomas smiles, trying to reassure his son. "It is only natural the woman wants to know all about you. After all, you will be a good catch when the king promotes you, which I am sure he will."

"Promotion, or no, I will not sleep with her."

"You will, when you are married — it will be your duty."

"I have heard reports she never bathes."

"I am sure that cannot be true." Thomas Boleyn sighs. "That is your only argument against the match?" He takes another sip of wine and sets the glass back on his worktable.

"Seriously, Father, you cannot make me marry her. She seems a vile girl and her family are far too ambitious."

"George, if that is your only issue, I will speak with Anne, and when she returns to court, which she will, if Jane lacks manners, I am sure Anne could have a kind word with her. Besides, Lord Morley has assured me Jane is all the things required to be a Boleyn, and I am sure she does not need educating on the finer points of bathing!"

Anne grips my arm, but I wave her off and focus back on the father/son interaction. Thomas walks around his worktable and stands in front of his son, then pats his shoulder — a blatant effort at reassurance, but George shrugs him off.

Thomas grimaces at this rejection. "What will happen when I am gone, eh? Who will carry on looking after our estates if you have no son and heir?" He tries a heartening smile, but George averts his gaze, continuing to fiddle with the toothpick.

"I know I will need an heir, Father, but it will not be with *her*." His neck reddens as his temper flares. He leans closer to Thomas. "I will *not* marry her."

"Come now, George." Thomas holds both hands out. "I have done my best for you. Jane is a pretty little thing."

"If you want her to sleep with a Boleyn so badly, *you* sleep with her."

His father's jaw drops. I don't think he can believe what he has just heard. "You are wilful and ungrateful, George!"

"No, Father, I'm not! All I want is the prerogative to choose my own bride."

"Now, George, you know this is not how our world works. The king has already agreed to your betrothal." Thomas strokes his beard, as if searching for the right words to turn his son to his way of thinking. "The king has gone to a great deal of trouble — even supporting Lord Morley with Jane's dowry."

To me, it feels as if Thomas hopes that mentioning the king enough times will persuade George to see sense.

He lifts a rolled-up scroll, which bears a large red seal and ribbons. "The king has signed the agreement with Lord Morley. All we need do is sign this document together, and all will be settled." He tries to hand the document to George. "The king loves you — we all love you and have your best wishes at heart."

George grimaces, then turns on his heel and storms out of the room, barging past Anne and me.

"George, come back here!" Thomas Boleyn is not a happy man. I feel sorry for George, and my heart breaks for him as I watch him disappear towards the kitchen. "George!" Sir Thomas strides out of the room but stops in his tracks when he sees us, the scroll still in his hand.

"Anne, I need to speak with you."

Anne winces. "Now, Father?"

"Yes. Mistress Wickers, please go and help Lady Boleyn with the supper. We will join you shortly."

I dip a curtsy as he guides his daughter into the room and shuts the door behind me. I cannot leave. I am here to bear witness so I cannot resist listening in on this conversation, too.

"We need to talk about Henry Percy," Thomas says, his voice now hoarse.

"Do we, Father?" Anne asks, so innocently I have to bite back a smile.

"I understand why you wanted the Northumberland marriage and why you tried to arrange it."

A silence ensues. He is probably taking another gulp of wine.

"I was doing my best for this family," Anne says.

"But, daughter, as you know, a marriage of a senior noble is a matter for the state, something only the king can decide."

"But, Father, no one else knows about this — apart from you, Mistress Wickers, and Cardinal Wolsey."

I smile at that because we both know there were many other people in Wolsey's chambers that day.

"Daughter, how can you be so foolish to believe such a thing? What were you thinking?" Thomas knows how gossip spreads at court.

"As I said, I was doing what I thought best for our family, and for me."

"You should have left such a delicate matter of your marriage to me. Now the whole court knows of your disgrace." That must be a lie. Surely not everyone knows about her pre-contract with Harry Percy. Or maybe they do.

"The Butler proposal fell through — what was I to do?"

"You should have spoken with me first."

"I would have, but the Countess of Salisbury and the queen tried to support me in this matter."

"I know. I heard about that from the cardinal."

"Father, I was not trying to embarrass you, I promise." Her voice wavers. *Don't cry, for goodness sake, stay strong.*

"I hope your reputation is not ruined." There is a short silence. "You have not consummated the relationship with Percy, have you?"

"No! I would never lie with anyone other than the man who would be my husband."

"At least your mother has taught you some pride." He sighs. "Any scandal would have destroyed your prospects. Mary is fortunate that she is a married woman. I never approved of her becoming the king's mistress, and I have failed her as a father because of it, but at least the child she carries can be passed off as William Carey's, even if it is not."

"I know," Anne says. "I have seen how Mary is treated. I will never be a mistress to anyone — you have my word."

There is a long silence. Hopefully because Thomas is embracing and forgiving his daughter.

"Then let this be an end to the matter."

---

Later, supper is fraught with painful silences, uncivil discourse, and wary looks. Mary and William spend most of the evening in their bedchamber, while Elizabeth and Thomas are deep in conversation in the parlour. George is sulking in the library, probably having discourse with the wolfhound, or has his nose stuck in the latest book from France. I did debate whether I should go and console him, but I feel I would be adding to his hurt and creating more problems — something I'd rather avoid.

The sun has sunk low in the sky, leaving it tinged with pinks, purples, and golds. Agnes has made a fire in the bedchamber earlier in the evening, and I savour the warmth from its dying embers. She helps me undress and prepare for bed.

The atmosphere was so thick with discontent that Anne has already tucked herself in early. When I climb in, she barely says a word, except goodnight. With her shoulders hunched and tense, I don't cuddle into her for warmth as I have so often done. Instead, I grip the edge of the mattress and cry silently into my pillow, until, eventually, I drift off to sleep.

# Nineteen

### New Year's Day – Hever Castle

"Why did we not visit Allington with your parents and George?" I ask Anne.

"I declined the invitation because I have no desire to see Thomas Wyatt, and you need to avoid my brother."

"Do I?" She stares at me and says nothing. Her words prick at my conscience, and it hurts.

"You pretend to be ill, but your mother will see through it. She was rather put out that we didn't join them."

The Boleyns have been away for a few days and returned here to Hever on the early evening of New Year's Day. There is much excitement in the house, for New Year's Day in Tudor England is the day gifts are exchanged. We are called into the parlour, a private retiring room with Tudor panelling and stone fireplace, where Lady Boleyn sits before the hearth.

As I enter this private space, the early moonlight refracts silvery hues onto the wooden floors at the opposite side of the room, and warmth and light radiates from the small hearth, making this room feel almost cosy. Mary has come downstairs from a guest room, where she has been curled up in bed with William, exchanging their own gifts and idle chatter. William smiles at me as he follows Mary into the room, his tall, thin frame barely visible in the glow of the fire.

"Mistress Wickers, how are you?" he asks politely, plumping a cushion up for Mary to lean against as she sits down. Carey is a handsome fellow, with a narrow face and dark brown eyes. His clothes are plain but made from quality fabrics. He helps Mary settle into a chair and rests his hand on her shoulder as she watches the festivities. There is clearly a fondness between them, despite any rift the king may have created.

I perch on the edge of a settle and watch Anne embrace her mother. Thomas stands in front of the fire, warming his legs. George lies on the floor, resting against some large cushions, avoiding eye contact with Anne — his foolish pride tying him to a game of pretence. Every so often, I catch him sneaking a peek in my direction, and when our eyes meet, his mouth turns up in a wry smile. His parents are oblivious to the charade, but Anne scowls when she catches us exchanging glances.

"Children, as is the tradition for this time of year, we have gifts for you," Lady Boleyn says, handing me a beautifully presented parcel wrapped in gorgeous crimson and gold paper. I didn't think about buying gifts for them and I blush with embarrassment and gratitude, not expecting a gift, guilty that I haven't returned the gesture.

"My Lady, you are most kind." She must notice the rosy hue of my cheeks as she pats my shoulder.

"It is nothing, Beth," Thomas says, his smile broad and genuine. "You are a wonderful companion for Anne and have shown great love and loyalty to us all."

Anne takes her turn and stands before her mother, her gaze on the floor.

"These items —" her mother hands her a parcel wrapped in yellow and gold paper, with a blue ribbon tied about it — "were ordered some time ago for you, my darling. We had intended to save them to give you upon your marriage, and give this to you as a gift to remember your heritage, but as your nuptials have yet to come about, we have changed our minds." She looks about the room at all of us. "We want you all to have these particular gifts now."

Anne blinks fiercely as her eyes brim with tears, but she accepts her parcel and begins to unwrap it. I am just as excited as I sit next to Mary, and she watches me loosen the ribbon on my gift and pull open the crimson paper. My package contains a bolt of fabric — the softest velvet — of the most unusual colour of midnight-blue, which will contrast perfectly with my skin tone. Beneath the navy velvet is a bolt of deep yellow, almost gold, satin, and tissue.

Holding it up, I can't contain my delight. "What a fabulous gown this will make!" I get up, nearly dropping the bolt of fabric, and wrap my arms around Lady Boleyn, thanking her for her excellent choice of present. I tentatively give Thomas a quick peck on the cheek, and his smile broadens in response.

"Ah, it is nothing," he says. "You can ask the Master of Wardrobe of the Robes to measure you for a gown, which you shall design yourself."

This cloth must have cost the earth. And did I hear him mention court and me in the same breath? Could we be going back to court?

Anne heard him, too, because her gaze darts to me, giving me one of her knowing looks. She strokes the velvet as she holds the bolt of fabric against my décolleté. "This colour will be wonderful on you!" Then Anne opens her smaller package to discover a brown leather box covered in Italian gold-leaf scrollwork. With great care, she lifts the lid.

Inside, nestled on a bed of black satin, is a magnificent collar of large, radiant pearls, and from this circlet hangs a gleaming and polished gold "B", beautifully crafted. Dangling from the lower loop of the "B" are three pear-shaped pearls, striking for their size and high lustre. As if that isn't enough, attached to the circlet is a long strand of equally captivating pearls, which are meant to be draped over Anne's collarbone and tucked into the bodice of a gown. I'm not sure if it's real gold, but it certainly looks it.

I cannot believe what I see and blink at the realisation that, here, Anne holds the famous strand of pearls and cypher necklace that she will make so renowned.

Thomas hands George a package wrapped in paper. "This is for you, dear son."

"Thank you, Father." He wastes no time unwrapping the present and pulling out some leatherwork, which decorates and holds a small dagger with an embossed and gilded hilt. "This is beautiful!" He turns the dagger and tugs it out of its sheath, then runs his finger down the edge of the blade. "It is sharp!" He laughs. "Thank you both." He gets to his feet, embraces his mother, and kisses her cheek, then turns to his father and gives him a firm hug. Thomas is somewhat surprised with this sudden show of appreciation.

"Your turn, Mary." Lady Boleyn passes her eldest daughter a prettily wrapped parcel, tied with red ribbon.

"Thank you, Mother." Mary beams, tugging at the ribbon and pulling open the paper to reveal a pile of linen baby gowns, with exquisite blackwork embroidery. William peers over her shoulder at the bundle of linens now resting in her lap.

"Thank you, Lady Boleyn," he says. "They will be most useful."

"I embroidered those myself!" Lady Boleyn smiles.

"Mother, all these gifts are remarkable," Anne says. "My necklace is gorgeous, and certainly much too costly."

"I wanted you all to have something I know you would each cherish. Something you might all use every day." She looks on proudly at all her children. "I wanted you to have your necklace, and to wear those pearls in good health and fortune, darling Anne."

"It is beautiful, Anne," I say, tracing my fingers over the metalwork of the "B", gobsmacked at the item I'm touching. Lady Boleyn notes my amazement at the necklace and reiterates how beautiful the cloth is by comparison. She doesn't realise that I delight in the jewellery because of its provenance, not because of its worth.

"Beth, a gown made in those colours will flatter your flaxen hair, and everyone will take notice of the extraordinarily beautiful young woman you are." Lady Boleyn looks delighted with the colour of the fabric she had chosen for me.

"I am most grateful, Lady Boleyn." I don't let on that I noticed George smirking at his mother's comment. I help secure the pearls about Anne's slender neck, and she sits the "B" flat against her chest, before resting the pearls in the right position and tucking the excess of the strand beneath the neckline of her gown.

"Goodness, sister," George says, "you will need to look after that!"

"I will." Anne cradles the empty necklace box in her hand.

"Anne, it looks wonderful on you — treasure it, and remember your father and me always by it." Lady Boleyn radiates with pride. "Let us hope that perhaps, someday, you will be blessed by having a beautiful, accomplished daughter of your own who will wear this pretty necklace, proud of her Boleyn heritage."

As I stare at the larger pearls on the necklace, I think of the possibility of her daughter, Elizabeth I, wearing them. It breaks my heart to know that someday it will be broken to pieces, transformed from its present state, and several of the larger pearls will adorn the Imperial State crown. I want to blurt out what I know, but I pull myself back, needing to hold both my tongue and my nerve.

Anne gratefully embraces her father, and he returns her gesture with a tender kiss on the forehead. The love within this family is so evident, and I am delighted to be present in their home at such a time.

I can't deny that it is extra-pleasant to feel the warmth of George's surreptitious glances, too.

# Twenty

### STILL AT HEVER CASTLE

A few weeks later, Anne is summoned to the parlour, where we find Sir Thomas reposing in his great chair by the fire. He directs Agnes to light a few candles around the room to dispel the gloom from the descending dusk. Anne looks pensive sitting on the settle, and I wonder what Thomas wants with us.

Moments later, George appears and stands behind us, my back tensing when he rests his hands behind me on the settle. Lady Boleyn is in the kitchen preparing supper with Mrs Orchard and the other servants.

"Sir, would you like me to bring you some wine?" Agnes asks.

Sir Thomas nods. "The red burgundy will do just fine."

Agnes scurries away, closing the door behind her.

A bit of an awkward silence ensues, which leads me to worry even more. What has happened to have Anne's father act this way?

"Daughter, there is something you should know," he says, but goes no further as Agnes returns. She sets a jug of French wine on a small table beside him, then leaves. "I prefer you to hear this from my lips." He sits back when Agnes returns with four glasses, tapping his fingers on the arm of the chair as she sets them on the table.

"Should you like me to pour the wine, sir?" she asks.

"No, that will be all, Agnes," he replies, both hands tapping now. She gives a short curtsy and leaves. "Right, where was I?" He strokes his beard.

"What is it, Father?" Anne asks, clearly frustrated at his delay in coming to the point. I shift in my seat as George steps forward to stand beside me, his expression giving nothing away.

"I shall come straight to the point," Sir Thomas says.

Anne clears her throat. "I wish you would!"

"Well, I had a letter from Wolsey today." Whatever colour had been in Anne's cheeks has now gone. "It seems Henry Percy is married. The wedding took place days ago at Alnwick Castle, Northumberland." Anne is biting her lip.

"Don't cry, Anne," I blurt out. "I cannot bear it."

She tries to smile through her pain. "Father, how am I to endure this?"

"It will get easier as time passes." Thomas Boleyn's eyes soften as he endeavours to ease his daughter's turmoil. "All has been done for the best."

This doesn't seem to placate Anne, who visibly bristles. "I appreciate you telling me, Father." She takes a sharp breath through her nose, and I feel a 'but' coming. "I am glad I have heard this from you, rather than anyone else, but I still think Wolsey is to blame for this debacle, and mark my words, Father, he will pay." She gets up to go, but George catches her elbow.

"Sister, sit down." He pats her shoulder.

She sits, and we all look to Thomas Boleyn.

"Now that Mary is coming closer to her time, you will assist your mother when your sister goes into labour. William is happiest with her here at home. Greenwich is not suitable for a woman in her condition." His mouth half-curls in a smile. "You are better off here, supporting your family at such an important time."

"Yes, Father," Anne says in a muted reply.

"William is neither blind nor deaf to know that the child may be the king's," George adds. "Mary is uncertain of the child's parentage, but to save William's feelings, we will not be discussing it around him. It would not be fair."

Thomas Boleyn nods, continuing to caress his beard. "Master Carey is looking forward to the birth of his child, and his feelings should be spared. Is that understood?" His tone is brusque.

"Yes, Father," Anne answers.

"William loves Mary," George says. "I know this is a terrible burden to bear for the family, but the king has sent only a few gifts for Mary since he found out about her pregnancy, and we must not take it for granted that he might recognise the child."

"I understand," Anne responds, while I just sit there nodding along.

George is obviously happy with our acquiescence. "We are all hoping that as Mary becomes absorbed with caring for her child, she will forget the king and focus on her husband."

"We will lead the court to think the child is a Carey, even if it is not," Thomas says with a swish of his hand. "It is best for Mary and best for the child."

We all nod. Historians debate the parentage of Mary's children even now, and until I set eyes on the child, and can watch it grow, I will agree with those who suggest the child is William Carey's.

"Now, on to other business." To my surprise, Sir Thomas looks at me. "Mistress Elizabeth," he says, addressing me directly, stroking his beard again, "as Anne has been banished from court, I would like you to attend on Queen Katharine in Anne's stead and return here to Hever when Mary's baby is due."

I swallow back a ball of apprehension and stare at him, then glance at George. Anne looks alarmed and not a little angry.

"Why should Beth go back to court when I am banished?" Her eyes are intense, her fists balled at her sides. "That really is not fair," she snaps, like a toddler stamping her little feet. Considering the news Anne has just been given about Henry Percy, is it any wonder she is in a temper?

"Daughter, it is for the best." Sir Thomas plucks at the anglets on his doublet. "You need to stay here — it is Wolsey and the king's express command. We need someone who supports us, who can go unnoticed about the queen's apartments, and be able to report back and tell us how the land lies with Mary. The family name is at stake, and we must know where we stand, for the sake of the forthcoming child."

"But, Father, I am better placed to go, and with far more experience."

"No, Anne, it is decided." He glances at his son. "George will accompany Mistress Wickers when we leave in a few days. I will ride on ahead with them, then George can return Beth to Hever safely when Mary's time comes."

"A few days? You all leave so soon? But you have only just returned home!"

My nerves are in shreds as I realise my dilemma. What will happen if I return to court without Anne? And what if I'm alone with George? How will I resist him if he comes on to me again? I need to be resilient and oppose his advances at all costs — keep him at arm's length, no matter what. Anne won't be pleased with me being alone with him. She'll be even less happy that I'll enjoy all the court revels while she is forced to remain here.

I keep my head down, curtsy to Sir Thomas and his children, leave the room, then disappear as fast as I can to avoid another tongue-lashing from Anne. The trouble is, do I go back to court with George just for the sheer experience of it, or should I stay here and try to find the cypher ring? I have searched so hard for it these past weeks, with no joy. As I run, my stomach is both in knots and bursting with excitement at the prospect of spending time at King Henry VIII's court, with George Boleyn.

Within moments, footsteps sound on the stairs and Anne appears at her bedroom door.

"You cannot go to court without me!" She steps into the room and pushes the door behind her.

"Anne, it is not my fault, it's what your father wants."

"You certainly cannot go on your own with my brother." She picks up a jug of wine and pours herself a glass.

"Why not?"

"Why not? You know exactly why not!" She looks angry, clenching her glass so I can see the whites of her knuckles. "Before the month is out, once you get to Greenwich, he will be in your bed!"

"Anne, how could you suggest that of me?"

"It's not you I worry about, it's George! He will take advantage of you, given an opportunity." She takes a sip of the wine, places the glass on the small table near her bed, then slumps on the end of the mattress, dejected.

The bedroom door swings open.

"Did I just hear my name being mentioned?" George asks, a big smile lighting his beautiful face. "Are you not excited that we are going to Greenwich together, Beth?" His smile broadens, and it is apparent that he is delighted with himself.

Forgetting myself, I smile. "Yes, I'm really looking forward to it."

Anne watches us from the corner of her eye and huffs. "Well, is this not lovely?"

Oh, God, she's angry with me. This isn't going to go well. I look away from George and settle myself in a chair before the fire.

"Beth, I should have let you go back home when you had the chance," she says. She rubs her brow and groans. "I'm never going to get back to court if you go in my place."

All I can do is shrug — there is no use arguing her point.

"Sister, do not be so ungrateful. Mistress Elizabeth and I go together to court for Mary's benefit!"

"Your own personal gain and benefit, you mean."

"That isn't true, Anne!" I snap. "We do this to protect Mary's relationship with the king. This is what your father wants."

She takes another sip of wine, clearly unhappy.

Now I'm getting cross. I'm only doing as I'm told. It's not my fault she has been banished from court. She's so wilful, no one can tell her what to do, let alone control her.

"Ladies, come now, be kind to one another."

"I am sorry, George. I want to come with you and Beth. This whole situation is so unfair."

I almost laugh. This whole situation has been brought about by Anne insisting on marriage to Henry Percy. I should have been more forceful in my warnings to her about him and told her about Wolsey interfering before he did so, but I was afraid I'd upset her. I remind myself that I am not to meddle — to change nothing — but the desire to win a better outcome for Anne and a chance for her to live longer weighs heavily on my conscience.

I sometimes wonder what other people would do in my position. What would Rob do? I mustn't think about him, or about home. There is no chance of me going back to Carshalton now, not with the ring still missing and Sir Thomas giving me a commission.

"Sister, I will look after Beth, I swear, and I will protect the interests of Mary at all times. And if I can, I will recommend you to Wolsey, and to the king, by telling them how sorry you are for defying them." He places his arm about her shoulder and squeezes her. "All will be well, you will see."

She tries to smile. "I hope you are right, brother."

He raises his eyebrows and grins "I know I am."

"Leave us, George, Agnes has to prepare and pack a trunk for Beth's journey." Anne nudges him. "Perhaps you should be preparing for that journey to Greenwich, too."

# Twenty-One

### Travelling to Greenwich

The litter is being loaded with our belongings by the Boleyn servants, Robert Cranewell and Agnes. The horses are chomping at the bit, liveried up and raring to go. Their hoofs crunch in the gravel beyond the drawbridge as I hug Lady Boleyn goodbye.

"Remember, Beth, you will do well if you heed my advice and listen before you act once you are at court. You are charming and beautiful, and everyone will not fail to love you. Queen Katharine, especially, will love you."

Thomas chuckles. "Wife, do not fuss so!" He embraces her and kisses her cheek. "Look after our girls," he says, as he sees Mary watching us through one of the casement windows above. "Mary will need you more than ever, my love." He pats her arm.

I watch as George leans in to kiss his mother.

"Be a credit to your father and return Mistress Wickers safely when Mary's time comes."

"Yes, of course, Mother."

George then embraces Anne.

"I wish I was going with you." She's sulking, and Thomas Boleyn doesn't look best pleased about it.

"Now, Anne, we have discussed this. It will not be long before George and Elizabeth return to us. Just be patient."

"Yes, Father." He hugs her, then kisses her cheek. She rubs the spot afterwards because of the prickliness of his beard. Tears fill her eyes as she grabs my hand and pulls me in to hug her. "I will miss you, sweet friend."

"And I you."

"Please be careful around George," she whispers in my ear. "Do not let him close. You do not deserve to be hurt."

I sigh. "I will be careful, and you are right."

"Come now, Mistress Wickers, we have said our goodbyes." George helps Agnes into the litter.

Thomas Boleyn mounts his horse and waves his bonnet in the air as he begins to trot down the drive, setting the pace with his servant, Robert, who rides alongside him. Griffin barks persistently, striding alongside Sir Thomas, who shouts at the wolfhound. "Griffin, go back to your mother. Stop that infernal noise!" He raises his horsewhip in a comedic gesture. "Griffin, *go!*" The dog finally obliges.

"I'm coming!" I shout, giving Anne one last hug. Griffin is soon about our skirts, circling us.

"One thing, before you go…" Her gaze is both secretive and insistent, and she digs into the leather purse belted about her waist.

"What is it?" I take in a sharp breath as she pulls out a shiny gold ring, its rubies glistening in the sunlight — the 'AB' cypher visible to me once more. I glare at Anne, my face burning. She tries to stay pokerfaced, but smirks, which makes me boil.

---

How I managed to keep calm as I was bundled into the litter, I'll never know. My face must be a sight if the heat is anything to go by. Wringing my hands in my lap, it takes all my strength not to leap from the litter, rush towards Anne, and strangle her. They smile and wave from the drawbridge as the clattering of livery and horses' hooves carry George, Agnes, and me towards Greenwich. Anne thinks we've parted on good terms, but I can't believe she forced me to stay in her time, against my will, when she had the ring all along! How dare she.

I sit here, beside George, with the ring clenched in my hand, visualising the London of my time. How I miss it. As I stare at how white my knuckles are, my stomach lurches and I unclench my hand when I realise what I'm doing. Christ! I could have unintentionally transported myself back to the twenty-first century in front of Agnes and George. What the hell was I thinking? I could have been gone in the blink of an eye.

Without drawing attention, I slip the ring into a little velvet pouch I have tied about my waist and breathe a gentle sigh of relief. Things are different now that I have the ring back. I have options. With that in mind, I sit back to enjoy the journey, promising myself the experience of court before thinking about heading home.

All in all, I've been in Tudor England for over two years, but have only been gone from the twenty-first century for a few days. It feels like forever since I sat watching Professor Marshall lecturing on the Tudors, but in reality it has only been a few days.

Now, I have no choice but to continue this journey. Thomas Boleyn knows nothing of my time-travelling adventures. No one in Tudor England knows my secret, except for Anne, who has convinced everyone I came from France just after her to be a companion, and servant. She thinks I'm going to help her in this life, because I'm from the future, and know everything about her. But I will never divulge all that I know. I've be warned not to mess with history.

I glance at George. Anne doesn't want me to be alone with him. She's right, having witnessed that kiss. I shift in my seat to create a little distance. I need to behave myself, ensuring that I don't cause problems at court. That wouldn't do, particularly because I don't want to change history. Who knows what would happen if events deviated from the path they are meant to follow? George looks out of the window, his family becoming small specks as they watch from the front of Hever.

Agnes just smiles as I sit in silence, leaning against the side of the litter, wondering how many hours it might take to get to Greenwich Palace. The horses trot on at a gentle pace. Hever is about 29 miles from Greenwich, a fifty-three-minute drive from here, on the best route, in my time. At the pace the horses are going, the journey, by my estimation, is going to be eight hours or more.

I sigh, wishing I had my iPhone so I could listen to my favourite playlist to while away the time. The battery died a long time ago, and unless I can pair it up with the battery pack to charge it, when no one is watching, that's the way it will stay.

George breaks the monotony. "Anne will be a comfort to Mary and to Mother while we are away." He squeezes my arm. "All will be well, Beth, you will see."

His smile placates me, for now.

The litter lurches over the hard-packed ground, and Sir Thomas Boleyn rides ahead with Robert Cranewell. Considering Thomas is in his mid-forties, he seems incredibly fit, especially when, at his age, he is approaching what the Tudors consider to be old age.

I pretend that things are the same way with George, before the kiss. We have an audience sitting opposite us — Agnes — who, in her naiveté, appears nonplussed by the strained atmosphere, so tries to make small-talk.

"Are you looking forward to returning to court, Mistress?"

"Yes, but it won't be the same without Anne."

"I am sure you can endure it," George says, reaching for a leather poshote pot. He removes the lid and gulps back the ale, which has been curdled with milk. Nutmeg and cinnamon fragrances fill the cabin as he offers me some.

"No, thank you." I lean tighter to the side curtain.

"Do you have a cold, Master Boleyn?" Agnes asks.

"No, I am trying to keep one at bay." He frowns, then nudges me. "Why will you not speak with me, Mistress?"

"I'm fine, George," I reply, trying to feign innocence, as if he doesn't know what the problem is. He can't have forgotten the kiss already. I cover my velvet purse with both hands, just to make sure the ring is still there. When I get the opportunity, and when George isn't looking, I'll transfer it onto my middle finger.

"Have it your way." He sniffs, then tucks the poshote down near his feet. The silence is deafening as I stare out the window, looking at a family of deer in a nearby field. George watches them, too.

"They would make for good sport, if His Majesty were here." He nudges me, and I give him a whisper of a smile.

The dappled, early spring sunlight flickers through the trees, and all we can hear is the intermittent chirping of birds and the thudding of the horses' hooves against the frosted ground. We pass other travellers on horseback and I hear Anne's father in conversation with several of them. He passes pleasantries with a rider in court livery, who doffs his cap as our litter passes. George leans out of the window to see who it is.

"Looks like a messenger with dispatches from court." He sinks back into his seat. "I heard him mention Penshurst to Father."

"Why did the messenger not give the dispatch to your father?" I ask.

"It is obviously not meant for him. It may be that the king wants to visit for hunting, and is letting the servants know so they can prepare for his arrival."

"How often does the king visit Penshurst?"

"Not as often as he once did during its previous ownership."

"Does the king come to Hever?"

"No, never."

"Not even because of his relationship with Mary?" Should I have mentioned that in earshot of the driver? With him sitting upfront, with the clopping of horses' hooves, he'd not be in a position to overhear quiet conversation. Come to think of it, with Agnes snoring opposite us, she'll not have heard me, either. "Not one single visit — even before she was pregnant?"

"Not one," George replies.

How odd. I thought the king would have pursued Mary at Hever, out of sight of his courtiers. Perhaps with the labyrinth of passageways and many small chambers at Greenwich, or at Richmond, and with a handful of loyal men of his privy chambers, the clandestine meetings might have been easier to arrange.

I don't want to think about Mary and the king. She is safe and secure at home with her family, and the birth of her impending child will be a blessing for them. One which I hope they will accept as a Carey, whether it is or not.

"You know, George —" I incline my head towards his — "it doesn't matter if the king doesn't recognise the child." He looks at me, his brows furrowed. "Mary will be the happiest of all when that baby is cradled in her arms. I'm sure being a parent will make her the kindest and gentlest of mothers."

"And what about you?" He shuffles in his seat to get a better look at me. "Will you marry and be a mother?"

"I don't know, especially now that —"

Thomas Boleyn shouts to the driver. "We shall stop shortly at the next tavern."

"Yes, sir," the driver shouts back.

On the other side of the litter, Robert Cranewell reins his horse closer to us. He smiles in at me. "Mistress Wickers, it will not be long before we can stop to refresh ourselves and eat."

"Thank you, Robert." I return his smile, and pull the furs I borrowed from Anne around me for warmth. He is still a young man, probably around twenty-five years of age. With Cranewell being a 'Robert', I'm naturally reminded of Rob, and the trouble he got me into with Professor Marshall when he insisted I bring him through the portal. Thankfully he was dragged back home to the twenty-first century. Sometimes I miss him, but as I glance at George, I realise I'm content enough being here beside him.

"I am famished!" Agnes says, rubbing her stomach. "I could do with some cheese and bread, and a good drink."

George smiles at her. "The tavern is not too far from here, where Father and I always stop for refreshment."

Agnes is clearly excited about serving me at court, but the whole scenario makes me feel uneasy.

"You know, you never finished answering me," George says.

Agnes sees my discomfort. "Are you hungry, Mistress?"

"Yes, but you mustn't worry about me, Agnes. I am of the same status as you. I'm not titled, and not from an important family."

"You are important to me," George whispers, leaning closer. I don't show it but my heart melts. I can't stay angry with him for long. "And," he adds, "you are a firm friend of my sister."

"That is true, but my connection to you, your sister, and family will not make me important in the eyes of the king and his courtiers."

"Wait and see." He smiles. "Besides, Anne has told me you have quite a fortune in your own right."

I sigh. If only he knew that twenty-first century currency rates and inflation bear no resemblance to Tudor coinage. My meagre student loan would be worth millions in their world.

After a while, Sir Thomas, and Robert Cranewell trot on past us again. Within what seems like an hour or so of travelling, the litter grinds to a halt outside the tavern, allowing us all time to rest, and to water and feed the horses. Sir Thomas opens the door and offers me his hand.

"Mistress Wickers, how do you fare?"

"Very well, sir, although I would be grateful to relieve myself and have some food." I straighten my crumpled skirts as George helps Agnes to the ground.

"Agnes, you go with Mistress Wickers and I shall go with my father and Robert."

"Yes, Master George," Agnes replies, rather shyly.

She walks in front of me and leads me through the inn, which is dimly lit with many candles. Weary travellers' repose in wooden settles, and on benches and stools in front of tables soaked in stale wine and spilt milk. We find a serving woman who kindly directs us to the privy. I'm relieved I've avoided the stench of the communal pits. I suppose it's better than going behind a tree. Poor Agnes is in a bit of a state.

"What's wrong?"

"It's my monthly courses," she says, releasing a long sigh. "My fluttering rags need changing."

"What do you mean?"

"You know, Mistress — my wallops, because of the bleeding."

All I can do is nod. Her period, or courses, as she calls them. The poor woman needs to change her 'rags'. I find it fascinating how women of this era cope with menstruation. I'm lucky, as my contraceptive implant stops me from bleeding each month — a blessing with all my time-travelling escapades.

"I do not suffer with monthly courses," I say.

Agnes stares at me, then at my belly. "But … you are not with child!"

"No, I'm not." Should I explain? Have I said too much already? "I just don't bleed, and haven't for some time."

Her mouth opens, then closes. She frowns and shakes her head. "I wish I did not!" She leads the way into the privy, which appears to be a wooden row of boxes, built with a pit underneath, where all the waste drops into. I've visited some primitive toilets at summer music festivals and … well, some smells can't be unsmelled. This has the same feel, a version of a garderobe — not exactly luxurious but it does the job. I turn my head as Agnes enlightens me that most women wear a simple girdle belt, which is made from fine Holland linen and tied at the sides, like tie-sided knickers, I suppose. I can't help giggling.

"What is it?" she asks in her country tone.

"Nothing," I say, thinking of the gaudy Ann Summers' tie-sided knickers my sister has sold in her time as a sales rep.

Agnes appears to have sorted herself out. Now she stands there, still talking to me while I'm sat on the privy, trying to have a wee. The woman has no sense of decorum, nor is she aware she might be invading my personal space.

I laugh with embarrassment. She looks at me, her expression strange. I straighten my skirts and wish there was somewhere I could wash my hands. This is when I miss the modern conveniences of home.

"Mistress, would you mind if I ride upfront with the driver for the rest of the journey? He's an old friend of my family and it will be nice to have a chat before we arrive at court."

"Of course not, Agnes." What else can I say? I can't deny her time with a family friend, can I?

As I lead the way back inside, I push away the thought that I'll be alone with George for the rest of the journey. Everything will be fine. I can handle him — I hope.

"Mistress wait for me!" she calls as I duck through the back door. She thanks the serving girl and, as we walk through the stuffy small rooms full of sweaty weary bodies, I see that George and Thomas Boleyn have secured the best table, and have already been served their refreshments. George stands when he sees me.

"Come sit with Father and I."

I nod and pull my skirts in as I struggle to slide into the settle, next to Sir Thomas. George sits opposite me and tucks into a chunk of bread and cheese. Agnes sits next to Master Cranewell, and nibbles on a morsel of bread between sips of wine.

"Here, some wine," Sir Thomas urges, passing me an empty goblet and a flagon of the red beverage. "The journey will soon be over — after all, we left this morning. We are nearing Blackheath, and Greenwich is not so far from there. We may well reach Greenwich at dawn."

"Dawn, Sir Thomas?" This must mean he is expecting me to sleep in the litter with George as we travel overnight. I can't possibly do that! What made me think the journey would be like jumping in a car? How stupid am I? Heat rises in my cheeks, made worse by George noticing my embarrassment.

"Beth, trust me —" he smirks — "I am here to protect your honour."

"All will be well, Mistress Wickers. Why do you think Robert and I flank the litter?" He smiles reassuringly. "There are few robbers on the roads this time of year."

"Is Blackheath not far from where you come from?" George asks, chewing on a mouthful of crusty bread.

"Erm, not far, George." I half-smile, flicking him a look in the hope the questioning won't go any further.

"Father, we could call on the Wickers, could we not?" he says.

"No, we have no time for that — the king has summoned me, and we cannot have him waiting."

Common folk sitting adjacent to our table overhear Sir Thomas and stare at him as we get up.

"Sir, you know the king of England?" one of them dares to ask as we pass his table.

"Yes, I'm the king's ambassador. My name is Boleyn. Sir Thomas Boleyn."

The man looks gobsmacked, eyeing Thomas's fine clothes and sword. He grabs Thomas's arm. "Would you mind taking a petition to the king?"

Thomas looks at the hand on his arm, then at the man. "Certainly not, my dear man." While he is being polite, his face is puce with impatience. "I am afraid, though, that I have no time to deal with your business." The man shrivels back onto his stool. "But, if you have a written petition, I could pass it onto Cardinal Wolsey."

As I watch him converse with this stranger, it dawns on me that Sir Thomas Boleyn is not the Machiavellian character history has so often painted him. He's gracious, compassionate, and always willing to help others where he can. The man pulls a folded parchment out of the bag hanging from his belt and hands it over.

"Thank you, sir." The man bows.

With that, Thomas ducks through the doorway and out into the early evening light with his entourage following. He unfolds the parchment and scans the childlike writing, then folds it back up and stuffs it into a leather saddlebag on his horse.

"What was that all about?" George asks.

"A dispute the man wants resolved over some boundaries of neighbouring land."

"Can you not deal with it?"

"It is not in my jurisdiction — Wolsey is the best man for the job." He tugs his leather gloves back on while Robert Cranewell holds his horse. Then he calls up to our ever-patient driver. "Get George and the ladies to Greenwich as soon as you can. I want us to be there by dawn."

"Yes, m'lord." The driver jumps down from his position to help Agnes onto the seat beside him.

George takes my hand to assist me into the litter. My heart flutters as I glide across the seat to a spot on the far side. Heat flushes through my face, and George must notice as he slides in next to me and slams the door shut. I edge away, trying not to give him any encouragement.

The horses trot off, their hoofs thudding against the dirt and grit, as Robert Cranewell and Sir Thomas ride ahead. A moment later, the litter jolts and I find myself hurled against George, who chuckles brazenly at me.

"See, you are sat where you are meant, are you not?" He embraces his opportunity and pulls me close.

"George, no!" I try to push myself away from him, but his hold is too strong.

"Beth, what hurt would it do?" He looks down at me with those dark, mesmerising eyes, which twinkle with elation.

"Look, you must stop this." I push against his chest, and he releases his grip a little and stares at me with his puppy-dog eyes.

"Why must I? You know how I feel, I've made no secret of it."

"But it's wrong." My nostrils flare. "You are now engaged to be married."

"Ah, but betrothed is not married," he says, chuckling. "It's a long way from bended knee to the altar, you know."

"That is as maybe —" my shoulders slump — "but I don't want to get on the wrong side of Jane Parker. She barely knows me."

"I wish she barely knew me!" he says.

I glare at him. "Don't be so mean!"

"There you go again, always chiding me." He laughs. "You are worse than Anne."

I take the opportunity to break free to sit on the opposite seat. Being able to look straight at him makes me feel more comfortable, even though his striking looks are more dangerous head-on as he leans towards me, chattering on.

For the rest of the journey, I'm more relaxed. We discuss everything, including his interest in theology — he's definitely a Lutheran. He enthuses about Thomas Wyatt's poetry, and a manuscript he and Tom are compiling. I listen as he shares his hopes and dreams for the future and his ambitions for his family.

"Why do you not talk of your impending wedding?"

"It is a long way off — there will be time for all that soon enough."

"Have you spent any time with Jane? Alone, I mean?"

"Not really, we have only exchanged pleasantries."

"What do you think of her … really?"

"She has nothing in particular to commend her." He sighs. "She is not like *you*."

I sit up. "Whatever do you mean?"

"I doubt I could talk to her as I talk with you or Anne." He grins. "She does not discuss politics, and says little on religion, although I think she supports the old faith."

"You mean she is probably a Catholic?"

"Undoubtedly."

"Perhaps, George, you could educate her."

"In more ways than one!" He chuckles.

"George!"

"Well, she is most certainly a virgin. It won't be like putting my person in a grizzled-up leather bag — more like a silk purse!"

I can't believe he just said that.

"Stop looking at me like that — it was a joke!"

"With your humour, George, I feel sorry for the young woman."

"I don't know what you mean!" He laughs again.

"How do you get away with that kind of talk at court?"

"I don't." He smiles. "I am well-behaved at court."

"Really?"

"You have seen me. As the king's page, I am diplomatic, courteous, and gracious."

"I suppose if you weren't, the king would not have you in his service."

"Indeed not."

Dappled twilight streams through the windows, and sparrows swoop over the fields in search of a cosy roost, even though the early spring air is damp, and the mist is closing in. The creeping cold makes me shiver and I pull the fur rug over my lap.

"Talking of diplomacy, what is our commission at court?"

"You heard what my father said." He nods at the window. "He wants us to keep the king's mind on Mary. With Henry's bed cold, we cannot allow others to parade their daughters under the king's nose."

"But your father didn't want Mary to be his mistress in the first place."

"You are right, he didn't, but since Mary has secured that position, she needs to keep it."

I am struck be a sudden thought. "I hope your father does not expect *me* to impress the king?"

"You will make a profound impression at court, if you stay there long enough. I know it."

"I am not of the disposition to divert or beguile a king!"

George squeezes my hand. "Beth, you will enchant him. I've seen him captivated by you before!"

I make no reply. Surely that can't be true. This commission is ramping up my anxiety. I hope the Boleyns don't expect me to sleep with the king. No, Sir Thomas wouldn't expect that. After all, he has been against Mary's affair from the beginning and, no doubt, when Henry's desires rest upon Anne, it's highly likely her father will be against that relationship, too.

I look out the window, hardly able to believe I'm in this situation. A part of me wants to order the litter to turn around and head back to Hever, so I can run through the portal and go home. I twist the 'AB' ring on my finger. "Do you think he likes me?"

"What are you worried about?" George grabs my hand this time and leans closer. "You are lovely, dear Elizabeth — why would the king not like you?"

"Is the king not fickle when it comes to the opposite sex?"

"No, not when he has been married to the queen for nearly twenty years. The king of France has had many more mistresses than Henry."

"I think the king likes to be in love."

George stares at me. "You do? How so?"

"He was raised by women and has lived with women most of his life. He is adored by women."

George nods. "That is true."

"So, it is obvious that the king might be infatuated with the idea of being 'in love'."

"Women love men of power."

"Men just love power."

George gets up and sits beside me. "You have a funny way of looking at things, Mistress Wickers." He pulls the fur coverlet over our laps and we lean closer together, like old friends.

After what seems like hours, I'm jolted from my sleep by the wheels of the litter clashing against stones. I rub my eyes and realise I've had my head on George's chest, snuggled against him — his arm about my shoulders. I jolt upright, pulling the fur tighter around me.

"Why are you moving?" His brows knit together. "You looked so peaceful sleeping against me."

"It's too intimate — I don't mean to encourage you." I shiver, and he notices.

"Look at you. Now you have moved, you're cold." He pats his doublet. "Come here and cuddle against me — no one can see — we aren't doing any harm." He looks at me through lowered lashes. "Come on — go back to sleep." I look at him rather sheepishly. "There is no reason to be shy. Not now."

"I suppose not," I say, closing my eyes as I lean in against him once more. Between his cosy heat and the gentle rocking of the litter, it's not long before I sink into a comfortable slumber.

# Twenty-Two

### Greenwich Palace

My heart flutters when I lean out of the litter window and see the sprawling, turreted palace of Greenwich come into view. It's the king's pleasure palace and my jaw drops as we roll through its gates.

The entrance is guarded by liveried men, just as Richmond was. Our driver halts the horses, and I hear Sir Thomas talking to the gatekeeper who, from his response, obviously recognises him. The sun is rising on the horizon and the stacked silhouette of the red-bricked turrets and chimneys takes shape through the early-morning mist from the river.

Sir Thomas glances at me and explains who I am. George remains sitting beside me, waiting for us all to be ushered through the gates.

"Are you catching flies?" he asks, chuckling at my open mouth.

"No, but it's my first time here," I reply, my gaze following the woody smoke wafting into the air.

The driver takes us forward and we stop in the cobbled courtyard. Sir Thomas dismounts, pats his horse, and passes the reins to Master Robert, who leads both animals away to the stable block. "George, show the ladies to the apartments," Sir Thomas says after opening the litter door, "then take Mistress Wickers to the queen."

"Yes, sir." George alights and takes my hand as I step down. Agnes follows on behind us. He leads the way towards the Boleyn chambers allotted to us by the Comptroller of the Household.

"We Boleyns are on the rise," he whispers. "The king has given our family new lodgings here, which are better than the last."

I have an adjoining room to Sir Thomas, and George's apartment is closer to the king's private apartments, so he is only a moment's call away when needed.

George waits outside as Agnes helps me freshen up and change into a gown of black damask, a favourite fabric of the queen. Agnes dabs her fingers against my neck, planting drops of rosewater onto my skin, the sweet-smelling scent filling my nostrils.

"There, Mistress," she says, viewing her handiwork, "you look fit for a queen."

George grins as I come out of the chamber. "You look adequate, I suppose."

Agnes frowns at him and scurries back into the rooms as the servants arrive with the rest of my trunks.

"George, you always know exactly what to say to make a lady feel good about herself."

"Sorry, my lady. I promise I will be on my best behaviour."

I roll my eyes, straighten my back, and lift my chin, remembering who I am representing. He escorts me through the galleries and rooms, which are bright and welcoming. Rich tapestries adorn the walls, and the decoration is spectacular, if not a bit gaudy. Fine walnut furniture graces all the chambers as we pass their open doors, and Turkish carpets cover the rush-matted floors. George leads me up the stairs of the donjon to the door of the queen's apartments, where he gives my name to the usher, who then announces me.

"You will do well," he whispers, backing away.

My breath is shaky as I watch him disappear down the stairs. Now, suddenly, I am on my own. My heart is in my mouth as I enter this hallowed room, hoping the queen will be as pleasant and welcoming as she has been previously. Butterflies fill my stomach as I approach Her Majesty. I don't feel so confident here without Anne. Panic surges and I fear my senses will be overwhelmed, but as Queen Katharine looks up from her sewing, my fears disappear at the warmth in her smile.

"Welcome, Mistress Elizabeth," she says, extending her hand to be kissed.

The rooms are dark, with oak-panelled walls decorated with grandiose friezes, and painted leatherwork embellishing the ceilings. The heady fumes of burning beeswax candles mixed with incense fills the room — probably the reason for Katharine's ladies-in-waiting standing in an obedient stupor.

The queen is dressed in rich damask, the colour of midnight, with a black velvet bonnet in the style of her favourite gable shape — a traditional English style, which she has long since adopted and made her own. Her face looks worn, but her expression is cheerfulness itself, and I catch a hint of her greying chestnut hair peaking from under her hood.

As I rise from my curtsy, I feel a little out of place because all the maids and ladies are dressed in a similar style to Katharine, and I wonder if the queen will object to me wearing gowns made in the French style — gowns which Anne has given me. She looks me up and down but being the paragon of grace that she is, she says nothing before turning to the Countess of Salisbury.

"You remember Mistress Wickers, the Mistress Anne Boleyn's companion?"

"Yes, Your Grace." The countess looks at me and half-smiles. "You are a delightful young woman, but your manners are so foreign to me." She blinks and remains silent, as if waiting for the queen to agree with her.

"Mistress Elizabeth —" the queen gives me her full attention — "you will soon fall back into the routine of court. It is a great pity that your mistress and friend could not accompany you, but I have no doubt that Wolsey will relent on Mistress Anne's banishment once William Carey's child has been delivered."

"I expect so, and hope so, Your Majesty."

The queen nods, then crosses her hands. "Mistress Parker," she calls to the other side of the chamber, "make friends with Mistress Wickers. She will need to be chaperoned."

My heart races when Jane Parker scurries across the rush-covered floor to greet me. As she approaches, I wonder if she is this strange and dangerous woman history has painted. Maybe I'm being unfair to her. She's a young woman of about nineteen, with mousy-brown hair and light-blue eyes. Her gown is a natural 'sheep' colour that blends well with her fair skin tone. As far as I recall, she has not been here for too long and is yet to learn of the rewards, pleasures, and dangers of a public life in court.

She blinks at me, then smiles demurely. "Mistress Wickers, I am Jane Parker. I believe you are the ward of my future father-in-law, Sir Thomas Boleyn?"

"Not his ward, Mistress Parker — rather, a companion to his younger daughter, Anne." I force a smile.

"I see." She nods once. "We are around the same age, I think?"

"I am a couple of years older."

"I was born in Norfolk, and am the daughter of Lord Morley. It is he who has made the match for me with George. He wishes me to marry into the Boleyn family." From the way I have seen her obsess over George — watch over his every move and fawn over him — I wonder if it is she who has forced her father to make the match.

"The Boleyns are an up-and-coming family," I say.

"And well-educated," she adds. "Not to mention that both Mary and George are very handsome." She blushes.

"You don't think Anne attractive?"

There is a pause before she answers. "Anne is truly wondrous!" I can't believe that she's actually gushing. "Not beautiful like her sister, but she is clever, witty, and intelligent."

This startles me — not what I was expecting to hear at all. I thought she would hate Anne but, no, she gives me a totally different interpretation of their relationship which, on Jane's part, appears to be one of great admiration.

A short while later, we sit at the far end of the long walnut table in the Great Hall at Greenwich Palace. I admire the tapestries with their imposing murals, and the tall, ornate oriel window that affords stunning views over the river. So much to take in. I marvel at the brightly painted yellow ceiling, noticing the eavesdroppers carved into the hammer beams. What conversations have they been privy to?

Jane nudges me but I pretend to ignore the courtiers nearby. George is amongst them and he stares way too long to be appropriate. One of the young men notices and wanders over to us.

"Ladies." He bows, doffing his cap. "Who might you be?" Tall and bearded, his eyes sparkle as he takes us in. He's certainly good-looking and knows it.

"Master Wyatt, you jest with me," Jane says, her hand at her neck. "You know who I am. You are friends with my brother, Henry Parker."

"I was teasing you, Jane," he says, laying his lute on the table. "It's your friend I do not know."

"Mistress Wickers, I would like you to meet Thomas Wyatt — musician, poet, and friend of the Boleyns."

I offer Thomas my hand and he gestures for me to remain seated.

"Master Wyatt, I have heard much about you from the Lady Anne."

"Only good things, I hope?"

"Yes, sir — your families have been good friends for many a year."

"It is true, I have known the Lady Anne for a long time." He chuckles.

"Ah, yes, but how well?" a man of around the same age pipes up from behind him. The group stifle their laughter. Jane blushes.

"My mistress and friend would not like to be talked about so," I say, letting him know by my tone that I'm not impressed. "It is not her fault she has been banished from court."

"Ah, I heard about that." Wyatt gathers himself. "All because of that Percy fellow. And now he, too, is banished to Northumberland. Pity that."

More laughter follows his blatant sarcasm.

"Tom, I wish you would not discuss my sister's private matters so," George says, his annoyance evident that Thomas would make such a delicate matter public.

"No doubt your sister will be back at court to tease us all before long, eh, George?" He winks at the group of courtiers behind him. "While we are waiting, I have composed a poem for her."

Jane continues to stare at George, but he won't meet her gaze, which makes him look on me all the more.

"Another poem?" he asks, and the men laugh.

"There's a surprise," Sir Francis Bryan says. He appears rakish, which is why his nickname around court is the Vicar of Hell.

Tom Wyatt looks diffidently at them, pulls out a small piece of vellum from his doublet, and clears his throat. "This one is different. Special, I tell you." He looks at me as I take a sip of wine, probably hoping he will impress me enough that I will write back to Anne and confide in her all he has written.

"Come on then, Tom, let's hear it."

"It's called 'Forget Not Yet'."

His voice has a musical tone, and it isn't surprising that many of the ladies of court are attracted to him. Some may consider him favourably if he shows any interest in them, possibly even go to bed with him, but as he is a married man, I know Anne will never entertain him. She told me she liked him, but not in *that* way.

George told me before how Tom is a good friend of the family — friends since childhood, and neighbours in Kent. Also, he shared that Anne was a confidant of Margaret, Tom's sister. I, of course, was already aware of this, but could not let on that I knew of Tom through my studies.

Anne would never waste her time on him, no matter how charming he is. She confided in me that whenever she was in his company, she rejected all his overtures, and there's no reason why she wouldn't continue to do so on her return to court. Tom, however, is persistent. As he reads out his poem, it's obvious who he has written it for. He probably wants me to hear it, knowing I am a friend of Anne's and that I would likely write to Anne to let her know that Thomas Wyatt still pines for her.

"Forget not yet the tried intent
Of such a truth as I have meant;
My great travail so gladly spent,
Forget not yet.
Forget not yet the great assays,
The cruel wrong, the scornful ways;
The painful patience in denials,
Forget not yet.
Forget not then thine own approved,
That which so long hath thee so loved,
Whose steadfast faith yet never moved;
Forget not this."

The small group of men around the end of the table applaud, crying 'bravo!', but Tom is looking to me for my reaction.

"What did you think of it, Mistress?"

"I liked it very well — but do you think Mistress Anne would be rather put out to be the subject of your poetry?"

"I rather hope she will enjoy being the centre of my attentions."

"Tom," George says, patting him on the shoulder, "my sister is not for the taking, nor the sport, for she will never go with a married man."

"You can't blame me for trying." He sniffs, folding the parchment, then stuffs it back into his doublet.

George chuckles. "I admire your persistence, Tom." He stares at me and my face grows hot.

Jane notices, much to her chagrin. "George does not talk to me!" she moans, brushing her skirts.

"You know how men can be when they are with their friends." I smile to reassure her. "They forgo affection to their betrothed in public."

"Why?" Her face is red, and she looks like she is about to burst into tears.

"They have a reputation to uphold." I rub her arm. "To show affection to you might be seen as a weakness."

"Yes, but I have seen the way he looks at you."

"Whatever do you mean?"

"He looks at you as if you are his betrothed."

"Come, Jane, you are mistaken — we are just friends." I look back over at George, who is still talking to Tom Wyatt and Francis Bryan. They seem engrossed in conversation and do not notice as Jane gets up, her arm outstretched towards me.

"Come on, Mistress Elizabeth, I do not want to listen to any more trifles. You have a gown fitting with Master Skutt and Master Cotton." With that, she defiantly grabs my hand and takes me towards a part of the palace I've not been to before.

She knocks before we enter the tailors' workrooms at the back of the palace. I see Agnes has already delivered the bolts of midnight-blue velvet fabric and the yellow-gold satin tissue Lady Boleyn gave me as a present for New Year. They sit on the workbench.

"These are beautiful satins and velvets," the tailor says, stroking the bolts of cloth. "My name is Master Cotton. I am Master Skutt's apprentice." He's a tall, lanky man, with broad shoulders, dark hair, and an extremely long beard for his age. His dark-brown eyes are mysterious and brooding, yet he has a soft-spoken manner. "We have copied the kirtle you sent to us for fit and have made a pattern in buckram of both the kirtle and an overgown."

"Already, Master Cotton?"

"Please call me Paul." He smiles, leading me over to two mannequins, which I presume are dressed with my toiles.

An older man, shorter and stouter, turns to me from another bench, shears in hand. "Mistress Wickers, we have been expecting you." He lays down the shears and looks me up and down. "I see you are dressed in the French mode." He frowns. "We shall need to change that."

"This is a gown Mistress Anne Boleyn gave me, sir."

"Well, that explains it," he says, his eyes lighting up with his smile "I am the Master tailor here. My name is John Skutt."

"Are these your permanent rooms?"

"No, we trade in the city, but when we are called to court to fulfil any requirements of the king or court, we come here." He walks over to the mannequins and instructs Master Cotton to take the patterns — toiles, as I'd call them in modern terms — from their display in order to fit them on me.

"Take your maid servant with you, behind that curtain there, then we can pin you into the pattern to see the fit."

Jane huffs, not happy to be called my maid, but follows me behind the curtain anyway, as Master Cotton hands the patterns through to her. Once I have stripped down to my shift, she helps me into the heavy buckram kirtle and I step out into the middle of the room, where the tailor and his assistant are waiting.

They bustle around me, pins in their mouths, pinching seams together where there is gaping, marking how high the neckline should be with a piece of chalk, then standing back and inspecting their handiwork.

"What say you, Master Cotton?" Skutt taps his bottom lip with his forefinger.

"I think the neckline needs a slight raising," he replies, both eyebrows arched, "then the gown will sit better over her bosom."

Heat fills my cheeks as I stand before them.

"Yes, Paul, the gown must be new-bodied. You are right to suggest altering the neckline. It is our quest to get the lady's clothes to fit close and smooth." He folds his arms and nods. "And no cleavage!"

Paul smirks. "We did not have this trouble of gaping necklines with the larger ladies like Lady Guildford and Mistress Seymour when they first arrived."

I hold my tongue as they discuss my body as if I'm not here.

"A lady's attributes must be softly rounded in such a close-fitting dress," the master tailor replies, which has heat rushing to my cheeks again. "Turn around, Mistress Wickers."

I do as I'm told. Master Skutt is on his knees, tugging at the pattern's train.

Master Cotton puts his rough hand on my shoulder, a bevy of pins protruding from his mouth. "Master Skutt, do you think the train needs to be longer?" I try not to laugh at his garbled words. He leans around to me. "Would you like a longer train, Mistress?"

"I put myself in your hands, gentlemen. Whatever you think would suit." More tugging ensues, with pinching and pinning of the thick unbleached linen as the pattern of the gown is put over the top of the kirtle.

"See," Master Cotton says, as his senior pins the bodice's neckline just under the neckline of the kirtle, "raising the neckline was the perfect move." He beams, admiring my gently swelling cleavage. "You have taught me well, sir."

"That I have." Skutt leans back and admires their work, then walks around me, looking me up and down, inspecting the pinning with an eagle eye. "I think that is all we need, Mistress Wickers. Will you trust me with the cloth you have given us?" He rubs his hands together and glances at Master Cotton.

"Yes, sir. I am very happy." I look over my shoulder at the masses of buckram laid out behind me, which circles me in a beautiful train.

# ❧ Twenty-Three ☙

As Jane and I follow the queen's entourage, all she can do is witter on about George. We have become friends, of sorts. At times she can be chatty, is always observant, but is prone to gossip. The fabric of her clothes are plain, usually dark colours in wool or damask, and her jewels are simple. Her air can be haughty when she has an opinion to voice, which I put down to being a follower of the old faith and a staunch supporter of Queen Katharine. Her main topics of conversation are the queen, other courtiers' wrongdoings, and George Boleyn. It's usually George this, George that — I wish she would shut up about him.

As we tiptoe across the gravel, towards the tiltyard, I look back at the towering donjon that houses the royal apartments. The palace is spectacular — I have to pinch myself at times to believe I'm here — and my mood plummets when I consider that all this splendour will be turned to rubble and lost to history.

"The king was born here," Jane says as she walks beside me. It is a welcome change for her to discuss someone other than George, although I can't blame her — all the time she's looking to see where he is sat, he's with Thomas Wyatt, Francis Bryan, and William Compton. The men are laughing together, waiting to see who will be advanced because of their deeds in the tournament.

"Why is George not taking part today?" she asks me.

"I really don't know."

"He would make such a chivalrous knight," she says. "I would like him to wear my favours one day." She's pained that she hasn't been given the opportunity to see her betrothed in a suit of shining armour. I understand where she's coming from — I'd like to see George in some armour, too. We take our places in the royal stand, a bench along from the queen, who sits with her closest ladies-in-waiting admiring the men as they come out on their chargers.

A hush descends and all we can hear is the rattling of armour and the thudding of hooves in the thick mud as the men who are to take part in the joust are introduced. Jane and I are thrilled to be soaking in the atmosphere of the tournament, but I am heartbroken that Anne cannot be here to enjoy it.

There is no doubt about it, Henry VIII is a superb athlete, and as we sit in the royal box in anticipation of who is to ride in the lists, we are on the edge of our seats waiting on the informal event to begin.

The king's horse is without trappings, which appears to please Queen Katharine, who looks relaxed watching her husband as he enters the yard.

He surveys the crowd, spots for his wife, and nods to her. Then he looks along our row. Who is he searching for? Anne? Surely not. Not Mary, anyway, as he must know she's in confinement at Hever.

His gaze flickers to Jane, then rests upon me. He lingers, watching me for what seems like an eternity, then smiles. I nod back, so as not to draw too much attention to myself, but the queen glances down the row to see who her husband has spotted. I avert my eyes, as if what just happened didn't occur.

Cheers rise from the crowd as Henry parades before us all. The reason for the display is so the king can show off the new armour he's had made to his own design and fashion, such as no armorer has crafted before. The joust has been ordered to test its design, making sure it is fit for purpose and is money well spent. The Lord Marquis of Dorset, the Earl of Dorset, and the Earl of Surrey are appointed on foot.

The crowd watches transfixed as the king comes to one end of the tilt and the Duke of Suffolk to the other. The king looks towards the crowd, sucking in their cheers of approval. Then we see a gentleman say something to the duke, Charles Brandon.

"Sir, the king is come to the end of the tilt."

"I see him not," says the duke, "by my faith, for my headpiece blocks my sight." With these words, God knows by what chance, the lord Marquis delivers the king a lance, the visor of his headpiece being up and not down or fastened, so his face is quite naked and open to the elements.

"Sir, the king is coming," the gentleman says to the duke. We all watch in fear as the king comes thundering towards Brandon at full pelt — but his visor is still up. Heavens, this won't be good.

The crowd holds its breath, and I shiver in the freezing March weather, pulling my furs about me as the wind chill hits. The duke sets forward at a great gallop, thundering over the mud, with sticky residue flying up as the horse charges and the duke holds fast in his saddle, his lance out. And the king, likewise, unadvisedly continues in the same fashion towards the duke. Then, when the crowd realises the king's face is still bare, pandemonium erupts, with everyone shouting and hollering in the hope that he will stop.

"Hold! Hold! Your Majesty, *hold!*"

The Duke of Suffolk appears to neither see nor hear, and the king doesn't flip his visor down. It must be a mistake.

The lance makes a loud *crack* as it impacts with the gap in the king's headpiece and splinters fly in every direction. I catch my breath and hold my hand out to touch Jane's arm as we see the king fall. Copious amounts of blood spout from around his eye and people come running from every direction to assist him as his body slams into the muddy ground.

All I can hear are screams of terror from onlookers. In that split second, it looks like the duke has struck the king on the brow, right under the guard of the headpiece — on the skull cap or basinet piece to which the barbette is hinged for strength and safety, the part no armorer takes heed of, for it is always covered by the visor, barbette, and volant piece, and thus that piece is so protected that it takes no weight.

The duke's lance has broken into shards and has pushed the king's visor or barbette so far back with the counter blow that the king's headpiece is full of splinters. Jane averts her eyes, as do I, until we see Queen Katharine race down the steps of the royal box, lifting her skirts in order to reach her husband quicker.

We follow on behind, as a crowd encircles the king. Sir Thomas Boleyn, George, the queen, and many other courtiers surround him. The Duke of Suffolk is now off his horse and shouting, "No! No! No!"

The armorers will be blamed for this, even though the king had forgotten his visor, and so will the lord Marquise for delivering the blow when Henry's face was exposed.

The duke disarms as he attends the king, his face ashen, probably wondering how much damage he has done, but the king is pulled up, and Suffolk grabs his head in each hand as he tries to access the damage at close range. The king allows him to study his eye and tries to make an encouraging smile for his best friend.

"I swear that I will never run against you again," Brandon shouts. But if the king had been even a little hurt, his servants would have put the duke in jeopardy.

"No one is to blame but myself, for I intend to show the crowd I have saved myself and my sight." But the crowd gasps when the king falters. Then he straightens and stands before Suffolk, who now grips the king by his shoulders to help his balance.

The queen leans in to mop the blood from her husband's brow to see what damage has been caused.

"My Queen, I am well." The linen handkerchief reddens with his blood. "I shall ride again!" Then he calls his armorers, who put all his pieces of armour together and give him a new helmet.

The onlookers return to their positions and the king, much to the queen's dismay, takes up another lance and runs six courses, by which all men can see that their king has taken no hurt, which is a great joy and comfort to all his subjects present. It is a great relief to the queen especially.

As Jane and I take our seats, I turn to her. "He doesn't appear to be seriously hurt, bar some damage to his eye and head, but he seems to have recovered well."

Jane looks vexed, probably concerned more for the emotional well-being of the queen than the king.

---

Tonight, the court is taken by surprise when the king's household make arrangements for him to visit Queen Katharine's bedchamber. When it comes to sleeping with his wife, the king follows a ritual involving a large amount of staff, including an elaborate procession through the corridors that have been cleared and guarded, and I keep my eyes lowered when I see him weaving through the courtiers to the entrance of her rooms. When he sees me standing in her presence chamber, he stops.

"Mistress Wickers." He strokes my cheek, his touch warm and light. "Is it not rather late for you to be up?" He is too familiar with me, but then I forget that he knows who everyone at court is, right down to the lowliest of servants.

"No, Sire. I am here to do the queen's bidding."

"You may go and have some good rest." He watches the rise and fall of my bosom beneath the neckline of my gown.

I can't believe I've just heard him grunt under his breath! This man is no prude. As I watch him step inside the door of her chamber, with his groom in attendance, I don't really want to imagine him undressing. He makes no such display when he visits Mary — she has relayed to me how things go and this visible dramatic entrance at Katharine's apartments is done to provide a diversion to what is really going on in his private life. In my time-travelling adventures, I know him to have bedded Bessie Blount, Mary Carey, and who will be next? This show of pomp and ceremony is in stark contrast to the occasions when he desires privacy when visiting the chambers of his mistresses, or when they are brought in secret to his chambers, for the pleasure of His Grace.

Henry's grooms are charged to remain humble, reverent, secret, and lowly about all tasks, and Mary tells me that two grooms sleep on pallets outside his door and Sir Henry Norris is charged with preventing all other gentlemen from entering the king's chambers. The only time the king is alone is when he orders his grooms out, once his mistress of the moment is procured.

With Norris's assistance, it seems it's not difficult for Henry to admit whomever he pleases into his bed, whenever he wants. But tonight, the king belongs to the queen alone. Whatever secrets his grooms know, they are loyal and never show any surprise when he shows favour to one lady, or another. By the way the king looks at me, I'm hoping I will not be his next target. When I started this adventure, little did I ever imagine that I might be the target of Henry's attentions. I must keep his mind off me at all costs and when and if Anne returns to court, I need to make sure that somehow, I put her in Henry's way, if only to divert his attentions from me.

---

A couple of weeks later, Margery Horsman comes to fetch me when a messenger arrives in the queen's apartments.

"Mistress Wickers, a Master Cotton is here. He is asking you to go to Master Skutt."

"Oh, my new kirtle and gown must be ready!" I say. "Would you accompany me?"

Margery is a young woman of good standing, who has served Queen Katharine for some time. She's petite, not particularly beautiful, but with a cheerful demeanour.

"Let me ask the queen's permission," she replies.

Within minutes, she rushes back from the queen's chamber. "We haven't got much time. The queen wants to go to Mass."

Master Cotton strides ahead as Margery leads me from the queen's apartments into Master Skutt's workroom. The room is full of clutter, fabrics, shears, silk thread, and pots of pins.

"We have your gown and kirtle ready, Mistress Wickers." He directs me to the back of the room, and as he pulls back the curtain, I'm astounded to see the mannequin dressed with my finished kirtle and gown. "We hope that you will be pleased with the design." Margery follows me in behind the curtain. "Please feel free to try it on — we would like to see how it becomes you."

Margery helps me to change into the new gown, and as I step out into the clear expanse of floor, I feel like a queen. Master Skutt and Master Cotton take a sharp intake of breath when they see me. I look down on the midnight-blue velvet, matched with a golden-yellow kirtle and dark-brown fur turned-back sleeves. To say I'm overjoyed would be something of an understatement.

I lift my arm, inspecting all the tiny natural pearls which have been sewn into the fore-sleeves, shimmering in the well-lit room. As I stand here, Master Skutt pulls the train out to show its full effect. He circles me, nodding to Master Cotton, who smiles at their handiwork.

"This is more than adequate," Skutt says. I can't help but stroke the plush silk velvet, feeling its luxurious texture.

"You look incredible," Cotton says, a wry smile curling his lip. He turns to Skutt. "I think this is one of your best creations, sir."

"Are you pleased with our efforts?" Skutt asks me.

"Sir, there are no words to express how exquisite this gown is."

"To finish off this ensemble —" Skutt turns to Master Cotton, who is now reaching for a small box on a shelf above their heads — "we have also created a bonnet, in the design the queen prefers — a gabled English style." With that, Master Skutt opens the box and pulls out a pearl-encrusted gable hood, accentuated with gold and yellow-hued tissue and a rich black velvet. He comes towards me, bonnet in hand, and decorates my coifed head with his incredible creation. Then he hands me a small mirror and what I see takes my breath away. The hood highlights the curvature of my cheekbones and my high forehead and slender neck.

Margery Horsman sighs. "I think the queen will prefer you in this, Mistress Wickers."

"I think she will, too."

---

A couple of days later, I throw myself into preparing for the entertainments and decide that my new gown will be perfect. As the queen leads us out into the Great Hall, Jane and I walk with Margery Horsman. The musicians play their melodious turns, and as we watch the revels, Jane notices George saunter in our direction. He's left Francis Bryan, Will Compton, and William Carey near the king, in case their services are required. He bows directly to me, but before he has the chance to speak, I am shocked to see the king now standing beside him.

Jane and I dip into deep curtsies and my heart is in my mouth as I stare at the king's kid-leather, soft shoes. To my surprise, I feel his forefingers gently lift my chin. He is tall, broad, and magnificent in his suit of red cloth of gold — a confident man in his early to mid-thirties, with an air of grandeur and assurance that royal blood and years of wearing a golden crown has conferred.

"Mistress, there is no need to avert your face from me. For it is such a beautiful face." Surprisingly, he bows in an elegant, courtly fashion that enhances his majestic dignity, even though he shows deference to me.

I sink into a deeper curtsy. The kaleidoscope of colours twirling past us begins to slow, as I realise most of the court's attention is now on me. From the corner of my eye, I see George fixing his gaze on the king, then on me. I feel faint and unsteady on my feet. The king must realise this, as he reaches out for my elbow to steady me.

"You look lovely this evening, Mistress Wickers." He looks at me with a gentle, reassuring smile. "I am pleased to see you in English fashions."

"The gowns that Mistress Boleyn had given me have become a little worn, Sire." My face burns. "Lady Boleyn gave me some bolts of fabric as a New Year gift, and your master tailor has created this gown from them."

"I am glad that my tailors have worked so hard for you." He makes no pretence about surveying my gown from neckline to hem. "You may send me the bill." He looks down at me with such intensity, his blue eyes are piercing. The scent of fresh herbs fills my nostrils as he leans in close to my ear. "I would like you to visit my chambers this evening," he whispers.

My face flushes as my jaw drops. "Your Grace, I am not worthy of such an honour. It would be wrong of me…"

"I shall decide who is in the wrong," he whispers.

"But Your Grace, I can't … erm, I cannot."

"Henry Norris will come to collect you, after the entertainments tonight." I open my mouth to reply, but he stops me with his forefinger on my lips. Our eyes lock. "Now, Mistress Wickers, will you do me the honour of joining me in this dance?"

I want to refuse him, especially in front of George, but no one refuses the king, not even me.

George stares in disbelief. "Your Grace, Mistress Wickers is new to the court and does not know the dance." He tries to hold me back from taking the king's hand, but the king growls at him. I give Henry my hand, bowing my head so he won't see the discomfort, nor the thrill of it in my eyes. One dance, and that would be it. Nothing more.

"Boleyn, you think me not capable of leading this young woman in the dance?"

George shrinks back, his face shocked at the turn of events — I do believe he is jealous!

The king leads me out onto the dance floor. I look back at George, and shrug. Then I glance at Jane Parker. She stares at me, then at George, looking like someone has pierced her heart with a knife. For the moment, George is my dearest friend, but how long it will last, especially after tonight, who knows?

---

Agnes fumbles with the ribbons and cords on my dressing gown as I stand in my chambers, preparing myself to be collected by Henry Norris for my midnight audience with the king.

"Calm down, Agnes!" I squeal. "What's wrong?"

"Mistress, I know it's not my place, but…" Agnes says in her country accent.

"But what?"

"You should not be visiting the king at so late an hour, and on your own, without a chaperone!" She's still fumbling with the turn backs on my brocade sleeves. "What would Sir Thomas say?"

"Sir Thomas is probably well aware of the king's request."

"I doubt it — he would only know if Master George were to say something."

"George will not tell his father," I say. What am I doing? What if he wants to kiss me, touch me, or sleep with me? He can't possibly want *me* in *that* way. Surely not? This isn't about sex, this is about reminding the king of Mary, or indeed arousing his interest in Anne. This is about the Boleyns, not me. My heart leaps when someone bangs at the door, which Agnes goes to answer.

"Is Mistress Wickers there? I need to see her, urgently!" This male voice is insistent.

"Master George — this is highly inappropriate — especially at this late hour!" Agnes argues. "George, you must wait here!"

George doesn't wait, and barges into my bedchamber. "Beth, why is it when I tried to stop you dancing with the king tonight, you ignored me?" His face is pale, his eyes red, as if he's been crying.

"Please, George, you know as well as I do that no lady-in-waiting can refuse the king. You should not have taken my ignoring you as an insult — how can any woman refuse the king?"

I try not to show the panic in my voice as he continues pressing his argument. This isn't how things are meant to be turning out. I could have really messed up the bloody timeline of events by even accepting a dance with the king. Who knows what a butterfly effect this will make? How did I get into this mess? I could just run out into the night, twist the ring and be out of here, out of this whole sorry debacle!

"You could have refused him, especially if my affection for you has meant anything to you!" He whines. "Am I not pleasing to you?"

"You know I adore you!" I wish I didn't have such an honest heart, but I can't help myself, as I blurt out how I feel. "Until that kiss at Hever, I never dreamed that you thought of me in any way beyond the ordinary — up until then, I thought of us as good friends."

He strides over to me. Agnes nervously potters about the bedchamber, folding gowns and tidying things away. Bless her heart, hanging around to protect my modesty and my reputation.

I stiffen, not wanting to give the game away to her, unsure how much she's already overheard.

Mercifully, George takes my hand. "You cannot go to him. Anne would want me to protect you from the king. Look how he has treated my sister Mary — I do not want that for you!"

"George, that is very sweet of you," I say, pulling away from his grasp. "But I can look after myself!"

His eyes are now blazing with anger. "As your friend, and someone who loves you, I forbid you to go to the king." He wrings his hands as he stands before me. "You must not do this."

"Why ever not?"

His face softens. "I do not want the king to hurt you."

"This audience may not even be about *me*," I say. "He might want to ask of news of Mary and her pregnancy. Have you not thought of that?"

"No, I had not." He looks thoughtful.

"It's a possibility, isn't it?" I sigh. "Is this not what your father asked us to do? To keep Mary in the uppermost thoughts of His Grace?"

"Yes, yes — he did."

"Then do not worry." I move closer and embrace him, which startles him. He tries to kiss me, but I pull away.

"I'm sorry," he says, "please forgive me?"

"Do not take advantage of the situation — we are here for your family's sake. But most of all, we are going to do whatever it takes, for Mary and her unborn child."

"I under—" Our conversation ends when we are interrupted by another knock at the door. Agnes rushes to answer it, and George hangs back in the bedchamber, so he won't be seen.

"I have come to fetch Mistress Wickers, on command of the king." It's not difficult to recognise the familiar voice of Henry Norris. I check the bows on my dressing-gown, give a nervous half-smile towards George, and head out to the outer-chamber door where Sir Henry is waiting. I gulp back a ball of nerves as he makes a bow and smiles.

"Mistress, the king is waiting for you."

As I walk alongside Henry Norris down the labyrinth of passageways, past flickering torches, my heart is in my mouth, and my questions to Henry Norris must give my nerves away.

"Have you escorted many ladies to the king's private apartments of a late evening, sir?"

"You must know the king has acquired tastes when it comes to women — but I cannot tell you the king's secrets, my lady."

"Then, sir, how am I to please him?"

"When I introduce you into the king's bedchamber, I can only say that, as a woman, you will know how to please him. He is a man, like any other, after all." He gives me a knowing smile, that of an attendant beyond his years.

My nerves are heightened as I realise that George might be right — what if the king expects me to have intercourse with him? I'm not sure I could do that, even if he is a king.

I'm glad I have my silk slippers on — the soles slap against the flagstone slabs, which are cold and damp. The embers of glowing fires dissipate, their woody fumes lingering in the air. Mist settles on the Thames, as stars illuminate the geometric hedging in the gardens. The palace is quiet, and many courtiers are either in their own beds or ones belonging to their friend's wives. I have no idea what to expect, meeting the king in such a private way, as I've only spent time in his company when he was surrounded by his entourage.

My heart skips as Norris walks in front of me, escorting me through the state apartments. We walk through the state bedroom, which is maintained to impress visiting sovereigns. I gaze at the state bed — a colossal construction with a canopy fifteen-foot-high, hung with gorgeous and expensive tapestries. I can't believe I'm in here.

We walk through a smaller pair of oak doors, guarded by two of the king's privy servants in full green and white livery. Entering the king's innermost sanctum, the air is heavily perfumed with musk and herbs. A small fire crackles in the grate, as Norris and William Compton prepare the room for the king's arrival.

"Please sit, Mistress Wickers." Norris waves towards a chair covered with damask cushions. I do as I'm told, sitting on the edge of the chair, pulling my dressing gown tighter about me. "The king is at his bath — he will be here shortly."

I shouldn't be surprised that Henry has a bath on a regular basis, as I'm aware from the records that he has a Turkish bath at Hampton Court, so he probably has one here, too. I try not to imagine him naked, lying in the sunken bath of hot water and floating rose petals. He's probably having his genitals perfumed with essential oils and rose water, which the Tudors believe is medicinal and wards off infection. Although, I have to say, it's a relief he isn't the morbidly obese king he will later become. His legs are muscular, his chest broad, and I'm about to see and experience them, first-hand.

As I wait, I watch Henry's privy household, his specific attendants of his bedchamber, prepare his bed.

"How many of there are you?" I ask Norris, his key swaying on his blue ribbon as he pulls back the linen sheets.

"Six of us." He smiles, then lies on the bed and rolls across it. "There are always attendants in the king's private bedchamber," he says, somewhat out of breath.

"What are you doing?"

"Checking for assassins with knives!"

"Oh." I grimace. "Where do you and the other servants sleep?"

"Either on this small, wheeled bed pulled out from beneath the royal bed —" he pulls it out a foot or two to show me — "or favoured servants such as myself share the king's bed, when it is required."

"You are very intimate with His Grace, then?"

"Yes, indeed Mistress," he replies, then smiles, as the other servants make the king's bed ready. He sleeps on a pile of eight mattresses. William Compton and Norris lift the sides of each mattress to confirm there are no hidden enemies with daggers lying in wait.

"So, the king has little privacy?"

"I am the king's Groom of the Stool. I guard the king's privacy in his privy apartments. It is my job." He reaches for the badge of office, which is a gold key on a blue ribbon hanging from his neck. "This gives me the ultimate authority to demand that no other keys for the bedchamber be made or allowed.

"How many servants of the bedchamber do you control?" I ask.

"There are a handful of servants here at all times. We prepare his bedchamber when he wakes, for sleep, and if he needs our attendance at night." He says this somewhat sarcastically.

Intrigued, I watch as Norris sprinkles the sheets with holy water and makes the sign of the cross over the bed. William Compton warms Henry's nightshirt before the fire for a few minutes as an owl hoots its goodnight from outside. Other attendants draw the long and heavy drapes across the casements, shutting out the night. Attendants deliver trays of sweetmeats, sliced apricots and asparagus, and place them on a sideboard. Finally, rose petals are scattered across the bed.

"Norris, I shall attend His Grace with his nightgown," Compton says.

"Very well."

Butterflies flutter in my stomach while I watch an attendant light numerous candles about the room with a small taper. The warm glow, mixed with the room's heady, musky scent, creates an intoxicating atmosphere. Perhaps this is the effect Henry is after. I glance over at the servants as they hurry around carrying out their ritual tasks. They keep staring at me, probably assuming that I'm to be the next courtier Henry will bed.

Behind me, large oak doors swing open, and there in a dark red dressing gown, enters Henry VIII. He towers over all of us. I rush to stand and drop in a curtsy at his feet. Norris hands the king a full goblet of red wine.

"Thank you, Norris." Norris bows. "Mistress Wickers, I am delighted to see you."

The king smiles, extending his free hand, which is covered in rings. I stand up and take his hand, then plant a brief kiss on the biggest ring that glitters before me.

"Your Grace."

"Call me Henry. No need for formalities here." He nods. "And I may call you?"

"Elizabeth, Your Grace … erm, I mean, Henry." I pull my dressing gown about me, to cover myself. He notices.

"Do not fear me. I am no rapist, my dear." He shocks me with that remark.

"What makes you think I would consider you in that way?"

"I heard rumours that a certain Boleyn girl thinks me capable — does she?"

"Which Boleyn girl, Sire? Mary, or her sister Anne?"

"Anne. She alleges I forced myself on Mary. George told me. He said that Anne thinks I could not possibly have honourable intentions towards her sister."

"Sire … Henry." I wince. "I believe that Anne thinks you have treated her sister badly, because since she announced her pregnancy, you have ignored her and sent her packing to Hever."

"I see." He frowns. "Does Anne not consider that the child Mary is carrying might be William Carey's?"

"I do not know, Sire." My brows feel heavy as I frown. "She might realise it is a possibility."

He walks over to his bed, tapping the covers. "Come and sit beside me." He smiles. His eyes twinkle in the candlelight, their cobalt blue lighting up his face. His beard is neatly trimmed, and his hair is cut short around his ears in the new fashion. Through the opening of his dressing gown, the neckline of his nightshirt peeps through, with its intricate blackwork stitching around the collar. Short, red chest hair winks at me, but it isn't inviting me in.

"Gentlemen, you may go. I bid you goodnight, and good rest." He waves his attendants away.

"Your Majesty, if you need anything, you only have to call," Norris says, taking a few steps backwards through the open bedchamber doors, closing them firmly behind him.

The king turns to me. "You have no need to fear me." This big, powerful man looks as different as a schoolboy, sat in his night attire, making a humble, earnest plea. "I asked you here, hoping you will take pity on me, for these are unfair slanders laid at my feet." He takes a sip of wine from his goblet, then retrieves a kerchief from his dressing-gown pocket and wipes his lips.

I settle next to him, pulling myself up on the coverlets and furs on his bed, which are covered in rose petals. "Sire, Henry, you are my noble Lord and King, why would I need to pity you?"

"One Boleyn sister think badly of me," he says in an imperious voice. "Mary gave herself willingly to me. I would never force myself upon a lady, especially one I so admire."

"You are ever gracious, my Lord," I say, rolling one of the rose petals between my fingertips.

Henry gets up and sets his drink on the sideboard. "It was amiss of Norris not to offer you some wine… Would you like some?"

"Yes, please, Henry."

He picks up an empty goblet and pours the contents of the jug into it until it's almost full to the brim, then passes it to me.

"Thank you, my Lord." I have to pinch myself, because I'm having trouble believing that I'm sitting all alone with Henry VIII in his private bedchamber. I shake my head in disbelief, then take a sip of the spicy, fruity red wine.

"Would you please implore your mistress that I would never harm a hair on her sister's head? I admire Mary, for her beauty, sensitivity, and grace."

"From what Anne believes, there was more force than fondness between you and Mary."

"I am fond of Mary, but would never do such a thing!" His eyes are blazing. "This affair with Mary, for the time being, has come to an end due to her pregnancy. It has run its course." He plonks back on the bed beside me.

"Anne has pushed Mary for answers for months," I say, tugging at my dressing-gown sleeves. This is a conversation I wasn't expecting. "Besides, all Mary says is that she loves you."

"Does she, indeed?" Henry beams as he takes another sip from his goblet.

"But Anne thinks that your Grace gave Mary no choice." We all know that it's impossible as a woman to refuse the king, otherwise I wouldn't be sat here. Oh God, Anne is going to kill me for being so honest, and what the hell was George doing retelling all his conversations? I shake my head.

His face flushes. "Is that what Anne really told you?"

"It has been implied in conversations, Your Grace."

"Henry — please." He seems frustrated. "Elizabeth, you must know I am a gentleman and a knight, I will not gainsay her, but do not think ill of me."

"I do not … Henry."

"I'm glad." He smiles once more. "And Mary loves me. Well, I was not expecting that!" He chuckles. I know he thinks a lot of himself, so that statement is a lie. "Anne will poison Mary's mind against me. You must reassure Mistress Anne that her sister came to me willingly enough."

"Like me … Henry?" I smile, trying to lighten the mood.

"Ah, I do not think you come to me with any expectations." He raises a brow. "If my heart was currently not with Mary Carey, it would be yours!" His eyes light up.

My face flushes hot, and my décolleté reddens. The heat from the fireplace is overwhelming. This is what it feels like when Henry VIII hits on a woman! "My Lord, what a compliment you pay me." I nod. "But I don't think it is my favour you look for." I need to turn his attentions towards Mary, and eventually Anne.

"No, how so?"

"You look for the approval of Mistress Anne Boleyn," I reply. "I have seen the way you watch her. You have been admiring her for some time."

"You are right, but only to win her affection, for her sister's sake." He sighs. "I had feared approaching her because she seems cold towards me."

"Sire, I mean … Henry, she is cold towards you because she believes you ordered Cardinal Wolsey to interfere in her affair with Henry Percy."

"I did not!" His face grows puce. He gets to his feet and refills his goblet from a flagon of wine that sits on the sideboard. "Would you like more wine?"

"No, thank you, Your Grace." I smile, covering the top of my goblet with my hand.

"That is a beautiful ring you are wearing." He comes to sit back next to me, and I want to shrink into the tapestries on the wall and disappear. "May I see?" He takes my hand and inspects the rubies and cypher on the top of the ring.

"The 'AB', what does that signify?"

"It is a cypher, my Lord." I half-smile. "After Anne Boleyn, for being part of her household." He buys my lie, thank God.

"'Tis a beautiful thing." He stares at it, but I don't want him to inspect it any closer, and I snatch my hand away. "I think you are a loyal friend to the Boleyns."

"I am, Sire."

"I have been glad to show favour to that family. Thomas Boleyn serves me well." He sips more wine. "I am prepared to be more generous still, once Mary has had her child."

"Should you like to resume relations with her?"

"Why ever not?" He chuckles. "She is a beautiful woman — declares her love and loyalty — so what is there not to desire?" He smiles. "But, I am not one for being around women who have been in confinement, nor in labour. It is an unclean thing." He grimaces. "I shall send word to Mary once she has been churched, and when we know the child and she are healthy."

So, he has not closed the door on a relationship with Mary. That surprises me.

"It seems," he says, "from my recent conversations with George, I must make more of an effort with the Boleyns, especially the women!" He grins. "Do you think that would please them?" He takes another sip of wine.

I nod. "I know it would please Mary, Your Grace."

"And what about Anne?" He leans in closer to me.

"Sire, Anne is her own person. She protects her family name fiercely, but she has a renegade tongue."

"I see." He laughs. "A strong-willed woman, and one not to be crossed, it seems." He leans closer and kisses me on the cheek. Heat floods my face.

"Henry, you are very forward!"

"Fear not, that is a thank you for being so honest with me." He blushes, too. "I think you and I could be good friends?"

"You would want me to think of my King as a friend?"

"Of course. You may ask anything of me, at any time when you need anything, all you must do is ask." He smiles again, the honesty radiating from his pours. Then he stands, takes my hand in his, and pulls me to my feet. He places my hand against his bare chest through his nightgown and I feel his heartbeat. *Gagoon, gagoon, gagoon.* He bends to kiss me on the lips, and his hands slide down my waist as he draws me to him. His hold is strong, and in that moment, I understand how difficult it might be for a woman to refuse intimacy with him, and how vulnerable that makes me feel.

I go rigid in his arms, the thought flashing across my mind that, despite his declarations for Mary, he may want more.

"I want us to be good friends — if for now, we can mean nothing more."

So, he does want me — not now, but at some point, he will. My body stiffens, and for a moment, I'm frightened.

"Sir," I cry, shocked that he might think he could get away with sleeping with me. "I am your good subject, nothing more."

He lets me go, standing back and looking at me with such a wounded expression that I almost take pity on him. To think that, in this moment, I have a power over this man who holds the lives of thousands in his hands. I do not want him like that. I have to think of a right and proper answer to the evening's discourse. I have to think of an answer that will bring his thoughts back to Mary and Anne. I have to deflect his interest in me, without offending him.

"Henry, would you not be happy with friendship between us, for now?"

"Friendship it is," he says, rather reluctantly.

# ❧ Twenty-Three ☙

Morning sunlight cascades through the window and I rub my eyes, wondering just how early it is. Back home, I'm so used to having my iPhone to check the time but, of course, it's at Hever, and wouldn't be any use, anyhow, with time here being so different.

I slide out of bed and curl my toes into the plush rug. Where's my dressing gown? My head wasn't right after my late-night audience with the king. Luckily, I didn't have to slide between the sheets with him. He certainly has a way about him. What will Anne think? She's going to kill me when she finds out I've shared how she feels about his treatment of her sister. I need to go to her and let her know how last night went, because someone will have told Anne I was with the king last night. Knowing Anne as I think I do, she'll be worried.

Agnes potters around my bed chamber, fetching underpinnings from my trunk.

"Agnes, I need to find Lady Anne — do you know where she is?"

"Asleep in her bed in the chamber next door, no doubt." Agnes replies, shrugging her shoulders, as she picks out a pair of stockings from a drawer, and places them in a pile on the end of my bed.

"Mistress Beth, once you be dressed, you can go and break your fast with the Lady Anne."

"I will, Agnes. Thank you." Our conversation is broken by the sound of knocking on my chamber door.

"I shall send whoever it be away, and tell them to come back when you are dressed, Mistress Wickers." Agnes hurries to answer the door as the thudding on it grows louder. "Yes, yes — give me a moment!" Agnes calls out. As she opens the door, I hear argumentative voice rise as Agnes tries to calm the person down, but I can't quite make out exactly what's being said. Within moments, I can hear Agnes' hurried footsteps as she scurries back through to my bed chamber.

"Mistress Elizabeth, 'tis Jane Parker. She insists…"

Jane, looking flustered, pushes past Agnes. "Who exactly do you think you are?" she screams, standing at the foot of my bed, hands on hips.

"Pardon?" I pull my plaited hair over my shoulder.

"You heard me." Her eyes are ferocious. Her lips are tight, and white, and as she begins reprimanding me, little flecks of spit begin shooting from her mouth. "You have upset George, and he will not speak with me." He avoids speaking with her at the best of times, but I'm not going to tell her that.

"Steady on, Mistress Parker, say it do not spray it!" Jane stares at me with a puzzled expression, but I carry on. "Why would George being upset be my fault, exactly?" I ask, reaching for my dressing gown, which Agnes has found. I wrap it over my shoulders and shove my arms through the sleeves. Agnes ties it up on me.

"George was angry when you danced with the king last night!"

"And?"

"I know he cares for you… I-I'm not stupid!" Her eyebrows knit together as she squints at me through the slanted sunlight.

"Do not screw your face up like that, you will spoil your beauty," I quip. "George and I are friends. You know this."

"It is more than that, I can feel it." Her scowl darkens her eyes. "I have seen the way he looks at you … how you exchange glances."

She's right, I know, but I have to draw her off our scent. Besides, it's not my fault we fell for each other, and it was long before she met him.

"I am his betrothed," she snaps. "Soon to be his wife!"

"I know, Jane." I walk over to her, arm outstretched, wanting to give her some reassurance, but she stiffens and backs away.

"Do not be charitable to me, as if you feel sorry for me," she says. "I have told George he is to have nothing to do with you again. You are not to socialise with him or spend any time alone in his company, whatever!"

"That is not for you to command," I reply. "Only Sir Thomas Boleyn can tell me what I should or should not do regarding his family."

"Ladies, perhaps it would be best for you both not to be arguing?" Agnes pleads. "Mistress Anne would not like it, and neither would Master George!"

I can't stop a chuckle. "Agnes, George would love it. You know he enjoys being the centre of any attention."

"Now you are making fun of my betrothed!" Jane shouts. "Have a care, Mistress Wickers."

"If George were here, he would be laughing, too. It just shows how little you know him."

"And you know him better?"

"I like to think so." That probably wasn't a wise thing to say.

She paces up and down the bedchamber, and starts to rant. "You come from France. No one has heard of you, yet you have money in your own right. Your parents never visit court, and no one has ever met them. You align yourself with the Boleyn family, who take you in without question. You make friends with Anne and my fiancé … goodness knows why?" She's fuming now. "You bewitch George so that he falls in love with you, even though you know he is to be married." Her voice must be heard on the next floor at this stage. "According to the Boleyns, you are a servant — yes, a servant! — yet you swan around the court, dancing with the king, and now I have heard you met with him in his private chambers and, I do not doubt, have probably been in his bed!" She turns to me, her eyes blazing. "Who do you think you are?"

"I have cast no enchantment on anyone. I am a good friend of the Boleyns, nothing more." After this tirade from Jane Parker, there's no way I will have an opportunity to speak with either George or Anne. Jane will block me at every turn.

Agnes strides back into the room, her brows furrowed, ready to put her two-pennies' worth in, which is nice to see. "Mistress Wickers has been nothing but loyal to the Boleyns … and, as far as Master George be concerned —" her country accent comes stronger with her ire — "'tis him who flirts with Mistress Wickers, not the other way around. He pushes himself upon Beth, I have seen it with mine own eyes."

"You are lying!" Jane cries.

"No, Mistress Parker. I never lies."

"And another thing!" Jane shouts, swinging back to me. "You conspire to not only take George from me but after last night, you plan to come between the King and Queen!" She is spitting feathers now. "How dare you come between a good Catholic marriage, that the Pope has blessed from the very beginning."

"I have done noth—"

"I knew you were an evangelical as soon as I set eyes on you!" She persists in shouting, her ire twisting her mouth. "You turn George against me, and now, for your own ends, you are prepared to turn His Grace against his beloved wife!"

I hold my hands out to her. "Jane, you have this all wrong, I swear!"

"Well, whatever the case, I shall petition the king and ask that you be banned from court, so that you will never return!" If Jane succeeds with her plan, I will never get a chance to explain my side of last night's events with Henry VIII to Anne, or her brother. So, if I leave and go back to my time, no one will find me, so there's nothing Jane can do to destroy me.

"Ye cannot do that!" Agnes shouts.

"Watch me!" Jane snaps at her. She swivels back to me. "If you have charmed the king, then I will go to the cardinal myself and tell him of your misdeeds, so he can ban you from court." She's beside herself as she paces the chamber.

"Jane, this is all jealousy against me, which is completely unwarranted."

"Elizabeth Wickers," she almost growls, "you have proven to me what a brazen and wanton opportunist you are. You are not fit to serve the Boleyn family, and I will tell Sir Thomas what a deceitful, goggle-eyed whore you are, who should be locked in the Tower and the key thrown away!" She glares at me before storming out. Christ! I wonder who this woman will bitch about me to? I will never be able to rehabilitate my reputation now, if she has her way. The cow has truly stuffed things up for me.

Agnes follows after Jane, making sure she has gone, then bolts the door behind her. "I am so sorry, Mistress, please forgive me?"

"It's all right, Agnes. This isn't your fault." My legs are shaking. "If anyone else bangs on my door, do *not* let them in, understood?"

"Yes, Mistress Beth."

"Now, help me dress." I must try to go to Anne, to Hever.

Agnes hurries around the chamber. "Which gown would you like, Mistress?"

"The dark mulberry one," I reply, "with the sheep-colour sleeves and black French hood."

"And the petticoat and kirtle?"

"The plain, red-wool petticoat, and the damask, sheep-colour kirtle."

"Very well." She soon finds the garments and lays everything out on my bed, then proceeds to help me into each item at their allotted time. "Mistress, why are you in such a hurry?"

"I do not know," I lie. "I feel the need to get some fresh air." I want to get back to Hever, and go back through the portal to avoid confrontation with Jane again, or with George. But what if Jane carries out her threat? Perhaps going back to Hever isn't a good idea, either. I want to avoid all the questions from everyone. And I don't want to think about what Sir Thomas would make of me visiting the king in the middle of the night.

Neither do I want to answer questions from George about what might have happened. What if Jane Parker goes to the cardinal or, God forbid, the queen? I will be done for — thrown in the Tower under false allegations. Wolsey would never believe a newcomer to court. He would side against me because he dislikes the Boleyns. If I'm locked in the Tower, I may never get out. I may never get back to my own time, especially if they strip me of my possessions. The ring might be lost for eternity, and I would rot in a prison cell with no hope of ever seeing my family or freedom again.

Agnes fumbles around, her panic mirroring my silent distress. She finishes dressing me, just as she's done so many times before.

"Sit down, Mistress. I shall do your hair."

I sit at the dressing table, holding a small vanity mirror as she pulls my hair into a tight bun at the back of my neck — no time for fancy braiding. She sits my French hood just in the right spot, tucking the edges over my ears.

"That looks well on you, do you not think?"

"Beautiful, Agnes," I reply, viewing my reflection in the mirror. I turn to her. "Would you mind fetching some bread and cheese from the kitchens, so I can break my fast?"

"Of course, Mistress Elizabeth." She turns to go into the outer chamber.

"Agnes, what time is it?"

"Nine of the clock," she answers. "I just heard the chimes in the courtyard."

"Thank you, Agnes." How did I miss that? I give her my best smile. "And, Agnes, thank you so much for all your support."

She glances back at me, delighted in herself. "I shall be back in no time at all."

I know I haven't much time, so I check all my personal belongings, making sure there's nothing incriminating left amongst them. Then I pack everything together in the trunks, ensuring the chambers are left tidy.

My conscience is at me. I need to escape the problems I've caused here. Should I just go? I've not said goodbye to Sir Thomas, nor to his wife, or Anne or Mary stuck at Hever. Then there's George. What do I do about him? If I say goodbye to him now, that's only going to open up a huge can of worms, especially with Jane. If he'd just waited to see what happened with the king, rather than jumping to conclusions, then Jane might have left well alone. His jealousy of Henry has driven Jane's jealousy.

Oh, it's all such a mess. I know I've overstepped the mark — probably even messed up that time-space-continuum stuff, and things might not be the same when and if I try to go back to my time. Do I take a carriage back to Hever to use the portal, or should I see if the ring works on its own, like before?

My heart leaps at a pounding on my chamber door. George is roaring my name, his voice rising above the hammering of his fist.

"Beth! Beth, open the door. I need to speak with you, as a matter of urgency."

I don't answer, but tiptoe to the door and turn the key in its lock.

"Beth, open the door! Please talk to me." He groans, and my heart is fit to burst. "Jane did not mean to be so harsh. I beg you, open the door." A silence ensues for what feels like minutes. What do I do? Something shuffles outside.

"Mistress, open the door. I have your food, just as you asked." Agnes. I'd forgotten she'd gone for food. "I know you are in there!" she says, knocking on the door. Goodness, between her and George, the rest of the palace will be wondering what's going on.

"Mistress Wickers, has the cat got your tongue?"

I remain silent as they continue to call my name and bang on the door. Damn it, what am I to do? I rush back through to the bedchamber and shut the door, then grab my bag of essentials and sit on the bed. Time to go.

I twist the cypher ring and rub the ruby stones. What do I think of? Where do I think of? I want to go back to my time, so where's the safest place I can return to without anyone being suspicious? Nine in the morning at home — what would be happening? Mum and Dad will have already left for work. The only one in the house will be Rutterkin, and where will he be? Probably comatose on my bed, snuggled up on my duvet.

I'm sat in a locked bedchamber now, so maybe I should think of my own bedroom. Yes, that's it, my comfortable bed, with my warm duvet, and Rutterkin curled up, right in the middle of it. Eyes closed, I visualise my room and a normal university morning when I've got up late. Agnes and George continue banging on the door and shouting, but I mustn't be distracted. It's time to go home. I focus as hard as I can: bedroom, bed, duvet, Rutterkin…there's no place like home.

My breath catches as my mind swirls and tumbles, then everything settles, and I open my eyes, look up, and see the familiar smooth, white Artexing of my bedroom ceiling.

Home. It worked, I'm home. I look to my right and, there, on the pillow beside me, Rutterkin is curled up in a black ball of fluff, his stomach rising and falling with each deep sleepy purr. His ears are twitching — it must be a good dream. I look down to see that I'm lying on top of my modern, crisp, clean, and flea-free duvet, and I'm dressed in my mulberry gown. I'll have to get out of that. The French hood is intact on my head, and my leather cow-mouth shoes are still on.

The most unimaginable headache is pounding through my head. I get up to look at myself in my wardrobe mirror and pull off my hood to reveal the little bun Agnes so neatly created at the nape of my neck. *Thank you, Agnes, you looked after me so well.*

I grab for my linen bag and dig around the bottom of it to pull out my iPhone to recharge it. Damn it. Where is it? I wanted to check the last few photos I took. Don't panic, it's bound to be in here somewhere. There are a dozen shots of Anne, and Hever, and George, sleeping near the fire in Anne's bedchamber. Then I remember, I'd left my iPhone in a bag, under Anne's bed at Hever. Damn it!

I sit back on my bed. This was no dream I've been living these last few months. These people I'd been living my life with are all real, and I will miss them so much, especially Anne. I could have messed things up with my stupid meddling and I know I can't go back. It's time to return the ring to Professor Marshall.

# Twenty-Five

## St. Mary's University, Twickenham

As I make my way towards Twickenham in the bright sunshine, a beautiful rainbow forms as a sudden downpour falls in sheets. Typical English winter weather. I switch on the wipers, relieved to be getting back into the routine of study, hoping I can slip back into submitting my history assignments, even if they might not be handed in at the right time. I know the professor will give me some leeway. It's not like he doesn't know where I've been. And then there's Rob. The last time I saw him, the professor was dragging him out of Anne's antechamber. My heart does somersaults at the thought of seeing him again. Then I get a flash of George's sweet face. The essence of his image floats across my mind, and I smile at the sight of him, but I have to push aside the bittersweet memory and focus on the road ahead of me.

Strawberry Hill House, Walpole's Georgian Gothic Revival castle, and the familiar blends of Victorian and modern architecture come into view as I find a space to park. As I stroll through the entrance of St Mary's, I swallow back my nerves, look around, then follow the labyrinth of corridors that lead through to the history department. The passageways are thronged with students, chatting in their usual friendship groups and faculty huddles. Many of the faces are familiar yet everything feels vague and disconcerting. With all the travelling back and forth between centuries, I've been out of the loop, and at a time that is so important, when I need to achieve module credits towards my qualification. I should feel at home here but, as I wander towards the professor's office, I feel disconnected, at odds with the twenty-first century.

I pull my bag tighter to my side, keeping my head down so my hair partly obscures my eyes. Fooling myself into thinking no one can see me makes me feel safer. And I'm less likely to get a bollocking for my absence if I manage to go unnoticed. When I reach the door of my tutor room, someone tugs on my elbow.

"Beth?"

I'd know that voice anywhere.

"You're back, then?"

"Shhh!"

"Oh, that's nice — don't text me to let me know how you are." Rob frowns. "I suppose you didn't think I'd be worried about you?"

"Well. Yeah. Of course, I know that, but I told you I've mislaid my phone." I offer an apologetic smile. He looks tired. A late night down the pub, or in the SU bar. Or perhaps he's been keeping up with his coursework, who knows? "How are you?"

"I'm okay," he answers, "but I've got to say, I've been concerned about you." His cheeks flush and I believe him.

"I'm sorry." I look down, trying to hide my embarrassment.

"I asked Professor Marshall if he'd heard from you." He brushes his hand through his hair, then pulls the strap of his bag higher up onto his shoulder. "I even begged him to let me go back through the portal to get you, but he refused!"

My absence has annoyed him. I know I haven't been gone long, so I don't know why he's getting his boxer shorts in such a twist.

"Can't you keep your voice down?" I urge, pulling him aside to let some fellow students into the room.

He sighs. "Look, I'm sorry — you can't blame me for being worried about you." His face regains some of its colour. "What sort of a friend would I be if I didn't care?" He flicks his hair again, then digs both hands into his jacket pockets. The bell rings for the second session of the morning.

"I have to go," I say, hesitantly, not wanting to upset him but knowing I need to use my time wisely, to catch up on my work and assignments.

I head towards the small hall for the lecture where Professor Marshall is waiting to begin. I find a seat, pull a notebook and pen out, and hang my bag on the back of my chair. My hair is in a state so I grab a scrunchy from my jacket pocket and fix a messy ponytail, then wait.

Fractures of sunrays stream through the windows, creating a kaleidoscope of colours across the floor. Other students take their seats and the collective chat stills.

"Good morning all." The professor smiles. "I hope you have remembered that today is the deadline for your assignment?" He looks around the room, and his gaze rests on me. "I know some of you may have a good reason not to be submitting the essay today but most of you have no excuse." He scrutinizes the sea of faces before him over his glasses, and I avert my eyes. He'll want to talk to me before the day is out, and that's fine, but for now, I need to focus on the matter at hand.

He whips out his whiteboard pen and writes in large letters across the top of the board: THE ASCENDANCY AND IMPACT OF CARDINAL WOLSEY. With that, he turns to face his audience and gives us our next assignment. "The questions I'd like you to answer are these: What ecclesiastic reforms did Wolsey undertake? And was he serious about Church reform?" He looks about the room, searching for a face that might shed light on the answers he's looking for but everyone remains silent, and not one of us raises our hand. Perhaps it's because some students are afraid of getting the answers wrong. There's so much I could say about Cardinal Thomas Wolsey, considering I've met him first-hand. I couldn't say what he thinks about Church reform because I haven't had any in-depth conversations with him. Neither have I overheard him in the council chamber to be able to ascertain his thoughts, but I know what he thinks about Henry Percy and Anne Boleyn.

I open my notepad and scribble down the title the professor has written on the board. Some students use laptops but I can't be bothered with technology at times — it always fails on me. Using a notebook, I can scribble random things, make sketches, and create diagrams. So much more freedom to connect with details coming at me from the lecturer. I sketch my impression of Wolsey when he confronted Anne and Henry during that meeting in his chambers. Professor Marshall pings up a portrait in PowerPoint of the great man himself. I smirk to myself, on seeing that it doesn't resemble the cardinal I've seen.

Without waiting for a response, he continues his short introduction to the man. "I want you to consider Wolsey's ecclesiastical policy — how far his policies included plans for reform, and how he used his powers as *legate a latere*."

I write that down in big letters, LEGATE A LATERE. The professor walks left to right in front of us, waving his marker in the air. "I want you to consider how these powers were also used to create his own central authority in the Church." He looks straight at me.

The professor stuffs his marker back into his jacket pocket and folds his arms. "Fellow historians, for your next assignment, I want you to review the primary sources you have been given so far." He paces the platform, checking every student is listening. "Then, I want you to read John Guy's essay on Wolsey's domestic policy, and from it, consider what ecclesiastic reforms he undertook, and whether or not he was serious about reform."

He whips his marker out and writes these points on the board, along with the deadline of the assignment, then turns and faces us again. "Additionally, in light of what you have previously learnt about the different aspects of Wolsey's career, return to this question to conclude your assignment: Was Wolsey both a radical and successful reformer?"

As he writes this on the board, I jot it down in large letters — CONCLUSION: WAS WOLSEY BOTH A RADICAL AND SUCCESSFUL REFORMER?

"I have the printouts of John Guy's essay here." He waves a few sheets of paper at us. "Please make sure you take a copy on your way out, folks." He smiles. "Now, do you have any questions?"

As students raise issues on the assignment, I find myself recalling that episode in Wolsey's office with Anne, and then my mind turns to the night

I was summoned to the king's private bedchamber, and how gracious and kind he was until he had me in an over-friendly embrace and I had to break away. It seems to me that, advisor or no advisor, Henry was always determined to make up his own mind, on any matter, and wasn't slow in airing his opinion on anything. My mind drifts as I remember the musky smells in his room — the pungent taste of the wine I was offered — the rose petals strewn across the furs on his bed. I recall Sir Henry Norris's knowing look as he closed the doors on us, and my anxiety when I realised I was alone with King Henry VIII, then how at ease he eventually made me feel until he implied that he quite fancied me. I didn't expect that.

That was one of the reasons Jane Parker became so angry with me — because the king had shown favouritism to me. Or was it because George had been jealous of me being with the king? My thoughts blend into a muddle, like sugar dispersing into a cup of stirred tea. I don't want to think of George. Why should I upset myself? It's just not worth wishing for something that will never be. My focus snaps back to the present as Professor Marshall's voice resonates across the lecture room.

"Put your assignments on my desk here!" he bellows, tapping an empty spot beside the pile of printouts. "You have a month to complete the Wolsey essay. Go and have a break, and I will see you all in here after lunch."

The room fills with the chatter of students filtering out in small groups. Most take copies of John Guy's essay. Some pass the professor offerings of paper stuffed into document holders. Others are empty-handed, and that's where a short, sharp conversation is exchanged, excuses given, and deadlines shifted. I'm the one he's going to be moaning at next. I stride towards the exit but he beats me to it.

"Miss Wickers, could you see me in my office, please?" He looks at me over the top of his glasses.

"Now, sir?"

"Yes." He picks up his bag and heaves its strap over his shoulder, then grabs his laptop and all the ink-stained essays off the desk.

We elbow past groups of students and solitary members of staff in the bustling passageways until we arrive at his office.

He puts the laptop, paperwork, and document folders by his computer, dumps his bag on the floor, and looks at me over his glasses as he leans against the edge of his desk. "When did you come back?"

"Come back?" I ask, as if I don't know what he means.

He frowns at me. "From being with Anne."

I sit on the high-back chair opposite him, cross my legs and put my bag on the floor. That's when I realise that my jeans have got caught in my leather boot, because I dressed so fast this morning.

"I arrived home late last night, sir." I keep looking at the floor. The last thing I want is an inquisition. I sit back, pull my jacket around me, then fold my arms.

"Why did you come back so soon?" He leans forward. "According to my calculations, you've only been missing from here since yesterday. You haven't missed much work."

I sigh. "Professor, I have no idea how the time-slip works between here and there. I'm always careful to leave a note for my parents to say I'm staying at a friend's for a few nights, so they don't grow suspicious. Trouble is, when I've returned to Anne, months have sometimes gone by, even years, yet here, time doesn't seem to move on much at all. It's all too strange and complicated for me to try and work out."

"Yes, that is the confusing part of the phenomenon." He wiggles his eyebrows, then his frown betrays that he is as nonplussed as me. "That being said, though, I am very careful how I proceed with it. You still haven't told me why you've returned home so soon."

"I've tried to do what you say." I bite back a sigh. "I try to observe and do my utmost not to change things."

"That is all I meant you to do — however, I feel a 'but' coming on." He leans towards me, his arms now folded, mirroring mine.

"I thought it best to come back when I did." I pinch the bridge of my nose and wonder whether it's a good idea to go into detail. "Because I'd … annoyed Jane Parker."

He rolls his eyes. "Why, what did you do?"

"It's not what I did, sir," — I groan in my head, worried about how much I may have to elaborate — "but what I was asked to do." I wring my hands in my lap, then bring them up to my lips.

He frowns again. "Go on."

This isn't going to be pleasant. "Well, you know Anne becomes secretly engaged to Henry Percy, and ends up being banished from court for a time?" I'm apprehensive, resting my hands back in my lap.

"Yes…"

"While Anne was hankered down at Hever, Thomas Boleyn asked me to go to court in her place, to keep the king's mind on Mary." I turn my palms towards him.

His eyes widen. "Really?"

I shrug. "The Boleyns seem to trust me."

He smiles. "That's a good thing but, surely, you didn't go alone? Who accompanied you?"

I take a deep breath, not really wanting to answer him, but blurt his name out, anyway: "George Boleyn."

The professor's brows furrow as he blinks several times. "What is the issue with him? Why would George be a problem?"

"It's not just George. It's the king."

He chuckles. I glare at him, not amused that he's finding my predicament funny. "I'm sorry but let's face it, Bluff King Hal was always going to be a problem."

"Now you tell me!"

"Let's go back to George first. What happened with him?" He cups his chin between his thumb and forefinger and gives me an expectant look. Maybe he has an idea of what's coming.

"He … likes me," I whisper.

"What?"

"George likes me — like that," I say, emphasising with some gusto so I don't need to mention the love word. I can't believe I'm having this conversation with my professor. I shake my head and fold my arms in front of me again — there's no going back now the cat's out of the bag, so to speak.

"That's not good," he says, grasping my full meaning. Before he can ask another question, I move the discussion on to the king.

"I realise anyone fancying me might be difficult, especially when, one evening during the entertainments, the king asked me to dance."

"Doesn't he ask most ladies of the court to dance?"

"Yes, but he doesn't ask many to visit his bedchamber afterwards, late at night."

The professor blushes, no doubt realising this goes way beyond his safeguarding remit as a tutor and university lecturer.

"But, sir, please don't be worried." I try to keep my tone upbeat. "Nothing happened."

"I should hope not!" The red in his cheeks fade. "So how were things left? You still haven't explained why you returned here so abruptly."

I tuck a loose strand of hair behind my ear. "There was a problem."

"What sort of problem?" he whispers, leaning in closer. I don't know who he thinks might be listening.

"George got jealous." I sigh. "He told Jane Parker, his fiancée, about my meeting with the king, and she was furious."

He lets out an exasperated groan. "What happened next?"

"She accused me of leading George on, enticing him away from her." I wince at the memory of it. "She even accused me of sleeping with the king, and coming between the royal couple."

"She accused you of coming between Henry and Katharine?"

"Yes. She started threatening me. Said she'd tell Wolsey about what I'd done. Threatened to ask questions about my family — she wanted to know where they lived, what my station in life was, and why I was at court. The last thing she shouted at me was that she was going to make sure Wolsey had me arrested and put in the Tower."

"Christ."

"What would I have done if they'd thrown me into a prison cell? They'd have taken my belongings away and, heaven forbid, confiscated the ring. I wouldn't have been able to return home. What then?"

The professor nods. "Indeed."

"I had no choice but to come back as fast as possible." I reach into my jacket pocket, grasp the ring, and hand it to him. "You'd better have it back." I can't help releasing a sigh of relief as he takes it from me. "I suppose, and I hope, that with me not being there, there is no way I will have altered the history now."

"Let's see." He grabs his copy of Eric Ives' book on Anne Boleyn from the bookshelf. I jump as the force of removing it from the bookcase makes the whole thing pivot open, just as it did before, swinging wide to reveal the dark passageway through to Hever.

We both stare at the opening, then face each other. I shut my open mouth. He turns his attention back to the book and flicks through to the chapter on Anne's downfall.

"It doesn't look as if anything has changed." He takes the ring from me and puts it on his desk, then closes the portal door. "I think you are right. We need to leave the past in the past."

I nod and quickly leave his office, tears suddenly blurring my eyes. Of course, the professor is right, but I already miss Anne dreadfully.

As I head to the library to complete my overdue assignment, I can't help wishing that maybe one day I'll see her again.

Want to carry on Beth Wickers adve
with the Timeless Falcon Dual Timeline

# COMING SOON:

Volume Two: The Ring of Fate.

Volume Three: A Turbulent Crown.

Volume Four: An Enduring Legacy.

# A NOTE TO THE READER

Dear Reader,

Thank you for reading *The Anne Boleyn Cypher.*

This is my second novel, but my first historical novel, which, as a series, has been a long time in the writing. It began years ago, with my interest in Anne Boleyn and the dramatic story of her fall, reading the likes of Jean Plaidy when I was a child of nine. My study of Anne and of history has never diminished. I know that Anne's life history is an interest shared by many: the crowds who visit Her Majesty's Fortress, the Tower of London, compelled to see the supposed site of Anne's scaffold, or visitors who flock to Hampton Court Palace where Anne stayed in triumphant days, or to Hever Castle, her family home for a time. The fascination with everything Anne Boleyn is evident in numerous websites on the internet. The insatiable appetite for all things relating to the Tudors, from raunchy television series to opulent films, to the West End musical *Six!*, continues unabated.

I have consulted academic works and research on Anne Boleyn and personalities of the Tudor Court by successful historians like Eric Ives, Suzannah Lipscomb, Amy Licence, Elizabeth Norton, Lauren Mackay, David Loades and others, to frame a number of real events in Anne's life, to bring her story around Beth to life. Primary sources are also fantastic devices to learn of historical context, and analysing sources is the closest we will get to remove the veil between these historical personalities and events, in order to conclude anything which remotely resembles the truth. The highlight of my research was looking through and holding the twenty-six pages of Anne Boleyn's indictment of her trial, and seeing the indents in the vellum where the Duke of Norfolk had ticked the jury off with his quill as they entered the king's Great Hall at His Majesty's Royal Palace and Fortress of the Tower of London. My primary research included documents from websites such as British History Online and the National Archives at Kew. The icing on the cake in terms of research, was having the opportunity to sit in the front row of The Aldwych Theatre and watch Ben Miles as Cromwell in the stage adaptations of Hilary Mantel's *Wolf Hall* and *Bring Up the Bodies* — on the last night's performance — and knowing Hilary Mantel was in the audience. What an incredible experience that was. The play was an atmospheric-inducing device, and historical aspects of the drama were thought-provoking.

It is this insatiable appetite by both historians and enthusiasts for Anne Boleyn, that compelled me to write a completely different take on her story, rather than the usual regurgitation of Anne's story, from her point of view. Moreover, it is my protagonist's story, from Beth's point of view, which enables us to observe Anne in a different light. What would we do if we had the ability to time-travel back to the Tudor period and meet Anne? Would we behave ourselves and not tamper with history as we know it, or would we wreak havoc and try to save Anne from her well-documented downfall? These are the dilemmas that face Beth Wickers. Her story is one I felt obliged to write, and although I include primary events, it will never be close to the truth of Anne's life, as unless we were there at the time, we can never know all the facts relating to Anne Boleyn. Furthermore, I wish to stress that although the historical aspects of this book are loosely based on original sources, digital archives, and academic accounts, Beth's character and her experiences in the Tudor period were used as an entertaining device to creatively retell Anne's story, and is written purely for the readers' enjoyment, and to entertain.

Reviews by readers these days are integral to a book's success, so if you enjoyed *The Anne Boleyn Cypher* I would be very grateful if you could spare a minute to post a review on Amazon, and I love hearing from readers, and you can talk with me through my website or on Twitter (@PhillipaJC) and follow my author page on Facebook (Phillipa Connolly Historian).

Phillipa Vincent-Connolly, Poole, Dorset. November 2022

# ALSO BY PHILLIPA VINCENT-CONNOLLY

THE TIMELESS FALCON SERIES:

Volume Two: The Ring of Fate
Volume Three; A Turbulent Crown
Volume Four: An Enduring Legacy

Disability and The Tudors: All the King's Fools

# ACKNOWLEDGEMENTS

Firstly, I want to thank my readers who have supported me by reading and reviewing any previous editions of volume one of this series, for believing in me and my work, and for loving Beth Wicker's story enough to continue reading the whole Timeless Falcon Dual Timeline series. Secondly, thanks to fellow historian and writer Dr Lauren Mackay, for her inspirational guidance and contributing to the editing, and to Alison Weir for her initial support through email correspondence and answering queries, for face-to-face advice, and for so generously helping me edit the first chapter of this book when I first embarked on writing this novel.

Thanks to Eamon Ó Cléirigh from ClearView Editing, who persevered and supported me in slowly transforming this novel, and the subsequent series to come, into its final incarnation. Thank you for your patience.

Thank you to Richard Jenkins for his beautiful photography for the cover of the book.

I also want to thank Professor Suzannah Lipscomb for allowing and approving a cameo of herself to appear in this book, and for letting me know that she thought this story to be 'delightful'. And to historian Tracy Borman for coming up with the name Rutterkin, for Beth's black Persian cat.

I had the opportunity to learn how Beth might have felt wearing Tudor clothing for the first time when Tudor Dreams Historical Costumier, Gina Clark allowed me to dress up in full Tudor dress and be photographed inside Hever Castle. I have dedicated this book to Gina because our mutual love of history and costume has blossomed into a close, life-long friendship. Thank you also, to John Gillo, a friend who has encouraged and supported me to keep going with this series of books, when I could have so easily given up!

Lastly, special thanks must go to my family and friends, who have all put up with me during the writing of this book, particularly my wonderfully supportive boys, Joshua and Lucas, who have trailed across the south of England, staying at Hever Castle, visiting the Tower of London, Berkeley Castle, Sudeley Castle, and Hampton Court Palace on numerous occasions, and generally absorbing my enthusiasm for Tudor history. You have all been wonderful in so many ways — thank you.

# ABOUT THE AUTHOR

Phillipa Vincent-Connolly is an historian, writer, and published author of historical fiction and nonfiction. She is a consultant on many exciting projects across a broad spectrum with a special interest in disability and is becoming the 'go-to' broadcaster on this subject, especially recently with the publication of her book, 'Disability and the Tudors'. Published by Pen and Sword history imprint, currently, this is the first book in a series on disabilities in specific eras and benefits from Phillipa's own experience of living with Cerebral Palsy.

She achieved her degree in History and Humanities in 2011 and her PGCE, QTS, in 2014, and NQT 2019, in teaching (secondary), and part of her MA Graduate Diploma in History in 2020, and is currently working towards her PhD at Manchester Metropolitan University specialising in Tudor disability history. She has spoken at the National Archives and the British library to great acclaim. Her experience in teaching makes her an authoritative and engaging public speaker. She is a Fellow of the Royal Historical Society.

Phillipa has written for History Today, Blitzed Magazine, has been interviewed regularly for BBC radio, and has appeared in mini-TV documentaries.

Among her many interests, she has a deep and abiding love for all things historical, archives, artefacts, architecture, fashion, and royalty. Phillipa is also a keen activist, giving a contemporary voice to disabled people of the past, and those who currently feel disenfranchised. Her own disability has allowed her to identify and empathise with those who have not been heard and she is passionate about equality for the disabled. She lives in Poole, Dorset, but is not solely UK centric, as she has a broad spectrum of knowledge and research on which to draw.

A rising star in historical fiction too, with her eagerly awaited 'Timeless Falcon' historical fiction series of books, Phillipa has both the research and writing abilities to adapt to any project and is the future of the past.

https://phillipavincent-connolly.com

# REVIEWS FOR THE ANNE BOLEYN CYPHER

**Professor Suzannah Lipscomb** says Timeless Falcon Volume One The Anne Boleyn Cypher is, 'a delightful story' – Suzannah Lipscomb is a Professor Emerita. Historian. Broadcaster. Author & editor of 7 books. Host of NotJustTudors podcast.

**You're wasting time! You could be reading the book right now!** – 'I honestly can't put how much I love this book into words. I've read tons and tons of books about the Tudor period, and Anne Boleyn is one of my favourite people. After reading for years though, I pretty much know her story front to back (similar to the book's main character, Beth). This book zoomed to the top of my all-time favourites list before I even finished it. It has a new, refreshing, and such an imaginative angle about Anne that it's easy to get lost in the book. I have lost count of the times I've read the book. I don't want to really summarize the book as I think picking it up & diving in is the fun part. I'll just let you know that I think anyone with an imagination who loves the Tudor period will want the Kindle version, physical version, AND audiobook of this story! So go buy it. Chop, chop! :D' – TERRIE M, AMAZON REVIEW

**A Favourite of the year so far!** – 'Okay, okay. I think we have a new contender for my favourite book of the year?! If you don't read the essay I'm about to produce (apologies in advance) and go further than the first few sentences, I'll just say: read this book! You need to, and you won't regret it. Now I love a historical fiction book. And I love a historical non-fiction book. I just love history. And this book hit every mark I could possibly want. The Tudors are such an interesting area of history and the whole premise for this book is outstanding. I love the plot and the set up as a whole and will send out my plea now for the author to never stop writing these books (pretty please). I could read them ad infinitum. I'm also going to be staring into the void now waiting for the next book to come out. Wish I had a time travelling ring so I can go into the future and read it stat! I loved how this history was portrayed and how us as readers, could get an insight into what Anne Boleyn's character may have been like, discovering the 'living' world of the Tudors right along with Beth. They may be names in history textbooks when it comes to Cardinal Wolsey, Cromwell, the famed Henry VIII and so on, but this book brought them to life. I also adored Beth's character and she was very easy to like. This whole book was just so easy to slip into and lose yourself in. I never wanted to put it down and I both never wanted it to end, and wanted to read it as fast as I could to see what was going to happen! I tried to slow it down without much success and just devoured it. Certainly, need this addition to my physical shelf as it sure as hell will be a reread in the future as it was such a joy to read. I will force my essay to its conclusion now as I think I could wax lyrical about this book forever, so I'll sum up: much enjoyed, 10/10 and it's a great book you won't regret getting stuck into.' – NICOLA WILTON, Amazon Review.

**Outlander meets the Tudors** - 'I bought two of these one for me and one for my sister-in-law. She's Anne Boleyn obsessed so figured she'll love the book and I thought it sounded interesting (despite me not being a huge fan of AB). However, I can honestly say I'm hooked!! The first time I started reading it I got to chapter 4 before I put it down. The story is already captivating, it's like Outlander meets the Tudors and I look forward to reading on. I would thoroughly recommend it to all Tudor fans. Phillipa Vincent-Connolly has well and truly created something special here.' – KAREN EASTER

**Amazon - make this a Prime Original series!** – 'Start reading this on a Friday after you are finished working and have no other plans for the weekend. You will not want to put this down until you reach the last page. When you have read the last word on the last page of this incredible book it will leave you begging for another volume; so, you can continue to walk in this world where the beautiful writing made you feel like you were right there with the characters in the book. Timeless Falcon is a breath of fresh air in the line of Tudor historical fiction.

I am eagerly looking forward to the release date of the next instalment of the series and actually would already love to see it as a TV series!! Maybe even an Amazon Prime Original!!!!!' –AMAZON REVIEW

**Outlander meets the Tudors** – 'I absolutely love these time travel books, being transported back and looking at history through the eyes of the modern traveller. This book does not fail to please. You can almost feel the historical characters, know what they are saying and what they look like. This might be a work of fiction but incredibly well researched. Who doesn't want to be transported back to their favourite era and this book helps you achieve that goal. I am so looking forward to book two. – AMAZON REVIEW

**MUST HAVE for any historical fiction reader** – 'I've just read Timeless Falcon. It's amazing, I love it so much I'm so gutted it's over. It's left me with so many wonderings about volume two it will be a MUST HAVE! Congratulations on such a wonderful read. Can't wait for volume two!!!' – ASHLIE NEWCOMB, Greenwich University Literary Student

**Superb storyline... a must for any Tudor addict** – 'What a great read.. if your addicted to reading anything Tudor fact or fiction.. this is a must. I could not put it down.. ready and waiting for volume 2' - JESS FOXWORTHY

**A must read** – 'Ever since I received an audible version of the Timeless Falcon, it has been like opening a box of luxurious chocolates. I dip in and find another unexpected luscious adventure of Beth, the history student time traveller, to unwrap and see where her friend Anne Boleyn's journey is headed. Guided by Philippa Vincent-Connolly's expert descriptions of the Tudor England, Hever Castle and the Royal Court, Timeless Falcon is a gripping novel for all history lovers' – PHIL ROBERTS, Historian and writer.

**Phenomenal** – 'I picked up this book because of my intense adoration of all things Tudor England and Anne Boleyn - and I was blown away. I first listened to the audible narration, which is absolutely fantastic, and I highly recommend it, and then purchased a copy to read on my own. By the time I had finished, I was GUTTED to find out there's not a release date for book two. I have my fingers crossed for soon though and I've followed all of the authors social medias and such to keep up. I'll be the first in line for book two!! I need this series!!!! It's everything I have ever dreamed of, and honestly, it's a joy watching Beth go back and forth and manage the difference between her two worlds. I need to know what happens!!!

Please release the rest of the series and get the same audiobook narrator!! I'll be getting hard copies and the audiobook copies as well. Hurrah!' – AMAZON REVIEW

**Phenomenal and Original** – 'Timeless Falcon is just as good, if not better, than anything Gregory or Weir has written. I was hesitant about the time travel aspect, as it is so often done badly, but Vincent-Connolly does this very well. I also loved that it was a refreshing, different way of telling Anne Boleyn's story. I started reading and couldn't stop. Can't wait for the next one!' – JENNIFER DUNLO

**Tudor Time Slip** – 'In "Timeless Falcon", Phillipa Vincent-Connolly retells the well-known story of Anne Boleyn through the eyes of a modern-day woman, Beth, who travels back in time to Tudor England where she meets the real Anne. Now, Anne Boleyn's story has been done to death, so to speak, and there are countless novels recounting the story of her life. But this one is different. Vincent-Connolly offers a story skilfully weaved around real-life characters but with a surprising twist. The detailed and vivid narrative transported me to a time period that I love, and allowed me to experience Tudor England like never before.

"Timeless Falcon" is very well-researched and fabulously written. It's a page-turner enhanced by flawless narrative and an absorbing plot, making it a perfect choice for fans of historical fiction, Anne Boleyn and Tudor England. I highly recommend this novel to everyone who loves everything Tudor.' –AMAZON REVIEW

**A Time Travelling Delight** – 'What can I say about this delicious literary morsel but wow! Jumping right into the Tudor world without abandon, Beth eats up the past with a silver spoon and makes friends easily with one of the most fascinating and fashionable Tudor queen, Anne Boleyn. Twisting between past and present, this student of history lives all historians dream of watching infamous events unfold before her eyes. I loved every moment and can't wait for volume 2!' – JANEL VANHIMBERGEN

Printed in Great Britain
by Amazon